THE RING OF FATE

A Timeless Falcon Dual Timeline Series

Volume Two

PHILLIPA VINCENT-CONNOLLY

Copyright © 2023 Phillipa Vincent-Connolly.
Copyright © 2015 Cover photography Richard Jenkins
Copyright © 2023 Cover design by Megan Sheer: sheerdesignandtypesetting.com

First Edition

The author has asserted their moral right under the Copyright, Designs and Patents Act, 1988, to be identifiedas the author of this work.

All Rights reserved.

No part of this publication may be reproduced, copied, stored in a retrieval system, or transmitted, in any form or by any means, without the prior written consent of the copyright holder, nor be otherwise circulated in any form of binding or cover other than that in which it is published and without a similar condition being imposed on the subsequent purchaser.

This book is a work of fiction. Names, characters, businesses, organisations, places, and events, other than those clearly in the public domain, are either the product of the author's imagination, or are used fictitiously.

Any resemblances to actual persons, living or dead, events or locales are purely coincidental.

A CIP catalogue record for this title is available from the British Library.

❧   **Gina Clark**   ☙

Thank you for your incredible friendship, wit,
never ending encouragement, exceptional tea-making,
and continual supply of champagne and strawberries

❧ One ❧

Mid-December, Present Day – Carshalton, London

If I don't catch up with her now, I will lose her forever, as will history. This moment will change England for all time, and it will be my fault.

My heart is pounding so hard, I'm terrified it will burst through the reed boning of my kirtle as I struggle to catch my breath in this damned constricting dress. It tangles around my ankles, hindering my pace, so I gather up my petticoat and skirts, scrunching the silk velvet in my fists, my cow-mouthed shoes pounding the familiar concrete paving slabs of one of London's most famous bridges. Onlookers gasp as I push past them in my authentic Tudor clothes, desperate to rescue my charge.

The sky grows black as thunderclouds gather, angry and ominous, and it's only moments before spits of rain spatter my skin. Determined to take on my responsibility, I continue fighting my way through the crowds, ducking, and swerving as umbrellas spring open to shelter individuals from the predictable and dismal London weather.

St Stephen's Tower, with its famous inhabitant Big Ben hanging inside, chimes its melodic tones as the afternoon approaches, while gossiping tourists tut at each other, nudging elbow to elbow as I scurry past. I must look a strange sight – a young woman in full Tudor Court dress, rain-soaked, sprinting along the pavement of Parliament Square. Stranger still is that I have no camera crew chasing me, no areas cordoned off for filming, no director or producer. Nothing. It's not the film set of *The Mirror and the Light,* it's just me – pursuing one of the most famous women in English history. As the gap between myself and Anne shortens, I flinch at the sound of my mum's voice:

"Beth!"

I look about as I run, half-expecting to see her behind me.

"Wake up!" she shouts again, her voice edged with impatience.

I snap around, my vision blurred, convinced I'll see the lady Anne. Then, out of nowhere, Rutterkin's wet prickly tongue flicks my cheek, prompting me to wince as he pins me against the softness of my cotton pillow. His needle-like claws dig into my collar-bone. He won't stop, at least not until I've nudged his weight from my chest with my hand. He's not impressed and lets me know with a grumpy purr. I turn my head, my eyelashes brushing the pillow. Mum picks him up.

"You're late!"

"What time is it?" I mumble, giving my eyes a good rub.

"Eight a.m."

I look at her, standing over me, hands on hips.

"Really?"

"Yes," she says. "I'm late, too. Goodness knows why the alarm didn't go off."

Dad must have had an early meeting in Westminster and woke neither of us before taking the taxi to the station.

"Oh, God!" I moan, blinking, watching Mum walk over to the windows. She opens the curtains to let daylight in.

"You'll get stuck in traffic if you don't hop up now." She walks over to the door and rests her hand on the brass handle. "I'll do you some toast, and a cup of tea. Is that okay?"

"That would be lovely," I reply, sitting up against my pillows, flicking my tousled hair from my eyes.

"Would you like your toast with marmalade?" she asks as she leaves the room.

"You know me so well!" I respond, unable to hold back a smile.

"Ten minutes, no longer – okay?"

"Yes, alright then."

She shuts the door behind her, and I let out a long sigh, relieved that chasing Anne was only a dream. Yes, the lines have been blurring between the past and present lately but dreaming about Anne now is ridiculous. Why would I be chasing her through modern London?

My time-travelling experience was no dream, that's for certain. I have the clothes to prove it. Only Professor Marshall and Rob know the truth – that I'd been living in sixteenth-century Tudor England for what was essentially years, though only days have passed in twenty-first-century time. If Rob hadn't met Anne Boleyn for himself, in her time, he'd never have believed me. The past to me is familiar – not a foreign country but a vivid reality, where they do things so differently. These historical figures I've met are tangible – flesh and blood. The Boleyn family and their rise and fall, are one of the greatest stories in English history – it is an extraordinary Tudor saga. An epic of hubris and pain. I've been spell-bound watching each member play out their parts – Thomas, the ambitious, yet respected patriarch. Elizabeth, the doting mother. George, the fearless son. His sisters – Mary, the reluctant mistress of kings, and Anne, the calculating courtier, and finally, their brutal uncle, Thomas Howard. I've been learning so much about these personalities during my university degree but, to talk with them, live with them, and experience their lives in real-time, is something 'otherworldly'. The Boleyns:

Thomas, Elizabeth, George, Anne, Mary; other courtiers; even King Henry VIII have been accessible to me. Several are friends – confidants, even – but I will not miss them. I can't miss them. No, I refuse to be dragged into the time-slip again. Besides, I've probably messed things up with my stupid meddling. There is no point going back. What becomes of Anne Boleyn, is not my responsibility – none of them is, really. I know from history, that the family played a dangerous game and paid the ultimate price, but with or without me, they will leave a remarkable legacy, changing the course of English history, and taking their name from obscurity to the apex of power. However, I do feel a pang of guilt, because as a history student, I do have a responsibility to how their 'histories' play out. *That* is what I'm struggling with, more than anything else.

It's not long before I've showered, dressed, and am ready for the day, swigging my tea down and chomping on my toast before I run outside and jump into my little vintage Figaro car, which is exactly where I left it after my last time-slip. No, hold on, I have a funny feeling the professor might have driven it back here, rather than leave it in the university car park, where I think left it. Or maybe it was Rob? I realised some time ago that time-travel screws with your mind, as well as your emotions, and as I throw my bag onto the passenger seat, I'm glad my life is regaining a semblance of normality.

I only have my ipod to plug into the aux lead, and choose a track, because I think I left my mobile phone in Tudor England. Christ, how am I going to get that back? I try not to think about anything but the present moment, when thankfully, I turn the key in the ignition and the engine jumps to life. I really should change to a modern electric car, but as a student, I just can't afford it. Music blasts through the speakers as I drive off from my parking space, into the road, and eventually filter into city-bound traffic. I must look ridiculous to other drivers when they spot me singing along to the music, but I can't help myself – I've really missed moments like this from my *real* life. The music automatically changes to the next track on my playlist. Listening to familiar songs makes me feel like my old twenty-first-century self.

As I make my way towards Twickenham I'm not surprised to be driving in a sudden downpour, as the rain falls in sheets. This is our usual kind of English weather. Rain. I switch on the wipers, relieved I'm back in my time ready to continue with my routine of study, even if the weather is rubbish.

I think of Rob. He keeps warning me about time-slipping. We argue about it since I've returned. Now, I've decided it's best to not even bring up the subject with him. I don't need him complicating my life, like the last time, when Professor Marshall had to drag him back through the portal. Even though we've had our disagreements, I'm always pleased to see Rob. Then I get a flash of George Boleyn's sweet face. The essence of his image floats across my mind, and I smile at the sight of him, but I have to push aside the bittersweet memory and focus on the road ahead of me.

Strawberry Hill House, Walpole's Georgian Gothic revival castle, and the familiar blends of Victorian and modern architecture come into view as I find a space to park. As I grab my holdall from the passenger seat, I'm ready to focus on the here and now. I secure my mobile phone in my pocket and thread the earplug leads up underneath my jacket and over my collar.

A glance towards the building to my left tells me nothing much appears to have changed. The breeze whispers through the nearby trees, then wafts gently across my cheeks. I'm conscious of the line of cars, buses, and delivery vans queuing from the A309, waiting to make their drop offs onto campus. I lock my car and turn to join the groups of students across the car park. It's so busy,

Once inside, I pass through the reception, relaxing with the familiar sights, sounds, and smells that greet me. I make my way towards my tutor room in the history department for my first lecture of the day. Students are massing, with everyone greeting friends. I look around, and it's not long before I catch sight of familiar faces. I hope Rob hasn't told any of them he went through the portal. He swore he would never say a word.

Voices ebb and flow around me. For a moment, I could swear I can hear someone call my name.

"Beth?"

I look around, to see a friend of Rob's walk up behind me. "Eh? Oh, sorry, Marc, I was miles away."

He rolls his eyes, then smiles. "Are you okay?" He grins. "Thought you might be with Rob? No?" Marc's brows knit together. "Look, I'm going to find him. I may catch you later."

His girlfriend grabs for Marc's hand. "Come on!" They manoeuvre through the crowded corridor, and as I watch them walk away, I think of Rob, who I've liked since the beginning of my first year here. I would never tell Marc. Not a chance. All the girls seem to fancy him, but I no longer even know if we are friends now, because of my time travelling adventures. Jealousy is a horrible emotion, but Rob knew I could never let him go with me to the sixteenth century, at least, not for any prolonged period of time.

I don't have to swallow back my nerves, as I'm feeling confident since being back in my usual university routine, as I look around, then follow the labyrinth of corridors that lead through to the history department. The passageways are thronged with students, and as I stride through the groups of people, I see Professor Marshall.

"Miss Wickers, could you see me in my office, please?" He looks at me over the top of his glasses.

"Now, sir?"

"Yes," he replies, handing me his keys. "I'm dying for a cigarette and having a chat with you will give me the excuse to have one." We elbow past groups of students and solitary members of staff in the bustling passageways until we arrive at his office.

"Can you open the door?" he asks.

"Of course."

He watches me fumble with the bunch of keys. I'm all thumbs but manage to locate the right key and unlock the door. The familiar smell of his stale cigarette smoke hits me as we enter.

"You know, I've told you before sir, you really should stop that disgusting habit." I glance at him, pinching my nostrils.

"Never!" He smiles. "It's one of the few pleasures I have left." He puts the laptop, paperwork, and document folders by his computer, dumps his bag on the floor, and looks at me over his glasses as he leans against the edge of his desk.

"What did you need from me? I haven't finished the latest literature reviews you asked me to write."

"No, it's not that." He shakes his head. "I need to make sure that since we last checked history hasn't altered since the last time you time-slipped."

Out of the corner of my eye, I'm glad to notice that the bookcase, or should I say, 'portal' in the office is closed. No matter how much my heart is pulling me back to George, my mind has to dissuade itself into walking through that portal, and back through time to Hever. I shake my head. Surely, the time-slip wouldn't open without the cypher ring. I made certain I'd never go back through it. I gave his cypher ring back to him, last time we discussed about messing up the history.. Professor Marshall eyes me curiously.

"Why, sir?" I frown. "I told you before, I didn't particularly want to discuss my time-slipping in any more detail – and for God's sake, the portal is closed now. Let's keep it our secret?"

"Of course, this is our secret, unless you have told more than Robert Dryden about it?"

"No, I'd never break your confidence!"

"Good, I understand." He picks up his copy of the Life and Death of Anne Boleyn by Eric Ives, that's face down on his desk. "I wasn't sure if you had altered anything, except, you need to look at this." His eyes look anxious as he turns the book over, showing me the cover, and I can hardly believe my eyes. I stare at the image for what seems like a few minutes.

"What is that?" I whisper. I'm amazed to see a portrait of myself on the cover, staring back at me. "*The Life and Death of Elizabeth Wickers,* by Eric Ives?! How can that be?"

"I don't mean to alarm you – you must have changed the narrative of Anne's story, because it's as if she no longer exists and you are in her place!" Professor Marshall's eyes are wide.

I can't say a word – I'm dumbfounded. A shiver runs up my spine. WTF? All I can do is shake my head.

"Not only that, but a couple of blank pages in the book exist, with only their page numbers printed at the bottom." He opens the book to the blanks and shows me. We stare at them, then he looks up at me in disbelief. "But what if you have changed something? The change in title of the book, and the different portrait on the cover, must mean something. What has gone on, then? Please tell me you haven't slept with Henry VIII?"

"No way! I'd never do that. I don't understand what's happened either," I say, shaking my head again. "Have you come across this phenomenon of blank pages before, when you've time-slipped?"

"No. And this worries me." He frowns. "You can't leave history as it is in this book. You appear to be the second wife, for God's sake!" Professor Marshall's face is puce with anger. "You have no choice but to make sure Henry marries Anne."

"What?" I stare at him, my mouth hanging open.

"I'm serious, Beth, you have to go back. History may be about to rewrite itself because of your actions. It looks like you have taken Anne's place and have become Queen of England!"

"But I..." I grasp for words but am hit by this morning's dream, sprinting through the rain to catch Anne Boleyn, in modern London.

"What is it?" he asks. "What are you thinking?"

I slump down in one of his office chairs, and release a long sigh. "You're right, sir, I can't leave things as they are. And there's the problem of me having to retrieve my holdall with my books."

His eyes widen again. "You left those books and all that paperwork you took with you there?"

"I did. I'm sorry." I wonder if he thinks I've done that deliberately. I stare at him, still worried by the difference the time-slipping has made to the book, if that's what's happened. "Professor, are you sure the blank pages aren't a production error? Why would pages be blank like that?"

He goes back to the first few pages of the book and flicks through it at a slower pace, seeing if he can spot any other significant changes. Is he hoping the pages will be full this time? He must have been mistaken before, or it must be an error during printing. The information can't be missing. The title can't have completely changed, with a portrait added of me, that is entirely new.

"I, erm..." He stops flicking. "Look! Those sections have definitely disappeared." He turns the book to face me, offering up the blank pages.

Yep, all I can see are the printed numbers at the bottom of each page. Gawd, this isn't good. What the bloody hell can he do about that?

"But," he says, "it does mean there's still time to rectify things before history is actually 'rewritten'." He seems determined as he snaps the book shut, nodding to himself. "You definitely left all your belongings there?"

"Erm…yes, because the ring flipped me from the palace, straight to my bedroom. I only brought back a small linen bag. Nothing more."

He groans. "Oh, dear. Do you mean to tell me you left every single scrap of historical paperwork there? And those modern books I'd given you?"

"Yes, sir." I grimace, embarrassed by my stupidity. "And…you aren't going to like this – I left my mobile phone there, too."

"Shit, that's not good at all." The poor man looks flustered, and I suspect he wanted to use something stronger than 'shit'. "Do you think Anne might read those papers, or flick through the books?"

"Sir, I have no idea. I hope not." My nerves are rattled. "I warned her enough times not to press me for answers on her future, so I'm hopeful that she's had the common sense not to look at any of them. I think I hid them well enough – under her bed."

"Do you really want to take that chance?" He shakes his head, pushing his glasses back over the bridge of his nose. The thought of me perhaps having altered the history fills me with a strange sense of fear, and urgency. I need to see for myself if anything has changed. I can't leave my modern-day stuff there – if anyone discovered them it might cause a disaster. A nauseous feeling rises in my stomach. No, I can't leave things the way they are.

He grabs the a rolled up piece of kitchen roll from his desk drawer, unwraps it, and offers me the cypher ring. "You're going to have to go back."

I nod. The thought of going back to the Boleyns excites me and terrifies me all at the same time. How can I share with the professor how worried I am about landing back into a situation that might place me in extreme danger? I can't risk being arrested, held as a traitorous prisoner, never to be seen again – or worse, executed by being burnt at the stake as a witch! How can I risk going back, even with the cypher ring?

"I can't!" I stare at the rubies in the ring as they sparkle under the fluorescent lights.

"You can't let your fears override what needs to be done – you can't leave things as they are, and I'm not just referring to leaving your personal belongings in the sixteenth century. You certainly can't risk not going back – especially when we know that history is in the process of being altered." He jabs the cover of the book with his forefinger.

"Stop justifying my going back, Professor, it's not fair!" I glance at the bookcase, and thought I saw it opening. No. That would be weird timing.

Perhaps it only swings open every time someone pulls that Ives' book from the shelf? Strange. Perhaps time itself is trying to tell me that it needs me – that history needs me – and I have no choice but to return to Hever to set things straight.

"Look, Beth, how can you possibly put the history on the right track without knowing if you've derailed it? We know something's not right, because of the blanks, and the cover of the book.' Professor Marshall picks up the book from his desk and waves it in front of me for emphasis. "You know you changed history. The evidence is here. Isn't it your responsibility as a historian, that history is played out as we already know it? You are there to observe, like I've told you so many times before. It's a learning experience, and you're not supposed to meddle."

He fixes his glasses and turns the book over in his hand. "You have to go back, not just for your sake but for Anne, and for the wider history. What if Henry and Anne never get together now, and Elizabeth Tudor is never born? You leaving history in this present state," he continues to wave the mistitled Ives' book at me. "You have, our lives and those who came before us to think of, and if you don't re-write the history of this country, by time-slipping again, you will have changed irreparably."

My mouth's dry, and a lump has formed in the back of my throat as fear and apprehension threaten to overwhelm me. If I can't rectify history, and make amends now, it will be my fault.

"I understand, Professor. History simply can't be allowed to rewrite itself, because the consequences for modern England, and the Empire, are too horrific to even consider."

"Exactly! You have no choice. Go back to Hever, get your stuff, rectify the situation, then get out – that's your objective. If things are altered, you may have to tell Anne her future to set her on the right path again. Tell her she is going to be Queen of England and that she will be mother to a great Tudor monarch but give her no more detail than that. If you leave things as they are then we will have no Gloriana – no Armada." His eyes widen. "No English Civil War. No Queen Victoria, or Queen Elizabeth Mountbatten-Windsor, or Diana, Princess of Wales, and even King Charles III. Imagine that!"

I shudder. Christ, it would all be my fault. Professor Marshall seems to be trying to light a fire under my boots to get me racing back to Hever. And it's working!

"I admit that I messed up." I glare at him. "But you gave me this responsibility!"

"And you gladly accepted it. You need to pick up that mantle of responsibility again, and soon."

I rub my temples, my mind in a whirl. "Go right now, you mean? Get my stuff, tell Anne the truth, then leave?"

"Or, you could stay with her for a few days, just to let the dust settle, and see which way the wind is blowing."

"The best-laid plans…and all that?" I stare at him, then at the ring, realising that if someone comes across my modern stuff, it's going to give my identity away. Poor Mrs Orchard would get into such a fluster if she came across my phone, or even that book with all those familiar Tudor portraits. What if Lady Boleyn sees the book, or the papers, and shows her husband? God, that would be a nightmare, which Anne or I would not be able to explain away.

"One last thing, sir."

His eyebrows arch. "Yes, what is it?"

I reach into my pocket and pull out my keyring with my car keys and house keys. "Can you put these somewhere safe? Just so I know where they are?"

He nods, takes them from me and places them in the top drawer of his desk.

"Just so you know," he says, "there's a spare key to my office door in here, in the event you arrive back when I'm not here." He looks at the bookcase, then holds out the ring to me.

I bite my lip and take it from his outstretched fingers, knowing that I must accept the inevitable and return to Tudor England.

Two

FEBRUARY 1526 – HEVER CASTLE

Equal levels of trepidation and excitement bubble inside me at the thought of seeing the Boleyn family again. To block out the eery stillness of the portal passageways, I pop my *Airpods* in, and in my music app on my *iPod Touch*, select '*Spellbound*' by Siouxsie and the Banshees – it's a favourite 80s track of my Mum's. As Siouxsie's voice echoes through my brain, I take tentative steps, following the flickering flame of the torch I'm carrying, its soft light guiding me through the murky passageways, towards and through the door with the lion's head handle, and up those thirteen steps, which have now become so familiar to me. The cypher ring is on my middle finger but that is the only thing that looks remotely Tudor about my appearance. All I can feel is the solitary pounding of my heart. All I can hear is Budgie's rhythmic drumbeats, and Siouxsie's melodic tones, as I push open the door to the antechamber leading to Anne's bedchamber.

My hope is that no one but Anne will see me. I'm going to stick out like a sore thumb wearing my modern clothes, just as I did at the beginning of this time-travelling adventure, arriving here at Hever. It feels like months have passed since I was last in her company, but it's only been one night. How far will her time have leapt forward? She'll probably be infuriated with me, realising I left the court before I was meaning to, if she doesn't know what happened to me already.

I ease her bedchamber door open, to silence, apart from the music pounding in my ears. I take the time to have a look around. Thank God, I'm alone. I peer through the window to the familiar views of the gardens below. It's cloudy outside, and it must be winter, judging from the dismal colours of the landscape beyond, and the trees' skeletal branches stretching towards the windows from the orchard below. I stop the music playing, and tug the *Airpods* from my ears, stuffing them into my jacket pocket, for safe-keeping with my *iPod Touch*. Now, all I can hear is the cry of birds as they fly from the roof of the castle towards the hedges beyond the moat, then back again. With no one here, I'll have time to search for my holdall and all the stuff I've left behind. The room smells heavily of woodsmoke and sage. Mrs Orchard and Agnes must have been on a cleaning spree. The rushes on the floor look fresh and crisp. Fresh greenery fills a vase, and the hearth has been swept. It's funny the details you notice when you are actually concentrating on looking for something entirely different! Trouble is, where would Anne have put them? My bag's hardly still under the bed. No, she wouldn't have left it there. Goodness, I've left so much of my modern belongings behind – at Richmond Palace, under the floorboards of Anne's bedchamber. No, we rescued those before moving on to the next palace. Most of the toiletries and make-up have probably been used by Anne. It's my mobile phone, the books and paperwork I need to retrieve, otherwise they'll give my identity away, and reveal that I know future events.

If I didn't have this extended mission, I could escape as soon as I've located it all. I'll tell Anne how things need to be, then I'm out of here. It's not like I owe Jane Parker any explanations, even if she did give me a dressing down for spending an evening with the king. Still, I doubt she'll get over knowing that her husband flirts openly with me.

As I look about the bedchamber, I'm hit by the guilt of knowing that I'm letting Anne down. I can't stay with her for too long. It hurts me to think about it, but I can't even stay here for George. I need to get my stuff, find out what's happening with Anne – tell her the truth – then go. That's it. That's all. Come on, Beth, pull yourself together and find your damn gear.

I open the lid of a large trunk placed close to the wall on the other side of the room but, as I turn over the linen shifts, silk gowns, and satin kirtles, I realise my stuff isn't in there. A nearby chest is next, and I rifle through each drawer, my throat tightening as panic rises at my inability to find what I'm looking for. I take a moment to survey the room. The only place I haven't looked is under the bed. Did Anne take it out and hide it? Did Mrs Orchard find it? Surely, she wouldn't have crawled under there. Grasping hope, I drop to the floor and scan the darkness, swiping the lavender-scented rushes aside as I reach towards what might be my holdall. The only way to know for sure is to lie flat and pull myself halfway under the bed. There's something there but the stupid thing is right at the back, beneath the mesh of ropes that hold the mattress in position on the frame. The musty, dusty smell irritates me, and I press my nose and mouth into my shoulder as I stretch. There isn't much wriggle room, but I manage to grab a hold of the strap. Wooh!

"That's a really nice view!" a familiar voice says.

I freeze. George. What's he doing in here? And my bottom and legs are in full view. My face grows hot, and I shift, hitting my head on the mattress. "Christ!"

"Erm...I am not so sure our Lord and Saviour can help you," he says, chuckling. I pull myself further into the darkness, tucking my backside and legs under the bedframe so he has less to see. It's suffocating under here but I can't let him see anymore of me, at least not in my modern clothes. How do I get into such stupid predicaments? I turn my head, noticing his cow-mouthed shoes as he shuffles closer. Then his face appears as he looks into the gloom at me.

"Is that you, Mistress Wickers?" He chuckles again, squinting into the darkness. "If it is, why have you been gone from us for over two years?"

Two years? How on earth have two years passed? I've only been gone one night. I shake my head, trying to remember what happened to Anne during that time. I could check the books in my holdall, just to be sure, but I realise I can't with George here – it's also too dark and cramped under here. Why didn't I pay more attention in some lectures? If George wasn't waiting for me, I'd be able to scurry out into the light to take a quick look. Dammit!

I shove the holdall further into the shadows. Ok, what to do? I can't possibly come out from under this bed. I'm in skinny jeans! For goodness sakes, skin-tight clothing would give even a young man like George a heart attack! I stifle a giggle. This situation is ridiculous, and embarrassing.

"I know you left London abruptly, without explanation," he says. "I was not sure when I would see you again." Frustration edges his voice. "Of all the places I might find you, I certainly did not think you would be hiding under my sister's bed!" He straightens and shuffles from one foot to another. "Are you going to come out from under there?" He's insistent, I'll give him that.

"No, George!" I can't let him see me dressed like this.

"You can't stay under there forever." He laughs again but it's a nervous one, sounding as embarrassed as me. "Are you sure you will not come out?"

"I can't explain why I'm under here," I say, realising too late that I forgot to speak *Tudor*. "Or why I cannot come out. Stop laughing!"

"Mistress, I shall return with my sister."

I'm convinced a smile came with that comment. He turns on his heel and I'm left alone in the dark, my heart pounding through me. I pull myself out from under the bed, as fast as I can, then grab the first linen thing I see from a nearby chest, rip my jacket, T-shirt, and bra off, throw them to the floor, and shove the shift on over my head. After a quick pause to check for sounds outside, I tug my boots off but my objective to look authentically Tudor before I'm discovered, is thwarted when voices filter up from the stairs. Without thinking, I kick my boots under the bed, then dive to my knees and push my jacket, T-shirt, and bra after them into the gloom. Footsteps draw closer and my gut flips. Someone's whispering.

"It is really her?" Anne asks, her French tones an immediate giveaway.

"Yes, sister. But why she has returned to us now, God only knows."

"George, I understand you are angry, I truly do, but I did explain that Beth had been summoned home to her family as her father was seriously ill."

I pull myself into the shallow stillness beneath Anne's bed, needing to get these jeans off. But it's no good, there's no room, and the denim fits like a second skin. My heart is in my mouth. I don't want George to see me in anything modern. I wait. Listen. From the sounds of it, Anne has covered for me – lied for me again. How bad must I have made her feel just leaving her as I did, with no word, no explanation? Nothing. Some friend I am. Jane Parker put me in a terrible situation, I hope Anne knows that. Did George tell her what happened with Jane?

This situation is so frustrating. I can't believe two years have gone by since I was last here. Why can't I control this butterfly effect – this jumping at random, from year to year? Perhaps it's because I used the portal, not the ring on its own, where I'd have to think of a specific place, time, or event. Damn. I really need to remember that. The sound of someone entering the bedroom snaps me back to the moment.

"Beth?" It's Anne. "Beth, are you under my bed?"

I groan. "I'm afraid so, yes."

George chuckles. "Sister, she will not explain why she will not come out!"

"Do not worry, George," Anne says, "I shall sort this out."

I shift about and watch as she pushes him out through her bedroom doorway. When she shuts the door behind him, I manoeuvre myself out from the musty darkness. My jeans are covered in dust, and my ponytail is tangled up in knots.

"Why in God's name were you under my bed?" She stares at me. "And why did you not get word to me that you had left Court?" Anger and frustration knot her features. "Why did you allow George and Agnes to come back to Hever without you?" Her nostrils flare. It's an infuriating habit but she only does it when she's livid. She stares at me, hands on hips.

"Anne, calm yourself," I say, trying to keep my voice low so George won't hear me. "Before I can fully explain what happened, I must change out of these jeans. I can't let George see me like this." I try to smile as I nod at my jeans.

"No – you look like you are a horse-rider, again." She frowns, and I giggle, but she doesn't see the funny side.

"You know, it's a good thing Agnes had the sense to bring all your proper clothing and belongings from Greenwich." She goes over to the trunk I'd been rifling through earlier and pulls out an array of my garments, which I now recognise, and she proceeds to dump them on the bed. I jump with fright when George opens the door without knocking, probably wanting to find out why I was hiding under his sister's bed. He stands there, eyes out on stalks at the sight of me in my tight-fitting, skinny jeans.

"What are those?" He blinks, barely able to comprehend what he's seeing. Anne acts fast, herding him backwards through the doorway.

"Brother, they are new riding clothes." She says this as if it's something everyone should know. "A new fashion from a foreign land."

How true that is. I admire her quick thinking and ability to remain calm under pressure.

"That looks like fashion I have never seen!" he says. He chuckles as he tries to peep through the gap in the door.

"Do not worry, brother – you will not be viewing Beth in them again."

"More's the pity!" He laughs, and Anne giggles with him.

"Now, go away and let me help Beth change!" She steps back in and closes the door on him before rotating the key in the lock. Then she turns to face me. "You know, he will never look at you in the same way, now he has seen you in *those*... What do you call them?"

"Skinny jeans," I reply, stifling a giggle. I pull my socks off, then start pulling my jeans off. Anne looks aghast because my jeans are so tight, I literally have to peel them off. My knickers are the last to be discarded. I throw everything on the bed. It looks like I'm staying, for a while, anyway. Also, now George has seen me, it gives me no choice.

As Anne helps me change, her questioning becomes more insistent.

"You haven't told me why you left George and Agnes to return home alone. I know it has been two years but, what happened?"

"You won't – I mean, you will not like it, mistress." I shiver as she ties cuffs closed on the sleeves of my shift.

"I may not, but it would be a kindness to have an answer." She passes me a petticoat, her jaw set firm as she awaits my response.

"I had to get away from Court." I put the petticoat on over my shift and start lacing it up.

"Why, what happened?" She frowns for a moment, then walks to a small side table and pours herself a goblet of wine. "Would you like some?"

"Yes, please," I reply, fixing on my kirtle. She pours a second glass, then comes over to ladder-lace me. I hug the bedpost as she pulls the lace as tight as she can. By the time she finishes, I'm practically gasping for breath. Next, she eases my arms into a matching overgown of brown silk velvet.

"You were explaining why you left Court," she says through a mouthful of pins, forcing me to continue telling my sorry tale.

"George was jealous – he made the whole situation very awkward." She begins to secure the placard in place with pins. "Should Agnes not be dressing me?"

"Never mind Agnes – did I not warn you to stay away from the advances of my brother?" I twist to glance at her, and she doesn't look happy.

"You did. Ouch! That hurts." I wince as she secures the last pin into the placard.

"I am sorry."

Hmm, I'm not sure she is. I sit on a chair and pull up the woollen stockings she has given me and tie them with garters. Next, she hands me a pair of leather slippers, and just as I slide my feet into them, the bedroom door swings open. George again.

"I have no wish to disturb you, ladies, but, sister, you know that there were rumours at Court that Beth had slept with the King?" It's obvious that he's been listening, and he doesn't look happy.

"George, I never went to bed with His Majesty!"

"Then, if you did not sleep with him, what did His Majesty want when you spent the night with him?"

There's no doubt he thinks the worst of me. "Your father asked me to keep Mary in the King's mind while we were away at Court. I did exactly as I was asked." I refuse to avert my eyes as he stares at me.

"But Jane told me you went to the King's bed."

"She would, wouldn't she," I snap back.

"George, you cannot blame your wife," Anne chides. "She only grumbled about the situation because you had made such a fuss about Beth!"

Wife? My heart sinks. I should have known with two years having passed. The ceremony has taken place, then – of course, it has. My mouth is dry, and my heart feels as if it's in my mouth, but I'm relieved that I was away long enough for the event to pass and I didn't have the stress or the pain of attending the wedding.

George glances at me as if he's a little lost. "Mistress Wickers, you must know, I never married for love – it was on Father's insistence. I did not have a choice. The King had made the match. If she'd been a horse in a bum-roll, I still would have had to marry her!" He groans through a long sigh. "And in my life, I could not have imagined a wife I would have loved – unless she could have been you."

His sentiments astound me. Anne stares at the two of us, probably just as shocked by her brother's statement. A heavy silence lingers between us for a long moment, until one of us plucks up the courage to speak.

"You will come to love Jane eventually," Anne says. "And in my case, I would like to please Father by making a match that would mean advancement for us all."

"Anne, you would take pleasure as a widow!" He chuckles. "Marry an old rich lord. Then, when your husband dies, you will be able to take your pick of the rest of the gentlemen at Court. All the men love a widow!"

"Oh, George!" she cries. "You would spend my virginity on an old man of a corpse!"

I wince, rubbing my cheek. "Like the King's little sister with Louis XII?"

"Never!" Anne says. "I felt sorry for her. How could she have his decrepit body rising and falling on her every night?"

I shudder at the thought but it's a vision I'm finding difficult to eradicate from my mind. It makes me think of a time not that far off when women will be repulsed by the smell of Henry's ulcerous leg.

"Louis' body was only fit for burial – that's the truth of it!" George laughs again.

Even I laugh at that but Anne glares at me, assuming that I'm being just as disrespectful as her brother. I need to change the subject – to find out where I am in her story, and what I have missed.

"What year is it?" I ask her. I just want confirmation. She doesn't seem surprised by my question and doesn't bat an eyelid. George, on the other hand, looks at me, his eyes widen, not understanding why I wouldn't know such a basic fact as the year.

"The year of our Lord, fifteen-twenty-six," he says, his eyes shadowed beneath a deep frown. "Why would you not know the year we are in?"

"And the month?" I ask, ignoring him.

"February," Anne answers. George's eyebrows knit together as he twists a toothpick between his fingers. A usual habit for him.

"George, it's easy to lose track of time when you are consumed with looking after loved ones. Don't be so hard on Beth."

"I'm not being unkind!" he grumbles.

"You were unkind to her at Court – Agnes told me." She leans towards him. "Jealous of the King, weren't you, George?" It's nice to hear her defending me.

His face flushes. "I could not help my feelings."

"But, George," I say, astonished, "you know your jealousy was unfounded."

"Clearly, you did not see the situation from my point of view," he retorts, not at all pleased. "All eyes were on you with the King, and I saw how he looked at you!" He continues fiddling with the toothpick.

I giggle. "George, Henry looks at all women that way!" I don't think he's finding it funny.

"Brother, you see the King dance with many ladies of the court, yet you are never angry like you were on that occasion." She raises a brow. "Agnes told me how incensed you were, shouting at Beth through the door from outside her chambers."

His shoulders slump. "I could not help myself." He looks lost as he stares into the fire. Poor George – he's no longer the seventeen-year-old I'd first met. He must be about twenty-one now, or thereabouts. "You know how I feel…"—he pretends to ignore me but then flicks a look my way—"about Beth." Heat rises in my cheeks. I wish he hadn't said that.

"I have told the both of you before, this affection you have for one another cannot go on." She looks at me, then her gaze rests on George. "Brother, you should not dote on Mistress Wickers, who can do as she wills. You need to remember that you are married, where she is not."

I cough into my hand, heat rising in my cheeks. Anne sure knows how to embarrass a person and put them in their place. My heart goes out to George.

"What was your wedding like, George?" I ask.

He sighs and shakes his head. "I was throwing up."

"My brother was never ready to go to church," Anne says. "He was drunk!"

"I was sick!" He looks from her to me. "And…I intended to stay that way for as long as possible."

Anne glances at me. "You know, Beth, George was out of his chambers all night before the wedding."

"How so?" I ask, remembering to speak Tudor. Even though I've only been away for one night in my time, it's like my twenty-first-century visit has knocked the Tudor out of me.

George holds his open hand out, palm to ceiling, as if questioning why he has to answer such a query. "I was at Southwark."

"Tippling houses, and Southwark stews – George never takes care, Beth."

"I did not care!" he growls. "Anything to take my mind off marrying Jane Parker."

"George, that is no way for a member of His Majesty's Privy Chamber to talk."

"Who will hear how I talk?" he asks.

"We hear it," she answers. "Father and Mother will hear you. They say the King highly favours you, and, as such, you cannot speak of your wife in such a way."

He slumps back in a chair, still twiddling the toothpick between his fingers. "I know the King favours me. He likes it when I lose to him at cards!" He smirks.

Anne smiles. "George, the King likes it when anyone loses to him at cards. Your wedding, brother, was a celebration for all, including the King."

He snorts. "Celebration? Hardly. You know, sister, that I was with Tom Wyatt, drowning our matrimonial sorrows."

"Why did you marry Jane if you dislike her so much?" I ask. "Clearly, she is taken with you."

"That, Beth, is what makes it worse!" He holds his head and groans in frustration. "Remember, Father gave me no choice in the matter, and *she* couldn't wait to get her hands on me. At least Wyatt never has that concern – his Elizabeth Brooke is handsomely taken elsewhere in an extramarital affair."

"You know," Anne says, "I'd pity Jane Parker if she wasn't a vixen in a mild disguise."

George stares at her. "I knew you hated Jane!"

"Have you always despised her, Anne?" I ask.

She shakes her head. "Not despised or hated, Beth. Disliked, maybe – I just do not understand how she deserves my sweet brother."

"Jane was worth a good opinion for the match with Father, Uncle, and the King. They say my marriage was good enough for a fine wedding present." He chuckles. "Henry gave me Grimston Manor. That is worth one night with any drab – even Jane!" He laughs to himself.

"How can you insult Jane so?" I ask, somewhat shocked.

"My relationship with Jane is a painful one, but it's politics – the Parker's had the right connections, so Father said. Wyatt is lucky, he never sees his wife." He looks at Anne. "You know, sister, Wyatt loves you. He always has."

Anne reddens as she coughs into her hand.

"Where is Jane?" I ask him, trying to bring the conversation back on line.

"At Court, serving in the Queen's household."

Anne steeples both hands at her chin. "At least, with my sister-in-law not here, it will give us time to discuss what has happened, Beth, with you having been away, and for you to speak with my parents – apologise to them, perhaps." Her eyes widen as she nods at me. I'm not looking forward to facing them, sure they will be mad with me. I know it.

"What did you both tell them?" I ask.

"What we already knew," she says, "that you had gone home to care for your father." That was a well thought out lie but I hope it doesn't bring some kind of prophecy to pass against my real-life father – she knows my Tudor family doesn't exist.

"We even placed candles for your father at the altar in Saint Peter's," George says, looking at me, maybe in the hope that his generosity might be appreciated.

"That was most kind of you, George." I feel guilty for yet another lie but what can I do?

"Beth?"

"Yes, Anne?"

"You never told us exactly what the King wanted with you." She pushes a loose strand of hair from her eyes. "If he did not lay with you, what reason would he have to summon you?"

George rests his elbow on the side of the chair and leans his chin on his hand, waiting for my answer.

"He wanted to speak with me – to find out how Mary was."

"And?" George asks.

"And…to find out what Anne thought of him."

"Me?" Her eyes are wide, her mouth open. "Why?"

"I think the King has been trying to work out for a long time what you think of him." I'm not lying, and I need to get things moving – I have a serious mission to complete.

"But…why? Why does my opinion matter to the King?"

"He cares about how he is perceived," I answer.

She leans closer. "I have no idea why His Majesty would be interested in what I think about him." She plays with the tangled girdle belt hanging from her waist, her brows joined by her frown. "What reply did you make?"

I can't lie to her. Here goes nothing. "I told him that you thought he had forced himself on Mary."

Her face turns puce.

"You did what?" George asks.

"I was honest with the King!" I splutter. "What else could I be?"

Anne glares at me. "Now you sound like my sister. Always trying to please others!" She shrugs at George. "Brother, now do you understand why the King has asked after me – why he pesters you about my wellbeing?"

He nods. "It makes sense now."

"Trust me," I say, butting in, "the conversation was not as bad as it sounds."

"Why ever not?" Anne asks, her tone leaving no doubt that she's annoyed.

"Because I told him that Mary loved him." I smile at her. "He was pleased by that."

George chuckles. "He must have been because Mary is pregnant again."

"Is she?" I ask, as if I didn't know. Her daughter Catherine, must be about two years old now.

Someone taps on the door. Anne gets up to open it, and Mary enters.

"What are you huddled in here for, I heard voices, so wanted to be in on the conversation." She clutches her rounded belly. "I did not know Mistress Wickers had returned to Hever."

"Neither did we, sister," George says. "Until now."

She smiles. "I hope you are well, Beth?"

"I am very well, thank you," I say. "And you look like your baby is growing well." By the size of her bump, this latest baby doesn't look like it has much longer to spend in there.

"Now, what were you all talking about?" she asks.

"You," George says.

"I hope you are saying only nice things about me." She sighs, sounding tired, as she lowers herself onto a velvet, cushion-covered chair. "I need to talk to you all." She groans as she settles herself against the back of the chair, no doubt uncomfortable with her time fast approaching. George gets up and walks to the small sideboard where the jug of wine sits. He selects an empty wine glass and pours the burgundy liquid in.

"Does anyone want some?" he asks, lifting the flagon up.

"I will, thank you, George." I pass my empty glass to him.

"And I, brother." Anne passes her glass to me, and I give it to him.

"Just a small glass for me, George," Mary says. "I'm sure milk must be better for this small babe." She rubs her belly. George hands the refilled wine glasses around and settles back into his chair, taking a small gulp from his goblet.

"I am sure it will not be long before this babe is here with us." She sounds confident. "It is nice to see you back, Beth. How is your father?" Anne must have lied well because she doesn't seem put out by my long absence.

"Well, thank you, Mary."

"Anne and Beth, you will be with me when my time comes, will you not?" She nurses the glass of wine on top of her belly.

"I am not sure mother will allow us." Anne sounds concerned.

"Mary, you have done this once before." George wiggles his brows in jest. "You will be well, it's not like you do not know what to do!" Even at times of stress, he never fails to make us all smile.

Mary nods. "I am hoping the arrival of this child will be successful. And this time, it has to be William's."

"Are you certain?" Anne asks.

"As certain as I can be."

George laughs. "If this new baby has hair the colour of Catherine's, then you can be sure it's a Tudor!"

"Does William know your time is close?" I ask.

"Not yet, he is still at Court, though I expect he will return to Hever in a few days. I have written to him, and Father has sent Robert Cranewell to him with my letter. He will soon know that my time is near."

"Have you told the King the baby might be his?" I'm not sure I should be asking such an impertinent question.

"Yes, I told Harry – I mean, Henry – before I left Richmond." She shifts, glancing around the room as her cheeks flush. "He knows there is a possibility the babe might be his, but I have had no word from him since, not even a letter." She stares at the wine glass resting on her bump. "Perhaps it is over with him." She sniffs.

Anne looks at me, then back at Mary. "But he could show some responsibility!" Her anger carries across the bedchamber, her neck reddening. "He cannot allow things to end like this with you – just like that."

"Why not?" George asks, rubbing the back of his neck. "He is the King." Mary looks as if she is about to burst into tears on hearing that remark.

"George!" I shout. Why does he have to say unkind things, at the most inappropriate time? It may be a truthful statement but can he not spare Mary's feelings? Even though he's two years older than when I last saw him, he's still acting like a petulant teenager. So annoying.

"He will not own it, George," Mary says, her voice rising as she fights back tears. Her hormones must be getting the better of her. However, these people have no knowledge of such a concept so I can't share the reason for her sensitivity. "We only have to look at Catherine to see she is Henry's." She leans across to the small table beside her and sets her wine glass down. "But you know the legal presumption because I am a married woman. Any child I bear is my husband's so the King can avoid scandal." She sounds resigned as she rubs her belly, then wipes away a stray tear.

"What is it?" I ask, giving her shoulder a light squeeze. "It can't be that bad." She shrugs her eyebrows and her shoulders.

"Do not tell us you have come away from this affair with nothing for the child," Anne says, glaring at her sister. "Knowing you, your conscience has disallowed you from petitioning the King for any financial assistance, again. It is just like last time."

"Anne don't upset Mary further," I say, all too aware of my haughty tone.

"I am not," she shoots back. "I am just being practical." She tilts her head and frowns. "Father will be disappointed, again."

"Please do not tell Father, at least not until I have spoken with William."

"You do not do yourself any favours, Mary," George says, shaking his head.

I rub her arm in reassurance. "At least you have confided in us."

"You look tired," Anne says. She sips her wine.

"Come on." I extend my hand to Mary and get up. "Let me help you go back to bed. I can tuck you in."

Anne sets her glass on the table and helps me pull Mary up, and we walk arm in arm towards the bedroom door.

"Don't worry, Mary," I say, "you should be happy, you are having another child."

She grimaces at me. "Women die in childbirth, you know."

"You won't be one of them." I can't hold back a chuckle. Anne looks at me, as if I'm some kind of witch predicting the future, and, to her, I suppose I am. It makes me shiver.

"Everything will be fine," George says as we leave the room.

"Yes, brother. Thank you. William is hoping for a boy this time."

I'm not going to give the game away and tell them that Henry Carey will be arriving soon.

We stand beneath the portcullis as we wait to greet Thomas Boleyn. He appears at the gatehouse entrance, as a dot in the distance, with Robert Cranewell, his servant. Within minutes, he alights from his horse and hands the reins to Robert, who leads both horses to the stables. Thomas crosses the drawbridge, passes under the portcullis, and makes his way to Anne, who throws her arms wide in welcome. He wraps her in a gentle embrace but with equal enthusiasm, with Anne burying her face against his velvet gown.

"You smell wonderful!" he says.

She smiles. "It's a new perfume, Father."

He inhales the creamy scent of vanilla and cinnamon, unaware, of course, that it's a twenty-first-century scent, heady and luxurious – gifted to Anne by me.

"It reminds me of Christmastide." He chuckles as he leans in to hug me. "Good morrow, Beth, it is good to see you." He whispers in my ear, "How is your father?"

"Much better, thank you, sir." Why was I ever worried about how he would be with me? He's a kind and gentle soul.

George fakes a loud cough. He doesn't like being ignored. "Father." He pats Thomas on the shoulder. "How was your journey?"

"I am tired, son." He sighs. The ride back from Greenwich, through Blackheath and back down to Kent, must have been exhausting for him.

"Father," Anne says, "is there any news of when I can return to Court? Have you spoken with the Queen, or even His Majesty?"

"Daughter, you know what my answer will be." He removes his cap and steps into the inner hallway, resting his hand on her shoulder and giving her a tender look. "You cannot go back to Court until Mary has given birth to our second grandchild." He smiles, no doubt to ease the pain. "Besides, you need to help your mother look after little Catherine, with Mrs Orchard."

"Of course," she says, her shoulders slumping.

"Where is your mother?"

"In the library, sir," Agnes answers, bobbing a little curtsey, her cheeks a rosy hue. She carries a pile of dirty linens, busy with her chores. "Good morrow, sir." She sounds buoyant, which is nice to see considering how hard she works.

"Agnes." He nods. "I hope you are keeping well?"

"I be very good, sir." She bustles off in the direction of the kitchen.

He places his feathered cap on the settle in the Entrance Hall and runs his hand through his fine, greying hair. "Children, Mistress Wickers, give me a moment with my wife – I promise, we will all spend time together later." He slips a leather folio under his arm and thumbs the buckle of his belt.

"Of course, Father," George says. Anne and I watch as Thomas finds his wife waiting for him in the library, one of my favourite rooms, with its walnut panelling and shelves full of precious, leather-bound books. He places the folio on his desk, then goes to her. "Embrace me, then?" he asks, opening his arms to her.

I love the tenderness between them – it makes me happy to see their closeness – it will make them stronger in the years ahead.

She allows his arms to enfold her, and they embrace for a long moment.

"Husband, it is good to see you," she says, standing back from him, lit by the warmth and glow of the small fire crackling in the grate. "You must be cold and tired."

"Yes, Liz, I am," he replies, as Anne eases the door shut.

She gives me a sweet smile but carries a touch of melancholy in her dark eyes. I can tell she yearns for the kind of love her parents share – the kind of love she believes she lost in Henry Percy. To love someone, as she loved Percy, and for him to be unable to return her feelings, must be painful for her. I wonder if she is over him. Unrequited love makes me think of George.

Perhaps there's a kind of beauty in that sort of love. It burns bright in those who experience it. I know I long to be loved in that unconditional way. It's clear to see that Thomas and Elizabeth experience that 'once in a lifetime' kind of love daily – even now in their late married life. God only knows if that will ever happen for me.

Three

I spend my time waiting for the arrival of spring, enjoying Anne's company, with her family. In the evenings, after supper, we gather in the cosy parlour, in front of a crackling and popping hearth fire. Being with them all like this, makes me think of my own parents. Of my sister Jo, and my little niece. I miss them all. It's weird because, when I'm here with the Boleyns, I feel like I'm home, and my modern life doesn't seem real. I think of Rob when I look at George – they are such different characters. George is so full of life – even Ambassador Chapuys, who will later become Anne's most bitter enemy, will love him. Everyone loves George. After all, what is there to dislike about him?

My heart skips a beat when he joins us in the parlour, reclining next to me in the settle, his feet stretched towards the hearth. He has good legs. I can't help but glance at his codpiece, stifling a giggle. They are such strange appendages to have on clothes, but they do draw the eye to a man's jewels, which is exactly what they are intended to do. He notices me glancing, and chuckles.

"Do you like my new clothes, Beth?" He smirks. His eyes are bright and his smile broad as he jokes with me, whereupon the conversation and gossip become lively, infused with everyone's laughter. In all this good humour, I mustn't forget my mission, which is ultimately to bear witness to how things are in their lives, and to ensure history runs true to how we know it.

He tells us he has been awarded the sum of an additional twenty pounds a year for him and his wife to live on. I chuckle to myself at what that would buy me in modern England – dinner, and a couple of drinks! He smiles at me, probably wondering what I find funny. I'm pleased to hear of his good fortune, and Thomas looks proudly on his youngest child. And, as they sit together, the acrimony I'd witnessed between them before I left appears to have dissipated. George delights in teaching me several new card games he has learned in his time at Court, while Thomas reiterates how he has witnessed his son impressing the king.

During the day, when the weather permits, Anne and I walk with her mother in the gardens to gather herbs and early spring flowers. Lady Boleyn's attitude to Anne has thawed. Their relationship appears to have improved and, ever-gracious, she offers sympathy for her thwarted marriage plans with both James Butler and Harry Percy. To my relief, she has stopped berating her for being drawn into such mistakes and misdemeanours.

"Mother, you know I seek a marriage based on love, like yours and father's – for passion – and I understand how James Butler did not work out for me, and any pre-contract with Henry Percy was ultimately not permitted." Her remarks cause her mother to cast a look of both admiration and pity. "But can Father not arrange another suitable match?" She sounds despondent.

"I want you to marry for love – I am not sure your brother is happy with Jane." She frowns. "I hope your father has not made a bad match there. Believe me, I do not want any of my children to be unhappy." She throws a side-glance at me, but I have no idea what she means by it, then focuses back on Anne. "However, I am your mother, and I am obliged to discourage you from the notion of a love-match. And the truth is, many men are seeking brides much younger than you."

Another back-handed compliment Elizabeth Boleyn seems to relish giving out so freely. Anne must be twenty-five by now. As such, that's not old, at least not in my mind, but by Tudor conventions, her age is causing her to be overlooked on the marriage market for younger women of the court, unless Sir Thomas can manage to arrange another match, and soon. I know, or have an idea, how things are in that regard. However, I'm surprised she's never matched with any other men. It puzzles me why her father doesn't receive offers of marriage for his younger daughter every few months. Will she become wrapped in another arrangement similar to one she had with Henry Percy, before I manoeuvre Henry to snatch her up? Sources have never been found to record such a match happening, so I'm determined to make sure it's Henry who makes a play for her next, so history takes its right path.

My thoughts nudge me back, reminding me of the purpose of this visit. I'm angry with myself for being distracted by silly frivolities. I need to remember how things must go.

Lady Boleyn picks a handful of daffodils from a nearby flowerbed and drops them in her basket. "Girls, we well know that noble-born women from households of means have little say in selecting husbands. As far as my husband is concerned, marriage is strictly a matter of creating lineal and financial arrangements." She sounds decisive. "I wish for both your sakes things were different."

Anne giggles. "Mother, I knew you could not stay mad at me forever!"

Her mother gives her a reassuring smile. Thank God everything seems back to normal with these two. It's not easy walking on eggshells around them. Since Anne's banishment from Court by Wolsey over the Percy matter, her mother seems to have enjoyed telling her off, and even ignoring her at times.

She turns to me. "What of your marriage prospects, Beth?"

I glance at Anne, not knowing how to reply. Save me, Anne.

"Mother, can we concentrate on my lack of marriage proposals first, rather than Beth's?"

"Only if Beth does not want to discuss such matters?"

"I mean no disrespect, Lady Boleyn, or should I be calling you Lady Rochford?" I'm hoping my questioning will take her mind off my love life. Fair play to Anne for getting me out of what could have been an awkward predicament.

"Please, Beth, Lady Boleyn is sufficient. It is my married name, after all – Lady Rochford is my title." She smiles. "However, in close company, as we are now, you may call me Elizabeth." She nods once.

"Elizabeth, concerning a match, I am happy to tarry a while." I smile, hoping she doesn't pick up on my unease. "Marriage, for me, at this moment, is not important."

"You have a very independent attitude," she says, "and I am uncertain your parents would approve of such an opinion, on such a significant matter as marriage."

"Mother, leave Beth be." Anne scowls. "What about me, or do you not care about that?"

"Anne, I am confident that your father will yet find you a desirable husband."

Anne sighs, knowing that she may miss her chance if her father doesn't deal with the matter soon.

"You worry too much! Besides, your father is widely recognized at Court as a consummate negotiator and tactician." She gives her daughter's hand a reassuring squeeze. "He has made a good match for Mary, and for George, no matter what your brother may say, and I am sure he will make a beneficial match for you just as equally." She turns to me. "Then we can help Beth make arrangements just as significant for her, in marriage!"

My face burns and I can't bring myself to reply.

"Mother, is it not our place to decide on such a thing?" She glares at her mother. "Perhaps Beth's parents should be the ones negotiating such a match?"

"All marriage negotiations and matches should be advantageous for all parties," her mother says, "and both families, as well as being a union of love. Why should all young people not be happy with their spouses as they set out together on this journey of life? Should it not be an advantage for all?"

"Lady Boleyn, if everyone entered into partnerships and marriages with your attitude, we would all be the happiest of people, would we not?" I link my arm through Anne's as we walk across the meadow.

"It is encouraging that my husband does not see marriage just as a political advantage, as many husbands and fathers. My brother Norfolk pushes Thomas to think like him – that marriage is about political ambition, and nothing more, but my husband has always had a kinder heart." She looks at the sky and smiles. "However, I know he hopes for love to grow in his children's marriages, and if they bring political advantages, he says 'tis all the better."

"Mother, I am glad Father does not listen to Uncle. Look how Norfolk treats his wife – there are rumours he beats her, and we have all heard how unhappy their marriage is."

"Yes, Anne, 'tis a pity, because I think my brother would have mellowed a little had he had the comfort of a loving relationship with your aunt."

"I think the unhappiness lies more with my aunt than my uncle, Mother."

Lady Boleyn doesn't reply as we begin to make our way back towards the castle. Her wicker basket is full of spring flowers ready to decorate our bedrooms. The Boleyn women love spending time in the gardens, and enjoy the work, though Anne tends to watch rather than get her fingers dirty. We cross the bridge spanning the moat, and walk through the courtyard.

Once inside, we find Sir Thomas is in the parlour with William Carey, who has returned from Court after receiving his summons from Mary. The poor man is pacing the floor, anxious. Lady Boleyn leaves her gardening gloves and the basket of flowers on the sideboard, and goes upstairs with Mrs Orchard and Agnes, who has settled Mary into the bedchamber ready for her confinement. It's a waiting game now.

I knock on the door and ask Sir Thomas and William if they would like any wine or bread. Both nod to me, so I walk to the kitchen and fetch a wooden plate laid with cheeses and a flagon of red wine. I place the refreshments on a side table, and, just before I leave, Sir Thomas addresses me. He fills two goblets with wine and passes one to William, then stands before the fire as the flames crackle and whip in the grate. Having spent copious amounts of time with Anne, I haven't had the opportunity to spend much with her father. He's clever, cultured, and able, entirely the kind of man King Henry likes to have about him.

"What think you of the King's dalliance with my daughter Mary?"

He watches me, waiting for my reply. This man is of a gentle disposition and does not appear to be cunning, manipulative, or cruel. In fact, Thomas Boleyn often appears somewhat timid, and 'not of a warlike disposition'. No doubt, he has drive, with ambition to be an even more successful courtier, but from what I have seen of him, the overbearing man depicted on television and film belongs in the realm of fiction.

"Sir." I take a shallow curtsy before him. "My opinion counts for nothing."

"Beth, come now, you have been living with our family for some time. I am sure you cannot help but observe the goings-on in our household and at Court. You must have an opinion." His lip curls into a gentle smile. "We heard about your late-night audience with His Majesty." His look is direct. "George told me." My face burns. This isn't good. What must he think of me? "I am giving you an allowance to be a companion to Anne, and sent you to Court in her stead, remember?" He rests his goblet on the mantle.

"Yes, sir." I dip a sharp curtsy, wanting to avoid any confrontation, which I'm surprised hasn't happened sooner. As I turn to go, he cups my shoulder with his hand.

"Stay," he says. "Converse with William and me for a while." His tone leaves no room for refusal. "Besides, do you not think you owe me an explanation as to what happened with you and the king?"

I shrug, astounded that he's been so blatant with the question. Having William in the room makes things extra-awkward but I do as I'm asked, settling myself in a chair near the fire while the father-in-waiting continues to pace.

"The king asked me how things were with Mary." I flutter my eyelashes as I try to hide my nervousness.

"Really?" William says. "What did he want to know?"

Sir Thomas gives him a stern look, as if to say, 'Let me do the talking', and he indicates that the man should stop pacing and sit.

"And what reply did you make?" Sir Thomas asks.

"I told the king that Mary admires His Grace as much as any other of his subjects."

"And?" William asks, exasperated.

"William, be quiet," Sir Thomas growls. "Let me handle this."

"I told him that she is well, and that was it, sir." With Mary's husband sat in the room, I couldn't exactly tell Sir Thomas that I told Henry she was in love with him. That would not be fair.

"Did he ask about little Catherine, or perhaps he indicated what might happen to Mary once this new baby is born?"

"No, sir. As you know, I had this conversation with the king long before we knew Mary was pregnant again."

"Of course." His mouth curls up at the corners. "Did Henry talk of anything else?"

Hmm, so curious. What is he really asking? "Yes, sir. He did ask after Anne."

"Anne?" He frowns. "Whatever for?"

"I think he was trying to find out what she thinks of him."

He grunts. "Come now, Beth, why would he want to know what Anne thinks of him?"

"Perhaps he wants to know if he is liked," I suggest. "For himself?"

"Indeed, the king is liked — what a ridiculous question!"

William bristles. "You are calling the king ridiculous, sir?"

"No, no!" Thomas grumbles as he looks towards his son-in-law. "I'm trying to understand what the king wants from us, William. I am trying to ascertain what he will want from the Boleyns next."

"Obviously, now he wants Anne!" William snaps. "Since, it appears, he has finished with my wife!"

"Now you are being ridiculous, William!"

"Could it not be a possibility, sir?" William sounds deadly serious.

Sir Thomas turns to me. "What say you, Mistress Wickers?"

"I say the king can do what he wants, sir. After all, he is the king, and what the king wants, he gets, does he not?" I produce a meek smile, hoping my answer will satisfy his curiosity.

"It is the correct reply, of course, but not the one I am waiting on."

His expression is serene and calm as he waits for me to speak. I'm not sure what to say. Goodness, will he chastise Anne for entertaining a relationship with the king? I gather myself.

"Sir, with respect, it is not my place to comment."

He looks at me with curious eyes and takes another sip of his wine, then settles the goblet on the mantel.

"Do you think I have manipulated Mary for my own ends?" He tilts his head, his gaze fixed on my face, then looks at William, then back at me. "Do you think I would offer Anne up to the king, as Norfolk did with Mary?" I glance at William and remember Mary once telling me how angry he'd been about her becoming the king's mistress. I wonder how the poor man feels about the possibility of this forthcoming child having royal blood.

"No, sir, I do not. Your diplomatic record speaks for itself – you do not need your daughters to align themselves with the king to achieve anything."

He smiles at me now, seemingly pleased with my answer. "Beth, you are aware of my responsibilities to the king since he came to the throne?" He cups his chin with his thumb and forefinger, his other arm folded behind his back. A proud man, he seems keen to show he is not the manipulator those at Court may believe him to be.

"Yes, sir, I am."

"Did you know I was present at Katharine of Aragon's wedding to Prince Arthur?"

"No, I did not." I lean forward, resting my elbow on the arm of the chair, wanting to catch every single phrase he utters.

"Or that I escorted Margaret Tudor, Henry VII's daughter, to Scotland to marry King James IV?"

"No, sir," I reply, with some surprise, and lean back again against the cushion.

"I was appointed an esquire of the body before Henry VII's death, and our present king chose to keep me on. I was knighted by his majesty, and my good lady wife, Elizabeth, served as one of the baronesses of the Queen's chamber at the coronation of Henry VIII and Katharine."

"Sir, you astound me with your diplomatic prowess."

"As well as this, Beth, I was appointed keeper of the foreign exchange in Calais and served as Sheriff of Norfolk and Suffolk. I participated in revels in honour of the queen and dressed up as one of Robin Hood's men!"

He smiles with pride and, to my amazement, continues reciting his list of accomplishments, astounding me with his complete diplomatic record and service. I wonder what's got into him, telling a woman he hardly knows all this personal information. Maybe the prospect of becoming a grandfather again has gone to his head, along with the wine?

"I was involved in arranging the jousts to celebrate the birth of Prince Henry, Duke of Cornwall, and was also a chief mourner and one of the knight bearers at his funeral in February fifteen-eleven. Indeed, I was also given rewards and grants in that same year, which included the keepership of the park of Beskwode, Nottinghamshire, the manors of Borham, and powers in Essex, Bushy in Hertfordshire, Purbright in Surrey, and Henden in Kent. Not forgetting Culverts and Little Waltham in Essex. To add to this list of accomplishments, I was appointed Sheriff of Kent." He picks up his goblet and takes a long sip of his wine. I catch a look between him and William, confirming that he's having a bit of fun with me with all this boasting.

"Sir, what a day of joyful celebration for the king when Prince Henry was born."

"Yes, and utter despair for the king and queen when he died but fifty-two days later. The country went into a black mourning that day. Court was a dismal place for such a period." He looks into his goblet, having reached the bottom of it.

"Forgive me, William," I say, "what if the child Mary is carrying is His Majesty's, and what will happen if it turns out to be a boy?" I ask this almost in a whisper, hoping that mentioning the 'elephant in the room' will not get me banished from the Boleyn household.

He shoots up from the stool, glaring at me for even mentioning the possibility of such a thing. I don't think either of them expected a woman to imply such a thing in their presence.

"William! William! Sit!" Sir Thomas urges, his voice low but firm. He walks over to William's side and places a strong hand on his shoulder until he sits. I hope they don't think I am insulting the Boleyn-Carey alliance by asking such a question – I only want to know what historians have debated for nearly five-hundred years!

"The baby could be William's, just as equally as it could be the king's. It makes no difference. The king has never granted any titles or lands to a family related to a bastard child, until the birth of the duke of Richmond by Bessie Blount. As a family, we expect nothing from His Majesty. I have always been granted favour based on my endeavours to support the king and not, as Norfolk would suggest, by the virginity, chastity, and advancement in favour of my daughter Mary!"

His face has turned an indignant scarlet at my implied presumption that he is trying to advance his family through his eldest daughter placing herself in the bed of the king.

"My worth to His Majesty is beyond doubt. I was awarded grants and appointments jointly with Henry Wyatt, including the office of constable and keeper of the castle and jail of Norwich, as well as being granted one half of the custody of the lands, wardship, and marriage of John, son, and heir of Sir George Hastings. I was then sent to the Court of Margaret of Austria, with John Young and Sir Robert Wingfield, to act as an envoy to her father, Maximilian, Holy Roman Emperor, to conclude an alliance between England and the Empire against France. During this alliance, I developed a friendship with Margaret that meant I was able to secure a place for Anne at her court. I was respected by Margaret, and Anne, in her turn, has benefited from this alliance."

He is now pacing the room. I am in awe of his record and how fast he has risen at Henry VIII's court and how respected he is by the French royal family and other courtiers. He is an intelligent, charismatic, hardworking renaissance man, and is to be applauded for his incredible achievements and for providing his children, including his daughters, with a European education and amazing opportunities that other courtiers' children have not benefited from.

Being a diplomat is his job – that is what a courtier in his position must do. The Tudor court is a dangerous place, where he must negotiate to survive. He continues with his list of accomplishments, much to William's amusement, who knows full well his father-in-law's credentials.

"Sir, I did not mean to cause offence," I say, lowering my gaze.

He jolts to a stop, his chin out. "I asked for your opinion, and you gave it." He looks to the father-to-be. "William, please forgive Mistress Wickers – I think she meant you no disrespect." He walks over and taps the younger man's shoulder, as William glares at me.

"I know Beth meant no harm. I…have had to live with this situation, and with Mary being with child twice now." He sighs. "I am hoping His Majesty's head will be turned by another…and soon."

I stare past him, raising my brows. Little does he know.

"Do not be so despondent," Sir Thomas says. "Catherine could as easily be yours! Besides, Mary is of strong disposition. Once the child has been born, and mother and child are doing well, then, perhaps you and she can go and live quietly in the country?"

"Sir, for all our sakes, I hope that will be so." His cheek dimples as he chews the inside of his mouth.

The poor man, little does he know that he'll be struck down by the sweat before he's had a real opportunity to experience the freedom he seeks.

Four

4ᵀᴴ March 1526 – Hever Castle

As I sit by the window in the gallery, I recall that it's been four years to the day since Anne's debut at the English Court. I still think it incredible that I had the opportunity to witness the Chateau Vert masque, and Anne's first meeting with Henry VIII after her return from France. With my eyes closed, I bask in the flickering warmth of the memory and the sun's morning rays streaming through the window.

I snap out of it when Anne touches my shoulder and offers me her hand.

"Walk with me, Beth." She guides me down the length of the gallery for some exercise.

"I love this space," I say, marvelling at the majestic art surrounding us.

"Father designed it so that it extended across the entire width of the Castle," she tells me. "It is very special in its design."

I'm impressed by the original panelling, and the elaborate plasterwork of the off-white ceiling. "It's beautiful."

"It is most modern." She turns on her heel and leads me back towards the other end of the hall. "Father wanted our home to be the height of fashion, for entertaining our guests, and taking exercise, as we do." She looks down at our swishing skirts and links her arm in mine. "And in time, Mother is hoping that we might commission one of the Court artists to paint our portraits, so we might hang them up here, on display." She gestures at the expanse of blank panelling on one side of the gallery. We stop in front of a painting of an older lady dressed in an early-Tudor gown. Her approving gaze is fixed on the observer.

"Who is this, Anne?"

"Agnes Howard, Duchess of Norfolk. She is my step-grandmother."

"Does she ever visit Hever?"

"Sometimes. Now that her husband – my grandfather, is dead, the Dowager Duchess is often at Court."

"Are you close to her?"

"Not as close as one might expect kinswomen to be." She grimaces. "We are a large family, all interconnected."

"Your cousins, on the Howard side, do you have much to do with them?"

"When we see them at Court, yes, but they do not come and visit here too often."

"The dowager takes in wards, does she not?"

"Yes, she does. She believes it is her Christian duty to help support lesser family members, and help the women especially obtain good marriages."

I shiver at the thought of Katherine Howard, Anne's cousin, who, if history has its way, will be the fifth wife of Henry Tudor.

Anne looks at me. "What is it?"

"Imagine not being brought up by your own parents. I have been so lucky with how close I am to my family. I couldn't contemplate life without them." For a fleeting second, I wonder what my parents might be doing, hoping the time-slip hasn't made my absence noticeable.

"'Tis an expectation in most families, that if anyone falls on hard times, other family members step in to help bring up their children."

"I can understand the logic of that."

"Yes, indeed. But the dowager seems to have had little direct involvement in the upbringing of her wards – especially the young female attendants."

I think of Katherine Howard, again. "Do you see any of the young women who live with her?"

"No, she keeps them all away from Court." She shrugs.

"It's maybe for the best," I say. "Do you ever see your cousin Katherine?"

"Little Kitty Howard?" She smiles. "No, she is only three years old. Why do you ask? Have you heard of her?"

"I know of her," I reply, "b-because of the Boleyn family connection, is all." I really need to change the subject. I lead her to the casement window. We lean against the sill, watching the grey clouds over the meadow, as hazy rain patters against the glass.

"Typical English weather," I say, turning to look down the length of the long gallery. "You are fortunate to live in such a splendid place, with a family that loves you. Your father has done well for you all."

"We are proud of him." She nods. "He has worked hard to give us a beautiful home. Mother adores it here."

"This really is the loveliest of all the rooms in the castle." I watch shadows flit across the floorboards as the light changes.

"George was but a babe when it was finished. Much of the extensions to the castle and the timber-framed buildings were completed around then, too."

Without warning, screams pierce our serenity, coming from the floor below. It's Mary. Her labour is continuing, though we've had relative peace for the last while compared to earlier when she nearly screamed the castle down. Anne looks at me, apprehension in her eyes.

"Mary will be well, will she not?"

"Of course," I say. "'Tis not like it's her first time in a birthing chamber."

She shakes her head. "I do not want to think on it! The pain sounds unbearable."

Oh, my dear Anne, you have all this to come. She stares into the void, in a world of her own. I take her arm and we start walking down the gallery again, our pace slow.

"I've seen my sister give birth," I say. "It's a natural part of life but, I agree that Mary's screams are disconcerting."

"Try and ignore it, dear Beth."

I think of something nice to talk about. "Did you know, in my time,"—I arch my brows at her—"in my modern time, I mean, I have always enjoyed visiting Hever." Hmm, perhaps I shouldn't have said that. That sort of comment is only going to lead to further questions. Before I can change the subject, she stops and faces me.

"What do you mean, you visit here in 'modern times'?" Her beautiful eyes are shadowed by confusion, and I cough into my hands as my cheeks flush.

"Well, what I mean to say is, your family are so well known, concerning English history, that people in five-hundred years come to see where you lived and where you grew up." I'm hoping my compliments will satisfy her.

"You mean to say that people of a lower position in life, in your time, come to visit my house?" Her brows knit together.

"Yes."

"And what of my Boleyn descendants?" She bites her lip. "Does George not have..."—she counts out five fingers—"great, great, great, great, great-grandchildren living here in your time?" She keeps direct eye contact, her hold on my arm firm. I need to answer her but it needs to be ambiguous.

"The Boleyns move on...after all the marriages." Now I know I've said too much. Me and my big mouth. If the professor finds out, I'll be in big trouble. Now I'm biting my lip,

"After what marriages?" she asks. The woman is such a pusher!

"Well, Mary has married – and will marry again." Her eyes widen. Ok, I shouldn't have said that, either.

"Mary will marry again?" Her face twists, and I nod. She stops in her tracks, her hand over her chest. "What will happen to William?"

"I'm afraid he will die!" I blurt out. I drop her arm and face her. She gasps. Oh, God! What am I like? Why did I say that?

"Why will he perish?" She leans closer, her voice at a whisper. "What will happen to him?"

"He won't survive the sweating sickness." I cover my mouth with my hand. I really have gone too far this time. Time to zip the lips.

"The sweat will return?" She rubs her temples as she tries to comprehend what I'm telling her. "When?"

"Two years from now," I answer. "But, Anne, don't press me for answers about the future – you know better than that, and it's unfair of you." I grip her hands. "Besides, the professor warned me not to dabble in your family history – he made me swear, remember? It may bring horrendous consequences upon you and your family, as well as me." I try to stifle a nervous giggle when I consider that even if history were to play out as intended, it will still mean dire consequences for Anne, her brother, and the early death of her father. Only Mary and her mother will get out of the shadow of the block relatively unscathed. Well, if history goes to plan.

Her cheeks have reddened. "I beg you, as my friend, to tell me what you know."

"Anne, I've told you – I can't!" I take a deep breath to compose myself. First, I need to remember to speak more 'Tudor', but it's difficult when I've just landed myself in such an awkward situation. I release her hands. "I would be no friend to you if I told you what I know."

She glances about, then leans back in. "I promise, I will not press you for further information, providing you confide in me who I will marry!" Her dark eyes almost sparkle in anticipation.

"Anne, you are impossible!" I shake my head and cover my eyes with my hand.

She giggles. "If only that ring could tell me what it knows." She points at the cypher ring on my middle finger.

"Okay," I say, holding her shoulders, which tremble with expectation. "All I can say is that you will marry well." I watch with some amusement as a half-smile lifts her right cheek.

"How well?"

I giggle as I roll my eyes. "Very well!"

She grabs my hand again. "Please tell me who my husband will be. You cannot leave me not knowing!"

"I can't tell you, Anne, on pain of death!"

"Why ever not?" She chuckles, though I see serious intent behind it. "You have a duty, as my friend, to tell me – you promised me when we first met, you would do everything to support me. Remember?"

"I can't, I've told you." I sigh, knowing I must put an end to this. "Do you want things to go wrong in your life because of the information I might divulge?"

"No! Never!" Her response is edged with fear.

"Then, let it be." I steeple my hands at my chin, then link her arm. "Is it not fun living your life the same as everyone else, not knowing what lies ahead?" I rub her hand. "Besides, I would be in great danger of being accused of witchcraft, fortune-telling, and divination if my knowledge of the future was ever discovered. Have you not considered the peril you might put me in by insisting that I reveal such details?"

Her smile fades. I can almost hear the cogs in her brain going ten to the dozen.

"I may know all but I wouldn't be able to pass myself off as some kind of female John Dee, erm…I mean, astrologer – it just wouldn't work."

"Please, I beg you!"

"No, Anne. I have already said far too much." The only way she's going to take any notice of me is if I drill it home to her. "Unless you stop pressuring me for answers, I shall leave Hever and never return!" She blinks at me. "Do you understand, Anne?" I don't mean to be so harsh but if she doesn't listen to me, there's going to be trouble that not even the professor will be able to get me out of.

"Yes," she replies, giving me a gentle nod. "I am sorry." She opens her arms, and we hug.

"Everything will work out for the best, I promise."

Goodness, this turned so serious in such a short time. I could have got myself into real trouble, not to mention how it might have played out for my hosts, compounding the damage already done. From now on, I have to watch what I say. And I mustn't forget that the Boleyns have been kind to me, accepting Anne's story of my dad being unwell, and although they weren't best pleased with my sudden disappearance, they've welcomed me back into their household. It's like I've never been away.

We look up when Mary's labour screams heighten to a crescendo. She has to be close – the hallways have been filled with her shrieks since late morning.

We head downstairs to see how things are. Agnes glides around with a taper, lighting candles on mantels and windowsills until all are illuminated. Then she and Mrs Orchard scurry into the bedchamber with fresh linens, pails of hot water, and woollen blankets. Mrs Orchard has been barking orders at the poor woman all day, and both of them look exhausted, though Mary must be almost spent, her squeals ringing out across the castle. If history plays out to plan, her bedchamber will later be used by King Henry when he comes to stay on several occasions during his courtship with Anne.

We stand outside, and Anne hesitates before pushing the heavy oak door open. I swallow a lump of apprehension as she beckons me inside. With some trepidation, I creep into the room and notice the wall panelling of dark walnut, similar to the majority of the rooms Sir Thomas has extended and renovated. However, as I look up at the ceiling, I realise it's the oldest in the castle, dating from 1462.

Mary is curled into a tight ball of misery on the four-poster bed, while her mother perches near her head, smoothing the matted hair from her daughter's face and shushing her through pursed lips. A midwife busies herself in the corner, preparing the cradle that awaits its guest.

"Sweetheart," Elizabeth Boleyn murmurs in hushed tones to Anne, "you should not be in here, but before you go, you can help me move your sister to the groaning chair."

"Am I allowed in?" I whisper.

"Yes, yes. Quickly, girls." She beckons us in. "This is Mabel Williams, the midwife."

Mistress Williams nods. The four of us move Mary into position on the birthing chair next to the bed so she can begin the task of pushing her child out into the world. Mary sets her teeth as she starts straining.

"Not yet, dear, the baby isn't ready," Mabel says, like a schoolteacher to a recalcitrant pupil. Her ruddy face is covered in beads of perspiration. "You will know when to push – you will feel it."

"Anne, Beth, you must leave us," Lady Boleyn says. "As unmarried women, you really should not be in here."

"Can they not stay?" Mary pleads, her knuckles white from gripping the arms of the chair.

"No, it is not seemly." She rubs Mary's back as Anne and I stand there gawping. The midwife rushes us from the room, and we're left out on the landing listening to Mary's grunts and groans as she struggles through the late contractions.

I look down into the courtyard from the window. Sir Thomas, it seems, has suggested to William that they have the horses saddled. George is with them. They fix their stirrups and prepare themselves for a distracting horse ride. We step back when they all look up, though I'm positive they've spotted us. Like us, they can hear Mary's echoing cries, and I'm sure I see expressions of relief as they lead their mounts across the yard, then under the portcullis, over the bridge, and out onto the meadow on a gallop away from the drama. Men, it seems, are not so good, even across time and space, when it comes to coping with *women's* matters!

Lady Boleyn, Mrs Orchard, and Agnes dart in and out of the bedchamber as they continue awaiting the arrival of this newborn. I step into Anne's chamber to find my bag of modern-day potions and lotions. She follows.

"What are you doing?" she asks as I transfer painkillers, hand sanitiser, and essential oils to a linen pouch, tying it to my girdle belt.

The door to Mary's chamber opens, so I clutch the bag and scurry down the landing, glad to see that it's Mabel. I stand right under her nose. "Can I come back inside to help you with Mary?"

She stares at me, her busty frame blocking the way. "You know of such things, Mistress?"

"Yes. I helped deliver my sister's child." It's true, and I'm certain I can do a better job of delivering Mary's baby than most sixteenth-century midwives, who are considered by some as witches or quacks.

She looks from me to Anne's room. "Tell Mistress Anne to stay in her room. It is no place for her." She grips the door latch. "I have asked Lady Boleyn to go downstairs and make up a flagon of fresh wine for Mary." I must appear authoritative or confident to her, as she motions for me to follow her as she opens the door. "I could do with some help."

Before I step in, I see that Anne seems shocked, biting her lip in frustration at the turn of events. I hope she doesn't feel hurt at being excluded. It's not my fault. She knows not to argue with the midwife. I can't dwell on it, as Mary's screams are growing frantic. I'm afraid for her, worried about not having modern medical equipment or real pain relief to assist in this baby's delivery. This is why women dread childbirth during this era and are prone to believing old wives' tales. We English are a superstitious bunch. In my time, not a whole lot has changed. The number of people who believe in the oddest 'cures' for all kinds of maladies. Crazy. I think it's human nature to be superstitious – to believe in things that cannot be seen or proven, even when science offers solid explanations. The Tudors know no different, of course, with their limited knowledge, so they fall back on prayers and supplications. I'm sure Anne is praying for Mary, begging God not to let her sister die.

Mary's anguished shrieks fill the bedroom. She is ready to push. I discreetly cover my hands in sanitiser and come alongside her, hoping she will allow me this close at such an anxious time.

"I have come to help you, Mary. I delivered my niece for my sister a few years ago. Your midwife has agreed that I can come in and support you, if you will allow me? Mary nods as she bites down on a stick, her face a sweaty puce.

"Do as the midwife says, and all will go well with you." I give her an anxious smile, taking her hand as she bears down, ready to push through her final contractions.

"Please go and fetch warm water and fresh linens," I say to Agnes. She picks up the wooden pail, half-full of soiled linen, and scurries out the door. Mabel tugs at the bedsheets, soaked in amniotic fluid, and turns away to throw them into a wicker laundry basket. I take the opportunity to press out four dissolvable paracetamol tablets from their plastic packaging and drop them into the remnants of wine in Mary's goblet. They fizz as I swish the liquid about. When it settles, I urge her to take sips between pushes. It's the best I can do for her, seeing that she gets some pain relief, even if it is only in a small way.

She spits out the wooden stick – the quintessential pain reliever of the time – and gulps back the medicated wine. The poor woman must be dehydrated. I don't know what's worse, seeing her face yellow as each contraction washes over her, or her grimace as she drinks the medicine. As she shoves my hand away, it dawns on me that she has never felt the healing powers of modern medicine. Goodness, what if she has an adverse reaction to it? How long will it take for the painkillers to kick in?

Mabel throws a dry linen sheet to soak up the gory blend of bodily fluids on the floorboards beneath the chair. Mary has to be fully dilated now. It's happening! I massage the small of her back just as she squeals, and her baby's head crowns. Mabel crouches in close, cradles the infant's head, and guides his shoulders and arms out as he glides from his tranquil home. It comes to me then that I'm the only one who knows that it's a boy.

With Mary giving one last push, Mabel catches the rest of his tiny body as he slithers free. In my head, the lack of Health and Safety screams at me as I watch her go about her business. While she's not looking, I sanitise my hands again, keeping watch at Mary's shoulder. We wait in anxious anticipation as the midwife clears his airway, and an instant later, the first cries of life fill the room as he balls his lungs out, informing the inhabitants of the castle of his arrival. Mabel ties a piece of cord around the umbilical, to the end near the baby's belly, to stop the blood flow, severing near that point on the umbilical cord, for a clean separation from mother, then washes him in a tub of warm water. Once he's dried, she wraps him tight in fresh linens and hands him to me. He blinks, trying to focus, then closes his eyes and whimpers. To soothe him, I ease my little finger between his pursed lips. This is Master Henry Carey, eventually to become 1st Baron Hunsdon in Elizabeth 1's reign – his first cousin; Anne's daughter.

Agnes returns with pails of water from the kitchen, where Lady Boleyn has been warming it over the flames of the large fire. I want to place the baby on his mother's chest, the way it's normally done in maternity delivery suites. Although he's taken his first breaths, I have to curb my urge to interfere, as I know I must adhere to what the Tudors would do. Mary touches the infant's cheek, then I step away as we wait for her to pass the afterbirth. Once the bloody episode is over, Agnes draws her a bath. When Mary settles into the water, I test the temperature with the edge of my hand, then unwrap little Henry and place him to his mother's breast so he can try to latch on.

The room is busy around us. Agnes thuds back and forth, lifting blood-stained linens from the floor and banging doors as she runs in and out. I know Anne must still be hovering outside, listening, and waiting.

Agnes flusters as she makes up the bed, then hangs a clean shift to air, for Mary to change into after her bath, before getting back into her bed.

"Mistress Anne wants me to tell her details of the babe, Mistress Carey. What would you have me do?" Agnes frowns. She doesn't quite know what the protocol is around revealing the sex of the child.

"Fret not, Agnes. I would be grateful if you would stay here with me." Mary tries to smile, wincing as little Henry latches on hard. Despite her discomfort, she seems relieved the boy is suckling, and thanks me for helping her. "Please, Beth, go tell Mother and Anne the good news."

"Thank you," Agnes says to me. "I did me best to ignore Mistress Anne, but she would be accosting me for news every time I left the bedchamber!" Mary smirks at her, which has to be a good sign.

Anne is on the landing, clutching the carved oak banister, her knuckles white. Lady Boleyn appears beneath us on the lower floor and starts when she looks up and sees us in the gloom.

"Oh, Mistress Beth…daughter, you startled me." She passes a tray of victuals – a jug of ale, and a platter of bread and cheese – to Agnes to carry up to Mary. "How is Mary? We heard the baby's cries. What news?"

I smile as Agnes edges past me. "Oh, yes, Lady Boleyn, it is a little boy. The prettiest thing you ever saw. I daresay Mary will want to see you, now her trauma is done with."

"I am glad her ordeal is over. You have done well, Beth." She dashes up the staircase, or as fast as her dress will allow her. "I am so proud of you," she says, caressing my cheek as she passes me.

Anne and I wait in her chambers as her mother visits Mary and her new grandson, her voice rising as she protests at Mary's behaviour – in her mind, it's not the proper thing for nobility to feed their babies themselves, not even for a boy child.

"Thank you for your service, Mistress Williams," we hear her say. "Your payment is in the kitchen – Agnes will fetch it for you."

Someone descends the stairs and I assume it to be Mabel and Agnes.

"You cannot breastfeed the boy!" Lady Boleyn's cries. "We have a wet nurse for that, a young mother from the village."

Anne looks at me, her eyes wide, before storming up the landing and into Mary's bedroom. I wait outside.

"Mother, let Mary be, at least until the wet nurse arrives."

"Very well," Lady Boleyn says, sighing in resignation. Good, Mary and the infant need peace and quiet.

As twilight approaches, Agnes and Mrs Orchard creep around the house replacing spent candles. In the dim light, Sir Thomas and William Carey and George slam doors and thud up the stairs, their swords rattling in their belts, spurs in hand after their ride. Lady Boleyn dashes out from the bedchamber to greet them, her brows furrowed.

"The baby – do you have to make such a noise? And who said you could all tread on my rugs with muddy boots, and your leatherwork still on?"

"Forgive me, my love." Sir Thomas smiles. "We are anxious to see the child – the servants have said the baby has a strong set of lungs!" His face lifts with a wide grin.

"Lady Mother, let me see my child!" William pleads, though he doesn't dare run past her. George is hot on William's heel, and he smiles at me before following Sir Thomas and William in to see Mary.

I leave them to it and return to Anne's chambers. With all the commotion, the fire has gone out and, with the staff otherwise employed looking after Mary and baby, I try to light it myself, persevering until a tiny flame takes hold under the kindling, blowing on it until it catches on and grows. We are so reliant on firelighters in my time, we've forgotten how to light a fire from scratch. I'm quite proud of myself, soaking up the heat as the wood is consumed. Wonderful! I add a few small logs, then lie back in a chair and gaze into the hearth, exhausted from the day's events.

Anne returns, and I find myself trying to placate her while she complains about how the king has used Mary. At least we have the bit of heat from the fire. Her feelings are fickle, and it appears she's finding it difficult to make sense of them. She's not happy, moaning about women's positions in society, and how they are beholden to men. How would she react to seeing how society has developed in twenty-first-century England? Anyway, it seems she has a lot to get off her chest, and Harry Percy doesn't escape her ire. She also grumbles about being the subject of Tom Wyatt's poetry. I hold my tongue, wondering will she ever know true happiness. She knows that she's not in a good position, understanding that she has drawn attention to herself at the English Court by trying to arrange her marriage, and now she doesn't know what to do having noblemen and poets press her for attention.

"My sister has everything." Is she jealous? I haven't heard this from her before. "Men adore her. Her husband loves her, and she now has two children." She takes a deep breath and lets it out in a long sigh. "Yet, I have nothing. Men who admire me are above my station for a match, or they are married." She folds her arms. "I feel as if I will never know love." She looks at me. "I wish you would tell me who I marry!"

Here we go again. "You know very well, I cannot."

She sniffs, not impressed. "My heart has a mind of its own, and my body even more so. I feel as if I will never be married and have children, unlike my sister." She stares into the blazing fire. "My heart used to leap when Percy held me, and despite my argument against my neighbour's son, I enjoy the attention when Tom Wyatt writes poetry to me, although I would never tell him so. I like being the focus of men's attentions." She shrugs her eyebrows and smiles. "My knees felt weak around Harry Percy, in his time, the same as when the King looked at me that first evening during Chateau Vert."

"You certainly never betray your feelings in public," I say, happy she has calmed.

"Margaret of Austria taught me to never encourage men. Yet my body grows demanding, and time slips by, when, by now, I should be a mother, like my sister. I find my desires difficult to contain."

"It will happen for you, be patient. It is normal for you to be attracted to the opposite sex, and to want to be a wife and mother. Believe me, there is nothing wrong with you. Trust me." I feel for her, I truly do, and I have no idea how she'll react when the king reveals his feelings to her, which is something I'm waiting for with bated breath.

"Like you are attracted to my brother?" She giggles, raising a knowing brow.

"That's different."

"I do not see what is different."

All I can do is shake my head and smile. With Mary and the baby resting, all is calm. We continue sitting by the fire, relaxing, until the sound of footsteps on the landing draws our attention. Anne goes to see who it is.

"Brother, what are you doing?"

"I wanted to ask you if I should carry the news of the child's birth back to Court, to the King?"

He's hovering at the door, peering over Anne's shoulder, probably to catch my attention. His eyes sparkle in the candlelight, and I have to admit that he looks handsome tonight.

"Should you not ask Father that?" Anne says, her hand resting on his forearm.

"Perhaps. Father will have the matter in hand, will he not?" He looks over at me again and I wonder if his inquiry is just an excuse to spend time with us. "I've been bored since you were attending to Mary."

"I was not. I…wasn't allowed to go in. Mother would not let me."

"You were with Beth, were you not?" he asks, still loitering on the threshold. He looks from Anne to me, and back. "Can I come in?"

Without waiting for a response, he steps into the room and walks towards me. The candlelight flickers as he passes the bedside table.

"Beth was helping the midwife look after Mary," Anne says.

His jaw drops. "In the birthing chamber?"

"Yes," I reply.

"That surprises me. I thought you would have stayed with Anne."

"Where else would I be now but with your sister?"

"But I thought… Ah, never mind." He shakes his head, his brows furrowed, possibly troubled that I have traversed some great convention – an unmarried woman in a birthing chamber. I'll not encourage him, feeding the need for explanations, which I can do without.

He sits back in a chair opposite me, his expression now relaxed as warm shadows dance across his face in the candlelight and the glow from the fire.

The night is closing in but the Boleyn siblings never seem to care much about the lateness of the hour when they are in each other's company.

"Did you know William has decided to call the baby after the King?"

"No, I did not," Anne says.

"I can't say I'm surprised." He stretches his legs out. "I'm so glad Mary's labour is over." He rolls his eyes. "That boy took his time, did he not?" Scratching at the door sees him getting up to let Griffin in.

"George, do not comment on things you know nothing about." Anne lies across the end of her bed, resting against a large cushion. Griffin wanders in, his space slow, his paws padding as he nestles at George's feet, tail flapping in the dancing light of the fire.

"Now we know the sex of the child, do you think little Henry looks like William, or the King?" He asks such impertinent questions.

"I don't know," I reply. "So long as he is healthy. Don't you agree, Anne?"

"Yes, Beth."

"Did you enjoy your ride earlier, with William and Father?" Anne asks.

"It was good to get out in the fresh air, but it was muddy, and we all came back once it started to rain again." He looks at me. "I should like to take Beth on a ride, when the weather improves." He smiles at me, and my cheeks burn. Anne notices.

"We shall take Beth for a ride when she has an accomplished rider like myself for company." She's trying to put him off the idea of being alone with me, for propriety's sake. "Unless, of course, you can both promise to behave?" He takes no notice, and I look away as my cheeks flush again.

"You may be good, sister, even sitting on the side, but I can jump any ditch or hedge as well as you." He grins. "Who better to take Beth out than me?"

"Wishful thinking, brother!" She laughs, the sound reverberating around the room.

"Stop arguing over me!" I shake my head as I smile. "You will both wake the baby."

George shrugs. "Let us change the subject."

"Please do!" I say.

He glances over at Anne, shifting in his chair. "Did you know that the king wants you back at Court, sister?"

She sits up, her eyes wide. "Does he?" Griffin pads over and she ruffles his head, the gesture rewarded with a lick of his tongue.

"How would you know, George?" I ask, watching fragments of firelight flit across his face.

"He told me himself," George answers, not holding back a smug shrug of his brows. "It appears, Beth, that your 'little audience' with him, all that time ago, when you spoke to him of my sisters, made an impression."

"Obviously, it did. I kept his mind on Mary, just as I was asked to do." I giggle. "Because that baby just might be His Majesty's!"

George laughs. "Very true, Beth. Absolutely true!"

"Yet, the child might be William's," Anne says.

I sit up. "Maybe, but you only have to look at his mop of hair to realise it is the same red as his sister's. It does not take a scholar to realise that Catherine Carey is a Tudor!"

"But does that make Henry Carey a Tudor, too?" Anne stares at me.

"Has the King acknowledged Catherine?" I ask, as if I didn't know.

"No," George says. He picks up a sprig of mint from a pewter bowl and chews on it.

Who is he hoping to kiss? Me? I push the thought out of my mind. "Then it is highly unlikely the king will recognise him." I glance at Anne. "Despite his hair colour, I am hoping he is William's."

"The king might only acknowledge this child because it's a boy," George says, chomping through another mouthful of mint. Watching him, I wonder if it's not a bit late for such a snack. Through his chomping, he continues, "He's only ever done such a thing with the duke of Richmond and Somerset – Henry Fitzroy."

"How do you know how the king might act?" I ask.

"I forgot, you would not know, would you?"

"Know what, exactly?"

"Two months ago, I lost my position in the Privy Chamber." He shrugs. "I spoke with father of the matter the other evening, do you not remember?"

"Yes, George. Sorry." As if I wasn't aware that this would have been a result of the Eltham Ordinances.

He chuckles. "However, I am still in the king's favour, for, in the very same month, he appointed me as his cupbearer!"

Anne taps the bedpost. "And, George, you forgot to tell Beth that in June last year, father became Lord Rochford." She beams with pride. "I, of course, did not forget to tell her." Her delight is clear at managing to convey good news before her brother. Neither of them knows that I received this news from their father earlier, along with his other many accolades.

"We Boleyns shall always be in the favour of the king, do you not think?" He stares at me.

"Of course, George." Goodness, I wish I was better at lying – I'll have to practice. I take a deep breath and try to make a joke. "So, what you are really trying to say is…"—I giggle—"that my 'little audience' with the king has no bearing whatsoever on the fact that your family are still in favour with His Majesty?"

George's expression is a picture. "I am not saying that your kind words about my sisters did not have any effect on the king. Rather, I would say that it has been, and will always be, father's standing with the king that has brought us to where we are."

"George is correct, Beth," Anne says.

I nod at her, allowing a smile. "I know both of you are right, I just didn't want my efforts to be for nothing."

George leans towards me. "They were never in vain, and you know from seeing for yourself at Court, that many a pretty girl makes an impression on the king."

"Both of you did warn me," I say.

"George, Beth has told me the king had singled her out for conversation on many occasions whilst you were away."

I cough into my hand.

"It was a long while ago, now!" he says, and I chuckle to myself, thinking of the time flip and how I jumped from the court to home for one night, yet, when I slipped back, I'd missed two Tudor years.

"Everyone at Court has missed both of you." He throws the mint stalk into the fire, the flames crackling and hissing around it. "You do know, sister, that the king asks after you all the time?"

"Really?" Her long neck seems to stretch as she waits for his response.

"And he asks after Beth."

I'm surprised at that, and my cheeks warm recalling the tender, yet forceful embrace he held me in when I last saw him.

"When I was last serving the king, he specifically told me he liked the look of Beth in English gowns." The corners of his mouth curl up. "I think he's taken a bit of a shine to you."

"No, George, how could the king possibly remember me? I've been such a time away from court." I almost snap, thinking of the attention Henry showed me.

"You must have made an impression on him." He winks. "I know I fancied you from the first moment I saw you!"

"George, leave Beth alone!" Anne scowls at him, aware of my embarrassment.

"I speak the truth, is all." He turns his open hand up. "The king also asked me when he thought you both might return to court."

Anne flicks a look my way, then stares at George. "What did you say to him?"

"I told him it was up to our father, and that neither of you would return to the queen's service until he had agreed to it."

"George, you cannot say that to the king."

"Why ever not?" He chuckles. "It's true, except that the king told me he could override any such decision Lord Rochford made!" We all laugh.

"You are not lying, then, George?"

"I never lie, Beth." He crosses his ankles in a slow movement that draws my attention to his strong legs.

"You think we will both be summoned back to court?" Anne asks, her voice quiet.

"Probably."

"If the king has asked for us, surely it will happen?"

I shrug, hoping she hasn't noticed me ogling his leg muscles.

"Well, we cannot go back until the king or Katharine summons us. Besides, we need to wait for Papa to give his consent." She giggles as little Henry Carey's cries ring out. He's awake. Griffin's head springs up off the rug and he jumps to his feet on hearing the calls of Lady Boleyn from Mary's chamber. With a newborn in the castle, it's going to be a long night.

Five

STUCK AT HEVER WITH A CRYING BABY – MARCH 1526

Mary has gone through the ritual of being churched, although the process isn't as rigorous as it is when women give birth at Court. She has settled well into looking after a newborn again but, understandably, is reluctant to leave her baby at Hever with the wet nurse.

"It is no good, Mary being stuck here at Hever," Sir Thomas complains, slumping into his great chair in the parlour. "Besides, the King may move on to someone else if she cannot hold His Majesty's attentions."

"Well, husband," Lady Boleyn says as she leans back in the settle, "what a fine mess this is, with Mary left here, William gone to London, and Mrs Orchard helping to look after our grandchildren."

She's aggrieved. They are paying a young woman from the village, who recently gave birth, to come in and be Henry Carey's wet nurse. Anne leans forward, wringing her hands in her lap.

"Father, please let me go back to court." She seems a little more compliant than usual, and Sir Thomas must guess this is a ploy to get him to agree. "I miss it dreadfully," she says, her manner wistful. "It is what I am used to." She dabs an eye with the back of her hand, but it doesn't work on him.

"You can go back to Greenwich when the queen sends for you." He glances at her, then at me. "And Mistress Wickers, of course." He takes a sip of white wine from his glass. "In the meantime, you can go and inspect the new bolts of fabric I brought from London for you both." A cheeky grin lights his eyes. "Agnes has left them on top of the chest in your bedchamber."

Anne jumps up, rushes to her father, and embraces him, nearly knocking the glass from his hand.

He chuckles. "Steady on, daughter."

I don't embrace him but offer a nod in gratitude. Then I turn to Lady Boleyn and hug her instead.

"Do not thank me," she says with a big smile. "I did not buy them."

"Thank you, sir." I dip quick curtsy before leaving the room.

Time passes fast here, and as I reflect on the last few weeks, I think of my parents, of Rob, and all my other university friends, like Jessica. I wonder what they are doing and what I'm missing. Or has no time passed at all in Carshalton, or at University, while I've been here? I shake my head, thinking of all the modern conveniences I'm doing without: Hot showers; a cup of tea; driving in my car with my music blaring. I have to remember what the professor said, and live in the moment and enjoy it. So long as I reach my end goal, which is seeing Anne and Henry finally together, I will have accomplished what the professor expects of me and no more. I can't time-slip back to my time until Henry has chosen Anne. It's going to be a long journey but I have to keep in mind that I am the observer, and that's all. No more meddling.

———————•❋•———————

Over the next few days, Anne and I get to work on designing several gowns in the English fashion, as Sir Thomas has been kind to send for Master Cotton – Master Skutt's apprentice. We hope he will like our ideas. Paul Cotton enters the library, looking awkward. It's the first time he has met Anne, and to someone who has never been introduced to her before, she can be rather intimidating. He shifts his weight from one leg to another, his nervousness obvious, but as he starts discussing the designs, he relaxes, and I feel more comfortable in his company here than when we were formally introduced at Court. His beard seems longer than when I last saw him, and he has this habit of brushing it as he stands there inspecting the bolts of cloth. He takes a small, leather-bound notebook from his doublet and Anne shows him where the inkwell and quills are kept, on her father's writing desk.

"What would you have us make for you, Mistress Anne?" he asks as he sits at the desk, nibbling the end of a quill.

She glances at me, then looks at him. "A dress similar to the one you made for Mistress Wickers?"

"Ah, like the blue velvet, with gold tissue?"

"Yes, Master Cotton, exactly like that, but in the colours of my choosing." She pats the bolts of velvet and satins in her lap. He makes a note, the quill scratching across the paper.

"So, you'd like the Sea Water cloth made into a gown?"

"Yes."

"And the Willow into another gown?"

"Yes, Master Cotton."

"And, finally, the frost-upon-green with yellow satin sleeves?"

"Yes, green is my favourite colour," she says, beaming. "It goes well with my hair."

"The sleeves?" he asks, probably hoping she won't want anything too specific.

"Well, I would like several pairs of sleeves – cloth of gold, and cloth of silver tissue."

This process is complex, and I'm learning so much, I almost need a notebook to write down everything being discussed. They talk about tinsel, which is another name for a different kind of cloth of gold or silver that can also be green. I'm confused but Anne carries on, while Paul scribbles, dipping his quill in the inkwell as needs be.

"And," she continues, "a black velvet gown with pewter-colour kirtle, cream, natural pearls, and gold habiliments." She knows what she wants, I'll give her that. "But, I will have French-style hoods, not those English gable-style bonnets – they do not suit my face shape." She glances at me. "I am sorry, Beth, but they just do not suit me as well as they suit you."

"Can you make something for me in black, Master Cotton?" I ask.

"Of course." He smiles. "We can use the same pattern we used before, and make it in the same style as the previous gown, perhaps with a changeable satin?"

By 'changeable', he means a fabric similar to a shot taffeta. "Yes, that would be perfect. The Queen likes her ladies dressed in black."

"If that is what you desire?"

"Yes, that would be wonderful."

"Mistress Anne, I will take an old kirtle and gown you have so I can match a pattern to it. Would that be agreeable?"

"Sir, you are welcome to whatever you may need."

He lays the quill back on the table and stands. "If that is all, ladies?"

Anne lifts a hand. "One last thing, Master Cotton."

"What might that be?" He cocks his brow, as if totting up the bill in his head. My fingers are crossed inside that Sir Thomas's purse can stretch to such a large tailor's bill as this. I was lucky the king paid for the last gown the Royal Wardrobe made for me. Perhaps, when we are back at Court, I will contribute to the tailor's bill with the allowance Sir Thomas has already paid me.

"Can we also have new Hollande linen shifts, with some embroidery?"

He nods. "Mistress, I will see what I can do."

"Master Cotton, my mother will be offended if you do not take some refreshment before you venture out on the London road."

"That would be very kind, Mistress Boleyn." He takes the bolts of cloth from her just as there's a tap on the door and George strides in.

"My apologies, I did not realise you were busy."

"Master Cotton is just leaving."

The apprentice takes his leave of us, following Agnes down the passageway, towards the kitchens.

When the door is closed, George nods to himself and runs his fingers through his hair. "Ladies, would you care to take a ride with me, as the day is so beautiful? The sun is out, and all the trees are covered in blossom."

"Not today, brother, my courses have come, and I feel too ill. Take Beth with you, I am certain she won't mind keeping you company."

"Anne, I am not as skilled a rider like you and George."

George winks. "Do not worry, I can look after you."

I can't help giggling. "That's what I'm worried about."

He nudges me, giving me that predatory look that has got me into trouble with him before. "Come on, we will have some fun. Anne can rest a while."

"That is an excellent idea," she says, "but, as I said before, only if you can behave, brother!" I suppose because George is now married, she no longer minds if I'm alone with him. She tilts her head to me. "Beth, I will go upstairs with you and help you change into a riding habit – I am certain one of mine will fit." She gets up and walks to the door, and I follow. "George, Beth won't be long."

"I can wait. Besides, I need to clean my boots." He smiles at me as Anne whisks me away.

Half an hour later, my hair has been plaited and pinned, and I'm dressed in Anne's green riding habit, wearing a large plume in her matching velvet hat. As I descend the stairs to the hallway, I hear a wolf-whistle that sends fire into my cheeks.

"My, my!" George exclaims. "Look at you, Mistress Wickers – you will charm the birds out of the trees when they see you riding beneath them in that." A broad smile lifts his cheeks.

The next thing I know, he has my arm as we walk out to the stables. Simon the stable boy helps him saddle up Anne's Irish Draft horse for me, then prepares his chestnut courser, checking the girth strap and the stirrups. Anne's horse is as dark as her hair can look in the candlelight. I stroke its mane, then George offers me his cupped hands so I can climb up into the saddle. I'm not used to riding aside, and must look nervous perched on the soft leather.

"Sit straight and find your centre," he instructs me. "That way you will feel more comfortable as you ride."

I'm sure he's surprised that I'm not an accomplished rider, with this being the principle form of transport for Tudor people of means, but then he doesn't know my origins. My lack of confidence in the saddle must make him suspicious, wondering why my parents haven't had me schooled in the equestrian skills any noble lady would be expected to know.

"And, therefore, more confident?" I suggest, grasping the reins, keeping my pinkies free.

"Exactly that," he says, beaming. He mounts his courser and reins in alongside me. "We shall take it slowly," he declares, and we begin to trot, crossing the meadow, down through the trees, and passing St Peter's Church, where his brother Henry lies. He must realise what I'm thinking because he turns to me.

"You know, one of my elder brothers is buried in there." He points towards the entrance."

"I remember, George, you showed me the brass cross that marks his resting place."

"Ah, yes." He smiles. "I remember, we stood over his spot, before Sunday service."

He stops his horse just in front of the church's wooden gate.

"What happened to him?" I ask, reining my mount alongside him.

"I had two brothers. Thomas and Henry. Both died young." A note of regret edges his words. I wonder if it was a case of the sweating sickness. "Contagion hangs heavy on the air, especially with children. It is hard to guard against."

Hmm, should I pester him for details? Maybe not. "I expect your poor mother was devastated."

"Had Thomas lived, he was to follow in Father's footsteps, being the eldest son – Father was planning for him to be in service to the local nobility." He lowers his gaze and shifts in the saddle. "When Father was remodelling Hever, the family occasionally stayed at Penshurst, and during that time, he was organising for Thomas to be placed in the household of the Duke of Buckingham, to pursue the traditional rank of a knight."

Fascinating. I never knew any of this about the Boleyn boys, as so little has been written about them, although I'd read Hugh Paget's paper published in 1981. Should I ask what might be taken as an impertinent question? Before I know it, the words come tumbling out. "What happened to him after that?"

"Thomas died," he answers, shaking his head, almost in slow-motion. "So, between father and the duke, they decided to bury him in the small Sydney Chapel of St John the Baptist Church, on the Penshurst Place estate."

"I see." I stroke my horse's mane and look at George, lost for words.

"To avoid further distress to our mother, my brother was buried quickly, so that mother could visit him while they were at Penshurst."

This makes so much sense to me, hearing it from the horse's mouth, so to speak. Thomas Boleyn, the younger, not being carried the five miles for burial at Hever, because the family had been living at Penshurst at the time.

"It must be a comfort to your mother to have one son buried so close by in Hever Church?"

"Yes," he says, "once father's income increased a few years ago, he marked both my brothers' resting places with brass crosses."

"I expect it is also heart-warming to you all to remember them with memorials." I try to sound genuine in my understanding, and not the stunned observer from another time.

"Yes." He sighs. "And you are right, it is a comfort to our mother for her sons' memories to be commemorated in such a way."

"Do not sound so sad. Be happy that you and your sisters have full lives to lead and have such bright futures in front of you." I'm hoping to inject some light into our conversation but, again, it has to look natural. He mustn't detect any hint of a lie in my demeanour.

He pats his horse's neck. "Indeed, my mother fusses over her brood, making up for her loss, trying to nudge us in the right direction, so long as Father approves!" He taps the courser with his heels.

"At least she cares, George. Your father, too." We trot along the muddy track.

"I think you can safely say she likes fussing over you, too." He shrugs his eyebrows. "Mother considers you part of the Boleyn brood now."

"I am glad your parents think so highly of me," I say, unable to hold back a smile. "Goodness, I feel like an adopted daughter!"

"We all think well of you, especially Anne." His compliments send heat into my cheeks. "She thinks of you more like a sister."

As the breeze wafts across my shoulders, I try not to think about whether George considers me a sibling or something altogether untoward, especially with him being a married man. Time to distract.

"George, can we stop and look inside the church on the way back?"

"Have you not been in there enough times?" He takes a swipe at a horsefly buzzing about his head.

"You know I have. I just thought it might be nice to go inside for a time – alone."

He stares at me. "Why on earth would you want to be alone with me?"

I open my mouth to elaborate but nothing comes out. The moment stretches before he starts chuckling, nudging his horse on.

As we trot along, my heart races at being here, riding with George – it's not often we have an opportunity to be without other company. The church is pretty, and the services held there are less flamboyant than those Queen Katharine attends. They are also not yet Lutheran.

"I am glad we have this time alone, Beth. I…have wanted to talk with you for some time."

"Oh? What about?" I think I know what's coming. Maybe this outing wasn't such a good idea after all.

"I missed you while you were away." He straightens his back, as if preparing for his delivery. "If you had not left court when you did, I…would have tried to persuade father against my marriage to Jane."

I grip the reins tighter. "You know he would never have agreed to that. And neither would the king, for that matter." I tip the horse with my heels and urge it on to match George's pace.

"I wanted to marry you." His sincerity has my heart palpitating at the thought of opportunities missed.

"I would've married you, too!" I blurt out, realising too late that I've said too much. "But, a match between us would have been impossible." I can't possibly explain my reality to him – he'd never understand. "Besides, I think my father is negotiating a marriage for me, with a gentleman from my village."

His incredulous look makes me think he doesn't believe me.

"Hmm, I suppose we must all make sacrifices." He half-smiles but looks lost behind it. "I certainly did." He takes a deep, slow breath. "But it will never change my feelings for you. Come, why don't we try a gentle canter?" With that, he kicks his coarser into a faster trot, taking a lead down the track which will become Hever Road. "I will stay with you," he calls back.

My horse responds with little encouragement, and I find myself gripping the pummel, happy to be keeping up. But then he takes off into a gallop, grass and muck kicking up behind him. All I can do is hold on as my mount follows, equalling his pace. My bones jar as I fight to keep control, the leather of my riding gloves stretched as I try pulling the reigns. My heart is pounding. I can ride but this side-saddle business is altogether different.

Without warning, George swerves his horse and jumps a ditch, full of confidence because he knows the area well. I have no choice but to hang on as my mount follows. It leaps, as does my stomach as I feel myself in full flight. When we land, the impact is too much and I'm sent rolling over the horse's shoulder, hitting grass with an almighty groan, and winding myself in the process. As I gasp for breath, my body contorts in absolute agony. The volume of my gown has twisted around my legs, trapping me in a muddy upside-down world. My hat is some distance away in the grass, and some of its plumes are bent. Anne isn't going to be happy. The pain is horrendous, and my panicked efforts to breathe through a mouthful of damp grass doesn't help.

The sun blinds me, and a rainbow of colours swirl behind my eyelids as my head pounds. I scrunch my hands into fists as pain from my ankle shoots up my spine. What the hell have I done to myself? Why did I jump that stupid ditch? Why do I need to impress George? Why am I in so much pain?

"Beth!"

As soon as I hear his voice, my lids spring open and he is off his horse, his silhouette over me, obscuring the sun's rays from my sensitive eyes.

"Beth, are you well? Please speak to me!"

I groan, aware of my legs being visible. As much as I want to be with him, this is not how I've envisaged it. With substantial effort, I manage to right my clothing and sit up, still somewhat winded.

He chuckles, spots my bonnet a few feet away, grabs it, and strides back to me. "How did you manage to get down there? Here, allow me to assist you."

I take his hand and try to get up but howl when I put weight on my foot. It comes back to me then, that when I fell, I caught my left ankle in the stirrup. Perhaps I've sprained it. Oh, God, I hope I haven't broken it.

"Beth, what is it?" He looks worried now.

"This is no joke, George. My ankle is so sore."

"I know you do not jest with me. How badly are you injured?"

"I can't stand!"

"Are you certain?"

"Yes!" I hold up my hat. "I'm sorry, George, I don't mean to take it out on you, but the pain is terrible."

With that, he scoops me up in his arms. If his wife could see us now, she'd go crazy with jealousy. Right now, I can't think about Jane Boleyn. I cling to his neck, trying to keep a tight grip on my hat at the same time, and nuzzle my cheek against his shoulder as sharp pains rack through my calf. Maybe it's not my ankle. If it's only a muscle injury, it will heal faster, unless it's a tendon…?

I look up at George. When I'm with him, I can honestly say it's the only time in my life I have felt really, really, happy. I can't tell him how I feel about him, though he must know. He must sense it. A glow forms in my chest. It's got to be the love I feel for him, or maybe it's the sun as it warms my face. He makes our progress seem effortless as he walks through the tall grass, disturbing the bees and butterflies going about their business among the many spring wildflowers. If it wasn't for the pain, this moment would be close to perfect.

My knight in shining armour's expression is fixed as he takes me back towards St Peter's, with both horses following close behind. A few months ago, I would have shrunk from his touch, but now, even with the pain, it excites me. The closeness of our situation enthrals me but also fills me with apprehension, because my feelings are defying the professor's strict advice – to keep my distance.

Everything he does is considered and measured. Is this due to his fear of failure in the eyes of his father? Does he feel the need to make up for the loss of his brothers? Whatever he thinks of himself, it makes no difference to the way I feel about him. He's so perfect and selfless in my eyes – the mere sight of him inspiring a slow-burning flame in me, again. As my cheek brushes his doublet, I inhale the homely scent of cinnamon and nutmeg. It tantalises me, and I'm once again reminded that this man is nothing like history has painted him. He is accomplished at everything he tries and, apart from his warped humour, I can find no fault in his character, his flawless dancing, his articulate speech, or his masterful diplomacy. No wonder he captivates his wife, along with so many of the younger women at court, reducing the other maids to simpering idiots when they are in his company.

The horses continue to follow, apart from the odd moments when they stop to tug on tufts of grass. A quick call from George has them soon trotting after us, their affection for him apparent in their happy neighing. I close my eyes and breathe deep, as if it will help me etch this moment deep into my twenty-first-century brain. He looks down at me, his lips pursed, and I wonder if he's able to carry me much further.

"George, put me back on the horse if I'm too heavy for you."

"No, you are as light as a feather." He takes a deep breath. Maybe he thinks the fresh air will give him strength. Then he smiles, and the gold flecks in his eyes dance as he continues on.

"I don't believe you. Don't break your poor back trying to carry me all the way home."

"I can manage!" he says, exhaling through pursed lips.

I lean into his chest, gripping his neck tighter to help him and to stop me from slipping. "If I didn't know better, I'd suspect you are enjoying this moment of chivalry." I giggle through my pain. We won't know until we get back how bad the injury is, but I'm glad I had the foresight to pack some painkillers when I first came here. Anne had the wisdom to have all my personal and modern belongings brought back from Court, and the sense to hide them away. Aspirin, paracetamol, and other stronger painkillers will help.

He says nothing – just gives me a knowing look. Sweat beads on his brow, and his face is flushed as we pass the church gate and head down the hill towards Hever. It doesn't take too long before we cross the outer courtyard.

Lady Boleyn comes out to greet us, the lappets on her hood flapping. "George, what has happened?" She lifts her skirts and scurries towards us as John, George's servant, leads the horses to the stables.

"The horse took off with Mistress Elizabeth…taking her unawares," George says between gasps.

She comes close to me, her expression twisted with worry. "Where are you hurt, Beth?"

"I think I may have twisted my ankle." George grunts under my weight.

"Well, do not stand there, George." She flaps both hands. "Get Mistress Wickers upstairs to the bedchamber.

"That's a sentence I never thought I would hear my mother utter!" he whispers through his chuckle. I can't help but laugh.

"George, Beth, this is no laughing matter!" Lady Boleyn remarks as she clutches the door latch.

"Indeed, it isn't," I reply, winking at George. His mother shoos us through the hallway and upstairs to Anne's room, and I feel like I'm being carried by a hero in an Austen novel as he sweeps me into the bedchamber, with Griffin barking around us. The noise wakes Anne from her slumber, and she jumps up, eyes wide, mouth open.

"Beth, what has happened?" Her voice is panicked – her face screwed up in confusion.

"The horse threw me," I answer through a genuine moan.

"Heavens, are you well?"

"She cannot put any weight on her ankle," George says, laying me on the bed, visibly relieved at being unburdened. He slumps back in the chair, exhausted. Agnes hands him a large goblet of what I assume is water and wine, which he gulps back, smacking his lips when he's finished.

"I needed that!" he cries.

"You shouldn't have carried me all that way," I say, removing my gloves and laying Anne's bonnet beside me on the bed.

"George, you fool – you could have damaged your back." Anne glares at him, then turns to me. "Beth, do you need a physician?" She looks at my feet poking out from under my gown. "Agnes, come here, child." Agnes's response is prompt and she's soon stood beside the bed. "Take Mistress Wickers shoes off."

She does as she's told, and I cry out in relief as my toes escape their confinement. My left ankle has blown up like a balloon and I can't rotate it. What am I going to do if it's broken? I'll have to go home and have it seen to. That has me thinking. Hmm, would the injury be exclusive to the here and now, and maybe not transfer to my modern-day? I shake such silly thoughts out of my head.

George looks concerned. "Shall I go and get Mother?" He gets to his feet, unbuttons his doublet, and throws it across the back of the chair.

"That may be a good idea," Anne says. Agnes hovers, looking somewhat lost.

"Agnes, go and fetch some cold water and fresh linens, would you?"

"Yes, Mistress Anne." She follows George out. Anne lifts my skirts above the knee, unties my garters, and rolls down my stockings, easing them in turn off each leg.

"Your left leg looks so swollen."

I pull myself up against the soft pillows to get a better look. Such a sight, with dark bruising marbling my foot and lower calf. Lady Boleyn soon joins us, fussing around me like a mother hen while Anne hands her cold linen bandages, which she expertly wraps and tightens around my ankle.

"You will have to rest in bed until the swelling subsides," she says, giving the dressed injury a worried look. "Though your skin is not torn, you may have broken a bone."

"Surely not?" I reply, though I'm afraid that might be a possibility. I collapse back against the pillows, spent.

An hour later, Agnes has helped Anne undress me, and I perch against the crisp pillows in a linen shift, my injured leg elevated over a bolster cushion. Agnes pulls the coverlet over my torso.

"We cannot have you being on display!" she says, tucking the covers around me. There's a tap at the door.

"Beth, are you decent?" George asks. "I came to see how you fare." His voice is tinged with concern.

"Mistress Wickers, should I be letting him in?" Agnes asks.

"I think he will do no harm, Agnes." I smile at her, but she seems a little apprehensive as she walks to open the door. She curtsies to him.

"Agnes." He smiles as he walks in, with Griffin following. She returns a meek smile as she scurries from the room, closing the door behind her.

"I left my doublet in here, I think." He looks around and spots it is lying over the back of the chair. Maybe he's using his collection of it as an excuse to be in my company again. He comes and sits next to me on the opposite side of the bed. "How do you feel…my love?"

That takes my breath away for a moment. He has never used those words to me so blatantly before. I must look startled. His eyes sparkle.

"Erm, I feel much better now that your mother has bandaged my injury – I'm hoping it is bruising, and nothing more." I look down at my exposed knee, and heat flushes through my cheeks. We are alone – the room is quiet – apart from Griffin slumbering at the side of the bed. George chuckles and bends to stroke the dog's ears.

"Where is Anne?" I ask.

"Downstairs, in the kitchen with mother. As you were on your own,"— he pulls himself up onto the bed and lies close beside me—"I thought you might like some company." He takes hold of my hand, and his gentle touch takes me by surprise. "Are you in any pain?"

"Not while my leg is raised," I say.

He looks at my injured ankle. "'Tis a pity – you have such beautiful ankles." His eyes sparkle as he looks at me, and my heart races. I wish being this close to him didn't have such a profound effect on me. He turns to lay on his side, so he can draw closer to me. "You could be stuck here for days…weeks. What can I do but keep company with you when you are in such distress?"

I shrug, rolling my eyes at the same time. As I try to thump him, he anticipates it and grabs my wrist.

"Ah, err…no, I think not!" With a luscious smirk, he leans over me, licking his lips as he looks down at me. His action and expression catch me unawares. To my surprise, he leans in and kisses my neck, sending a gorgeous shiver through me. His hot lips press against the softness of my skin along my collarbone, and I breathe in the fragrance of his hair, tensing my legs as gorgeous tingles flutter through my inner thighs. After too short a time, he rises, looks at me, and smiles.

"We shouldn't be doing this!" I say, trying not to gasp.

"I had planned to kiss you when we went out riding." He smiles, his eyebrows arched. "Unfortunately, your fall put paid to that."

"You don't give up, do you?"

"Why should I, Beth, when I know by a simple glance or gesture, you feel the same way as me?"

"Yes, but—"

"But nothing!" He pins me against the pillows and presses his lips against mine. This is not just a peck. His tongue wets my lips, its tip stroking, teasing, until he eases them open.

Caught in the moment, I can't resist him as he caresses my tongue with his, breaking off to nibble my lower lip before re-engaging, his passion rising. I give as good as I'm getting, my fingers in his hair, gripping, feeling, and realising that only a woollen coverlet and the thin veil of my linen shift separate him from my naked flesh. The thought of it excites me but not as much as when he pulls the coverlet down and his warm hand skims over the flimsy fabric of my shift. As he caresses my breast, all I can do is grind my hip against his. If he feels my nipple spring against the linen – all that lies between the lightness of his finger – he doesn't let on. Instead, he moans and sucks on my earlobe, my name on his breath driving any sense of pain into the stratosphere.

His lightness of touch is intoxicating as his fingertips trail over my collarbone, then up the back of my neck. His fingers tangle in my hair, and I can't help but press into him again. He really knows how to turn me on. His kisses burn, and I don't want it to end, but if we don't stop soon, things may go too far. Even so, I can't help myself and twist towards him, running my hands through his hair, relishing the feel of his chest against mine.

Then it hits me: What am I doing? This is exactly the kind of thing Professor Marshall warned me to avoid. But being with George, like this, is addictive. I haven't kissed him like this in so long. I haven't kissed anyone like this in so long.

The sound of footsteps in the passageway outside jerks me to life. George breaks free and jumps from the bed, ending standing almost at attention, his chest rising and falling as he attempts to pull himself together. The latch on the door lifts and Anne carries in a tray, with what looks like some broth and bread for me. She startles on seeing George standing beside the bed. Griffin jumps to his feet, too.

"Oh!" Her face is a picture of surprise. "Brother, I did not realise you were here."

He brushes his hand through his hair to straighten it out, his cheeks flushed. "I came to retrieve my doublet, sister." He nods at his garment on the back of the chair.

"I hope that is all you came to find!"

My cheeks flush and I lower my gaze as she glares at me. She must guess what's been going on. George picks up his doublet.

"I am glad you are a little better, Beth," he says, bowing, doing well to cover his tracks. "Sister." He flings his doublet over his arm and walks out, closing the door behind him.

It's taking some time for my ankle to recover, and it will be longer before Anne, George, and I return to court. I don't want to think about how Jane will react if and when I go back. George told me he has informed her by letter that he will make her life extremely uncomfortable if she says a word out of place to me when we return to London. He has told her he won't spend any time alone with her, even in bed, unless she is nice to me. I think the threat will work – it would certainly work with me. I'm hot with jealousy at the thought of him being with her…alone, but what can I do? She's his wife, more's the pity.

As I lay back on Anne's bed and look out the window at the clouds rolling across the sky, I think about how lucky I am to experience this life – my life at Hever. Her bedroom is delightful to recuperate in, especially with such great views across the moat, and it's easy to understand why the Boleyn family love this place so much.

The door is opened after a quick knock, and George enters. Anne covers my elevated leg with a blanket. So much of Tudor behaviour is about protecting a lady's modesty.

"Ladies." He gives us his gorgeous, cheeky smile. "Can I talk with you?"

"You can speak easily to us, George," Anne replies. "You know that."

"I have had a letter from our cousin."

"Francis Bryan?" Anne asks.

"Yes." He sighs, though it borders close to a groan.

"What is the matter?"

He grimaces. "I was hoping I would never have to tell you both about this."

"What is it, brother? Out with it – you are vexing me."

"It is the king," he says. "He is making overtures."

Anne glances at me, then frowns at George. "Whatever do you mean? To which lady does he make his attentions? What is that to do with us?"

Her mouth remains hanging for a moment. "Should he not be giving his attentions to Mary?"

"I think his allegiances may have changed, somewhat."

"I do not understand," she says. But I do. I have an idea what he might be talking about, considering the month and year we are in.

"Anne, were you aware that the king rode out into the lists of the Shrove Tuesday joust just past, with comparisons aimed at either Beth or you?"

That snaps my senses to attention. Did he just say my name? He must be mistaken.

"No, George," Anne says, "why would I? We have been here at Hever."

"Francis has sent word of the matter to me." His eyes widen as he nods. "I did not want to confide in you that I had heard rumours but, until I had this letter, and read it with mine own eyes, I was uncertain whether to believe such a story."

"George, surely the king never meant me? Unless you have told him I've returned to stay with Anne here at Hever?" I'm aware that my voice is trembling. This can't be happening. I've been away from court so long. Why would Henry think about me? Professor Marshall won't be impressed. And what effect will it have on history? For all I know, more pages may be blank because of it.

"What was the joust about?" Anne asks, ignoring me.

"Its theme was unrequited love. Henry Courtenay – Marquess of Exeter – and his team of men wore green velvet and crimson satin embroidered with burning hearts."

Even with my worry, I can't help clapping. "They must have looked splendid. I am sorry to have missed such an occasion."

"You will be sorry when you hear the rest of the story, because above these hearts, a lady's hand was depicted coming out of a cloud and holding a watering can, which poured silver droplets on the burning hearts to quench them."

"Why would Beth be sorry for that?" Anne asks.

"Well, King Henry's team wore cloth of gold and silver richly embroidered with a man's heart in a press, surrounded by flames and bearing the motto 'Declare I dare not'."

"'Déclarez que je n'ose pas'," Anne says, nodding to herself. "That is indeed the courtly theme of unrequited love."

"Indeed – with the burning hearts being quenched by a woman, along with the motto, signifying that the king was wooing a new love."

"And who might that new love be?" I ask, hoping he will reply with Anne's name. My work will be done here, and I can get home, even if only for a while.

He stares at his sister for a long moment, then blinks and looks at me. "It is thought that this new love is most definitely you, Beth."

No, that can't be right – it's Anne he's now meant to be enamoured by, not me! George must have told the king I'm staying at Hever.

"The king never said so much to me!" I snap. "How can he possibly want me, let alone be in love with me? He has not set eyes on me in the last couple of years!" I think back to that clinch between us in his bedchamber. But we didn't… Oh, goodness, I can't believe I made such an impression. Okay, this has to be fixed. "If the king were to make such a declaration, I would reject his advances!" I look around to make sure no servants are within earshot. Why would Henry make a play for me when I haven't been at court?

George clears his throat. "The king knows you are staying with us at Hever." It's like he's read my mind. We seem to have such a connection.

"How, exactly?" I ask.

"I told him," He answers. "I was then given a commission to bring you a message, Beth – from the king, but I have been afraid to pass it on."

"What is it?" Anne asks, her tone sharp as a steak knife.

"I am afraid neither of you will like it."

"Try us, brother," she says, her demeanour hardening.

"Henry asked me to declare his feelings for you, Beth, weeks before, and for you to make a reply."

My face turns cold as realisation dawns. "You…never thought to pass this message on to me?"

He grimaces again and tilts his head. "As I said, I did not know how you would take it. I cannot help it when I say…I am a little jealous." He frowns. His eyes look like they are brimming with tears.

"You must understand, I never wanted the king's attention," I say, my tone soft.

Anne grunts. "George, you should have been honest with Beth about the king's feelings when she first came back to us."

"I had Mary to think of," he says, like a petulant child. "How would she have felt? Her pain would have been unbearable." He lifts both hands to chest height, palms up. "You know how she feels about the king!"

Did he hold off telling me because of how he feels for me? If that kiss from last week is anything to go by, I know he will not want to share me. What am I thinking? It's not like I'm going to even entertain the idea of being a mistress to a king. No, Beth, remember your mission. Yes, I need to nudge Henry's attentions towards Anne.

I hold my head, stunned by this turn of events. This was not expected. If Professor Marshall gets wind of this, the closest I'll get to Tudor times is in a book, with the pages rewritten.

Six

LATE MARCH – 1526

"Hever is dull," Anne says. "The only thing that brightens the place is little Henry Carey's cries echoing around the castle." She giggles, then groans, bored without George, who has returned to Court.

Lady Boleyn helps Mary with her grandson. Mary is out of sorts, with what I believe to be post-natal depression, which gives her mother little time for anything else. I'm relieved that the swelling on my ankle has gone down, the bruising less than it was. And thank goodness I can now put weight on my foot. I am often left alone, sat in the library, reading, so as not to overdo things. Sometimes, if I feel up to it, I spend time with Anne, and if I can manage it, we walk arm-in-arm through the gardens. I love the slow pace of life here, but time can drag.

Although the cypher ring is still on my middle finger, I often check the door back to the portal, but the stairs beyond it always lead only to the servants' quarters and not to Professor Marshall's study. Anne wonders why I bother, as I have the ring to take me back home to my time, whenever I want. I've explained to her how it works. It fascinates her, just as it puzzles me. I check the door to the portal for peace of mind, and to see if it's my feelings, or my reaction to the ring heating up that changes access to it. Christ knows, the situation confuses me. Although, at times, I do miss my family, friends like Rob, and, of course, my cat, Rutterkin. Thrilled by my Tudor experience, and the feelings my love for George evokes, I don't want to miss a second of time here, even though my heart often misses home. I sometimes wonder if I should time-slip back for a quick visit, but I'm equally concerned that the portal, or the ring, might never work again. I'd never see Anne or George again. And I can't leave, anyway, not until I've reset the true path of our history and convinced Henry that Anne is the one for him. Even so, the uncertainty of the intricate workings of the portal and the ring keeps me guessing, and, for reassurance, I can't help but pull back the curtain in the antechamber to see if the passageway beyond the door, which leads to Professor Marshall's office, will appear.

As my leg and ankle grow stronger, of an afternoon, I climb the hill and linger beneath the trees at the summit, remembering George and the way he stole that kiss from me as I lay as a patient in Anne's bed, unable to do anything but go with the flow of his advances. Not that I'd refuse him – what girl in their right mind would?

Anne is free of suitors here at Hever, and I want her memories of love lost to fade so her heart can heal. She is now resigned to not knowing the name of her future husband, and no longer presses me. With Henry Percy safely ensconced and married on his Northumbrian holdings, I suspect he has forgotten about her. Also, any enthusiasm she had for finding a husband has dwindled, which makes my objective a tad easier. I have to push her into Henry VIII's arms.

I put a hand to my brow to sharpen my view. From my vantage point on the meadow side, I see a horse-rider approaching the castle. Squinting doesn't help, and I can only guess that he is a messenger bringing letters for Lady Boleyn. Anne is a few hundred yards from me, playing with Griffin, who runs around her skirts, barking up at her. She quietens him when she sees the rider and makes her way to me, uncertain if the news he brings will concern us. We do want to attend Court. Lifting the hem of my skirts, I tiptoe through the emerging spring grass with Anne as the sun warms our faces.

The only thing missing is male company. If George were here, the silence would be filled with his talk of politics and theology, when he's not annoying us with his quirky humour. He is a learned man and has never hidden his opinions from his sisters or me. I hoard the information so that I can bring it out one day in my essays, though I've no idea how I'm supposed to reference it. When he's here, I like arguing with him about his theories on life, love, music, and literature. Before he left, he presented me with a new publication by John Russel, the brother-in-law of Sir Thomas More. It's a contemporary book, printed in 1526, entitled 'A Hundred Merry Tales'. I haven't read it yet, but I've left it on my bedside table. A most precious gift, personally inscribed by George: *'To my dearest friend, Beth Wickers, George Boleyn'*. He's even drawn a cypher of his name beneath the inscription. I haven't been so foolish as to show it to Anne – I don't want her to worry that things may be re-kindling between us. No, I can't let her know my feelings for him haven't changed, as I wouldn't want it used against me in the future.

Anne, now full of restless energy, skips downhill, startling a huddle of grazing sheep that scuttle off en masse to the far side of the meadow. I try to chase after her, but it's not easy, as my foot still feels weak since that fall from Anne's horse. Perhaps I should have allowed it to heal for longer. To keep up with Anne, and avoid tripping, I hold my skirts higher than is appropriate so as not to lose my footing. I'm breathless when I reach her at the orchard gate. My French hood has slipped back, and the rear of my gown feels damp from sitting on the grass. It takes a little time for my breathing to steady – I haven't had much exercise in the time it took for my ankle to heal. I straighten my hood, smooth down my skirts, wipe the worst of the mud from my shoes, then hurry through the garden after Anne and Griffin, who have run ahead of me towards the house.

Griffin barks as the rider stops by the stables. With his large bonnet, it's hard to tell who it is. He dismounts and notices us walking towards him. Ah, indeed, he is as tall as ever. His light-blue eyes sparkle, and his beard is well-trimmed. For a Tudor man, he is good-looking – his smile warm and inviting.

"Ladies." He bows. "Good afternoon."

"Thomas Wyatt, why are you not at court?" Anne asks, shielding her eyes from the sun with her hand.

"I had to return home on business for my father. Not only that, I thought I would visit my friends at Hever, as I have been suffering such heartache." He holds the horse's reins.

"Who might that be caused by – your wife, Elizabeth Brooke?" Anne asks, with not a little sarcasm.

"No, she caused me heartache long before now. It's your absence from court, I can't endure that anymore, Lady Anne." He shifts his weight from one leg to the other.

"I give you no reason to miss me, Tom," she says, a sharpness edging her tone. "You are a married man, sir. You must not speak of your desire for me."

I cast an eye over the man's solid frame as he stands before us, his rosy cheeks and windswept locks make him look the epitome of gallantry. His eyes are not as blue as the king's, and he has a crop of brown-sorrel hair, both on his head and chin. As he stares at me, I'm thinking he might not remember me from my time at Greenwich. He looks at Anne with questioning eyes.

"Mistress Wickers, this is Thomas Wyatt. I think you have met in passing before, at court?" I nod in polite acknowledgement.

"You are certainly pretty." His broad smile captures me unawares, and my cheeks boil when he stares at me in a manner that leaves little hidden. He certainly fancies himself.

"I am a distant cousin of Anne's," I say, the lie coming easy. "We were together in France."

He nods once. "Yes, I remember George telling me."

"Why have you come here, Tom?" Anne asks.

"To bring an invitation to your mother, and to see you, Mistress Anne." His eyes twinkle. "My heartache is fading and almost gone, and now that I have seen your face, I am fully revived." Yes, he's full of himself, I'll give him that.

Thomas Wyatt belongs to the circle that Henry VIII gravitates towards, and it is within this group that Anne and George formed a clique, before she was forced to return to Hever. There are rumours about Court that he has been in love with her since her return from France. However, he is married to Lord Cobham's daughter, Elizabeth Brooke. Yet, despite this, he has already written a poem entitled *'Of his love, called Anna'*.

Disconcerted, Anne turns away and I follow her. She holds out her hand to me and I take it as we walk over the drawbridge.

"Anne, can you not call a servant to take my horse?" he calls out after her.

"Tie him to a post outside the stable – I'm sure you will not be here for long!"

She seems amused by her own comment. I look back to see him tying the horse up, then start walking after us.

"Why does he follow us and not go straight to the house, to see your mother?" I ask.

"Thomas is another, like Percy," she whispers, "who follows me adoringly like a lapdog. I do not ask for it with Wyatt, I swear. My uncle, the duke of Norfolk, hates him, and wants to ruin him, as they have had a falling out. Thomas is a favourite of the king – his regular tennis partner – so His Majesty has told George."

My mind races, and I wonder how Wyatt will react when the king begins pressing his suit to Anne, if we ever return to Court. She will be bowled over by His Majesty's flamboyance, generosity, gifts, and letters. I can't wait for the story to unfold. Wyatt's voice breaks into my thoughts, calling from behind.

"What are you two whispering about?" he asks.

"Nothing," Anne answers after a long moment.

"I also bring news from court," he says.

She turns and gives him an expectant look. "What news might that be?"

He removes his hat. "Cardinal Wolsey has given Henry free rein at Hampton Court." He cocks his brow, awaiting a reaction.

"Hampton Court is grander than Richmond," I say. Hmm, Wolsey is probably trying to keep in the king's good books.

"Hampton Court? What is Wolsey after?" Anne asks, a smirk lifting her right cheek. She must have read my mind. "The king had better watch his first minister." She knows how cunning the Cardinal can be.

"The King had cast an envious eye on Wolsey's possessions. His Majesty is learned in statecraft – with his exalted status, he is aware he is way above his mentor, Wolsey, and should show it."

Anne nods her agreement. "The King is more magnificent than Wolsey – of course, he should show it!"

He chuckles. "I think the fine tapestries, the shining glass in the oriel window, and the vastness of gold plate on the buffet convinced Henry."

"What has happened then?" I ask.

"Only last week, the king laid out the deeds to Hampton Court Palace on the table, for all the members of his privy chamber to see. He smiled broadly as he told us that the Cardinal is planning a grand gesture of giving his master the palace."

"What other news do you have?" Anne asks.

"Princess Mary has been sent to Ludlow for her education."

"Queen Katharine will be beside herself with grief," I say.

"Queen Katharine has retreated to Woburn Abbey, to seek solace for her troubled soul."

Anne tilts her head to the side and shrugs her brows. "The queen will spend many hours on her knees, no doubt praying for strength in her denial. Nothing changes, Thomas."

"No, nothing changes, not even my love for you." He grins, and Anne groans. "I have written a poem for you, Anne." He fumbles beneath his doublet of tawny silk and draws out a folded parchment. The wind kicks up and almost whips it from his hand.

"Another one? Do not all young men at court write poetry?"

"How many has he written now?" I ask her, knowing his intent. "Is it better than the last?"

I stifle a giggle and she tells me to shush. "You will never get it published, Thomas."

Her hurtful comment, no doubt, is in hope of discouraging her unwelcome visitor. Should I tell her later that his poetry will still be published nearly five-hundred years into the future? No, she wouldn't believe me. Should I ask her outright if she's ever slept with Tom Wyatt? Maybe not a good idea. Besides, from their chemistry, I'd say that's a big fat no. Wyatt notices me smirking.

"Your friend is a cruel mistress," he says to me. He clears his throat. "It is better than the last poem, although 'tis not quite right yet, although I have the idea of it. Are you both going to listen?" He leans against the bridge rail but Anne turns and continues walking under the portcullis, into the inner courtyard.

"Anne, wait!" He pulls off his stiffened, cream-brocade coat, trimmed with sable, and throws it over his arm, then dashes after us, vellum in hand.

"Why should I listen to you, Tom? We have been through this all before." She glares at him. "I do not want to know what you write. I should strike you down for writing bawdy ditties in my honour!"

I'm somewhat surprised when he takes no notice and begins praising her with gentle speech.

> "And wilt thou leave me thus?
> "Say nay, say nay, for shame,
> "to save thee from the blame
> "of all my grief and grame.
> "And wilt thou leave me thus?

"Say nay, say nay!
"And wilt thou leave me thus,
"that hath loved thee so long
"in wealth and woe among?
"And is thy heart so strong
"as for to leave me thus?
"Say nay, say nay!
"And wilt thou leave me thus,
"that hath given thee my heart
"never for to depart,
"nother for pain nor smart,
"and wilt thou leave me thus?
"Say nay, say nay!
"And wilt thou leave me thus
"and have no more pity
"of him, that loveth thee?
"Hélas, thy cruelty!
"And wilt thou leave me thus?"

Anne stiffens, her brows creasing. "Why do you portray me as a cruel mistress? I am not your mistress."

"He likes to do that, Anne," I say, realising as soon as it's out that it sounds smug, and that I don't know him well enough to say it. He stares at me but says nothing. Shadows move across the upper windows of the castle, and I suspect we are being watched.

"You loved me once, did you not?" he asks, rubbing his temples, as if he has a headache. Or is he composing another verse? I can't tell.

Anne's nose screws up. "Thomas, I warn you never to cross me. Whatever you may feel for me, you must never act on it and never talk about me to anyone, except my brother, when at court!"

"Anne, I think what Master Wyatt is getting at is that you tease him."

He grimaces in acknowledgement. "I would never compromise you, Anne, nor offend you, but you do tease me with your very presence. Mistress Wickers is right – you like teasing a man, Anne. That is your tactic. In the past, you have given me the impression you wanted my attentions. In fact, there have been times when you have solicited them. But once I catch you in an intimate moment, you then say no to me – you do not even allow me to kiss you. You dangle yourself like a carrot before the other men at court, so they yearn for you." He takes a shuddering breath. "Does your heart and mind belong to another?"

"Who else besides you looks at me?" she asks, tossing her hair back over her shoulder.

"Henry Percy did, and now, it seems, the most important man at court notices you." He scowls. "His Grace, the King."

"No, you mix me with my sister," she says. "You jest with me, Thomas!"

The sun's rays blink through the clouds and light his face as he smiles. "Perhaps."

"What you have seen is nothing," Anne snaps back. "The king looks at every young woman as if he is undressing her, does he not?" She pulls her cloak tight around her to avoid the chill as a breeze circles us.

"So, you are not going to whore it with the king?" he asks.

"I beg your pardon – I would never give into him! Besides, I have heard it is not I who interests the king but my companion here,"—she flicks a wave at me —"Mistress Wickers."

"Granted, the king can take a fancy to any woman he likes," Wyatt says, responding with an acknowledging nod. "I would never judge either of you."

"Well, I am not my sister!"

"And neither would I give the king permission to have his way with me," I say, "whatever ideas you may have of the king, Master Wyatt." I needed to say that. This twist has to be rectified.

"That is as maybe," he answers, "and you both say you would refuse him. You, Lady Anne, say that now, but what about when your uncle Norfolk decides to sell you for a peerage, or a casket of gold? Henry is king!"

"I have told you repeatedly, I will resist him!"

"We will resist him, you mean!" I giggle, but this is no laughing matter. I have to get a hold of myself.

"Can we talk of something else?" she asks. "Or better still, take your message to my mother, and then you may leave us."

"Anne," he says, his tone sulky, "you want rid of me that easily?" He chuckles. "'Tis not only Mistress Wickers the king looks at, but you, too. I have seen it. George has seen it. The whole court has seen it."

Her cheeks glow a rosy hue. "It means nothing. The king is not interested in me, believe me." She shields her gaze from him with the fur lining of her hood. "'Tis Beth he wants!"

My face flushes, and I grab the rail as a light-headedness takes over me. I can't deal with this – if Henry wants me, then the history will turn out all wrong, and things can't go that way.

Tom holds my elbow. "Are you unwell, Mistress?"

I stare at him, surprised at him being so familiar with me. "Yes. Thank you, Master Wyatt."

"Beth, perhaps we should go inside for some refreshment?" Anne says. We walk across the courtyard together, Tom still supporting me at my elbow. He's not backwards in coming forwards.

We step into the entrance hall and Anne throws off her cloak as Agnes appears, carrying empty pewter plates towards the kitchen.

"Agnes!"

She stops and bobs a curtsy "Yes, Mistress Anne?"

"Could you bring a flagon of ale and some goblets to the parlour, please?"

"Certainly, Mistress." She scurries off towards the kitchens. Anne enters the parlour, and sits in her father's chair, next to the hearth. Tom waves me towards the chair opposite, and he slouches onto the settle.

"You are kind, Tom, but misguided, and blatant!" Anne laughs, watching him fuss over me. "'Tis a good job you are such good friends with my brother, for he, too, is keen on Mistress Wickers, and I doubt would be happy at you showing her your attentions." She looks at me and my cheeks flush again. Why am I so prone to blushing? I think I have a headache coming on. As I rub my temples beneath my gable hood, I wonder whether a goblet of ale would be a good idea under the circumstances.

"Where is George?" Tom asks, as he removes his bonnet and slouches on the high-back settle.

"Still at court," I say.

"With his beloved, Jane," he throws at me. He looks at Anne but she only coughs into her hand – a retort not forthcoming. "Talking of women, I have heard rumours that the king no longer pays so much attention to your sister, and that he is definitely looking for a new love. I know it's either one of you two!" He plays with the feathers on his bonnet as it sits in his lap.

"SShhh! Neither Beth nor I am interested in being part of Henry's wider court. You have only heard gossip – it means nothing!"

He shrugs. "I like to commentate on what is happening at court." He starts folding his parchment but Anne whips it from his fingers, then tears it into pieces before his eyes. She smirks as she throws the fragments on the fire, and the three of us watch them burn, with some floating up the chimney breast.

"Now you cannot publish that verse, Thomas!" She laughs with gusto, her eyes growing obsidian – black and shiny – impenetrable in the glow of the firelight.

"Ah, but Anne, what you do not realise,"—he points to his temple—"is that I have every single word, and the order of the verse in my head. I can soon put it back on paper again." He laughs but she shrugs and looks away.

"You write of things you know nothing about. You write of me. You make me out to be a tease – to lead you on – when I have told you one thousand times that we are friends, is all. Why should I like something that makes me out to be something I am not?" She gets up and walks to the doorway, probably to see where Agnes is with the ale.

"I only write about what I see, Mistress Anne." His voice is softer now, almost apologetic, as he must know he has overstepped the mark.

"You do not know me, Tom Wyatt, and you never will." She scowls at him, then looks out the door again. "And as for the king, he has barely looked at me, let alone had discourse with me." I know that's not the case. "As I have repeated, it is Mistress Wickers who interests His Majesty."

"I always thought us a little more than friends, Anne?"

"Never anything more than friends, Tom."

"Mistress Anne, you can never say I have not tried with you. I am sure that you will make a good marriage, eventually. Yes, of that, I am sure." He snorts as he laughs, his backhanded compliment sprinkled with a hint of jealousy. I watch him, and he seems sincere, but Anne knows, with him being married, even if his wife cheats on him, he would never make a good match.

"The king and Wolsey will need to approve!" She pouts like a disgruntled child and returns to her chair.

"And what of you, my Lady?" He looks at me with that smile but my attention is caught when Lady Boleyn opens the parlour door.

"I heard voices – who is here with you?"

Anne looks up. "Master Wyatt. He has brought a message for you."

Her mother stands by the fire. "What have you been burning?" She looks at Anne.

"Wyatt's poetry, Lady Boleyn," I say. Mrs Orchard comes in with cheeses and bread, along with a jug of ale, and Agnes follows her with some empty glasses. She sets them on the sideboard and begins pouring the golden liquid.

"That will be all, Agnes, Mrs Orchard," Lady Boleyn says.

"Very well, Mistress." Mrs Orchard ushers Agnes out and closes the door behind them.

Lady Boleyn finishes pouring the ale as Wyatt slumps back into the settle before a dwindling fire. I'm sitting nearest him, feeling awkward as I fiddle with the cuff of my sleeve.

"How are your parents, Thomas?" she asks.

"In good health, Lady Rochford."

"And your wife?" Anne asks.

He bristles, then looks at his lap. "I have not seen my wife in some time."

We wait but he doesn't elaborate. I know from my studies that he and Elizabeth Brooke are separated.

"You are very quiet, Mistress Wickers," he says, directing his gaze at me, possibly in the hope of deflecting attention from himself. "Do you think of George?"

"What are you talking about?" I'm stunned that he'd say such a thing in front of Elizabeth Boleyn. Anne shouldn't have shared that with him.

"My son is married, Thomas Wyatt. Why do you vex Mistress Wickers so?" Her indignation is clear at me being so linked with George.

"Married, yes, but is he happy?" He smiles, as if this is simply a polite conversation.

"Is that really any of your business?" Anne asks.

Lady Boleyn grabs the poker and stabs at the embers in the hearth. Then she snaps straight. "Before I say something I might regret, I shall leave you all to your conversation." She steps towards the door. "Thomas, send my regards to your parents, and your lovely wife. I shall bid you good day, Master Wyatt."

He rises to his feet and bows, kissing Lady Boleyn's hand when she offers it, then hands her a small, folded note, which she tucks into the purse hanging from her girdle belt. With that, she lifts her chin and leaves the room.

"Tom, you are nearly as bad as my brother!" Anne says.

"I did not mean to offend your mother."

"I think you can safely say you have done so, since she has left the room!"

He raises his brows and nods. "So, Anne…before you burnt my poem, what did you think you of it?" I'm astonished at his inability to see beyond his ego.

Anne gasps. "You should not have written about me, and certainly not suggested there has ever been anything between us." Her dark eyes blaze in anger. "I am friends with you, but as I have repeatedly said before, only because you are a friend to my brother."

His face drops. Has it finally hit home that his poetry isn't touching her? Whatever his challenging comments, his hurt expression betrays his sincerity. At the English Court, it is fashionable to love in vain. All of the men, married or not, strut about the palace with their hearts on their sleeves, weeping and wailing over some woman or other. However, Tom, I suspect, is different. He has made the mistake of loving Anne in an all-consuming way…albeit in vain.

"Can I not write of a friend?" he asks.

"No!" Anne snaps. "Because you do not portray me as such."

"Look, Anne, the work still needs adding to. I will have to rewrite it, now you have torn it to shreds."

"Perhaps when you rewrite it all, Master Wyatt," she says, "you could take me out of it."

"Ah, don't be angry with me, Lady Anne." He looks at her like a lovesick puppy, hoping his pleas will allow him back into her good graces. I can't believe that I'm witnessing this. His ardour never seems to dim, and he seems to enjoy winding her up. I'm embarrassed for him. To avoid being pulled into the conversation, I get up and walk away, leaving them to argue alone. As I pull the door behind me, I see Tom get up, grab her about her waist, and lean into her.

"You are part of my childhood, Tom," she says, straight-arming him to gain distance. "Part of my memories, but I cannot love you. Kissing you would be like kissing George. You are too familiar, too close – almost kin – like a brother."

"You are so fair, Mistress Anne." His voice comes as a whisper, and I have to focus to catch everything.

"No, I am not. No one has ever called me fair. You are mistaking me for Mary."

Concerned about how this visit is going, I rush to find Lady Boleyn, who is in the kitchen helping the servants to prepare this evening's meal. I bob a curtsy.

"Lady Boleyn, I need you to come to the parlour."

"What is wrong, I have only just left?"

"It's Master Wyatt, Madam. I think he has outstayed his welcome – I'm not sure Anne can get rid of him."

She closes her eyes and sighs. "I shall see what I can do. He's always liked Anne, possibly a little too much. She has told me of how he has paid her too much attention at court."

"Madam, I think if Thomas had the opportunity where Anne is concerned, it would be more than a game of courtly love."

She guides me out of the kitchen. "We have been friends with his family a long time, but I will not put up with him pursuing my daughter, and neither will my husband. Thomas Wyatt should know better."

"He seems lost without her attentions, Madam."

"And there lies the problem," she says, shaking her head. As we approach the parlour, raised voices filter from the room.

"Well, Mary may be fairer but what you have, Anne, outshines her like the sun outshines the moon. The king can keep Mary – it is you I want."

"You think you want me, Tom?" she shouts "You are like the king, and the king does as he wills. My poor sister had his child, and the king takes no responsibility for the women he is involved with, nor with any children that he may have fathered!" We stand outside the door. "I told you, the king is nothing to do with me. In any case, Master Wyatt, I have my virtue and intend to keep it. Since the disaster of loving Harry Percy, I am done with all men!"

As Lady Boleyn opens the door, with me behind her, we find Wyatt's face close to Anne's.

"Anne, let me kiss—" He stops, realising he has an audience. His face is flushed as she pushes him away, her nostrils flared.

"Mother, I have told Tom we are just family friends. He will never be anything more."

He stands before her, clearly embarrassed.

"Master Wyatt, we have always welcomed you at Hever, but your conduct here is inappropriate and I would ask that you leave."

He steps away from Anne, his gaze lowered. Then he nods and puts his cloak back over his doublet.

"I beg your forgiveness, Lady Boleyn. I meant no harm." He thrusts his bonnet back on his head, its feathers fluttering.

"I should hope not, sir. If you bother my daughter again, I shall ask my husband to pay a visit to your father at Allington,"

"I am sorry. I have outstayed my welcome." He bows and rushes past us without another word.

"Anne, Beth – there you are. Where have you been?" Lady Boleyn doesn't wait for a reply but thrusts a pile of linen into my arms. She frowns when she looks at the creases in our gowns.

"Take that upstairs, all the servants are busy. You and Anne had better change into fresh gowns. Look at the state of your skirts – they will need to dry out before they can be worn again."

I bob a curtsy. "Yes, Lady Boleyn. Forgive me. Can they be dry brushed?"

"I will ask Mrs Orchard. She is knowledgeable with wools and velvets. Anne, your father has sent word that he arrives tomorrow in the company of the king."

My jaw drops. "The king?"

"But, Mother, we are not prepared to receive the king."

"You do not have to tell me that, daughter." Her eyes are bright but heavy with anxiety. "Now, help Beth to take those shirts to your father's chamber and then find Agnes, she must assist the other maids to change the draperies in the parlour." The lappets on her gable hood flap as she barks her orders.

"Yes, Mother," Anne replies, her voice low. She hurries ahead, shirts clutched to her breast.

As I reach the bottom of the stairs in a daze of disbelief, kitchen servants pass me with bushels of apples, bowls of walnuts, and platters of sweetmeats for the Great Hall table. I find Anne standing in the doorway of her father's bedroom, watching Agnes chasing cobwebs from under the four-poster bed.

Cobwebs! Oh, no. In a mad panic, I dump the linens and rush to Anne's room and scan the space under the bed, checking to reassure myself that she moved my stuff and locked them in a trunk before all this cleaning started. My heart. How could I explain my modern bits and bobs to Agnes, not to mention the books? I look around the room. What do I have to do now? I throw open the four casements and ask for the hearth to be swept, then step out to see Agnes looking flustered as she runs down the passageway, perspiration shining on her forehead as she endeavours to follow all the orders being barked at her by Mrs Orchard.

"Agnes! My mother wants you," Anne calls after her. The poor woman turns back and curtsies.

"Why all this cleaning? What news, Mistress Anne? Do we have guests coming?" She fixes her coif around her chin with the cord, her eyes bloodshot, cheeks flushed – close to being worn out, I would say.

"Yes, apparently, father has sent word that the king is coming here – now, get one of the other servants to assist my sister, please."

"Yes, Mistress Anne." She bobs again and leaves to find help.

Mary is beside herself, demanding that all her best gowns are made ready, as if we're not busy enough. When Agnes runs downstairs, thinking Lady Boleyn is in the parlour, I slip into Mary's bedchamber. Baby Henry is blue-faced and bawling in his crib, and little Catherine toddles about, chasing beams of sunlight streaming through the windows. I sort through a heap of gowns and sleeves on the bed, trying to help Mary find something suitable to wear. Why is she trying to make herself presentable? Does she think the king is still interested?

"Why are you so worried about your appearance, Mary?" I ask.

"With the king coming here, I want to look beautiful for him. Is it not a good idea to cultivate the king's good graces?"

This confirms to me that she thinks she has a way back into Henry's heart. Perhaps she thinks she never left it. "I suppose so," is all I can think to reply.

"The king coming here makes me feel insecure," she grumbles.

"Why?"

"I have not yet recovered from giving birth to my child."

"You mean that things don't feel the same, down there?"

"Yes, that is what I mean," she replies, her shyness surprising me.

"Your body will heal itself. It is nature. You know the king might not find you so attractive so shortly after the birth of a child. Men are strange creatures like that. Can you understand that?"

She nods. "Anne would say that a woman cannot be alluring if she smells of wet linen and is still leeching milk. She has told me that will turn the King away from me, for a time. Is that true?"

"Maybe." I sigh, thinking of how fastidious Anne is about bathing. "Mary, try not to vex yourself. You will see how the king is with you, once he arrives." Henry Carey's wriggles have grown furious in his crib. He screws his eyes up and clenches his little fingers into fists.

"Where is the wet nurse?" I yell above the child's screams.

Mary shrugs. "Helping Mother. Everyone is needed now Henry Tudor is on his way."

I pick up the infant and pace back and forth with him, looking into his swollen eyes, hoping to lull him to sleep. It seems to work. His eyes close, and

I think how babies are the same, no matter what the century – they still have to be fed and cuddled and cradled to sleep. Anne enters as I place him back in his crib. I swaddle him in linens and rock the cradle.

"That child makes an unholy noise!" she says, smiling down at him.

"All you require is patience." I nod at the child. "See, all he needs is a little attention."

"Like most men!" Anne smiles, as she touches my arm, then looks to Mary, and then at the gowns on the bed. "Fret not, Mary, the king will adore you whatever you wear."

Mary frowns, holding one gown after another against her in panicked efforts to choose the right one. She'd better make her mind up soon – there's only one more sleep before Henry arrives.

Seven

April 1526 - Hever

I flit from window to window in the staircase gallery, looking down at the inner courtyard in heightened anticipation. Sir Thomas emerges from the castle doorway, elegantly dressed in his usual black. He looks magnificent as he waits, arms folded, to greet his illustrious visitor. Moments later, hoofs clip and clatter on the cobbles, and I creep towards the closest window recess to witness the splendid display. Heart pounding, breath held, I hardly dare to look at the sight unfolding beneath me, a riot of colour and chaos. I try to keep myself hidden behind the curtain, observing the commotion in utter fascination: the conversation; hooves striking the cobbled stone; the clink of stirrups, all carried on the breeze.

Richly clothed riders dismount, and Robert Cranewell and other manservants rush around taking sweat-covered horses from their owners. One of Henry's pages, in white and green, weaves his way through the gathering, delivering flagons of what looks to be ale mixed with water to those who are dusting off their fine clothing after their arduous ride. They are in high spirits, and to accentuate the excitement, a raised pennant flutters high above the fray, displaying a splash of vibrant red embellished with three golden lions with blue claws and tongues. The pure gold thread catches the light, causing the flag to glisten as it shows off the royal arms of England.

In amongst this throng of male camaraderie, I spot a larger-than-life figure clothed in rich damasks and silks, wearing soft leather riding boots adorned with shining golden spurs. It is the king. You can't mistake him with his gold-linked collar hanging about his shoulders, while a silken sash secures a sheathed dagger at his waist. His bejewelled velvet bonnet is astounding, decorated about the rim with soft, white ostrich feathers that flitter in the gentle morning breeze. I hope he doesn't look up and catch me watching. He exchanges words with another man standing close by but I can't make out who it is.

Henry's features are chiselled and strong, hair as red as carrots, and eyes as steely blue as the sky, except when in shadow, when they are as dark as the moat surrounding the castle. The excitement of seeing him at Hever is too much – I am riveted – but before I have a chance to see any more, Anne yanks me away from the window and down the corridor, past a huge oak sideboard covered in silver plate. Keeping a tight hold of my hand, she swirls around and giggles at me, leading me to her bedchamber.

"Steady on, Anne!" I shout.

"Come on, Beth, no time to daydream. I must make you look beautiful for the king!"

I had forgotten how tall the king is. As he removes his cap, revealing his red hair that compliments his chiselled face, fringed with a reddish-copper beard, he glances about the Great Hall, where we are all beginning to assemble. Then his pursed mouth grows into a broad, beguiling smile when he sees me. His deep-set eyes are mirrors of the sky: blue, clear, glinting, and bright. He knows who I am as his cheeks redden when he looks me over. I feel as if he's reappraising me against our last encounter, so I sweep into a deep curtsy to avoid his generous gaze.

He is larger than life now he is here at the castle, his athletic frame filling the doorways he walks through, and such a contrast to everyone else in his entourage. His contagious laughter perfumes the air as he prepares to greet his guests lined inside the Great Hall. Lady Boleyn will be first, with William Carey and Mary next, then Jane Boleyn and George, followed by myself and Anne. Henry charms everyone without trying with his famous breezy manner – much like the English weather, with its sunny periods alternating with cloudy spells, but no bursts of heavy thunder, as yet. Now that I think of it, I have never seen his expression icy or cruel, to date.

Much to Anne's delight, George has told us that Wolsey is not amongst the guests here today. Henry prefers to look like a king than act like one, which is why he has left Wolsey at court to run the country. I'm aware that George's wife is watching as he whispers important information to me.

"You must know the king prefers the pursuits of archery, hunting, and hawking rather than governing."

If he's annoyed that the king has taken a fancy to me, he daren't show it, at least not while the man is here. The affability Henry Tudor eludes is the rib-poking, back-slapping, and bare-arm-around-the-shoulders kind. He stands amongst us, informally, as if with friends, which I suppose he is.

Sir Thomas begins the introductions, and George straightens, allowing me to see Henry offer his hand to Lady Boleyn to kiss. Then he moves down the line, drawing William Carey into a manly embrace, before he reaches Mary. To my surprise, he pays her no particular attention, and I feel sorry for her as he offers his hand full of gold rings and rubies to kiss. She flushes beneath his chilly greeting, not doing a good job at hiding her frustration, no doubt stemming from him not recognising what the Tudors refer to as his bastard children. His indifference must break her heart. Then again, maybe it's a usual trait of Henry's to cast off an unwanted mistress in such a way.

Her kiss on the back of his hand doesn't seem like one from a lover. She keeps her eyes lowered so as not to make the situation more unpleasant for herself. He gives a non-committal grunt when she summons Mrs Orchard to bring young Catherine to meet him. When he casts an eye over his daughter – if she is, indeed, his daughter – it is one of disinterest. Would he act differently if was introduced to little Henry Carey instead? I feel Mary's pain, and wish there was a way I could make things better for her, but with the king here, now is not the time to discuss it.

He smiles at Jane, who curtsies. George bows low.

"Welcome to the Boleyn home, Your Grace."

Henry smiles, then steps along at Sir Thomas's urging. I dip a curtsy too, like all the other gentlewomen, lowering my eyes as the king looms before me, keeping my neck bent, my focus on his feet, until he addresses me.

"Now, I remember this beauty," he says, and I look up to see him beaming at me. He touches my cheek, his flesh warm against mine, then bends to kiss my forehead. "The older I get, the more beautiful these young ladies become."

"Your Grace, this is Mistress Wickers," Thomas says. "She is a friend of Anne's, come from France."

My face burns as Henry lifts my chin with his large forefinger, and I have no choice but to keep looking into his eyes.

"Lord Rochford, have you forgotten that I know this fair creature?"

"Of course not, Your Grace!" Thomas replies.

Henry hasn't taken his eyes from me. "We have met before, have we not, Mistress Wickers?" He smiles at me as he raises my hand to his lips and plants a kiss, his beard prickling my soft skin.

"Yes, Your Majesty," is all I can manage to say. He moves on, and Anne's cheeks redden as he watches her dip into a great curtsy, her small bosom on full view for his delectation. She keeps her gaze lowered too, when Henry addresses her. To my surprise, blood rushes to his cheeks, too. Unexpected! Seeing this, I can't believe he's truly only interested in me – he can't be. Francis Bryan and George must have it all wrong.

"Anne."

She straightens her frame and, with a certain defiance, raises her gaze to match his. "Yes, Your Grace."

Once the introductions are over, he removes his chain of office and his heavy coat with the help of Sir Henry Norris, who has already acknowledged me with a glance and a half-smile. We can see that the king's doublet has its top buttons open, his skin glowing through the opening of the linen fabric of his intricately woven shirt. Agnes, Mrs Orchard, Robert Cranewell, and the other servants hang back, but their monarch nods and smiles at them.

He must realise we all know the truth, that Catherine Carey is his – but he expects us to play a game and acknowledge Mary's husband as the father of her children, particularly Catherine. The little girl is the spitting image of the king. Forced to conceal his scowls, now the introductions are over, William takes his leave, probably to walk around outside alone, trying to pretend all is well. Lady Boleyn asks if we should like to take a turn about the garden whilst luncheon is being prepared.

I ask Anne to stay close by my side as we head out into the mid-morning sun. My head feels light, and I take deep quiet breaths in an effort to retain my composure. She gives me a knowing nod, then turns to Mary, who glares daggers at me when the king holds out his arm for me. My heart thunders as I slide my fingers into the crook of his elbow. The silks of his doublet are so soft as I rest my palm on his jewelled, slashed sleeves, allowing him to escort me down a gravel path into the gardens. This isn't how things are meant to go. How can I get out of this?

Behind me, Anne links arms with Mary in a show of sisterly solidarity. I have no doubt that Mary is seething.

The king stops and looks behind. "What is it you ladies whisper?"

"Nothing of consequence, Your Majesty," Anne replies.

He nods and continues to walk. I can't help feeling small, his chest level with my eye-line. Regardless, I feel graceful in my taffeta russet gown as it billows out behind me in the breeze, and we glide down a narrow gravel path into the rose garden. Henry is all testosterone, his energy both burly and flashy alongside me, resplendent in his jewelled doublet. At that moment, the musky scent of his cologne transports me back to his private bedchamber that night I was asked to attend him. Does he remember everything from that occasion? He looks down at me, as if admiring my beauty.

"You are very quiet this morning, Mistress Wickers?" he says. "Have you suddenly turned mute? It is uncomely for a woman to be so quiet. They are usually so full of gossip and scandal."

"Sir, I am captivated just by being in your presence – that is enough to render any woman mute!"

He raises his brow at me and smiles. "That is so pleasant to hear, Mistress Wickers."

"Please call me Beth – we are friends, are we not?"

"Indeed, we are!" He chuckles. "I have not forgotten how kind you were to me, that night, in my privy chamber."

"Sir, it was the very least I could do." I'm hoping if I just show kindness, and avoid any flirtatious comments, he'll turn his attention back to Mary, or to Anne. I am *not* going to be *wife number two*.

He leans closer. "Beth, I delayed my hunting trip at Penshurst to pay you a special visit." His eyes sparkle as he whispers so only I can hear him. "Because I have missed you at court. I noted your absence, and George confirmed it. Two years I have been without your charming company." His eyelashes flutter. I can't believe I've been at the forefront of Henry VIII's thoughts – it's not good. "You have been looking after your father?" he asks.

"Yes, Your Majesty."

"I wanted to tell you how beautiful I think you are, both in the way you look, and in your heart."

Oh, goodness. My heart skips several beats, and I can't help blinking a rapid sequence, my eyelashes fluttering as I bow my head. This cannot be what Professor Marshall intended when he gave me the opportunity to be part of this time-slip. I feel the king's gaze burning into the flesh of my bosom, and my face flushes again.

"Have I said something to alarm you?"

"Your compliments have taken me somewhat by surprise, Your Grace."

"Did George not tell you how I rode into the lists, never daring to declare my love for you?"

"Yes, sir. He told me you had written to him telling him of your feelings – but he was uncertain whether they were aimed at Anne or me."

"Anne?" he whispers, flashing a glance behind. "No, the display was meant for you. Were you not pleased when you heard of it?"

"I feel honoured." That's all I can think of saying. He gives me a disconcerting look, and I'm not sure he believes me.

"I wish you had been there to see it!" he says.

The sun is warm on my face, heating my cheeks all the more. The weather has blessed us today, the clouds staying away as if unwilling to mar the monarch's pleasures.

"So, Mistress Wickers,"—he turns about to look at Mary and Anne, and the gravel grunts as his feet swivel—"ladies, when are you all returning to Court?"

"We do not know, Sire," Anne answers. "Mistress Wickers went home to be with her family after she left court. Then I sent word wanting her here at Hever, at the behest of my mother, to support Mary with the birth of little Henry Carey."

The king looks at me sideways, and I wonder if he thinks I've been deliberately hiding in the country, trying to avoid his attentions.

"Besides, I'm not sure Wolsey tolerates anyone at court associated with my family, apart from my father, Your Grace." She dares to look him in the eye.

The corners of his mouth turn up, showing how he admires her audacity. He must know that she's referring to the debacle Wolsey made of annulling Percy's suit to her and his securing of the marriage to the Talbot girl.

"Pay Wolsey no heed, Mistress Anne. He is a stubborn man and makes his mind up on people before getting to know them. You must all return to court – I insist on it."

"That is in my father's hands, Your Majesty. We await his pleasure." She slips me a conspiratorial look. It seems that she's enjoying me being the centre of Henry's attentions. I can't believe it – this is going to send history all topsy-turvy!

"And what of my pleasure?" He chuckles. "Does your father not consider that?" He stares at me for a moment, then bends towards a rose bush and exclaims at an early bud, drawing our admiration to the deep red hue peeking from its wrapping of green.

"You are like this rose, Mistress Wickers, beautiful and not to be hidden away at Hever." My cheeks burn again at his declaration. "Summer is not long away, Mistress. That is good to see. The sunshine brings out the best in us all, does it not? I will speak to Sir Thomas and tell him that Mistress Wickers and Mistress Anne are missed." He turns to Mary and Anne, all smiles. "We need beautiful women at court. In any case, it keeps me young. I will speak with your father, Anne, and not the Cardinal, about you all returning to Court."

He turns back to me and pats my hand in the crook of his elbow. "Nay, I will demand that you both…"—he turns to look back at Anne—"return to court immediately. I shall command Lord Rochford make arrangements to have you back in London in no time. I can't think how you all amuse yourself all day, buried here in the Kent countryside."

Poor Mary looks dejected. The king didn't mention her and court in the same breath. Her expression is easy to read.

Henry loves the company of women and revels in our compliments. He is a ladies' man, and this is the way he will be remembered by history, for his wives, and less for his political acumen. From the way he's holding my arm, hanging on my every word, I'm not sure he will give up his pursuit of me. I try to put on a good act, though, to be honest, I don't mind being the focus of his attentions. He is all graciousness. Underneath this façade of smiles I'm presenting, however, lies panic. My thoughts whirl at the way he is with me. I need to change his mind and send Cupid's arrows in Anne's direction. This must be the time in the original history where it begins with her. He's making it obvious he no longer carries affection for Mary, judging by how he's side-lined her so far today. The poor woman hangs onto Anne's arm like a lost child. I feel guilty. Will the history books see me as another Bessie Blount – a scarlet woman, sacrificing my friendships to gain the attentions of the king? No, this is all for Anne's sake, not mine.

The silence is broken when Mary asks to take her leave to return to the house to see to her baby. She bobs a curtsy to Henry, then repeats it to us all before retreating in haste, I suspect in tears. The king watches her disappear back up the garden path, towards the house. As I bend to pluck an early rose from the border, I feel his eyes bore into me. I lift the flower to my nose to smell its fragrance.

"What exactly do you do here at Hever?" he asks me. "I would imagine it dull when you could have the likes of Tom Wyatt and others to entertain you at court."

"I do not care much for Tom Wyatt, Your Grace."

He roars with laughter, the jewels on his doublet bobbing as his chest heaves.

"He visits Hever infrequently," Anne says. "Wyatt is more a friend of my brother, to be fair, Your Majesty."

"Ladies, please call me Henry – we are alone, there is no harm in it."

"If you are sure, Henry?" I say, but Anne glares at me as if I've said something atrocious. He smiles at me, then at Anne, probably trying to work out which of us Thomas Wyatt would be interested in the most.

"If you do not like the company of certain gentlemen, what do you do here all day?"

"Sire – I mean…Henry – Anne and I like to walk when the weather is fair, and when it is not, we read. The Boleyn family has a fine collection of religious books, and we read poetry, too."

"Books? Do you both enjoy reading theological books and poetry? That is something I would not credit."

"Yes, Your Majesty," Anne says. "George brings me things to read, too, mostly so that he has someone with whom to share his wisdom of theology." Her eye-contact with him is direct, as if challenging him to counter her. "Also, Beth takes great delight in seeing if she can beat George at an argument."

He bellows with laughter again, his strong frame shaking in the process. Then, when he has sobered a little, one hand gripping the hilt of his dagger, he playfully pats my hand.

"Oh, Beth, I had not expected that. I can well imagine George's anguish at being beaten by a woman in matters of learning!" He chuckles to himself, a dimple winking in his cheek. "I imagined your chatter would be of sleeves and silks, and here we are on the brink of something close to intellectual debate. But I see you are both like Margaret More: very educated and robust in argument and rhetoric!"

"Your Majesty, I thought you liked intelligent women?" I frown, then add a subtle smile, inviting his reply.

"Of course I like intelligent women, but there are so few among the queen's ladies, apart from the queen herself, that when I meet one, it takes me somewhat by surprise."

"Anne is a very learned lady, Your Grace. She has been well-educated." I had to get that tidbit in to further my mission. He smiles at her, and I almost let out a triumphant whoop when he offers her his other arm. I giggle inwardly at the thought that he is the thorn between two roses.

"Can you speak Latin and French, Beth?"

"Not very well, Henry. But I am learned in history, amongst other things." I hear Anne trying to stifle a giggle. "But you must know that Mistress Anne is very accomplished. She plays the lute exceedingly well and can dance many a galliard." I try to recall things that I know amuse and entertain him, remembering the David Starkey documentary 'Music and Monarchy'. "Anne can speak French, Latin, read scriptures, and is a proficient theologian."

"You should not exalt others above you," he says, looking down on me with a kind, genuine smile. "I also know, Mistress Wickers, that you are a good dance partner, for you have accompanied me in a few revels."

"My dancing ability is fair but not good, sir."

"What of your heart, is that close to God?"

"Yes, very much so," I answer, choosing to be vague so he can't figure out if I'm Catholic or Lutheran.

"Henry – I thought only kings and priests were close to God, and not so much the ladies?" Anne's cheekiness lifts my hopes further.

"Mistress Anne, I much admire the ladies of my court, but I like ladies to be faithful to God, not just to scripture. Faithfulness and love are important characteristics in a woman. How could you say that I do not like intelligent or religious women?" His disgruntled response flattens my mood.

"Sir, I meant no disrespect – I wanted to discover whether your heart was the same as mine on such matters, and I see that it is."

I lean forward enough to see that she has lowered her gaze in supplication.

"It appears I do not know you very well, Mistress Anne." He raises his brows and sighs. "I thought you were arguing with me on matters of religion."

"That could never be so, sir. For what ails the King's conscience, ails me."

I lean forward again and see that she is meeting his gaze, her eyes dark and mysterious. She is clever but seems secretive, and is playing him well, as if she can read his thoughts. Perhaps she has psychic tendencies I haven't noticed before. Whatever it is, it seems to be working. This is exactly how things should be developing.

"Is that so?" he says, his face open, showing a direct and forceful character. "I really do need to get to know you better, Mistress Boleyn. Perhaps we are kindred in character, what say you?"

I giggle, glancing at Anne. "Perhaps, then, Your Grace, your attentions should be on Anne!" He looks back and forth at us as if he has been ambushed.

"Like many daughters from nobility, Sire, I have been at the French Court, was well-educated in all matters of religion, politics, culture, and the arts by Queen Claude, and before that, Your Majesty, Marguerite of Austria, Duchess of Savoy, has been a great influence upon me."

"So that is where you get your ideas and manners from, Mistress Anne?"

"Yes, My Lord. I have been fortunate to be educated in such a way." She smiles, probably relieved she hasn't offended him.

"Then, I am fortunate to be in your company again." I lean out just enough to catch him beaming down at her. "Do not think I have forgotten our meeting during the Chateau Vert masque!"

"Did I make an impression, sir?" She laughs.

"That you did, Anne, that you did." His laughter fills the air but I'm hoping his intentions towards my friend will grow to be something more serious than a joke. However, she hangs back when she sees Griffin walking down the path alone.

Henry takes his opportunity, and turns to me, letting lose my arm, and I have to say that I'm relieved, but then to my surprise, he takes hold of my hand. "I like you, Mistress Wickers. I have tried to let you know often enough through George and others."

When he blinks several times in quick succession, my cheeks heat up once again. My goodness, what am I like? King Henry VIII is acting all soft and shy, and I'm reacting like a schoolgirl meeting her first date.

He lifts my hand to his lips. "It appears George did not do the job well enough, for, by your expression, it appears you do not believe me." The recent display at the joust relayed to me by George, confirmed to all the court that he was pursuing someone, but I never thought it would be me. "Beth, when you attended Court previously, I believe you impressed the queen with your intelligent and vivacious ways. She sorely misses your company. I will instruct Lord Rochford to bring you and Mistress Anne back to Court just as soon as he can."

Henry, ever intelligent, is quick to grasp the potentials of the situation. In my peripheral vision, I see Anne watching our interaction, as she strokes Griffin's head. This situation could go either way. It would be so easy to accept his flirtations, but I can't. It's impossible. No, I have to turn his focus back to her if I'm to ensure a correct historical outcome. My head is pounding with the possibilities of what might happen. No, it doesn't bear thinking about.

With that, Anne walks closer with Griffin following on behind her. Anne bobs a curtsy. "Your Grace, with your permission, would you like me to go and speak with my father?"

"Do you think my word will not be enough?" He chuckles, waving away his joke.

"Of course, it is enough, sir – I am longing to return to Court."

"Ah, that explains it. Be off with you then!" His eyes sparkle with enthusiasm. I mouth at Anne not to leave me alone with him, terrified that I'll say the wrong thing, or encourage him without meaning to. She smiles back in reassurance, turns away, leads Griffin by his collar, and glides out of the garden to find her father.

Henry tucks my hand once more into his elbow and proceeds to guide me around the gardens, pointing out primroses, and a clump of Lent-lilies beneath the hedge. I hope that by the time I return to the house, he won't have pinned me to a wall and ravaged my neck with a flurry of hot kisses.

My thoughts are drawn to Anne and her fate. I should be encouraging her into Henry's arms, not allowing her to facilitate him to do as he will with me. My mind races to her demise, and I shudder, but then a thought flits into my head: if I have an affair with the king, it might save her from such a horrendous end. I feel like a sacrificial lamb as I walk alongside him, in Anne's place. Looking up at him, it's hard to believe that he could harm anyone, let alone a woman he loves. I shiver as I consider the future.

"Are you warm enough?" he asks, pulling me closer.

"Just a breeze catching me unawares, sir."

"Let us find somewhere to sit, in the sun perhaps?"

"Whatever you wish, Your Grace." I look over my shoulder and discover we are alone. It's unusual. Where is his entourage – Henry Norris, George, and all the others? Shouldn't they be here, protecting him? Why have they all left me…to his mercy? Anne should be in my place, being swept off her feet by this monarch. Oh, my goodness, if this were to…develop, does it mean I will end up in the Tower on charges of treason, and Eric Ives writing that book about me? My mind boggles, and the professor's face looms as if he's in front of me. I must turn the situation around. There is no question about it – England's history needs to be about her, not me.

Maybe I should tell her that she will be the king's new wife. Would that convince her to flirt with him and win him over? Isn't that what Professor Marshall wanted me to do? Or maybe I could just open up and warn her of her future. No, we've gone through this, and she wouldn't believe me, anyway. This is such a dangerous time to be living in. I may be in the king's good graces right now but how long will that last? What if I contort the butterfly effect? I would never get away with it – and things could change all too fast.

As we turn a corner, I lean on his arm. He ducks beneath an arbour that will soon be smothered with roses, and we find ourselves in a secluded flower garden. The glint of sun on a window draws my eye to the castle, and I see Mary slamming shut her casement, the sound followed by the tinkle of glass falling to the hedge below. She is not slow to show her anger or jealousy – a family trait, no doubt.

Henry grunts. "Pay no mind to Mistress Carey. Her attachment to me was far too strong – I had to break it off." His brows furrow. "She's a sweet girl, but there is no future in a dalliance with a married woman – she was mine purely for entertainment."

I have never heard him speak so candidly before, and it surprises me. Henry Tudor is not how I expected him to be, at all. We walk deeper into the garden and stop at a stone bench beside a water fountain.

"Beth, would you like to sit with me for a time?"

I'm uneasy being alone with him. It unnerves me to be so admired by a man of such power. However, I must remember why I'm here – to steer Anne into his arms. He sits, patting the cold, empty space on the bench beside him.

"Do not be anxious in my company," he says, smiling. "I have your best interests, honour, and pleasure as my priority."

"Really, sir, I do not want to vex Mistress Carey."

"You are kind, Beth, but pass no heed to Mary. Come, sit." He takes my hand in his. His bejewelled rings sparkle in the sunlight, and his gentle manner confuses me. This man baffles me. It's not that I'm afraid of him – I'm afraid of what my presence in his life will do to change his history. Against my better judgement, I sit next to him. Within seconds, I feel a reassuring arm about my waist as he pulls me closer. He gets straight to the point.

"You have been occupying my mind for too often, Mistress, when my every waking thought should be concerned with more important matters of state." He sounds pensive, as if this is a problem that has been worrying him. "Since that evening with you in my chambers, I have thought only of you. I have been waiting to hear news of you, so I could see you again." He raises both eyebrows for a moment. "You see, I am of a mind to make you happy, but, in return, Mistress, I would like you to make me happier still."

His comment takes my breath away, as if the breeze has whipped away my tongue.

"I want to ask something of you, Beth." He pulls me even closer. "If it pleases you to be my true friend, and my loyal mistress – I should like you to give yourself up to me body and soul." I'm astonished as he looks deep into my eyes, his grasp around my waist even stronger now. "I promise to be faithful. I will take you as my only mistress."

"Like the French King does, sir?"

"Yes, exactly that – I will not have any thought or affection for anyone else. If you agree to be my official mistress, I shall serve only you."

A ball of nerves wells at the back of my throat on realising that George's *news* to Anne and I was true. Confirmation has arrived in the shape of this proposal, and I'm stumped for words. All I can hear above my heart thumping through my ears are the bees and birds doing their thing around the garden. Our only witnesses.

This handsome monarch is awaiting an answer. He's not rotund, impatient, nor angry, but intriguing, charismatic, and charming. Not the character history has painted. At this moment, I sense a pliable, malleable, and gentle nature – or is this how he is when he wants something…?

"Your official mistress?" I ask, only because I have to say something.

"Yes, and you will have everything within my power to give to you. All you need do is make any request of me you desire."

I want to laugh. This conversation sounds really cheesey – he's sounding like Jonathan Rhys Meyers in a scene with Natalie Dormer in the Tudors' television series, and it takes all my strength to keep a straight face. No doubt this stems from shock, and not a little embarrassment. I still can't believe the King of England fancies me!

"Your Grace, what have I done to make you proposition me like this?" I stare at him. "I have never given you any hope, have I?"

"What fault do I commit in presuming you might accept me? Why do you frown?" His eyebrows furrow in his confusion. "Please explain to me."

What would Anne, or Natalie Dormer say if they were here instead? I think fast. "Your Grace, I have already given my virginity into my husband's hands – and whoever he will eventually be, only he shall have it." I lower my gaze – I can't look at him – but he lifts my chin with his forefinger.

"But Beth…"

"Mary Carey will be called a 'Great Prostitute' because of her affair with you. I know how stories and rumour fly around London, and the counties – I understand how things go for women when they tie their colours to your lance." I manage to stifle a giggle at that remark. Have I gone too far? His cheeks flush on realising my meaning.

"I thought you would be flattered?"

Is he imagining me flat on my back? I shudder at the thought. The trouble is, I can't forget that he is the King of England. Young women of the court long to be singled out by him.

"I considered that you might accept me," he continues, looking disappointed. "Do you not love me?"

"Your Majesty, of course, I love you – I have loved you all my life." I'm not lying, I have learnt all I can about this man, starting at the age of nine with my obsession with fiction by the likes of Jean Plaidy. When I look at him, I still feel the need to pinch myself as a reminder of whose company I'm keeping. Now he's blushing.

"But you do not love your king enough that you could warm his bed?" All I can do is stare at him. "Do you not find me appealing, Mistress? Am I not all that you thought I would be?"

"Henry, I am not a worthy recipient of your attentions. Would you not prefer somebody with a position at court, and a title, and not some obscure person who has really only set foot in Your Majesty's circle? I do not think myself worthy of you. The compliment of your attentions has shocked me in the best possible way, but I feel your affections would be better placed elsewhere."

"I have tried other women but I lose interest. They do not compare to you. They do not captivate as you have." He sighs. Blimey, I think he really has fallen for me, or have I fallen for his charm? "I shall tell you a secret. I think that my marriage to Queen Katharine is unlawful in God's eyes. I have been seeking advice on the status of my marriage – my conscience is stricken and tender – and I think I offend God being married to my brother's widow."

"Queen Katharine is popular, sir, and the daughter of two anointed monarchs. Surely any implied stain against Her Majesty would never be accepted by your people?"

"The prince she had before me was my brother, and this, in the eyes of God, is an unlawful act. Do not argue with me on this point, Mistress, as my mind is already set!" He leans back a few inches, looking pensive. "The Queen can no longer birth any children, let alone a son." He rubs his brow. "Now Mary has birthed Henry Carey, and I have wondered whether this boy could be mine – it would confirm that I am capable of siring male children." He wets his bottom lip with the tip of his tongue. "I know the fault is with Katharine, it is not mine!"

"Sir, you have already achieved a son and heir, with Henry Fitzroy, the Duke of Richmond and Somerset."

"Yes. I am proud of my offspring, especially Henry – but he is another bastard. Just like little baby Henry Carey, up there…" He nods back towards the house, where Mary may still lurk at the damaged casement, possibly with her baby cradled in her arms. "As Mary is married, I could not say for certain he is mine, so, therefore, could never recognise the boy, even if I wanted to."

"Little Catherine looks like you, sir, do you not think?"

"A little." He grunts. "Sadly, the child is a girl."

"I think, perhaps, Your Grace, you could groom Henry Fitzroy to be your successor?"

He stares at me. "I have considered it." He strokes his beard with his free hand, the other still holding mine – his rings sparkling in the sunlight. "However, I might be inclined to keep trying with my wife, if she were still at an age for childbearing. I hope my conscience and matters with Katharine can be reconciled but, at this late stage in our marriage, I am beginning to doubt it."

"Henry, wait a while to see how your conscience feels, possibly some months from now."

He smiles, nodding once. "You are right, Beth. I knew, as my friend, you would advise me well." He kisses the back of my hand. "We are of the same kidney, and I had hoped you would consider giving me your heart, so I might start afresh."

I can't believe these words are coming out of his mouth. He's reading me wrong, thinking we're alike. Is this why he wants to be with me? What does he want? Me as his mistress, or is he considering me as wife material? My goodness, what have I got myself into? He should be saying this to Anne, not me.

"Would you allow me to hope?" he asks, giving me an expectant look.

"Your Majesty, I…" Before I have a chance to go further, Sir Henry Norris and George wander into the garden, and the disbelief on George's face is clear to see, even from a distance. As they approach, I get up, probably looking like a deer caught in the lights, and I feel as trapped as one. I make a deep curtsy before the king, and he rises. His features have the look of a puppy – soft, and hungry to connect – his eyes a piercing-blue in the sunlight, his stance less formal. My skirts billow around me as I take a step back.

"Your Majesty – with your permission, I shall take my leave of you." I keep my gaze lowered so his expression doesn't guilt-trip me into staying. He leans towards me in full view of our observers, takes one of my hands in his, then sweeps his other across my cheek, the contact like a soft breeze.

"Another time, Mistress Wickers?"

He sounds lost, and my heart breaks for him. I curtsy again and walk away, knowing that I'm the wrong woman for him. When I get to George, he extends his hand, but I sweep past him, my heart thundering. They must think me so rude but I have to get away. I need to find Anne – she's the only one I can speak with.

When I get to the garden entrance, I glance back to see the three men standing together, watching me scurry away.

The atmosphere is suffocating in the downstairs' hallways – the air stuffy with smells of roasting meat wafting from the kitchen. So different from the freshness of the garden. Elizabeth Boleyn rushes around giving orders to the servants, who are preparing supper for our illustrious guests, while Sir Thomas sits in his study poring over paperwork, no doubt attending to petitions for the king. I scoot up the stairs to Mary's bedchamber and give a tentative knock on her open door. She is slumped in a chair before the hearth, the fire has gone out.

"What's wrong, Mary? The glass from your window lays about the muddy grass outside, and look, I see there is glass upon the floorboards here." I'm getting better at Tudor-speak.

She scowls at me. "The king ails me. He does not see me when in your company. Have you noticed how he looks at you?" The venom in her voice surprises me. I thought she was a sweet-tempered woman but, when she mentions Henry, it seems she can't curb her need to vent.

Standing here, I consider that perhaps it's best to say nothing. I shrug, then shake my head, knowing full well the king's intentions towards me. It's not for me to confess his admiration for me. I turn my back on her and peek through her broken window, out across to the flower garden beyond. My neck is nearly burning knowing that her gaze is baring into me.

"Is he still out there?"

"The king?" I turn and nod. "He's walking with Henry Norris and George."

She eyes me beneath slanted brows, probably wondering what he was discussing with me moments earlier. Now I'm wondering what George is discussing with him.

"Do not court his attentions too much, for he will hurt you. He hurts those he professes to love – I have experienced it for myself!" Her voice cracks as she rocks little Henry's cot, the infant cooing in his linen swaddling.

"The king is affable to me, is all." I give her what I hope is a reassuring smile. "He is gracious with everyone – you read too much into things." Folding my arms, I turn back to watch the three men through the casement, as they walk around the flower garden, in deep conversation. They are too far away to read their lips, but if I could, I would.

"Mary, I was being courteous, is all. It is what your father would expect of me, is it not?" I turn to her, placing my hands on my hips. She tuts. I shouldn't roll my eyes, but I can't help myself, shaking my head at her wilfulness. "There is nothing wrong with being in the company of the king while he is here – after all, you have been gracious with him in your time." She scowls in response. "I know your father did not encourage the affair but, for a time, the king loved you, didn't he?"

"Yes, he did," she replies, nearly barking it out.

"'Tis, not all failure, nor an opportunity to bear a grudge against His Majesty." I turn to her, keeping my arms folded across my chest. "All is good with you and William?" I smile. She tilts her head as she chews on that, then gives me a half-smile. "There, now – your husband is good to you, and your little family is complete. I go to her and squeeze her tight. Little Henry Carey catches my eye, and he looks like he's smiling at me, or maybe it's just wind – I can never tell the difference!

I hope I've pulled this one off – made Mary feel better and reminded her she is loved and wanted by someone. If I put my mind to it, I can be convincing. The atmosphere feels lighter, the tension lifted as she gives me a genuine, heartfelt smile that has me relieved. I walk back over to the window. "You worry yourself too much."

Norris has walked off, admiring the early blooms, and George appears to be in a deep, heated conversation with Henry. Every so often, they glance up at the window but I'm sure they can't see me, or maybe just my shadow – a sense of someone. I hope they aren't discussing me. But wouldn't that be a good thing? It's hardly a disaster. I know George well enough to trust that he wouldn't encourage the king to follow his heart where I'm concerned. He would help my cause and steer Henry towards Anne, surely?

"I feel as if I have fallen out of favour with the king," Mary says.

I walk back over and kneel beside her, grasping her hand. "Trust me, Mary, all will be well. The king will have you return to him in no time, I'm sure. Give it time." I know the tone of my voice sometimes gives me away, and I can only hope that my words of reassurance convince her.

"I pray that you are right, Beth."

As she looks at me, guilt rakes through my bones. I shiver as a draft carries through the broken window. At least, I hope it's from that.

"I know I am," I lie again. "You know, your father will berate you for breaking that casement. We will need to fetch someone to fix it."

"Yes, yes, I am afraid my temper got the better of me."

"So, I noticed – as did His Grace!" She sighs, and I touch her hand. "Be gracious and smile in the king's presence and he will soon look on you favourably once more."

I have no choice but to convince her to lighten up. No man is attracted to unhappy, depressed women. I need to get everything back on an even keel – Henry has to be convinced he wants Anne, not Mary, and especially not me. Besides, her feelings need to be saved if she's to enjoy her time with William. It's only a year or so before he dies of the 'Sweat'. Would it be right for me to prepare her for that, in a slow, subtle way? Even when William dies, she has time; she is still the beauty of the family, a sweet-natured, brave, and passionate woman, who, despite everything, is loved by all who know her.

"Think of William – he loves you and stands by you."

"You are right, Mistress Wickers, I should be happy with my lot."

I squeeze her again, pushing any sense of the lie back. "Mary, you have nothing to fear."

The king and his entourage have left for Penshurst Place, and the servants are closing the house down for the night. One of them, John, has boarded up the broken casement, which will hold until Sir Thomas commissions the glazier to replace the broken panes. It's late now, and the house is quiet. Sir Thomas has called Anne and me to the parlour. The fire crackles in the grate and candles flicker on the mantle. Anne's father stands before the fire, its heat radiating onto his calves as he shifts his weight from one foot to the other. Lady Elizabeth is sitting on a plumped-up cushion in her chair, whilst Griffin lays his huge body at the hem of her velvet skirts.

"Daughter – Mistress Wickers – I have asked you both here at this hour to make a request of you." He looks tired – pale and drawn – probably all the excitement of the king's visit. It's past his bedtime, so this must be important to have him summon us at this late hour, after his nightcap. I have a fairly good idea of what it might be.

"A request, Father?" Anne asks, her eyes also heavy with fatigue.

"More of a command, actually." The man sounds nervous. He glances at his wife, and it's obvious that he's transferring authority on the matter to her, no doubt in the hope that she'll deal with this matter better than he can.

"Anne, after you came and spoke with your father, the King has requested that you and Beth come to Court to serve once more as ladies-in-waiting to Queen Katharine."

She is straight to the point, not mincing her words. Her well-educated upbringing enables her to deal with matters like this with confidence and authority. Anne is now wide-awake and up on her feet. She embraces me.

"Do not say a word to father about how the king was with you," she whispers in my ear.

"I won't, I promise."

She nearly squeezes the breath out of me. "You and me together," she says aloud, so her father can hear her. "Will it not be exciting?" Realising that I'm close to turning blue through lack of air, she apologises and embraces her father, then her mother. It takes me a moment to recover my composure before I can open my mouth to speak.

"Sir," I say, "would it be a possibility to take young Jayne, the daughter of John, to court with us, to be a companion to us?"

Anne looks at me, surprised that I have the fortitude to ask such a direct question. She shouldn't be shocked, as we've talked about supporting Jayne, because of the age of her father, and because of her disability – Down syndrome. I know Anne will be a great philanthropist as queen, so why not steer her towards a just cause?

Sir Thomas looks at me, puzzled. "Beth, do you mean the young, natural fool?"

"Yes, sir. I believe she helps Joan in the kitchen garden, and with general tasks like collecting produce from the village. I do not like the word 'fool' to describe her, sir." He blinks several times, his mouth open. "The girl is no 'fool'," I continue, "and neither is she foolish, nor an idiot. Jayne is a clever girl, who will be adored by all who meet her. I am certain of it!"

He wrings his hands. "I know the child." He is no doubt surprised by my forthrightness. "I would have to talk with John." He strokes his beard as he ponders the issue. "I cannot see a problem with it. In fact, I think it is admirable that you both desire to support this girl. Jayne is young." He looks at Anne, then me, leaning forward, as if to whisper. "You will both need to take responsibility for her care, and her keep." He raises both brows in expectation.

"You have no objection then, Father?" Anne asks.

"No, but my purse is light – you will have to fund Jayne yourselves, at first, with bed and board, as well as clothes." He glances at his wife. "I am not sure the Queen would stretch to such financial support. Would you both be happy to be official keepers for Jayne?"

Anne and I look at each other.

"I do not see why not," I answer.

"Then I will have to write to both Their Majesties to agree to the contract." He nibbles on his bottom lip for a long moment, then nods to himself and smiles, as if at a job well done.

"Thank you, Father!" Anne cries.

This is the moment we have been longing for: to go back to the English Court. Anne has had more than enough of the months dragging on here at Hever. I am grateful to the king for wanting us to return, but I don't particularly want to be placed in a position where I feel I must show him how grateful I am! And it's made worse by the fact that he declared before his close circle that it's my fault he's been struck by a dart of love. But then it's not about me, is it? No, this is about getting Anne close to him. Yes, my mission is back on track.

"Thank you for dealing with the matter of Jayne," I say, allowing a genuine smile. "All I ask, Sir Thomas, is, if you could determine with Jayne and her father whether she herself would be grateful and honoured to attend court." I must sound apprehensive, because he cocks his brow at me as he strokes his beard. "It goes without saying that I will endeavour to look after and support your daughter, also," I add.

In a rare show of affection, he embraces me, and I catch hints of that musky, woody smell about him. He must use a similar cologne to the king.

"I thank you for your loyalty to my family," he says. "But, more importantly, for your loyalty to the King." However, he has no idea how far Henry expects, or wants, my loyalty to stretch, at least not yet. "Anne, you must pen a letter to the King. Send our servant Robert to Penshurst."

She inclines her head. "At this late hour?"

He nods. "The King will be pleased to know that I have agreed to his command."

"But will Master Cranewell not be in bed, Father?"

"I will pay him a little extra this month – you can tell him so. Besides, from your letter, the King can then inform the Queen's household, so they can begin to make arrangements for your arrival. Do it now, and I will send Robert to Penshurst by first light."

Elizabeth Boleyn motions for Anne to follow her. Anne grabs my hand and pulls me along. Her mother goes to her writing desk in the library, and we watch as she removes a sheet of vellum parchment, which she places in front of her daughter. Anne takes an ink-soaked quill and presses it onto the cream writing surface to begin a letter for the king that will have far-reaching consequences.

Eight

Early May 1526
– The Palace of Placentia, Greenwich

Should I have tried the door to the portal before returning to court? I know I have the ring to time-slip in an emergency but it's nice knowing that I have that direct route back to Professor Marshall's office. Maybe I just need reassurance that the portal still works, for my own peace of mind. Oh, I need to stop analysing things and relax. All this tension is going to give me a migraine.

Knowing I am the centre of Henry Tudor's focus is a great boost for my confidence but the arrangement he is pushing for is not one I relish. His advances add to my problems. I didn't expect him to pay me so much attention, and this situation has thrown me off-kilter. Sometimes, I consider slipping out of the sixteenth century altogether but the period and its personalities are such a draw, even though I miss my family, and my mission to rectify the history is still active. The cypher ring is a serious piece of jewellery, with incredible power, and I avoid twisting it in case I prompt it into action, to who knows where? I've been in Tudor England for months but I don't want to go back to my time yet – I've got too much to accomplish, and it's all my own fault. So much for not meddling!

The strange thing about this time-travel business is that no matter how long I'm here, I don't appear to age much. I still look twenty-one, even though, by rights, with all the time I've spent in this Tudor time-warp, I should be around twenty-six or twenty-seven. Has Anne noticed that my skin is still smooth and youthful, even if my mind is seldom worry-free? If the time-slip remains consistent, little time will have passed back home, and my family and friends will have hardly noticed that I'm not around. At least I know there's not a colossal murder hunt across the nation for me. Is Rob worried?

I know I'll have to return at some point, even if it's just to re-orientate myself with university, and hand in those literature reviews. The only way the king will lose interest in me is if I'm not here to distract him, and Anne will get the opportunity to catch his eye! I need to make that happen before I return home, though. For the foreseeable future, I need to steer close to the path originally set out by history, and not meander along a storyline or fantasy created by myself. I don't want to be responsible for making our true history take such a radical turn. From now on, I must remain as an observer, just as the professor wanted.

As I help Agnes and the other servants load the trunks, Anne, George, and Jane are still inside, saying goodbye to Lady Boleyn. They are to ride in another litter to me. I think it's down to Jane Boleyn's insistence. And I'm not surprised, as she's hardly said two words to me since I've returned to Hever, politely ignoring me, if there is such a thing.

John assists Jayne into the litter. Sir Thomas obviously obtained permission from him for her to attend Court. She steps up first and sits at the curtained window on the far side pulling the fabric back. Her anxious father peers up at his daughter, Jayne, as I nudge up next to her. She squeezes my hand and gives me a worried look.

"Mistress Wickers, I am nervous about attending court."

"I will always be there to look after you, as will the Lady Anne, and so will the ladies of the queen's household. Agnes will be with us, too." I smile, put my arm around her shoulder, and give her a gentle squeeze. "I promise we will all look after you."

The corner of her mouth turns up in a nervous smile, and I consider how different she will be treated and elevated once we arrive at Greenwich, all because of her disability. Like Agnes, Jayne Fool – I hate using that as a surname – is a sweet-natured creature, with a sensitive character. As I hug her, she stiffens. I don't think she knows how to take my show of affection. I can't explain to her that I understand how she is 'different' because I don't know how she would take it, or even if she would understand. Like everyone, except Anne, Jayne must never know where I have come from. She peers through the litter curtain, down at her father, then Agnes steps up and sits opposite us. I will let her have the seat to herself, she deserves it with all the hard work she does, serving the Boleyns and me.

"We will have a splendid time at court," I say, breaking my embrace.

"Why might that be, Mistress?" Jayne asks, her manner shy.

"Because we will have new gowns made for you – you will look beautiful."

"Why would I need new gowns?"

Agnes shifts and leans forward. "I do not think the Lady Anne will have you doing the jobs of servants, Miss."

Jayne looks from her to me and back. "Not like I was with Joan, here at Hever?"

"No." Agnes smiles. "I think Mistress Anne will teach you to play cards, dance, and all manner of things." I could listen to her Kent country accent all day.

"I not sure how to be at court," Jayne replies. "I be scared." Agnes takes her hand. "Father has never explained how different life is there – and Joan, as she is not my mother, she feels it be not her place to tell me neither."

"Do not be afeared. Neither Mistress Anne, nor Mistress Beth will let anything bad happen to you."

"Anne and I would never let anything bad happen to either of you." I smile at them both. Although Jayne is reassured by my words, she will never know how my inner turmoil at returning to court stems from the king's *interest* in me, or how I'm going to get out of being his mistress. My stomach flutters at the thought of it.

It's almost eight in the morning, and the sunshine is trying its best to break through the clouds as the mist rises from the moat. I look through the window as Anne appears ahead of her brother. The sight of George walking arm in arm with Jane, under the portcullis and over the drawbridge, makes my stomach churn. The other litter sits alongside ours, so as I peer out, I can see what's going on. Robert Cranewell is helping Anne enter the litter, and Jane tells George she wants to sit next to him. I can't help smiling, glad to be sitting here with Agnes and Jayne, avoiding the constant glares from the jealous wife, and we been cooped up together.

Tears slip down Jayne's cheeks as she makes furious waves at her father when we get going. I hadn't considered that this is her first time away from home. Soon, he and Lady Boleyn are dots in the distance as I straighten out the knotted silks of my gown and we prepare ourselves for the journey ahead.

Our party are travelling to Henry's 'Pleasure' Palace, the Palace of Placentia, which will eventually be called Greenwich Palace. Like previous trips, it starts off somewhat arduous. The litter, like a primitive carriage, burdened with our baggage, constantly lurches from side to side. Jayne, her tears now dry, grips my hand, her head resting against my shoulder. At least Agnes isn't dozing like she so often does. I'm surprised she's been able to sleep on other trips with all the jolting. Though bumpy, it isn't too bad, and it helps to admire the typically English countryside, without cars, trains, or planes.

Hever gatehouse looks beautiful as the late-spring sunshine breaks through. Jayne pokes her head through the open curtain just as the inn opposite St Peter's church disappears from view. From my vantage point, I see the ditch where I was catapulted from Anne's horse, and George, like my knight in shining armour, ever gallant, rescued me from the mire. Is he looking out and remembering that moment, too? I lick my lips and recall the taste of him when he kissed me. Hmm, will we ever have a chance to be like that again? Just thinking about it sends a delicious shiver through me, so I push it from my mind and focus on the present.

The mist is lifting, and medieval cottages are visible through the trees as we continue on our way, all surrounded by lush greenery. Birds sing everywhere, and a few spring lambs are leaping in the fields as we ride through the blossom-filled lanes. Agnes sits upright, opposite us, eyes wide, taking everything in.

As we head out of the village, I think of my journeys to court with George – how I rested against him – and I recall his body heat as I fell asleep in his arms. I remember the feelings he released in me when I first became attracted to him. It feels wrong to think of him that way, now he's married, but we've already crossed the line of no return. There was so much in that kiss, it's impossible not to be affected by it.

What are they chatting about in the other litter? I expect Anne is gushing over the fact she will soon be back at court, after our long, lonely time at Hever. I need to be inconspicuous in the queen's company, not drawing attention to myself. I don't want her to guess or notice that her husband has taken a fancy to me. I hope for all our sakes her household is less dull, and that being in the company of her, and her ladies-in-waiting don't mean endless attendances at Mass, comparing needlepoint, or composing prayers. It might be nice to learn to play the lute – perhaps Anne will teach me. I wouldn't mind being taught how to play chess, or having the time to stroll in the palace gardens.

Henry's visit to Hever is just a memory now but I'm still wary of him. He's a busy man, which might be to my advantage. With so much happening, maybe when we arrive at the palace, he will have forgotten his request. I cannot be any man's mistress, let alone Henry Tudor's.

Soon, we're in the leafy hunting forest of Blackheath, which brings us through to the old Roman road from Kent. The Palace of Placentia is Henry's favourite, stretching two-hundred metres along the foreshore on the great sweep of the Thames, with splendid views of ships. But we arrive by road, with the palace being six miles from central London. Henry VIII has, since his father's death, added a tiltyard for jousting, together with an armoury, kennels, stables, tennis courts, and a cockpit. He has also established his Royal dockyards at nearby Deptford and Woolwich, cementing the area's importance to his naval and business accomplishments.

After hours of travelling, the familiar Tudor orange-red brickwork comes into view through the trees. The bricks range from deep purple to slate in colour and are laid in quarter-brick offsets in mainly English bond or English cross-bond, to form a diaper or chequered pattern within the palace's predominantly red brickwork. As the litter approaches the palace, I strain my neck to look out at the extravagant and elaborate architecture, epitomised by the spirally twisted chimney stacks for which the period is renowned.

It's been a tedious, long journey, and my back aches from being jolted about for six hours. We stopped to use a piss pot along the way, and pulled in at the now-familiar inn Agnes and I visited before, when we last travelled with George. Most of the time, Jayne and Agnes have been dozing. As the litter rumbles up the road towards the southern entrance, it must be around 2 p.m., they wake from their slumber, rubbing their eyes and yawning.

"Are we arrived?" Jayne asks, blinking.

Agnes looks out the window towards the redbrick turrets. "Why is the palace called 'Placentia'?"

"Good question." I lean out of the window as we enter the gates. "The palace was given to Henry VI's wife, Margaret of Anjou, in fourteen-forty-seven."

"Oh," Agnes says, none the wiser.

"Margaret re-christened it 'Plaisance' or 'Placentia', meaning 'Pleasure Palace'. And then the king's father elevated the manor to a palace at the turn of this century. He replaced the old buildings with a much larger house, centred on an inner courtyard containing royal lodgings, with the river immediately to the north, the hall and chapel to the east, and a gallery to the west leading to the House of the Observant Friars."

"You be very learned, Mistress Wickers," Jayne says.

"Must be all that reading you do, Beth?" Agnes adds.

"And here we are outside the detached gatehouse – the entrance to the palace." I look beyond the entrance, seeing the two new stable blocks and the walls of the tiltyard development to the south of the palace, with its twin observation towers connected by a gallery. There is also an armoury complex, the first of its kind in England, which Henry had built in 1517. It was designed to accommodate the accomplished foreign armourers already working for him at Greenwich, who manufacture suits of armour for both him and court, using steel from a Lewisham mill. He also commissioned other works to include the construction of a conduit house in the main courtyard, the remodelling of the chapel and library, and the addition of a projecting water gate to the donjon tower on the riverfront, contemporary with the tiltyard construction. From the palace's silhouette rising before me, it is easy to see why Henry loves it, and often uses it to receive foreign dignitaries.

Once we arrive inside the courtyard, Agnes helps Jayne and me down from the litter, and it is nice to feel the warmth of the afternoon sun on my back. George and Jane have walked on ahead, and he doesn't look happy with her barking orders at him. They have been stopped in their tracks by the Comptroller of the Household, Sir Henry Guildford, who has come out to greet us. I recognise him from his hairstyle, cut in the French fashion, and his familiar features and dimpled chin, which are so like his Holbein portrait. Anne walks across the gravel towards me, accompanied by Guildford. The comprehension in his eyes tells me that he remembers me from our first meeting at Richmond Palace. His glistening chain of office reflects fractions of the afternoon sunlight. I have to say, having him here is reassuring.

"Mistress Wickers, it is good to see you, and the rest of your party." He looks over his shoulder at George and his wife as they enter the palace. Anne links her arm through mine. Guilford smiles at me, taking no notice of a nervous Agnes and Jayne. "I know the king is expecting you."

He waves his cane, directing the servants to carry our luggage to our allotted chambers. We follow him inside. As he guides us down the passageways and corridors of the interior, it is plain to see that the palace is as opulent a place as any other of Henry's residences. We pass open doors and linen-fold walls, with interiors consisting of solid gold, gold leaf, and even cloth of gold.

I must be gawping, as a servant dressed in green and white livery turns to me. "Mistress Wickers, if you think these rooms are elaborate, wait until you see the Royal apartments – they are especially sumptuous."

We are directed to our rooms within the royal apartment complex, and the servants dump our trunks and caskets on the floor and leave us be. Agnes helps us unpack. As usual, Anne and I are to share, with Jayne Fool and Agnes taking an antechamber off our bedchamber. I'm glad they are together, because being a friend to Jayne gives Agnes a purpose, rather than just fetching and carrying for myself and Anne.

Although the furniture is sparse in these chambers, the quality of the mahogany and the carvings are exquisite. The wall hangings are made of olive-green silk, and the walls are painted in the style of religious friezes in the most opulent and vivid colours. From the look of the room, the high ceilings and huge, leaded windows, the king has made sure that Anne and I are here to experience the best of everything he has to offer. I'm thinking my work may be cut out getting him to transfer his attentions to my companion. I may have to up my game.

The next morning, I feel exhausted as Anne and I take a stroll around the gardens, close to the river. I was woken up in the early hours, by Jayne Fool, who wandered into our bedchamber, crying because she missed her father, and bewildered by her surroundings. I hadn't taken into account that she might not cope well on her first night away from home. It was a good job she came and woke me, because when I went to find Agnes, she was snoring away on her pallet bed – a bit of a let-down. I felt sorry for Jayne, and sat up consoling her for over half an hour, then told her fairy tales for the next hour or so until she fell back to sleep.

In the distance, as we walk, small merchant barges are docking. At the further end of this riverside path, there is a treadmill crane operated by men walking inside a drum as goods are off-loaded. The hustle and bustle of the servants bringing wares into the palace are non-stop, and it's clear to see that the river route is the easiest way to bring produce to the great kitchens here.

Budding blooms fill the air with their fragrance, and the breeze on my cheeks and the sun on my neck creates a moment of quality that I'm lucky to be able to appreciate. If I stood here in modern-day London, taking a deep breath would be a risky business with the fumes from all the traffic, not to mention the constant fallout from jet fuel.

Today, Agnes has dressed me in a yellow satin gown with golden accents and patterns. I turn to Anne. "Are you glad to be back?"

She nods. "Very much. I have missed it." She takes a deep breath through her nose and smiles. "The gardens are beautiful in the spring, are they not?"

"Indeed, they are."

"Now we are here," she says, "I really need to talk to you about Jane."

Butterflies flutter in my tummy. "Jayne Fool?"

"No. Jane – my sister-in-law." She tilts her head. "You must tell her that you want to be friends, and that George no longer takes any interest in you."

"Why should I lie?"

"I have told George to maintain the story that nothing has happened between you and him. It is easier that way."

I glance around to make sure we're alone. "I only kissed him but why should I have to lie to Jane?"

"Beth, just do this, for me?" Her brows furrow, and she holds my arm, stopping me from walking further down the path. "She is having trouble keeping George's attention as it is – she will not confide in me what is wrong in their marriage, but she is not happy." I want to shrug but stop myself. "She fears that you will take George from her."

"That is ridiculous!" I snort out a derisory laugh. "You know, despite my feelings, I have tried to keep George at arms-length."

As we start walking again, we see the king's barge moored at the landing. He alights from the craft, looking resplendent in silver silks and lightweight linens. His entourage gathers about him as the oarsmen tie the boat to its post. So much for hoping to keep some distance between us.

"And will you keep him at arms-length?" Anne asks, nodding at the gathering. The feathers in the caps of the male courtiers dance in the wind but the king has the largest plume. Norfolk smirks at him as they approach.

"I want to," I reply, "but how can I?"

Before I know it, Henry is standing before us, and I'm staring down at his muddy boots as Anne and I dip in reverence, our skirts billowing out around us in the breeze. He offers his hand to Anne, who kisses his ruby ring.

"Your Majesty!" she says, fluttering her eyelashes.

Henry Norris, Charles Brandon the Duke of Suffolk, George, and others, watch me. I wish I wasn't on the receiving end of the king's attentions but I am – there's no getting away from it. As I rise, he lifts my chin with his forefinger and stares into my eyes. His gaze fixes me to the spot and I'm speechless, my face burning, and it feels like ages before I find the strength to reply.

"Your Majesty."

He offers me his hand, and, like Anne, I follow suit, kissing his ring.

"Ladies, it is a pleasant day, is it not?" He glances up as the sun peeps from behind a cloud, then looks to Anne. "I am glad, Mistress Boleyn, that your father had the forbearance to send both you and Mistress Wickers back to Court." He smiles, resting his hand on the hilt of his dagger, as he so often does. "Otherwise, I would have been most displeased!"

"We are at your service, sir!" she replies. He nods and smiles.

Norfolk steps ahead of the group and coughs. "Come on, Harry, I need some refreshment. My throat is parched!" He waves his arm in front of the king, trying to get him to move along. "Your Grace?"

Henry eyes me again, his gaze lingering. It appears he may still have hope for a future with me. As he walks off, Anne looks at me.

"What are you going to do?" She doesn't hold back a smirk.

"Do? I…don't know." I sigh, knowing I have a serious job ahead of me. "What would you do in my position?"

She laughs. "Enjoy the attention!"

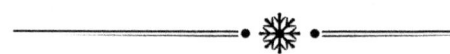

Bright rays of sunlight stream through the gap in the heavy velvet curtains hanging from the leaded windows of our bedchamber. As the clock strikes in the courtyard, the chamber ladies pull back the drapes and bring in rosewater for us to wash our faces. Agnes is helping Anne to dress. I watch the goings-on from the sanctum of the four-poster bed, sitting up against my pillows. Now dressed, Anne sits, mirror in hand, as Agnes braids her hair.

"What will you do this morning while I tend to the queen?" she asks.

"I know I should attend Mass," I answer, stretching my arms above my head, "but I think I might take a walk about the gardens and explore the palace."

"Alone?" She turns, frowning at me as Agnes tries to pin her long, brunette plaits high on her head.

"Yes, why not?" I shrug. "Can you make my excuses to the queen for me?"

When her hood is secured over her coif, she gets to her feet. The green satin of her gown looks beautiful on her, and the ouches on the neckline of her kirtle blink in the daylight as she walks past the window.

"Will that be all, Mistress Anne?" Agnes asks.

Anne looks at me, then back to Agnes. "I am sure Beth will need your assistance to dress."

"Yes, of course, Mistress."

"Take care of Jayne Fool after you have attended on Beth, if you would – make sure she has dressed appropriately and has broken her fast." She nods to herself. "'Did you both sleep well after Jayne's night fright the other night?"

Agnus frowns. "Mistress, what do you mean by night fright?"

I climb out of bed and shiver at the cold floorboards beneath my feet. This, I'm sure, I will never get used to. "You were snoring, Agnes – you slept through it!" I rub my eyes and walk over to the receptacle full of rosewater and wash my face. Agnes hands me a linen towel and I dab my skin dry. I give her a playful scowl. "I slept better last night, not being woken in the middle of the night!"

She stares at me, nonplussed, and I shake my head, smiling at her.

"Mistress, are you sure you will be comfortable walking around without a companion this morning?"

No problem changing the subject, eh? "Yes, Agnes, don't fret too much, I will be fine!" I pull off my night shift and she hands me a freshly laundered one, which I slip over my head. I'm excited at the thought of exploring Greenwich Palace on my own. I still have to remind myself where I am and what time in history I'm visiting.

It doesn't take long for Agnes's nimble fingers to lace me into my kirtle and a gown of moire satin and grey damask. I sit on the stool, mirror in hand, as she braids my hair, feeling sorry for the poor girl and the amount of work she has to do. All I can do is smile at her reflection in support.

"You be most fortunate to have hair the colour of flax, Mistress Wickers. It becomes you so well." She secures the last braid and sits my matching gable hood over my plaits, tucking stray wisps of hair over my ears and beneath the hood. I check myself in the hand-mirror, happy that I look a little more than adequate – even pretty.

"Thank you, Agnes." I glance up at her. "You always look after me so well."

With that, she bobs a curtsy, which always makes me feel unworthy. She smiles and goes to Jayne in the room next door.

As I step out into the passageway, the chapel bell tolls for Mass, and as I look out of the window, I see the queen and her ladies wafting across the courtyard on their way to worship.

Being here, like this, reminds me of when I've visited a National Trust property and forgot to pick up a pocket guide and a map on my way around. I'll just have to follow my nose.

Easier said than done. After walking down many passageways, heading in a northerly direction from the way we came into the palace yesterday, I find myself passing other courtiers, who bow, curtsy, and doff their bonnets. I don't recognise any but bob several curtsies in respect and smile back. Some of what looks like Wolsey's men are carrying leather folios under their arms, walking, and talking in whispers. They eye me as I pass them, and I soon find myself walking beneath the cloisters and out into the fresh air of the gardens.

At this moment, I am all alone, and it feels good to be in my own company – my mood is lighter. I'm rarely unchaperoned, with Anne as my constant companion. The gravel crunches under my leather cow-mouthed shoes as I walk towards what looks like a small fishpond. With the sun up, I already feel a little warm wearing all my layers of clothing. As I bend to watch the carp swimming around the lilies, my stomach tumbles when I notice a familiar silhouette reflect on the water. I would recognise that frame anywhere – the inverted triangular form of the king.

"Mistress Wickers, forgive me if I startled you. Would you take a walk with me?" His voice is calm, and low. To my surprise, Henry Tudor is alone, apart from his dogs, with no entourage or friends. No bishops or cardinals, either.

"Yes, Your Grace, it would be my pleasure." I smile, then inhale a steadying lungful of fresh air. He walks beside me, carrying soft leather gloves in one hand, his dogs' leads in the other.

"I had to walk my dogs before they pissed on my carpet!" He laughs. The dogs, 'Cup' and 'Ball', bound free ahead of us, their tails wagging like flags in the early morning breeze as they bark at the birds that swoop up from the river and fly overhead. We stride together, our pace brisk as we take in the smell of fresh blooms from the flowerbeds beside us.

"You look very beautiful in that gown, Mistress Wickers." I don't miss him eyeing my bosom.

"Thank you, sir." I smile. "'Tis the work of John Skutt's apprentice." He notices me blushing.

"Ah, Paul Cotton!"

It amazes me that he knows every name and intimate detail of each and every member of his court, privy council, household, and servants.

His greyhounds are now far ahead of us, and he taps his thigh with his gloves. "Cup! Ball! Here, boys!" He stops in his tracks, and they run back to him, barking, tails flapping. "I have missed you, Beth." He sounds melancholy. "I thought you would have given me your answer by now."

"Sir, as I said before, I am a woman of no consequence. I am flattered but I think I may not be the woman who could make you happy." I make the effort to ensure my voice resonates sincerity. It's not difficult because I mean every word I say.

"That day we spoke in the garden at Hever, I thought you would return to Court with a favourable view of my proposal." His attention is split between me and his dogs. "I am sorry – my boys…"—he looks around for them—"are prone to wandering off. Last month, they went missing for hours. I heard that they caught sight of a few rabbits and made haste after them. I had to offer a ransom for the servants to find them."

"I'm sorry, Your Grace!" I nod in understanding.

"This breed is fast – I use them as hunting dogs. They are good at that!" He keeps calling them back. I'm glad they are a distraction for him, as it means I don't have to answer any uncomfortable questions.

"I love the Boleyn family dog – Griffin – he is dopey but affectionate. A beautiful Wolfhound."

"Yes, I remember him well from my visit." He stares at me. "About that visit—"

"Sir, my answer might be favourable had I any family connections of renown, or perhaps even a title, but I have no such thing – I am just a companion to Mistress Boleyn, an employee of Lord Rochford – I am not worthy of a King."

"I say you are worthy." To my surprise, he takes my hand and leads me into a secluded part of the gardens, away from prying eyes. He clasps my hand in his bejewelled paws, looming over me. "Kiss me, Beth?"

Without thinking, I drop to my knees at his feet. "Your Grace, I beg you to consider that I am not a daughter of titled parents. They would say I am without blame or reproach of any kind – and I value their opinion of me, and on no account would I wish to lose it, even if I were to die a thousand deaths. Even though you may wish to kiss me, My Lord, I would ask you to reserve such a request, until such a time as God would be pleased to annul your marriage, so that you might be free to accept such tokens of love from a lady such as myself, and of your choosing."

I hope I'm sounding like a convincing Tudor lady: demure, chaste, and protective of my virginity, even though Henry doesn't know that is long gone! My face flushes from my anxiety. I'm rubbish at lying.

He raises me to my feet. "Beth, there is no need for you to be on your knees." He smiles. "My admiration of you, Mistress, is greatly increased. You have acted most properly – but it does not stop me from wanting to kiss you!"

He leans down and plants a delicate kiss on my cheek, which I wasn't expecting. At least he's behaving in a gentlemanly-like manner. My cheeks burn, and I break free from his grasp, curtsy, and take my leave. This is not how things are meant to be developing.

———— • ❄ • ————

As Anne and I settle down for the night, courtiers' voices filter in to us as they scurry down the passageways – whispering, chatting, even laughing. From beyond our chamber window, owls hoot, and a couple of foxes howl in the distance – a disconcerting sound, for sure.

"I've always hated that noise," I say.

"The foxes?" she asks.

"Yes. It sounds as if a woman is being attacked." In the low light, with the moonlight trying to slip in through the gap in the window hangings, I can see Anne frown at me.

"Attacked? What a strange thing to say."

"I almost sounded like that fox out there today."

She turns to me, resting on her elbow, her cheek on her palm. "Whatever do you mean? What has happened to you today?"

"I couldn't say anything before because we haven't been alone until now, but the King propositioned me again today, when I was out walking in the garden."

"I knew I should have come with you, instead of going to Mass." She sighs. "What did the king want?"

"Me!" I reply. "He wanted to kiss me."

She lies back on her pillow. "So, George was right, the king really does like you."

"It seems so." I move my head closer to hers. "I don't want this – I don't want his attentions, his admiration, or his kisses."

"You sound as vexed with the king, as I do with Thomas Wyatt!" She giggles.

"Tell me what I should do. How do I get rid of him?"

"If I were you, tell him you are engaged."

"I can't do that. That would be lying."

"It is a suggestion – what else can you do?"

Then it comes to me, and my tummy flutters at the possibility of a solution. "Henry likes modest, chaste women, does he not?"

"Yes. Not that I am an authority on what the king likes – such matters are beyond me, but I would imagine so."

"What if I was not chaste? What would he do if I told him I wasn't a virgin?"

She looks at me, her brows raised. "Are you chaste? Are you still a maid?"

This is so mad. I can't believe we're talking about my virginity. "Actually, no, I'm not."

She looks aghast. But, of course, why wouldn't she? It's unusual here for a young woman to admit she's had sex before marriage. Not being a virgin, and being unmarried, is not the done thing.

"In my time, Mistress, this is not considered a bad thing – to be single and to have been with men."

She gasps, and I'm not surprised, considering our worlds are five-hundred years apart in attitude!

"You mean it is common for women of your time to act like whores?" Her eyes are close to popping.

"Never whores!" I roll my eyes. "We are people in our own right, not property. The difference in my time, is that women have the choice in whom they sleep with. Our bodies are our own. We are no man's property, not even of our boyfriends, partners, or husbands. We decide when, with whom, and where we have intimacies." I'm hoping my explanation helps her understand.

"Hmm." She leans up on her elbow again, giving me a curious look. "So, there are no arranged marriages? You are never forced to do things with any man unless you want to?" Her brows furrow.

"No," I say. "Unless—"

"Unless…?"

"Men can still rape a woman, and, in my time, sadly, it still happens."

She lies back, her hand over her mouth momentarily. "It seems, my friend, that men, even over such a long period of time, never change."

"So true, Mistress." I pull the coverlet up to my chin. "The king would never rape me, would he?"

"I do not know." She sighs. "Mary told me he was gentle and caring."

"His Majesty would want his lovers to come to him willingly, do you not think?"

"Perhaps," she replies. "Which will make it all the more difficult to deter his interest in you."

She has a point, but I have a plan, and its potential is bubbling inside me.

The next morning, Agnes helps me to dress, as usual. I stand in the middle of the bedchamber as she fusses over me.

"Anne, would you mind if I don't go with you to attend on the queen this morning?"

She looks at me as she picks up her book of hours from the nightstand beside the bed. "So long as you take Jayne Fool with you. After yesterday, I do not wish you to be unchaperoned."

"Very well." I smile. "We can take a turn about the gardens. The weather looks fine again today, and fresh air and sunlight are always good for the soul."

"You being at your prayers would be better!" she grumbles at me. "I shall come and find you, once Mass is over." She heads out the door, on her way to the queen's apartments.

I find Jayne in the adjoining chamber. Agnes is fixing her coif over her shaven head.

"Why has Anne commissioned the barber to shave Jayne's hair?" I ask.

"Mistress Anne believes that in doing so, it means that Jayne is even closer to God."

"Like the monks in the monasteries?"

Jayne scowls. "I wishes you wouldn't speaks of me as if I were not 'ere! The Lady Anne says I am 'special' – special to God, because I speaks what's on my mind!"

Agnes's eyes widen as she ties the cord of the linen coif into a bow under Jayne's chin.

"I be very sorry, Mistress Jayne, if I offended you," she says.

I touch Jayne's arm. "We meant no harm. You are a particularly important member of the court, please never forget it." I take her hand as we begin our journey down many passageways, heading in a northerly direction from our chambers. We pass many courtiers, who bow, curtsy, and doff their bonnets. They give Jayne a sideways glance, which piques my curiosity. Is it not a Godly thing to be in the company of a disabled person during this period? I give a polite nod to courtiers I recognise, like some of Queen Katharine's ladies. Several men, dressed in black, walk together and talk in whispers, leather folios under their arms. Stephen Gardiner, Wroithseley, and others. They eye us with suspicion as we pass them, and we soon find we are walking arm in arm beneath the cloisters and out into the fresh air of the gardens.

"How are you liking court, Jayne?" I ask, her hand in the crease of my elbow.

"I likes it very much, Mistress Beth."

"And the queen's ladies treat you kindly?"

"Yes, very much so." She nods with enthusiasm. "Mistress Anne has been especially good to me – making sure I haves pretty gowns and hoods."

"That is as it should be. You are not a servant like Agnes, are you?"

"No, Mistress Beth – I thinks I am here to be a friend, and companion to Lady Anne is all." Just like me, I smile to myself.

We are alone as we walk together, and it feels good to be with her. Anne was right to suggest I chaperone her because, a few moments after walking past the entrance to the kitchen gardens, gravel crunches behind us and Jayne turns, jerks free from my elbow, and gets all befuddled as she tries to curtsy.

"My King!" she says, lowering her lashes. She's so cute, I love her. I look at Henry, standing before us in full majesty. The jewels on his doublet wink in the sunshine as he swats a fly away with his hand. Heat rises in my cheeks as he appraises me. I hope he's not trying to imagine me naked!

Before I forget myself, I dip into a curtsy, looking up into his eyes as I go down. I really should be more reverent but I can't help myself at times – it's the twenty-first century in me! The combination of his up-side-down, triangular form looming over me, the gold thread on his crimson cloak blinking at me, and those piercing eyes trying to work me out, all have me in a Holbeinesque spell. He looks like he's just stepped out of one of his portraits.

"Ladies, forgive me if I startled you." He beckons us to the arbour of what looks like the entrance to a walled rose garden. "Is Mistress Anne Boleyn not with you?" he asks, casting an eye over Jayne.

"No, Your Grace. She attends Mass with the queen."

"I see." He nods once. "Mistress Wickers, would you take a walk with me?" His voice is calm, and low. Like yesterday, he is alone, except for the company of his dogs. They dance around Jayne's skirts, and she flinches, bringing her hands up to her face to protect herself, in case they jump up. They circle me, and I pat their heads in turn.

Henry's gaze is fixed on me, which makes me a little nervous, especially now I know he has 'feelings' for me. My heart beats faster at the prospect of being alone with him again.

"Yes, Your Grace, it would be my pleasure." I smile, sucking in a quiet breath of fresh air. My response seems to placate him, and he stands beside us, watching his dogs as they run into the rose garden. Like yesterday, he's carrying soft leather gloves in one hand, and his dogs' leads in the other.

"Mistress Beth, shall I fetch the Lady Anne for you – perhaps she could walk with you both?" Poor Jayne seems concerned about me being left alone with the king. I hope she hasn't overheard any conversations I've had with Anne or Agnes.

Before I have a chance to answer her, Henry slaps his thigh with his gloves. "Jayne Fool, is it?"

"Yes, Yours Majesty?" she answers, her voice shaking. If only she knew how amazing and confident she is.

"No need to fetch Mistress Boleyn," he says through a broad smile. "Mistress Wickers shall be in safe hands with me."

That's what I'm worried about – Henry being alone with me. He looks past me, as if trying to see where his dogs have disappeared to. I wince inwardly.

Jayne flutters her lashes. "If that be your wish, Your Majesty?"

"It is – but, I wish some time alone, so I may converse with Beth. Would you mind going to see if you can spend some time with Mistress Anne and the rest of the queen's ladies?"

She raises her brows to the heavens, looking somewhat surprised, her cheeks reddening. It looks like I'm not going to get out of this.

"It's all right, Jayne. Do as the king says."

She curtsies, turns, almost in slow motion, her shoulders slumped, and walks back up the gravel path towards the palace. I hope she will be okay. She must know her way around by now. Henry offers me his arm, and I slip my hand through the bend in his elbow and smile. He ducks beneath the arbour, leading me into the garden.

"Here we are again, You Majesty – alone in each other's company."

"We are not alone, Beth, we also have the company of my dogs!" He chuckles. They are ahead of us, sniffing around the flower borders. "They had better not dig any of my roses up!"

"I'm sure they are well behaved," I say.

"Like you, sweet Beth?"

My face burns again. "Sir, you are too kind!"

"Beth, call me Henry – we have known each other long enough!"

He leads me to the other side of the garden. As nervous and anxious as I am, I can't help appreciating the intoxicating scent of the roses.

"I must confess, I saw you walking with Jayne Fool, and felt I could not miss the opportunity of talking alone with you."

I glance up at him, raising a brow. "You used walking your dogs as an excuse to spend time with me?"

He laughs. Cup and Ball bound about ahead of us as we take in the stunning fragrances hanging in the morning breeze. Their noses kiss the gravel and soil as they try to sniff out potential morsels, their tails springing up like ship masts when something is detected, followed by a flurry of digging in the borders.

The unmistakable sound of a male peacock comes from the other side of the wall. He makes a rustling noise, like a drumroll. The dogs prick up their ears, scanning the area for its source. Without warning, the magnificent bird swoops up onto the wall and emits a loud "Ah-AAAAAH!"

The dogs rush to the wall and start jumping and barking at the large bird, who is now tormenting them from his vantage point.

"Ah-AAAAAH! Ah-AAAAAH!"

I can't help laughing as Henry shoos his dogs away.

"You miss nothing, Beth!" He laughs, taking my arm again as we walk away.

"For what purpose did you wish to talk to me, Sire?"

"I am hoping you have given further consideration to my proposal, dear lady."

"Henry, I gave you my answer yesterday." I take a steadying breath. Here we go. "I am no lady, not titled, and have no connections – I am just a companion to Mistress Boleyn, and not worthy of your love or affection."

"And as I told you yesterday, that matters not to me." He takes my hand and leads me into a secluded part of the walled garden. Then he turns to me, his broad physique overshadowing me. "I want you, Beth – in my bed."

Before I can react, he cups my cheek with his large hand and bends so our lips meet. His tongue is persistent, and his beard prickles my chin. While his enthusiasm takes my breath away, I know I mustn't kiss him back. He tries his hardest to coax me, his arm wrapped around my waist, pulling me to him until I'm engulfed in his embrace. I manage to press my hands against his chest, and he releases me from his clutches.

Breathless, he stares down at me. "I thought you liked me, for myself?"

"I do, Henry—"

"But?"

"You have not considered that I may not be the woman for you."

"Dearest Beth, you are a woman without fault – and I value your opinion. You are a good friend to me, and I wish for us to be something closer."

"Sir, I wouldn't wish to lose your friendship – it means so much to me – but you have taken advantage of that friendship by kissing me today. My Lord, I did ask you yesterday to reserve such a request, until such a time as God would be pleased to conclude your annulment, so you are a free man, to choose love from wherever you may find it. But, it is not with me." I hope I'm sounding convincing without offending him. I'm not an early-modern lady, who is demure and chaste. I'm a twenty-first-century woman, with my own wants and desires, but I daren't tell him that it's George I really want. My face flushes with the stress of hiding the truth from the people I care about.

"You honour me with your friendship but I want you to honour me with your body. That kiss was exquisite. You stir such desire in me." He takes my hand. "I meant not to offend you, dearest Beth. Forgive me?" He bends and plants a delicate kiss on my cheek.

The man can be a gentleman when he wants to be. With my face burning again, I break free from his grasp. This is not working out the way I'd planned. I need a change in direction, to prevent the situation from developing the way it keeps doing.

I say nothing as I watch him reach into a leather pouch hanging from his silk belt. He takes out a small velvet box, which he offers to me.

"Open it!" he demands. "It is for you."

I take it and open the lid, and my breath catches at the sight of a small locket encrusted with many tiny diamonds and rubies. The gold work is stunning.

"If you open the locket, it carries my likeness – you can keep me close to your heart." He raises his eyebrows and smirks.

"Sire, as I said, I am not worthy." I close the box and try to hand it back to him but he shakes his head.

"You say you are not worthy to accept my gift but you think yourself important enough to argue with your King? I did ask the cardinal to look into your lineage, and it appears we can find no record of the Wickers' family." His brows furrow and he slaps a fly with his glove. "I had hoped your family might come to court, so I could verify their estates and titles, if they have any."

"Your Grace—"

"Call me Henry – we are alone."

"Henry, I am a woman without titles, and not one whom a King could love." I need to get out of this situation as diplomatically as possible.

He takes my hand in his, his touch gentle. "Who suggested I could never love you?" His eyes narrow, full of fire. "Titles are not always necessary. Mary Carey has no title."

"Mary Carey is married, sir."

"Titles can always be granted." He looks about him to check he is not being overheard. "You are beautiful, clever, and kind – what man would not long to be with you?" He sighs, his pale-blue eyes sparkling in the sunlight. I don't answer him, and he takes this for shyness. "It appears titles do not interest you. Was I wrong about you, and do you not want me?"

"Henry," I say, looking him straight in the eye. I have to put a stop to this. "I am flattered. What woman would not be, to be so fortunate to have the King's attention upon them? But I have a confession to make, and I could not live with myself if I did not divulge it to you. Sadly, I am no maid." I cover my mouth with my free hand long enough to convey my turmoil. This needs to be good. "Sire, in my past, I have had carnal relations with other men." He doesn't need to know the details – I just need to extinguish his fire.

His eyes widen, and he drops my hand like a stone, looking at me like I'm something he's just trodden in. The disappointment on his face is easy to read as he realises he won't have his way with me. He takes a step away, speechless. I offer him the gift back, and this time he accepts it, turning the box over in his hands, without looking at me.

"I think you and I are better as friends, are we not?"

He chuckles, and I've no idea what he finds so funny. "George Boleyn said as much!"

Ah, so that's what they were discussing when I saw them in the flower garden that day at Hever.

"Sir, I would agree with George."

He stares at me, his eyes soft. "I am sorry I was mistaken about you." Disappointment tinges his voice.

"As I said, sir, I am very flattered that you asked me to be your mistress, but loyalty and friendship would be a better fit between us two."

"Perhaps you are right, Mistress Wickers." He rubs his brow, then shoves the box back into his pouch.

"Which young lady do George and Norfolk think you should have asked to be your mistress?"

He shrugs his eyebrows and tilts his head. "Anne Boleyn."

Yes! "Sir, I think you have mistakenly loved me, but we shall keep this conversation between us." God, I can't believe I've just told Henry VIII he's in the wrong. I gulp back a ball of saliva.

"Do you think Anne a good choice?"

"Yes. Yes, sir, I do. I know Anne well enough, and she is everything your wife is not. The lady Anne is definitely a better choice for you than I." I lower my gaze in respect, crossing everything in my mind that he goes for it.

———————— • ❄ • ————————

Anne continues carrying out her duties as expected for the queen. We sometimes walk the gardens together and watch the gardeners tending the beautiful rosebushes, tying back clematis, and weeding the flowerbeds in the bright sunshine. Though we chat, I keep the conversation with the king to myself.

Mary, after leaving her children in Hertfordshire, is back at court. It appears, despite all the king said about her, that she thinks she's once again in his favour. Maybe my words back in Hever really hit the mark. I'm curious about them. It's obvious that she's besotted with him, but I know, after his conversation with me, that her feelings for him are no longer reciprocated. I've made a mental note of how she comes alive when he enters the queen's apartments, how she straightens her spine, her cheeks redden, and her eyes brighten, yet he gives no sign that he so much as knows her name.

One evening, George taps on the door and catches me unawares in our bedchamber as I sit reading my copy of the John Russel book he gave me.

"All alone?" He looks about the room, no doubt wondering where his sister is.

"It appears so." I smile, though I'm nervous about being alone with him.

"I'm glad," he says. "I have been meaning to speak with you on our own since that afternoon with the king at Hever." He walks over to the fireplace and thrusts the poker into the flames, then jabs it into his jug of ale, making the liquid hiss and spit. Not something I plan to try anytime soon. He takes a gulp from the goblet. I settle myself back into the chair as he pours wine for me from a bottle on the sideboard. He hands me a glass, then turns back to top up the ale in his goblet, from the jug.

"What is it?" I ask, taking a sip from my glass's fruity contents.

"I saw you talking to the king that day in the flower garden."

"At Hever, or here?" I ask, both scenarios swirling through my mind.

"Hever." His brows furrow as he studies me. I'm glad he has no clue what's happened lately between Henry and me.

"I know how he feels about you – he has told me." He steps in front of the hearth, taking a swig from his warm ale.

"Do you?" I sigh. "You don't know the half of it! It's not your undercarriage he's trying to fyrtle with!"

"He's not trying to fyrtle with what? It's not your what…undercarriage?" looking shocked, as he takes another gulp of ale.

"I'm sorry, George. Forget I said anything!"

George shakes his head. "It's not your fault, Beth. Has he been trying to take liberties that are not his to take?"

"You seem to forget George, the king is the king, he can take any liberties he likes, but he's not taking any liberties with my nether-regions!"

"Are you certain? You have told him so?" George smirks. "Henry did tell me you did not give him a straight answer…to his question." He places his goblet on the mantle.

"He lies to you!" My frustration is obvious. "I told him my husband would have my virginity, and that was it." More lying. This isn't good. I'm not going to reveal that I haven't been a virgin for some time now. My twenty-first-century love life is none of his business. I take another sip from my glass.

"Henry told me that you were allowing him to hope – that there might be some future in a liaison with you. Is that not true?" I say nothing. He looks at me, trying to read meaning into my silence. "Well?"

"George…" I get up and walk over to him, placing my hand on his upper arm. The velvet of his doublet feels rich beneath my fingers. His musky scent draws me in but I hold back – I need to stay focused. "The king's question took me completely by surprise." I take a few steps back and sit on the edge of the four-poster bed, staring at the last of the flames as they wither in the grate. They will soon be embers. He walks to the bed and sits beside me.

"I told you the truth, did I not?" He sighs. "About his non-declaration at the joust?" He pulls out a metal toothpick from his pocket and starts fiddling with it.

"You did, George."

"And now, you finally believe me?"

"Of course, I do."

"So, what will you do?"

How do I answer him? My mind is a blur. "You know, if the king were to catch you here – alone with me – he would not be happy." I feel my brows almost curl. "I cannot let you be put in harm's way."

"Is that because you love me?" he asks, turning the toothpick between his fingers, before tucking it back in his pocket. He slides his arm around my waist. "Tell me. If it is no, and you love the king, I will go."

"George, there is no need to ask me, you know exactly how I feel. However, my love is irrelevant and against my better judgement, because you are married. But you are right – I'm afraid I still love you."

"Then why do you entertain a dalliance with the king?"

"His Majesty gives you the wrong impression of me." I daren't tell him what occurred between Henry and me.

He shifts closer. "Are you certain?"

"Did you not say that you thought the king's declaration at the joust could have easily been a sign of affection in Anne's direction?"

"That I did." He plants soft kisses on my neck, and my thighs quiver as delightful tingles run the length of my body.

"Then…could we not turn the attentions of the king towards Anne?" His kisses become warmer and more persistent but then he stops and leans back.

"Anne? My sister?" He chuckles. "Has the King not had enough of Boleyn women?" His forehead creases. "He pays no mind to Mary anymore."

"Only because he was distracted by me."

"Whatever you said to the king in his bedchamber, all that time ago, must have made an impression." He kisses my neck again, and my body softens. "And I can understand why!" His breath warms my ear.

"George, enough!" I push him off me and tie the bow on my dressing gown a little tighter. "I have never led you on, have I?"

"You do not have to!" He smirks.

"We should not be together like this. What if Anne were to come back? Or if Jane were to come looking for you?"

He gets up, his face lighting with a broad smile. "Forgive me but I cannot help myself around you."

"Do not think of me. We need focus on creating the possibility of the king wanting your sister."

He sits in the chair by the ebbing fire. I remain seated on the bed, my arms folded across my chest.

"Could we make that happen?" he asks.

Now we're getting somewhere. "Why not? Anne is everything the king admires. She's intelligent, funny, vivacious, educated, and accomplished." I give him an expectant look. "She is everything so many of the women at court are not. What is there not for the king to love?"

"That is all well and good but how do we get her to notice him, in that way? You know she hated the way he treated our sister."

"I am sure it can be done." I can't hold back a half-smile. He jumps up, strides across to me, and kisses me straight on the lips. "George, stop!" I chuckle at his boyish behaviour, though he is all man. "Besides, I have told the king that he and I are better suited as friends."

"You did?"

"Of course, but you must keep that to yourself." I glance at the door. "I also know that both you and your uncle told the king that Anne might make a more suitable mistress."

"I have a confession to make," he whispers. "I did that to take his mind off you!" He looks at me, waiting for me to explode with rage, but I can't because Henry already told me what happened. George has done exactly what I needed him to do, without being asked. "And what else did the king say?"

"I think he appears to be considering the matter – but Anne knows nothing of it, and you must not say a word!"

He grins. "I love you, Beth. I am sorry to have doubted you." He walks to the door, and within that split second, I am on my own again. I pick up my book and begin reading but see nothing but those soft kisses on my neck.

A few minutes later, Anne bursts in. "Why did you not come and play cards with Lady Shelton and me? I played so well and won!" She smiles as she empties coins onto the bed from her purse.

"Perhaps you should play a game of cards with the king." I giggle. "Do you think you would win then?"

"Yes!" She squeals, picks up the coins, and puts them back in her purse. Then she walks over to her small casket, unlocks it, and places the purse inside. She then sits on the bed and removes the French hood which decorates her long hair. I remain silent, watching her tug at the ribbon in her braided hair.

"How is Mary?" I ask, unable to hold back, wanting to get things moving.

"Not good. Despite her leaving little Catherine and Henry Carey at home, the king is not enamoured of her anymore."

"I urged her not to worry," I say, "and to support her husband." I take another sip of the wine George poured for me.

"If I were Mary," Anne continues, "I'd not be able to forgive the King. As soon as her condition began to show, he turned as cold as stone and began sniffing around other women, especially you – and me. Henry Tudor makes no effort to hide the fact he is no longer interested in my sister. And when he came to Hever, he paid her no mind at all!"

I wipe my lips with a linen handkerchief, then scrunch it up into my dressing-gown sleeve. "I've tried to tell the king I am not interested in being his mistress and put him down gently." I nod to myself, confident that I've finally ended his pursuit of me. "If you were Mary, you would no doubt call Henry to heel and make him do as he is told, king or no." She laughs at my comment. "In fact, you would do more than bring him to heel – I fear he would not stand a chance with you!"

She makes a face at me for being impertinent. "What do you make of this relationship between Henry and my sister?" She tilts her head and places her hood and the ribbon on the bedside table, then lays back on the bed, resting her head against a cushion.

"The king seems shy," I state, reminding myself not to push her temper. "I think he genuinely liked Mary, perhaps even loved her for a time, but because she was married, he could see no hope in continuing the relationship."

"I think the king wants the rumours of the Carey children's parentage quashed!"

Wanting will not do him any good. Five hundred years from now, historians will still speculate about the parentage of Mary's children, but it's best to say nothing so I keep my mouth shut on that matter.

"Henry has had several mistresses," I point out, "but he is not as sexually experienced as the King of France. I think he genuinely believes in romantic love. Ideally, I suspect that's what he wants. All his dalliances are temporary but there will be someone who keeps his attention for a long time, of that you can be sure."

She snaps her head up from the cushion, mischievously staring at me.

"Do you know something I do not?" She smiles and points at me. "Of course, you must do. Tell me more, Beth!" She pats a spot next to her on the mattress, bidding me join her.

"What do you think of the king's decision to make Bessie Blount's boy his heir?" I throw this out, hoping to change the subject from Henry's potential next wife.

"What do I make of it?" She frowns at me. "You will do better to ask what the Queen has made of it. Henry Fitzroy is the king's illegitimate son. He may be a bastard but he is the only male heir the king is likely to have."

"The king has cosseted and promoted him. Young Fitzroy has his own household and has been granted many honours. Unless the king decides to seek an annulment and remarry, then perhaps Fitzroy will be his heir."

My little speech on the so-called bastard prince has created a heavy silence, as if I have sworn my soul to damnation. I'm well aware that Henry VIII desires to separate from his wife – he told me that day in the garden he was considering the matter. Not only that but his anxiety over his lack of male heirs has led him to question the validity of his marriage to Katharine – his concern based on her first marriage to his older brother, Arthur. History knows that he will focus on a theological argument – a minority opinion in canon law – that the papal dispensation allowing the marriage in the first place is invalid because marrying a brother's widow is forbidden in the Bible, and no pope has the authority to dispense with a scriptural prohibition. I know that once he lets it be known he is interested in Anne Boleyn as a prospective wife, and not a mistress, he will become determined to be rid of Katharine and obtain permission to marry Anne.

Henry changing his mind about me and moving his attentions towards Anne, making them public, is going to further antagonize Charles, The Holy Roman Emperor, and add fuel to the fire of ongoing problems. At the same time, he will naturally look to France for support, putting the French king in an awkward position. He will also need to secure the support of Pope Clement VII – a force to be reckoned with. Indeed, deciding to reject Katharine, he will dice with the crowned heads of Europe and the pope.

History says he gave up sleeping with her in 1524, although he had clearly been drifting for some years. She was thirty-nine then and had not conceived in seven years. Moreover, time has cruelly destroyed both her petite beauty and her gentle good spirits – she is now quite overweight and somewhat dull of appearance – and apart from a passionate concern for Mary, her one child, only duty draws her from religious observances to the frivolities of Court life. With no hope of children, nothing makes Henry want to sleep with her.

I nudge Anne. "You know that, from time to time, the king has solaced himself in the manner of monarchs by taking a mistress. With the final recognition that he will have no son by Katharine, his recent declarations to me show that his position has changed." I sit back and wait to see what effect my comment has.

"You mean the king's illicit pleasure is now no longer enough?" She blinks, then stares at me.

"Henry, and the country, need to have a son to succeed him. To do so, he has to marry again." Another seed to plant in her head.

"Whom will he marry, Beth?" she asks.

I consider whether to ignore her question and talk about Henry Fitzroy. "Does the king need to remarry?" I ask, trying to throw her off the scent. "Henry Fitzroy, whom he has brought out of obscurity and made the Duke of Richmond, could become his successor."

"Yes, he has given the boy precedence over everyone except any legitimate son that might be born to him." She brushes invisible dust off her lap. "The queen has been widely offended by it, and three of her ladies were dismissed from court for supporting Her Majesty in her anger."

"Didn't the Venetian ambassador report that Richmond had actually been legitimized?" I ask. "You know that any thought of ousting the Princess Mary in favour of the illegitimate Richmond involves extreme risk, and Henry has turned to a more conventional answer, a decree of nullity."

"He has?"

"Yes, and popes are always sensitive to the special matrimonial problems of monarchs, assuming plausible rationalization could be offered. Oh, on that point, Henry has discovered what he believes is irrefutable proof that his marriage with Katharine is defective and invalid in canon law."

She stares at me, probably wondering how I know all this. But then she must understand that I have the advantage of hindsight. Okay, let's continue with this.

"I have heard it said that the king believes with conviction, and compelling force, on the clear application to his position of a threat in the Bible: 'If a man shall take his brother's wife, it is an unclean thing…he shall be without children'. Leviticus 20:21, if I remember correctly."

"Beth, you know scripture well."

"Henry believes that quotes from scripture to be a direct word from God and that God has spoken directly to his condition – as a devout Christian, he has no option but to obey. He will, I have no doubt, be consulting his advisers, in secret, to take steps to divorce Katharine. He said as much to me at Hever."

"Did he?" She looks startled.

"I wonder if Henry would risk annulling his marriage and possibly invite a countersuit. I hope Katharine of Aragon does not know about the affair with Mary, as otherwise, she could use canonical impediment created by it, either in an attempt to block his next marriage, or to discredit his doubts of conscience concerning their own marriage."

Anne stares at me, her mouth hanging. I've dug deep to come up with accurate points to argue the political and romantic desires of the monarch. If she didn't already know that I'm from the future, she'd probably consider me a witch, or some kind of sorcerer, with all that I know.

We sit in silence, with Anne no doubt considering the consequences of the revelations I've just shared. Now and again, she stares at me, as if ready to ask a question, but then she looks away and goes back into herself. After a day spent largely outdoors, walking the gardens and sitting in the arbours, I'm tired, as I'm sure she is. When Agnes comes to prepare her for bed, it's a welcome intrusion.

Giant, swirling shadows cast by the mammoth fire, joust on the walls, dipping and dancing with those brought alive by the torches. The hubbub of voices and unsuppressed excitement lift all our spirits as the high-pitched laughter of the women is accompanied by the deeper rumbles of the men's conversations. Adding to all this hubbub are the minstrels up in the gallery, tuning their instruments in readiness for the king's enjoyment. When I turn to speak to

George, a serving girl passes with a tray of goblets full of wine. He grabs her elbow and relieves her of a goblet for me and one for himself, and although she is far beneath him in status, she smirks and simpers under his smouldering appraisal. I smile at him, knowing what a terrible flirt he really is. But I take no offence because he means no harm.

His chuckles go unnoticed, drowned out by a clarion of trumpets announcing a royal arrival. Everyone sinks to the floor in a backbreaking bow. My satin skirts fill with air and pool around me as I crouch before the passing queen, on her way to take her place on the dais. Anne and the queen's other women fuss around her, arranging her skirts, fetching a low stool for her slippered feet to rest on. Once she is settled, she flicks her hand, freeing everyone to resume their conversations.

Beside me, a woman is flirting with George, who leans against a carved screen – a decorative room divider made from walnut – his eyes fixed on her generous breasts. He proceeds to see how far he can lead her before she realises who she's flirting with; she is of the Howard line and, as such, is related to everyone. There are too many cousins at Court, and the Boleyns' tangled bloodlines often trip the unwary. To the left of the group, Jane Boleyn circles on the periphery until Anne beckons her to join us to watch the revels, by which time, the woman has moved on. Jane slides in between Anne and George, linking her arm through his, and leaning her head against his shoulder to show ownership. He pats her hand, his surprise at this public show of affection obvious.

"Wife, do not lean on me – can you not see I have a cup of wine to drink? Save your affections for the bedchamber!" An irked expression crosses his face when she scowls at him, then looks at Anne, back to him, and then to me, seeing if any of us will chide him for being disrespectful to her. I thoroughly enjoy my time with George and Anne. However, I can't say the same for Jane. At times, I find the former Jane Parker, now Boleyn, to be – at its most charitable – prickly. Maybe that's my fault. Whenever an amusement occurs, it seems to me she always has to interject, making the moment hers. If George or Anne tell stories of any kind, she must tell another tale that will surpass theirs. Nor do I like the way I often catch her inspecting Anne when she thinks no one is aware. Most annoying of all is the way she carries herself, especially her gestures, and her clothing often mimics any outfit Anne has designed. She seems quite a jealous girl, in my view, and I don't want to know how George is getting on with her in his marriage and will never bring up the subject in conversation with him. He must never know that I'm touched by the green monster, too. I realise I'm being a little spiteful towards her, but she brings it out in me. Makes me wonder if she has the same effect on others.

I clutch my wine and scan the company, noting who wears new jewels, gowns, and favours. What interests me most is who is playing cuckold to whom. Of course, the gossip is all about the king's secret matter, and the fact that he wants to annul his marriage, but none dare speak of it. I hope courtiers don't cite me as a reason for him wishing to terminate his relationship with Katharine. In the presence of the royal couple, we all pretend ignorance. However, as most will soon discover, this is not just another of Henry's games, and, this time, unlike other games, none of us are certain of the rules, not even him.

Another clarion announces the arrival of the man himself, and all except the queen sink to their knees again. He pauses at the great entrance, and I turn my head just enough to watch him enter, full of bonhomie, a beaming smile slashed across his chiselled face, his arm thrown around the neck of Will Compton.

As he moves through the hall, I bow my head, the back of my neck aching as I watch the royal feet approach. Imagine my surprise when they stop before Anne, who is beside me, and I find myself staring with some confusion at the king's square-toed shoes. They are made of the softest pale kid and encrusted with pearls. He's waiting. From the corner of my eye, I glance quickly in Anne's direction to see that Anne's cheeks are hot with embarrassment. Henry and Compton are smiling down at her. Blushing like a fool, she keeps her chin tucked to her chest as graciously as she knows how. Henry clears his throat, then taps his foot until she looks up at him.

"Mistress Wickers. Mistress Anne Boleyn." He doesn't quite meet her eye as he utters our names, his voice loud in the silent hall.

He nods to me, and I nod back, keeping my curtsy before him. Anne has no choice but to lift her head.

"Your Majesty," she says, deepening her curtsy, trying to get closer to the floor, but she appears to be as low as she can go.

My kirtle is digging into my flesh. To distract myself, I keep my gaze lowered in Anne's direction as Henry stands there just looking at her. Has he now really noticed her? It would be a great relief to know that his sights are definitively set on her, and that we are simply friends again. What a joy that would be. I can almost see those blank pages filling with text. Hmm, if this goes to plan, I might take the chance to return home to see how things are with that book.

He glances at me as he passes, smiling, and it's like a weight has lifted when he's on his way. We all rise. My heart is thumping, and Anne's olive-toned cheeks are still scarlet. A murmur surges around the room. Everyone is staring at her, whispering, speculating. She takes a sideward glance at me, looking like a rabbit caught in a poacher's trap. Then goosebumps erupt when hot breath caresses my neck, and I realise, with no little relief, that George is standing behind us.

"Well, well, sister and Mistress Elizabeth," he whispers. "Acknowledged by the king before the Court. Whatever next?"

Across the room, Sir Thomas Boleyn is standing in the shadows, conversing with the duke of Norfolk, but he scowls as Norfolk raises his goblet and smiles. Close beside them, Henry's sister, Mary, and her husband, Charles Brandon, do not hide their dislike. Cold floods through my body, followed by an internal heat, and sweat beads on my brow. Now that Anne has been acknowledged, will it be Sir Thomas or Norfolk who will make her replace Mary Carey if they can?

Anne grabs my wrist. "Beth, get me out of here!"

I look across to Henry, who now sits on his throne next to his wife, and notice that his focus is on Anne and me, or maybe just on Anne. The royal court seems spread before her in a carpet of stolen obeisance. He gets up and comes towards us, and she grips my wrist even tighter. I take a step back and ease out of her grasp, but she doesn't move. My heart is banging like a drum for her as Henry draws near. Is this it? Is this the moment things are set back on track?

She sinks back into her obligatory curtsy. Before she's halfway down, he takes her elbow and stops her.

"Mistress Anne, you cannot spend half your life on your knees. I am come to ask you to accompany me in the dance." He holds out his arm, which she accepts with grace. Yes! She rests her hand on his and he leads her onto the dancefloor, where others are forming for the first Volta. The minstrels strike up the drums and flute as the first few bars of the Basse Dance ring out through the hall. I have to say, the sound is almost hypnotic, and adrenaline rushes through my body, along with a nervous shock of excitement. As I wait to be asked to dance, I struggle to remember the steps Anne has taught me. Although I've been in the company of the king, on quite a personal level, there is something different about watching him with Anne in such a public scenario. The implied passion of the storytelling feels too intimate for safety. He seems more imposing now, dwarfing almost everyone in the hall.

My nervousness is accelerated when George approaches and bows, before Jane intercepts, chiding him for not asking her to dance. He's not impressed having to leave my company, and mouths 'Save me!' over her shoulder as he leads her onto the dancefloor.

I try to ignore him, thankful when his father rescues me from my solitude, taking my hand and leading me into the dance. Sir Thomas's grip is firm but gentle, and his hands are soft and smooth. He is confident in the steps and gives me a reassuring smile as he leads me through the dance. I keep my head turned a little to the right, to where, beyond the dancefloor, the onlookers have their heads together, busy whispering behind their hands.

"What do you make of the king's acknowledgement of Anne tonight?" He looks down at me in a kindly way, no doubt hoping for an honest answer.

"Sir, I think the king has good taste – there is no one at court, save Anne, with her manners and her grace. Is it any wonder that the king should notice her?" I grip his hand tighter as he leads me faster across the dancefloor.

"Of course, you are right, Mistress Wickers, but do you suppose the king has the same kind of interest in Anne as he has had with Mary?" He arches his eyebrows once, then looks across to Anne and Henry as they dance together in a swirl of excitement. Does he know that Henry asked me to be his mistress? If he does, he doesn't give the game away.

"I cannot say, sir, but I know that Anne guards herself well in the company of men." I hope he doesn't see the white lie in my eyes as I remember that scoundrel Wyatt trying to declare his love for her through his poetry.

"Ah, well, my brother-in-law Norfolk has asked me to place Anne in the king's way and have us use the situation to the family's advantage. What say you to that?"

"Sir, can I call you Thomas?"

"Yes, of course," he says with some urgency, wanting my answer.

"Thomas, I think you are a man of honour and that you would not use your daughter to your advantage. As you told me before, you and your family grew in the king's favour because of all your hard work and not for any other reason."

He smiles at that. There is no doubt that he is an ambitious man, for his family, too. He gave Anne the fantastic opportunity of receiving an education at the court of Margaret of Austria in Mechelen, and then was able to get her and her sister chosen to attend Mary Tudor, Henry VIII's sister, in France. These are amazing opportunities for a courtier's daughter, and Sir Thomas seems to be similar to Thomas More and Sir Anthony Cooke in believing that daughters should receive the type of education usually reserved for sons. He is a Renaissance man, for sure, who has shared his new ideas with me, such as humanism and the new religious views sweeping through Europe. Of course, such an education, and foreign travel, along with her family's wealth and connections, and her father's closeness to the king, makes her quite a catch in the marriage department, and that is what every Tudor man wants for his daughter: a good marriage.

"Norfolk has confided in me that he wants the king to notice Anne, in the hope she may become his mistress. But as Mary did not use the situation to her advantage, I am not certain it will work with Anne. A liaison with Henry is not something I desire for her."

He surprises me with his opinion, for history has always painted him as a pimp to his daughters, for his own personal gain. Our conversation is repeatedly interrupted by the other courtiers as they weave in between us during the dance.

"Do you think the king wants Anne for his mistress, sir?" I search his expression for the truth, as we are thrust once more into our meandering steps. He's not to know that I'm aware that George has spoken to his uncle about guiding Anne towards Henry, and vice-versa.

"No one knows what the king wants – only the king knows what is in his heart. If it is the case that this is what he desires, I will try to dissuade Anne from accepting his advances, as I would oppose her being any man's mistress. She has not been educated just to be an amusement to men."

"Perhaps it is nothing, and we need not worry ourselves?" I look up at him once more, remaining calm, pasting on a smile, and concentrating on the steps. Sir Thomas's breath is tinged with spiced wine as he plays the part of a pivot in the wheel I tread around him; my fingers unsteady in his palm. Each time I look up, I catch a melancholy look. The man is worried. His small mouth is tight and the furrows in his brow deepen as he glances at the king and Anne. Everyone in the hall is watching them, speaking in whispers, giving knowing nods as they witness the other Boleyn girl try and protect herself from her monarch's unassailable charm. Anne smiles brazenly and pays no attention to them, even when the music takes Henry from her to weave among other women. She watches him laughing and flirting with others until the steps lead him back to her, which she takes in her stride. Unlike the other women of the court, she doesn't seem consumed by his conversation or company.

As the dance continues, there is a flurry of activity at the dais as Katharine and her ladies are on the move. They sweep past in a flotilla of disapproval while the sound of the lutes dwindles away. The room falls silent once more, the dance and conversation coming to an abrupt stop as everyone left in the hall drops to their knees. Courtiers begin whispering behind their hands and in each other's ears, glancing in Anne's direction. Taken unawares, she doesn't have time to respond, and the queen passes her and Henry by without acknowledgement.

And that is how the change in Henry's preference began. After a night of dancing and on this fine morning, an equerry of the king calls to us in Anne's chambers. He enters the room, finding Anne reading aloud, trying to teach me Latin scripture – to no avail. The body servant of the king is shy, waiting patiently for her to respond.

"How can we help you, sir?" Feigning nonchalance, she goes forward to meet him. He hands her a velvet pouch and a letter embellished with the king's great seal.

"The King has asked me to bring you these gifts, which he asks you accept, along with his admiration."

She takes the parcel from him, thanks him, and places it on the table. I rush to her side as she unties the pouch, opening it to reveal several brooches and a necklace encrusted with rubies and diamonds. We gasp with excitement as we trace the precious stones on these exquisite works of art with our fingertips. She doesn't pick up any jewellery but breaks the seal on the letter with caution and reads the contents to herself.

"Anne, what does he say?"

Her brows arch. "The King has declared his great admiration for me and asks me to accept these gifts of appreciation." She reads the letter again, looking bemused at its contents.

"Does he say anything else?"

"No," she declares, handing it to me. She turns to the young man and thanks him for his patience, asking him to inform the king that she will reply to his letter as soon as she has a chance to put quill to paper. The equerry nods and leaves us to continue ogling the stunning gifts.

"Look at these pieces," I say. "They are so beautiful." I hand the empty pouch and the jewellery back to her, and she sits before the fire, staring at them in her lap.

"What will you do?" I ask, as she rereads the handwriting that will soon become so familiar to her. She folds the letter up, tucks it into the neckline of her gown, and places the brooches and necklace back into the softness of the pouch.

"I will send them back!" she declares, her nostrils flaring in indignation.

"Send them back?" I try to sound surprised, when I already have a good idea of what she will do.

"Yes." She snorts. "I thought the king was interested in you!" I'm sure I heard a growl rumble deep in her throat. "How dare the king presume I am to be enticed into his bed with gifts!"

"Anne, he did not send me gifts, yet he asked me if I would be his mistress!"

She stares at me. "Really?"

"Yes, really – you are lucky. I was never given jewellery such as this." Best not to mention the locket.

"He can send me trinkets, beg me for my kisses, but I will be no mistress, not to any man, not even a king." She gets up, places the pouch on the table, and walks to the cupboard, where she pulls her leather writing tray out. "These jewels are not worthy of my maidenhead. I will write to the king and tell him we are leaving."

"Leaving court?"

"Yes, leaving court!" Her nostrils flare again. "I can stay here not a minute longer – I do not want the king's attentions."

"What about Jayne Fool?"

"What? Can she not remain here?"

"I...suppose so," I answer. "It might be best. People with her condition don't like change. Too much disruption to her routine may distress her. You wouldn't want her to be upset again, would you?"

"Of course, not – we have a responsibility to her and her father, as her keepers, do we not?"

"Yes, without question. Do you want me to explain to her why she will be staying here, and not returning with us to Hever?"

She sighs. "You might make a better job of it than me."

"Very well."

Once she's settled at the table, the blank parchment before her and the nib of her quill filled with ink, she begins to write:

To Your Gracious Majesty,

It causes me much pain and grief to return the gifts you have bestowed on me. Alas, they are too beautiful, and I am unworthy to receive them. I think I never gave Your Majesty cause to give them to me, since I am nothing, and you are everything. Give them, I pray you, to a woman more deserving of Your Majesty's affections. I am leaving Court for my family's house at Hever Castle. I shall think of you on the journey there, and Mistress Wickers and I shall delight in conversation of our experience of Your Majesty's great court.

Your loving servant,

Anne Boleyn.

Nine

JULY 1526 – HEVER CASTLE

Anne and I are at a first-floor, inner-courtyard window when we hear the clatter of horse and cart as it passes the stables in front of the castle. We can just spot the visitors as they stop near the moat bridge. The cart is adorned with the king's coat of arms and accompanied by riders in royal livery. We remain silent, though excited, as these richly dressed men in green and white velvet dismount and stride towards the entrance to the inner courtyard.

A commotion breaks out with Griffin's loud barking as Anne's mother hurries under the portcullis and over the bridge. Anne drops her book on the bench and dashes down the stairs.

"Come on, Beth!" she yells, "we cannot miss this – it has got to be something to do with the king!"

My heart thumps so hard as I try to keep up with her trailing skirts in our rush to discover why such illustrious servants are paying us a visit.

"Gentleman, what can I do for you on this day?" Lady Boleyn greets the two liveried servants standing before her, their gilded uniforms of fine velvet stiff and starched as they bow in our general direction. Their faces aren't familiar.

"We are here on orders of His Majesty the King to seek out Mistress Anne Boleyn, My Lady." One of them peers over her shoulder as Anne and I step forward from the shadows of the doorway.

"This is my daughter, Anne," she says, as Anne stands next to her. "What does the king want?"

"The king has sent a gift for the Lady Anne, Lady Boleyn." The young man beckons us closer to view the cart. Two other body servants, still on horseback, doff their caps as Anne's mother lifts the corner of a linen sheet to reveal the carcass of a buck lying on a bed of straw.

"We have a letter for Mistress Anne, written in His Majesty's own hand." The principle servant pulls a large, folded letter from his leather folio, closed tight with a great red seal, just as her previous letter was decorated, bearing the coat of arms of the king. He hands it to Lady Boleyn, who finds the letter snatched from her hand by Anne.

"Mother, the letter is addressed to me, so I shall take it!"

Aghast at her behaviour, her mother looks to the heavens and sighs.

"You may tie your horses in our stables, where our stable boy Simon shall make sure they are fed and watered."

She calls out to Simon, who is all of thirteen. He disengages the horses from the cart and leads them to the stable block. Lady Boleyn seems flustered as she tries to direct all four servants towards the kitchen. They carry off the buck, hanging by its ankles from a pole, in the direction indicated, and when their job is done, they are offered a seat at a table in the castle's Great Hall, where they are given refreshment while they wait for Anne's reply to the king's letter.

I rush up the stairs with Anne, not wishing to be left out of this auspicious moment. She sinks onto her bed, breaks open the seal, and reads aloud the king's words to her.

> "'Although, my mistress, it has not pleased you to remember the promise you made me when I was last with you – that is, to hear good news from you, and to have an answer to my last letter – yet it seems to me that it belongs to a true servant (seeing that otherwise he can know nothing) to inquire the health of his mistress, and to acquit myself of the duty of a true servant, I send you this letter, beseeching you to apprise me of your welfare, which I pray to God may continue as long as I desire mine own. And to cause you yet oftener to remember me, I send you, by the bearer of this, a buck killed late last night by my own hand, hoping that when you eat of it you may think of the hunter; and thus, for want of room, I must end my letter, written by the hand of your servant, who very often wishes for you instead of your brother.
>
> "'H.'"

She stares at the letter, going over it again but in silence this time, just in case she has missed an important point in its contents.

"You did not tell me the king has written to you before!" I say as I run each line through in my head.

"The first letter was nothing, just a request for me to come back to Court. The king did not like that I had snubbed him by sending his jewels back." She sits up on her bed, handing the priceless parchment to me. My gaze dances across each word and phrase, wishing I had taken more heed during French lessons at school.

"You must reply, Anne. His Majesty cannot be ignored." I search beside the bed for fresh parchment, quill, and ink. The table legs thud on the floor as I bring it closer.

"What do I write? I do not want to encourage the king – look how he has treated Mary, and for that matter, you!" She screws up her nose in anguish, before dipping the quill into the ink.

"I shall reply in French," she says, pulling the table closer and beginning to write.

My French is not that great but, after reading her reply, it roughly translates as:

> *My Lord, how your tokens and signs of affection frighten me. How can I be to you what you think me to be? I may be of noble blood, but I think myself unworthy of your love, though the offer of it and the passion of Your Majesty's words and looks touch both my heart and soul. You have flattered me with so many and such wondrous gifts. Allow me to send you this token letter of loyalty, and gift, small though it is, and allow me to remain your ever-loving servant, Anne.*

"What do you think?" As she waits for the ink to dry, she pulls a ring from her forefinger and slides it into a small velvet pouch.

"I think it is very diplomatic, Anne. Although, you do not declare yourself either way, which, after his experience of me snubbing him, I have no doubt will infuriate His Majesty."

She laughs. "That is not the idea! I have simply told the king that I am his loyal and humble servant and will agree to be nothing more." She looks at me in a concerned manner, then gets up, folding the letter, and I follow her as she takes the pouch and runs from the room, through the house to the library, where her father's family seal sits on his desk. She doesn't bat an eyelid at disturbing the house. Her mother enters the room and watches her prepare the wax, heating it over the fireplace, before pouring it onto the letter, after which she presses the seal deep into the waiting substance. She goes to the king's men, waiting in the Great Hall, her head high, and hands the principal man the letter and pouch with all the grace I'm sure she can muster.

"Please give this letter and gift to His Majesty, with my sincere devotion." She curtsies to both men.

"We will, My Lady." They bow in unison as the principle man places the velvet pouch and letter into his large purse, closing the strap for safe-keeping.

"Please thank your lady mother for the refreshments."

With that, they take their leave and start their journey back to the king. I find this exchange of letters thrilling, because I know Anne's replies to the seventeen love letters Henry will send her are lost to history. No one but Henry, and now me, will know what she wrote, and he will destroy all of her replies when his love for her sours. Her words will turn to ash, blown away by the wind, never to be seen again. It is my hope to be present when she writes every response. The reality that I am witnessing the history first-hand sends a lump to my throat. On realising that she has enclosed one of her rings, I seem to recall stories of the king wearing it, but my memory of the research into it is fuzzy. At least, being here, at this time in history, I can actually view it as it happens.

A few days after, George arrives home with Jane, and they take supper with us all that evening, when we feast on the king's buck. Most of the time, Jane stares daggers at me. She has barely spoken with me since I returned through the portal. She is always going to bear a grudge. Despite her prickliness towards me, I try to ignore her and focus on the candlelight which casts dancing shadows on the wall, adding to the atmosphere of happy revelry as we dine on the bounty. Venison is an acquired taste, a bit like pheasant, and I'm not sure whether I will like it.

"Welcome home, George. We had not been expecting you." Sir Thomas raises his glass, taking in the faces of his family about the dining table. "I think we also need to thank His Majesty for such a splendid contribution to our family meal. To the King!" He raises his glass again, towards the ceiling.

"To the King!" we all shout.

"I certainly do not know what my daughter has done to deserve such a gift but perhaps Anne will agree that she has made an impression on His Majesty to receive such a present as this buck, killed by the King himself!"

Agnes enters the Great Hall and tells Jane that her and George's luggage has been unpacked.

"Thank you, Agnes."

I think she's glad to be away from Court. She seems more relaxed in the company of her in-laws, even if she hates being around me.

"It is good to be in the company of those who are dearly missed at Court," George says. He smiles, looks along the table, at Anne, his parents, then holds my gaze for a moment – long enough for his wife to notice. She glares at me, then at George.

"Jane, it is good to see you here, too," Lady Boleyn says, leaning across to Jane, squeezing her hand and smiling at her.

The dinner is served in three courses, and there are several dishes at each, with portions sufficient for all of us, which Agnes brings in serving dishes to the table. The poor woman is a slave to us all. She serves separate dishes of sweet and savoury courses, which she brings in at the same time, with hard cheeses and wine as an accompaniment. Sir Thomas has already carved a good-sized joint from the buck, with steam rising into the air like incense from the fresh-cooked meat. It is the mark of a gentleman to know how to carve such a kill. George helps Jane, then Anne, then me to the choicest portions of food before serving himself.

I take a long sip of sweet wine – an expensive one from Anjou. Ale and beer are also served at table. I stab at a piece of venison with the end of my knife and chew on a morsel – yep, definitely gamey – a bit too rich for my tastes.

After the main course, a sculpted confection of sugar known as a 'subtlety' is carried in to impress us – utterly spectacular when seen first-hand. They bring home to me how labour-intensive it must be to prepare such a meal from scratch. Everyone enjoys the excellent flavours and aromas, with the final course being pears in red wine, which looks delicious, as does the marzipan. The company is jovial and animated, wiping greasy fingers on large, linen napkins folded over the left shoulder, while we pass pewter plates up and down the length of the table, sipping at red wine and exchanging gossip from court and beyond.

"Lady Boleyn, may I please take my leave of this supper?" Jane asks. "I am tired from our journey, and I have a headache. Will you allow me to be excused to bed?"

George gets up and pulls her seat back so she can rise. She bobs a curtsy to her in-laws and nods to both me and Anne, then walks to the door, heading for George's bedchamber. She is about twenty-two, and, even in the summertime of her youth, she appears miserable. Her manner is strange – maudlin. If she feels depressed, then she wishes everyone about her to feel the same.

"Do not be long, husband," she calls over her shoulder to George, who sits back at the table, chewing meat from a rib with great pleasure.

"Children, please excuse me." Lady Boleyn rises, setting her handkerchief on the table before she beckons a servant to clear her place. "I must see if there is anything Jane requires before she retires."

"Mother, is everything all right?" Anne asks, watching her as she stands in the doorway.

"Not exactly, Anne. I am a mother with one son married to someone who is clearly not happy with him, another child who is the mother to two bastard children of a king, and the other, perhaps being pursued by that same married man. What else could be wrong, daughter?"

Shocked by her outburst, we all stand, nodding or bowing as she leaves the room. Sir Thomas follows his wife. We can hear them whispering in the hallway. George gets up and drags his chair to sit between Anne and me. He plucks yet another portion of meat from the serving plate and stuffs it into his mouth. His closeness is intoxicating and enticing.

"George, what does your mother mean of you and Jane being so unhappy?" I ask.

"It is nothing," he says, pulling his metal toothpick from his pocket and jabbing it between his front teeth. "Jane suffocates me, is all." He shrugs. "For a woman, she is ambitious, and expects too much of me. She is not content to be a wife at home. But no matter, how are you, Beth?" He places his hand on my shoulder, blind to everything else, and traces his fingertip down the nape of my neck, making me flinch, half out of nerves and half from excitement. Then he removes it, as if it never happened.

"Very well, George. We have missed you." I smile back before popping a grape into my mouth.

"Have you now? Well, there is someone who has missed my dear sister more," he proclaims, grinning as he pulls yet another letter showing the king's great seal from the inside of his doublet. He hands it to Anne, who circles the seal with her forefinger, then pulls at the red ribbon and opens it. Before she can begin to read it, he jumps up and snatches it out of her hands, holding it high above her head. I spring to my feet.

"George, give it back to Anne now!" I dance around him, trying to catch him out.

"No, George! Give it back, now! George, please!" Anne keeps her voice down so her father, who is probably now sat in his library, doesn't hear the commotion.

"I have given you my heart – now I desire to dedicate my body to you," George reads out loud, shielding Anne from it with his outstretched arm. We continue our protestations, begging him to give the letter back, but to no avail. He enjoys teasing us both and continues to read aloud, mocking the king's manner and causing such a stir.

"Written by the hand of one who in heart, body, and will is your loyal and most assured servant. H. R." He pauses, then raises both eyebrows. "Aww, and look…"—he smirks at Anne—"he has even drawn a little heart between the letters H and R. Oh…just imagine, the King of England writing to my sister, wanting to be her servant!" He nods at Anne, feigning sincerity.

"Give Anne back her letter!" I demand, glaring at him.

He smiles at me. "What is it worth, Beth?" He laughs. "If I give it back to her, you owe me a kiss!"

"Never!" I can't hold back a grin.

"George, give me the letter!" She pulls him towards her, trying to force his arm down to grab the missive. After a bit more play, he relents, handing her back the letter, which she folds, her face now flush, and places in the neckline of her dress for safety's sake.

"You are such a tease!" I say, knowing he will need to mature when the matter of his sister's relationship with the king progresses.

Huddling by the hearth in Anne's bedchamber, I've buried my nose in the John Russel book George gifted me. It's a precious possession but I've wondered why I've never seen it pop up in a British Library exhibition, or a viewing case at Hever in my time. I'm guessing it's because it only exists in my time-slip life, but if that's the case, what does that say about everything else about my experience here? Oh, too complex for my reading time. Best just to enjoy the book while I have it.

It's so different to holding Anne's book of hours. Just looking at a 'young' version of that ancient prayer book, which I've seen in modern times during my visits to Hever, stuns me to silence. The first time she showed it to me, I was speechless. All I could do was trace my fingers over the astrolabe she'd drawn in black ink at the bottom of one of its pages. And it's not just the books. At times, I can't help but stare in wonder at the items and precious artefacts I see and hold during my time here. Even though I've been at Hever for a long time, on and off, I don't think I will ever get used to 'Tudor Hever'. My passion for the period means I never grow tired or used to seeing such things in their prime.

I run my fingertips over the leather-bound cover of the John Russel book, as Anne asks Agnes to nudge the fire back to life and light some candles as the evening draws in. Agnes circles the room, lit taper in hand, lighting every candle she can find. I'm relieved because my eyes are straining in the low-level light, and the flickering flames illuminate the cursive print on the page. A clattering of hooves in the courtyard below has us looking up, and Anne skips to the landing, peering out through one of the casements to see who visits at such a late hour.

"Who is it?" I ask, my book in hand as I follow her.

"One of the king's servants, I think – in full livery." She sounds a little peeved as she squints into the gloom. "He appears to be handing a letter to Mother." She looks puzzled.

"Another letter from Henry Tudor?" I ask. Not that I should be surprised – she's going to receive seventeen or more over the next couple of years. Hmm, should I have prepared her for them? Perhaps, when she has all her letters, I could write a PhD on them, because I could write a hypothesis based on events and occurrences as they actually happened. I could document the letters, and Anne's replies just as they happened, sharing the intent behind the writing of each letter and its response. It would mean I could bring up the subject of historical accuracy, without other historians realising I'm basing my hypothesis on fact. Modern society is obsessed with historical accuracy and is dependent on historians 'getting it right' as they write up their research. I wonder if the point of my time-slipping is not just to keep Anne's narrative to the recorded history but also to clarify to my contemporaries how things really happened, and to produce a specific set of research. Of course, if I did this, I'd have to discuss it with Professor Marshall and not create further repercussions. I shake such thoughts out of my head, though I'm sure I'll come back to them at some stage.

"I hope not!" Anne replies, and it takes me a moment to realise that she's on about a letter from Henry.

Lady Boleyn calls for her, and we almost sprint down the stairs towards the hallway. I sometimes feel like her loyal lapdog as I trail around the castle after her. Her mother views the royal seal on the vellum with suspicion as she hands the letter over. The royal messenger waits, standing by the door outside. She asks him to wipe his boots on the iron stand, not wanting him traipsing mud in at this time of night. He nods as she waves him into the hallway.

"Go that way to the kitchens, sir. Agnes will serve you some hot broth from the pot." She turns to Anne. "Whatever could the King want at this hour?" She pulls her satin dressing gown about her as she stands in a draft, in the hallway, snuggling herself tightly in her slippers, waiting for Anne to snap the seal on the letter.

"Does the King's servant give any other message?" Anne asks.

"No." She sighs, then looks disappointed as Anne turns on her heels and runs back up the stairs. The king's servant is probably tucking into a steaming bowl of broth and a goblet of ale. No doubt, Agnes will get all the gossip from court. I expect she will hound him for news while the man waits for Anne to write her reply. His horse snorts outside. I'm sure Simon is looking after it while it waits for its master. It will need to be patient.

After a quarter of an hour reading my book in the low light of the library, my curiosity gets the better of me and I make my way up the stairs, guided by the light from a single candle, to find Anne alone in her dark bedchamber, lying on her bed. I ease the door closed behind me.

"Anne, why are you lying in here, in such gloom?"

Only one candle is lit. Perhaps Agnes blew them all out when we went downstairs, to save the wax. Poor Agnes, I feel sorry for her. She's so overworked. I put my candle in its holder on the nightstand and walk around the bed. Why would Anne want to lie in the dark? I pick up a candle from a holder at her side of the bed and light it from the fire, then set it back in place.

I sit on the edge of the mattress and wait for her to speak. What has her this way? She folds the letter and sets it beside her, concern etched across her face.

"What's wrong?" I ask, not liking the darkness in her eyes. "You are keeping the king's messenger waiting."

"No one understands," she complains, looking at me. She thumps a cushion to life, and pulls it under her head for more comfort.

"If you mean about the king being attracted to you – then I do, Anne." Her suggesting I don't understand how she might be feeling is hurtful. Ok, I didn't receive any letters but I have had tokens from him. And I know I didn't discuss it too much with her at the time, how he was with me, but I do know what it feels like to be the subject of his attentions. I know how uncomfortable it made me feel. Oh, I wish she would confide in me.

"He did not write to you, as he is now, with me – did he?"

"No," I reply, "you know he didn't." I lean towards her. "We are good friends, aren't we, you and I? Almost like sisters. You can tell me anything." I smile, taking her hand and holding it to give her reassurance.

"I wish things were as they used to be." She sighs, squeezing my hand in appreciation.

"Before I came here, do you mean?" I grimace, showing far more upset at her comment than I care to.

"No, dear friend, never!" She makes direct eye contact, her eyebrows high. "You know I tell you and George everything, but now, I am not sure I can share all my secrets."

"You can still tell me, Anne," I say, with the deepest sincerity I can manifest. "You can tell me anything you need to."

"I am not sure I can share them with George, though."

"Why not?"

"I know he would share them with Father or Uncle."

"Anne, what is it?" I'm growing more concerned by the second.

"The letter." She motions to it, then pulls it from beside her lap. "Read it."

I open it and straighten it out, my mouth dry. Then I read:

> "'On turning over in my mind, the contents of your last letters, I have put myself into great agony, not knowing how to interpret them, whether to my disadvantage, as you show in some places, or to my advantage, as I understand them in some others, beseeching you earnestly to let me know expressly your whole mind as to the love between us two. It is absolutely necessary for me to obtain this answer, having been stricken with the dart of love…'"

I sigh, my heart pounding as I hold the vellum, which shakes in my hand. Henry's really got the hots for Anne now, which has got to be a good thing.

> "'…and not yet sure whether I shall fail of finding a place in your heart and affection, which last point has prevented me for some time past from calling you, my mistress; because, if you only love me with an ordinary love, that name is not suitable for you, because it denotes a singular love, which is far from common.'"

I read the words aloud, hoping that in some way I can understand the French hand of the English king, and if I did so, the meaning will sink in. His famous script, splotched with blotches of ink from his quill, is hurriedly written so as to be certain of getting his request to Anne as soon as possible.

> *"'But if you please to do the office of a true loyal mistress and friend, and to give up yourself body and heart to me, who will be, and have been, your most loyal servant, (if your rigour does not forbid me) I promise you that not only the name shall be given you, but also that I will take you for my only mistress, casting off all others besides you out of my thoughts and affections, and serve you only.'"*

"Oh, my goodness, Anne!" I say with pretend surprise. "He wants you as his only mistress, forsaking all others, to serve you, alone."

"Is that not what he offered you?" she asks, her voice full of disdain. "The cheek of the king, he has had my sister already – he tried to get you - and now he wants me!" Her grimace looks painful. "How can he be so arrogant to assume I will accept him?"

"Will you accept him?" I ask, before continuing to read the sacred scrawl.

> *"'I beseech you to give an entire answer to this my rude letter that I may know on what and how far I may depend.'"*

I nod once to myself and look at her.

"No, of course, I will not accept him – even if he is my king, he is not God."

I'm shocked by her answer, knowing that all Lutherans believe that kings are placed on this earth to serve God and are second alone to God, set above all others to be obeyed. Then, I forget, she is a reformer and not a full-blown heretic. She will remain a Catholic until her death, no matter how much Henry upturns the Church to have her.

"Anne, lower your voice in case anyone hears you – you know how much it would trouble your parents if they knew of the king's intentions!" I look down at the rest of the script and continue to read, as the king expresses his final sentiments:

> *"'And if it does not, please you to answer me in writing, appoint some place where I may have it by word of mouth, and I will go thither with all my heart. No more, for fear of tiring you. Written by the hand of him who would willingly remain yours,*
> *"'H. R.'"*

"I will not meet with him," she says, "I will not give him such satisfaction." She fumes but, secretly, I think she is flattered by the request to be his mistress and wants nothing more than to be adored by a powerful and prestigious suitor. I can't blame her, as the Tudor Court is a bear-pit of primordial drama, highly political, and filled with horror and passion, just as the twenty-first-century historian David Starkey has described it. She's right to stay away from any intrigue, and I warn her that she would be blamed as the 'other woman' if she returns to Court.

"Please understand," she says, "it is not that I do not love the king. However, he already has a wife. I love the king as his servant."

"I understand – but what will you do?"

She folds the letter up and places it on the nightstand. "I must reply, and with rejection." The sorrow of such a task seems to be weighing heavy on her conscience. "I do not deliberately set out to hurt His Majesty, but I will stand by what God dictates in my heart for me to do."

"That is all you can do, Anne." She takes up the quill, which scratches against the vellum as she writes her short reply:

Your Most Gracious and Highest Majesty,
Your mistress I cannot be, both in respect of mine own unworthiness, and because you have a queen already. Your mistress I will not be.
Your most humble servant,
Anne Boleyn

Anne's response will no doubt be a surprise to Henry, who is reputed to have propositioned several women of the court at this time, trying to enter into these adulterous relationships because he desperately wants a son, and Katharine of Aragon, as we all know, is going through the change. He seems desperate for Anne, as he writes so many letters. The king is not usually one for writing personally to others, and he often gets his clerks to do such tasks – but not with Anne. His words are far too intimate to be shared with any other than the recipient. I'm sure he wouldn't be best pleased if he knew his love letters to Anne will be digitized on the Vatican Library website for anyone to read, almost five-hundred years later. I wonder what he'd make of that.

"Take my reply to the king's messenger," she requests. "Make sure the king knows that it is sent with my respect and admiration. I hope the messenger is still here?" She seals the letter and addresses it with a large italic H and R on the front.

"I presume so," I reply. "Agnes will have taken care to see that he has been fed well before he sets back on the road."

She sighs, though it sounds more like a groan. "Do not tarry – the king does not like to be kept waiting!"

Ten

July 31st, 1526 – Hever Castle

We are still at Hever, with Jayne Fool having remained at court under the watchful eye of the queen's household, as a temporary measure. The king's gifts and letters now arrive for Anne almost daily. She and I are alone in the gardens and the sun is high, flittering light across the surface of the moat as we emerge from the orchard, whose branches are now covered in baby apples. We hurry past the stable block, across the solid wooden bridge that connects the castle to the forest and the rich hunting grounds and marshland beyond the trees. Laughing together, we try to hold our skirts high so as not to soil them. It would not be seemly for us to show our ankles but no one sees us, as the family is busy inside. The Boleyns have a visitor – the king.

I imagine Sir Thomas is taking personal care of Henry, discussing the pile of petitions he has on his desk from France, or maybe they debate the latest court politics. Or perhaps the king is wondering where Boleyn's younger daughter might be. I imagine Mary arriving in his presence with a deep curtsy, explaining that Anne and I are taking air in the garden. How long will it be before he comes to find us?

I hesitate for a moment, looking about, but she takes my arm, leading me beyond the moat to the east of the castle, through to the formal gardens. With our skirts still gathered, we move as fast as we can along the path, down three short, stone steps, and through the arch in a mature yew hedge, cut many years before and maintained in pristine condition. We find ourselves in the secluded privacy of the flower garden. This is where we want to be, away from the chaos of the house, while the locksmith fits the king's personal locks to almost every door.

Whenever Henry stays in a courtier's country house, he makes it his business to have the main doors and his bedchamber door fitted with his own gilt locks, so he feels secure. It seems he is afraid of being assassinated. Not only that but most of the residents of the castle have been turfed out of their usual rooms, to accommodate his entourage. Where there is no space in the castle, some courtiers will reside at Penshurst, while others will stay in the nearby village. The bedchamber Mary gave birth to her children in has now been refurbished for the king's personal use. Apparently, Henry Norris and George will be sleeping on palate beds at the foot of the four-poster – I'm not sure George will find that comfortable. His mother and father will stay in the bedchamber next to the king, and Jane Boleyn is apparently staying in Anne's bedchamber, with us!

I found it fascinating earlier, watching the locksmith fit the lock to the Great Hall door. The latch has a smiling face on its surface, the engraving crisp, sharp, and brand-new. During my modern visits to Hever, the gilt lock is still in situ, yet the smiling face is worn – almost smooth – from the touch of many a tourist and visitor over the years.

The kitchen is a riot of steam and smells, with the few servants trying to keep up with the king's requests. In stark contrast, the gardens are in full bloom, the fragrance so heavy and sweet it stops us in our tracks. We find the stone bench where Henry and I once sat. It's a quiet corner, and we can bask in the sun whilst getting drunk on the colours and perfumes of nature. A stone fountain cascades water into a small pond at the centre of the garden, which is the only sound breaking the peaceful tranquillity of our secret spot. This little flower garden is set back from the main castle, and the sounds of Boleyn life, thrown into turmoil by the king's unexpected visit, do not intrude.

I walk deeper into the rose garden, towards the fountain, leaving Anne sitting on the bench re-reading Henry's latest letter, which she has plucked from her neckline. How I would love to hear her thoughts on the contents of his missives.

It seems that, as far as Henry is concerned, his romance with Anne is well under way. When will he offer her the position of maîtresse en titre? I hope I get to witness her rejecting him, which I know she will. I'm so lucky to be in such a unique position, to witness these events as they happen. I have so much knowledge about the events surrounding them, but I struggle to recall sometimes how things will pan out – I can't always remember every tiny detail. Anne will protest her honour, which she will declare will only be given to her future husband. Hmm, is she consciously playing hard to get, or is it the treatment of her sister by Henry that makes her hesitate? From spending time with her, I know she is no fool. The woman has seen her sister used and discarded, married off to a younger son with no titles, and, in her own case, Cardinal Wolsey quashed her first love of Lord Henry Percy, without sentiment, possibly on Henry's orders. She felt worthy of being a duchess through an advantageous marriage to him, but her plan of the heart was thwarted, possibly by the man who is wooing her now. I think of her and Henry, knowing she will never be his mistress, and, frankly, I do not blame her.

Whispered voices pull my attention back behind me, and I realise Anne is conversing with someone. Before I turn to see who it is, two hands cup my eyes, and hot breath sweeps across the back of my neck, sending delightful shivers through my shoulders.

"Beth, sweetheart, guess who it is!'

I take a quiet, deep breath, determined to remain calm, and turn to look at him as he removes his hands from my eyes. He grabs my wrist and pulls me to a hidden corner, beneath a large tree. I'm up against its trunk, and he is as close as a man can get – there's no mistaking his masculine excitement. He nuzzles into me, planting whispering kisses on my neck, then brushes his mouth against mine, light at first but then forceful, passionate, his tongue slipping deep – probing. He is beginning to make a habit of this, and I am beginning to like it.

"George, stop it!" I whisper, trying to push his hands away from my breasts. "Someone will see us."

"I do not care!" He takes my bottom lip between his teeth, pressing into me against the coarseness of the dark bark. "I gave Anne back her letter, and you owe me a kiss!"

"George, that was a few weeks ago, and I did not say I'd kiss you!" He grinds himself against me, hitting the mark. The man knows his stuff.

"Do not deny me – you know you want to kiss me!" He bites my cheek, soft and wet, the percussion of his growl vibrating through my skull. Against my better judgement, I close my eyes and rest my head against the tree, succumbing to the moment. He brushes his lips against mine again, then meets them with real passion, his kiss hot and probing.

"Please…stop!" I moan, easing him away, when all I really want is to drag him deeper into the shadows.

"I can't help myself," he says, closing the distance again. His breath is warm in my ear as he grinds into me, running his hands over my stiff bodice, cupping and kissing my cleavage in a flurry of activity that has me lost to anything but what is happening between us. "I have wanted you since the first moment you arrived here at Hever. I have tried to show you often enough!"

His hot lips brush mine again before his next kiss engulfs me. It's like I'm hanging from his gorgeous tongue, and I don't want to let go. His hands find my bottom and he pulls me hard against him. I take a sharp breath, visions of what might come next filling my head. But a noise from the other side of the garden brings reality crashing in, and I remember we are not alone. My eyes snap open on hearing the king's voice, and it's coming closer. I break free from George's grasp, even though it's the last thing I want to do. He steps back, showing no remorse.

"George, you have a wife!" I say, brushing my dress down. As much as I want to be with him, Jane doesn't deserve such treatment.

"Yes, a wife whom my father forced on me," he whines, his face screwed up. Right then, I wish I could alleviate his suffering.

From the shadows of our hiding place, I see Henry VIII, King of England, less than six metres away, standing before Anne, who is in a deep curtsy. He is a magnificent sight, dressed in the fine fabrics I am familiar with from his portraits. The man is so handsome, and still trying to hold on to the flush of his youth. His hands, as usual, are covered in a myriad of rings, and on the little finger of his left hand, he wears the ring Anne sent to him. He is resplendent with diamonds, rubies, and other precious stones, which glisten in the sunshine. I nearly have to pinch myself to be sure that I'm really here witnessing this. The man stands like a proud peacock, towering above Anne – near twice the size of her slight frame. He is sporting the same gold collar I've seen him wearing so many times before. I'm thankful that all his focus is on her, so he doesn't sense his hidden audience. Today, his complexion is fair but flushed around his cheeks. As always, his jawline is chiselled, and his eyes are like pools of bright blue as he follows my friend's every movement.

I shake my head in disbelief as I watch him. He looks tame, like a lapdog, and shows no anger or ferocity – attributes by which he will later be recognised. His mouth spreads into a huge, warm smile when Anne laughs, and his face radiates love and unrequited passion as they walk arm in arm in our direction. It didn't take him long to get over me – he must have been in lust with me, not in love, as I suspected. Men, how little they have changed.

At that moment, I know I have to prompt George to reveal our presence, but he pulls me away, deeper into the shadows, wanting to spy on the two lovebirds a while longer. Anne carries herself ably in Henry's company, her chin held high, smiling at her suitor. From the look of her, you wouldn't think she held any unkind thoughts towards him.

"Your Majesty is most welcome back at Hever. It is indeed an honour for us that you should visit us again, and so soon."

"It is no surprise what the king returns for!" George whispers through a raspy giggle.

"Shush! I'm glad it's not me!"

"Is this not our fault? Is this not what you wanted?"

"Yes, but perhaps your Uncle had a say in it too? Did you not suggest to him to have a word with the king?" I glare at him but can't hold back a soft chuckle.

"I did, but stop laughing!" he says. "They will hear you."

I'm glad that, finally, this couple seem to be promising themselves to one another – or maybe my assumptions are premature. Despite this, I'm happy to be here, witnessing this significant moment. We watch as Anne continues to captivate him, cocking her head to the side with a playful look.

"Perhaps Your Majesty left something precious behind after your last visit?"

He roars with laughter. "Oh, Anne, you are a tease. I swear, I thought Mistress Wickers to be appealing, intelligent, spirited, and courageous, but she is nothing compared to the likes of you!"

Humph. I can't believe he just said that. George glances at me, his lips pressed tight to keep his laugh silent.

"He knows you not as I do, does he, Beth?"

Anne is now looking straight ahead, giving Henry no inkling that she is pleased with the compliment. He moves in closer, holding her gaze as he takes her tiny hand in his and brushes the backs of her fingers with his lips.

"Anne, mine own sweetheart, it is true, I did forget something. And I have come to put it right."

"What do you need to correct, my Lord?"

"I want to say something to you – something serious."

I nudge George. "It is unfair to witness this conversation – should the king see us, we will be in trouble." I grip his hand, knowing there's nowhere else in this world or time I'd rather be.

"Shush, Beth. Our plan appears to be working!" He smiles and focuses back on the couple. "I want to hear what the king has to say."

"If it pleases you to be my true mistress and friend, for you to give yourself up to me body and soul, I promise I will take you as my only mistress. I will not have a thought or affection for anyone else. If you agree to be my maîtresse en titre, I promise I shall serve only you."

He stands before her like a statue as she frees her arm from his. I hold my hand over my mouth, stifling a giggle at hearing him saying the same words to Anne as he once did to me – in this very garden!

"'Maîtresse en titre' – your official mistress?" she says, brushing a loose strand of hair from her face.

"Yes, Anne. Then, I will make you a promise – and you will have everything you need." Does she think he's persuasive? "I will make sure that everything that is within my power to give, I promise, it will be yours. All you need do, is ask me." He stands resolute before her but his expression changes when she glares back at him, clearly upset by his persistence.

"What is it?" he asks.

"Your Majesty, I cannot believe you would ask this of me!" She scowls. "You used my sister, and you propositioned my friend, Mistress Wickers, in much the same way as you are doing to me now. What makes you think you can treat me like this?" She turns away, no doubt aware of the confusion on his face. I'm shocked by what she's said, landing me in it after Henry specifically asked me not to tell anyone about his propositioning me. This could backfire on me. God, no, I hope I'm not in trouble with him.

"Tell me what fault I have committed," he says. "Tell me!" he shouts, making her turn back to face him.

"Your Majesty, you use the ladies of the court – you do not truly love them." I can't believe she dares to say such a thing to him. What a woman.

"I will not be a mistress to anyone – I have already pledged my maidenhead into my husband's hands."

He stares at her, dumfounded. I wonder if, at this moment, he's reminded of my refusal of him. I'm only glad that my mission is on point – it has taken enough effort. Anne begins to pace the gravel path, her skirts swishing after her with every forthright step.

"And whoever my husband will be, Your Majesty, only he will have my virginity!" Her cheeks redden as her temper grows. "I will be no mistress," she insists. "I have seen your eyes wandering, My Lord, wishing first to have Mistress Wickers, and now, after her refusal of you, you want me? But I am not for conquering, like my sister, because it is a husband I will win."

That's it, Anne, dump me in it with the king – again!

He groans in dismay. "Oh, Anne!"

"No, Your Majesty, because I know how things will go otherwise. Whispers swirl around my sister, who is called a whore by the whole court!"

He tries to take her hand, but she pulls away. "I'm sorry if I have offended you, Mistress Anne. That was not my intention. I have spoken plainly this day of my true feelings for you."

With that, we watch aghast as he turns on his heel and storms out of the rose garden, leaving her standing alone, calling after him as he ducks beneath the arbour and strides back towards the castle.

George and I run to her.

"Anne, Anne, are you all right?" I ask. She looks startled when George grabs her hands.

"Sister, we heard all that the king said!"

I want her to look up, so I can see her face up close, to see the emotions behind her dark eyes, but before I can, she breaks away and almost runs along the gravel path, heading back into the castle, probably to prepare for the afternoon's hunt.

We follow, and are only in the door when Lady Boleyn sweeps Anne and me away and up to Anne's bedchamber. Hunting attire has been laid out around the bed for our inspection and approval. Agnes strips Anne of her shimmering green gown and dresses her for the hunt. Anne's mother starts to unpin my bodice but I face her, protesting that I would be no good on the hunt and that I will stay here in the house until they return.

"Please come with me," Anne begs. "I don't want to be alone with the king!"

"Child, do not be foolish – your father goes with you."

I nod. "I would prefer to stay here, Anne."

"If you are sure, Beth?" She slips on her leather riding gloves. This time, she wears a kirtle of lightweight wool, lined with linen, and trimmed along its edge with dark-brown velvet, overlaid by a dark-brown English gown of satin. It's stunning, and once again I almost have to pinch myself to be sure that I'm witnessing everything. The sleeves are puffed out with fakings at the top, gathered at the elbow, with narrow, velvet sleeves run close-fitting to her wrists. If my costume designer friend Gina could see this now, her eyes would pop. This outer gown is beautifully decorated with a trim of black-velvet ribbon, edged in gold cord, and fastened at the front with jewelled anglets, with a black-silk sash tied about her waist. I'm getting used to watching her being dressed and fussed over like some Barbie doll. However, preparing herself is no small task, as the intricacies of the many eyelets, hooks, and lacings that draw our dresses together are not something to be attempted alone.

While she waits for Agnes to complete her task, the hubbub of the castle carries on around us, alive with anticipation. The clatter of hooves reaches us through the open window, as fresh horses are brought in from the stables beyond the outer courtyard.

Agnes comes forward, holding out a pair of leather riding boots. I support Anne while she slips each one onto her stockinged feet. Agnes steps back, smiling as she admires her handiwork.

"I think you be ready, Mistress Anne."

I follow Anne down the stairs and out into the inner courtyard, where the king and his company await, impatient to be away. It is some spectacle. The horses are bedecked with fine leather saddles, set off with polished fittings. Simon, the stable boy, and several of the king's groomsmen, hold onto the reins of two or three horses each, as the men, including Henry Tudor, are assisted into their saddles. Anne is escorted to her ride, her beautiful, dark Irish Draught horse. It's an Irish breed, not like ones imported from the European continent today.

A strong-looking groom steps forward and offers her his locked hands, into which she places her foot. She is slim and lifts without issue into the saddle, whereupon she turns the horse and looks delighted to be sat on her favourite steed, knowing he is responsive to her touch. It isn't long before she finds herself at Henry's side; their earlier conversation apparently forgotten. He lifts his right arm and motions for the riding party to prepare to set off. The royal standard, carried by a lone rider, flutters in the breeze behind Henry and Anne, whilst the escort of armed guards, grooms, courtiers, and servants, fall in behind.

"Thank you," I hear Anne say.

Henry is impertinent, taking her hand and kissing it. He looks back at me. "'Tis a pity, Mistress Wickers, that you do not join us in the hunt!" He then turns back to Anne. "Mistress Anne, now we are complete." He shows no hint of his earlier hurt. "Let us away and tarry no more!" He looks around, then leans in. "And you shall ride by my side, sweetheart. I do not want you out of my sight." He laughs out loud. "How do you propose to ride safely, Mistress Anne, without a man to hold on to?"

"As you do, Your Majesty – I am a skilled rider!" She smiles. I'm unable to hold back a laugh as Henry stares at her, half in disbelief and half in admiration.

"Well, Mistress Anne, let us enjoy the hunt, and may our efforts be fruitful."

The entire party consists of the king, Anne, Sir Thomas, George, and others of Henry's household. He has decided on an intimate group, and since they are his close companions and confidants, I'd likely know many of them from my history books, but it is impossible to guess who is whom, from where I stand.

After my dalliance with George in the rose garden, I have to keep my wits about me, and keep my mouth shut, too, because, if it gets out about us, there could be hell to pay, especially with Jane Boleyn as a guest of her in-laws. As Anne rides out of the inner courtyard, all eyes turn towards her. She always has this effect on people when she enters or leaves company. This, no doubt, adds to the intoxicating allure of her presence where Henry is concerned. As I walk back to the hallway entrance, I notice George throwing a wistful look over his shoulder, smiling at me, probably wishing I'd attend the hunt with him. He knows I wouldn't be able to keep up. I'm thankful my riding accident has given me all the excuses I need not to be included. The party sweeps away on a tide of hooves over the drawbridge, with several hounds, including Griffin, weaving their way amongst them.

Eleven

31ST JULY 1526, HEVER CASTLE

To take my mind off the excitement of the king's visit, I go to find Jane, who I discover sitting embroidering in the parlour. Her little lapdog raises his head and wags his tail as I enter the room.

"Good day, Jane. Did you not want to join the hunt?" I pull the empty chair close to the fire grate, where a plate of sliced bread and cheese sits on a small table.

"No, Mistress Wickers," she snaps. I get the feeling she doesn't want my company. "I am afraid I am not good in the saddle, and do not hunt. George fairs well on horseback and it appears the king likes his company, as well as that of Mistress Anne." She lays her embroidery in her lap, then picks up the plate of bread and cheese, offering it to me.

"Thank you," I say, taking a slice of bread and a lump of cheese. "How are you, Jane?"

She ignores me as she resumes her embroidery, the crisp dark thread creating a spiralling pattern of swirls and flowers.

I nibble at the bread and cheese, the fire crackling through the awkward silence. "Why do you ignore me?"

"I like you not!"

"Why not?"

"You know why – you are far too familiar with the Boleyns, and with the king." She stares hard at me. "I am watching you. I warned you not to come back. I thought you might have heeded that."

"I'm sorry. I know you do not like my closeness to your in-laws, but they like me – I try to be friendly to you, for their sake, as well as mine."

"You are far too friendly with my husband, for my liking!"

I feel as if I should get up and leave her but maybe I should make an effort, for George's sake.

"What are you sewing?"

"A handkerchief for my *husband*." She looks up from her work. For a second, her gaze cuts through me. Hmm, perhaps she has her suspicions about me and George. I hope not. By the way she looks at me, and knowing how sharp a woman's intuition is, I bet I'm not far off the mark.

"He will like that, I'm sure. May I have a look?" She hands me the linen. "That is exceptionally fine. George will be impressed by such beautiful work."

"I doubt it, Mistress Wickers. Nothing I do is ever good enough for George Boleyn." She sighs, takes her work from me, then shoves the needle into the linen. "Why did you leave court abruptly? You did not return to my in-laws for such a time. Was it that you heeded my warning when I told you to leave?"

I can't believe she dares to come right out with what's on her mind. Then again, why wouldn't she be curious? One moment I was there, the next I was gone, for two years. I try to compose myself, hoping to steer the conversation positively so as not to arouse suspicion.

"My father was ill – I had to go home to help my mother look after him."

"Ah." She nods. "Very convenient for you, was it not, to flee court when the corridors were awash with rumours of you and his majesty?"

"Not really. Besides, you know the king and I are only friends!"

She releases a nervous laugh. "Unlike you and my husband!"

"You do George a disservice, speaking of him that way."

"My husband does not treat me as a husband should. I know he does not love me – I don't think he ever has, or if he ever will. I believe his heart is elsewhere." Her eyes have fire in them, and it's not just reflected flames from the grate.

"Again, Jane – I say to you, that, like his majesty, George is a friend of mine, and has been for a long time, since before you knew him."

She says nothing and sighs again, stabbing the linen harder as her frustration grows, until the thread tangles in her lap. If George is as promiscuous as history suggests, then it is no wonder she is utterly miserable. However, I have never encouraged him – he always comes on to me.

I finish the last piece of bread and wipe the crumbs from my gown. "Perhaps you try too hard, Jane. I do not mean to pry but maybe a Boleyn baby is what you both need."

"A baby?" She laughs, almost hysterically. "George rarely lies with…me." Her words catch and I suspect that she's lying. "Unless he begins to show me some affection, a Boleyn baby will be the last thing we share."

"As I said before, give him some time. I am sure he will find pleasure in your marriage soon. I have been away for some time – you cannot blame me for the failures of your marriage!" Maybe I shouldn't have said that, but I couldn't help myself. I wonder if she has fallen pregnant before and lost her babies. Perhaps that's where their problems lie in their marriage, apart from George wanting his way with me.

"Your existence is everything I blame for George barely showing me affection. We were starting to get along while you were gone." She frowns. "Even though you are back, it matters not because Lady Boleyn has given me advice on my marriage and I intend to make it work, even though I know George often finds pleasure elsewhere. He is known throughout court as being a rogue with women, bedding them and leaving them."

"Jane, that is unfair on George. I'm sure that he does not bed as many women as you suggest."

"Perhaps, but it upsets me that he never pays me the attention I deserve as his wife." She continues with her sewing, maybe wishing this conversation had never started. I feel sorry for the girl, knowing I'm partly to blame for her unhappiness because, if George was not in love with me, then maybe he'd pay his wife more attention. I have to remember, it's not my fault he knew me before her. Perhaps if I hadn't time-slipped, her situation would be content – but then, the history books have never decided either way if she was ever happy in her marriage. I need to forget about it – Jane's marriage is the least of my worries.

"Would you like me to leave you to your own company?"

"Yes, I would." She simmers as I get up to leave. I'll return to Anne's chamber, and wait for the hunt to arrive home.

The house comes alive again and, outside, horses' hooves clatter over the drawbridge and into the inner courtyard. I rush to a gallery window, delighted to see the king wrap his hands about Anne's waist and help her dismount from her horse. Her torso brushes against his before her feet touch the cobbles. For a few moments, she chats with him, then curtsies and hurries through the inner hallway door. I nearly run out but hold myself back to a fast walk, meeting her at the top of the stairs. She gushes at me, blurting out the delights of the hunt from the second she walks into her bedchamber, and continues talking ten to the dozen as Agnes helps her out of her hunting gear.

"We set out at a brisk trot, down a deserted lane that heads towards the forest," she explains. "It was hot by then." She pulls the pin from her hat and hands her headgear to Agnes, who gawps at her as she relays her experience of the hunt. "Our party passed only a few onlookers as we made our way along but those we did pass recognised the royal standard, and the exalted position of the noblemen, and all doffed their caps and bowed low." Her face is alive as she imitates their bows, then pulls off her gloves.

"I smiled down at them, but the few assembled would not meet my gaze. When we entered the forest, it grew much cooler than the open countryside. I even caught sight of a red squirrel darting across the boughs above our heads, and rabbits disappearing into the undergrowth."

"What was the king like, Anne?" I ask as I sink into a chair by the hearth.

"Henry," she says, in a familiar manner, "turned to his huntsman and began discussing the best direction to take in order to hunt down the best quarry.

He asked me to show him where to find the best chance of taking down a stag. Whereupon I directed him towards a path ahead and I galloped my horse down the winding track."

"You did what? You mean you went off riding without the king?"

"Yes, I did." She laughs. "At that moment, I did expect to hear Henry's thunderous roar call me back for my impudence and rudeness!"

"Anne, you probably scared his majesty half to death." I produce a mock grimace.

"I do not think his majesty would be scared of anything because…"—she sits on a chair opposite me, wincing as Agnes strains to pull her out of her muddy boots—"all I could hear was a swift crack of his whip against the flesh of his horse, and the king let out a 'HA!' and drove forward in hot pursuit, joining me in the chase. I do not know if it was the stag he was chasing, or if it were me!" She giggles. "I know it was a dangerous thing to do, to ride so recklessly, but I was showing off!"

Her boldness will always define her, and I admit that hearing of the hunt is exhilarating – I almost wish I'd gone with them now. I try to imagine what the experience would have been like, with the wind whipping past my cheeks, the mud being kicked up in my face, and my full skirts billowing around my legs. What would it be like riding a side-saddle in such a situation? I did it that time with George so I'm sure I would have coped. A giggle almost escapes at the thought that the only thing he wants me to mount… is him. The blood rushes to my cheeks, and I deflect her attention from it by breaking into a broad smile.

"Tell me more, Mistress!"

"With the king galloping to reach me, the entire party began following us, but not one courtier could keep up with Henry and me as we rode along the track, mud and dust thrown up in our wake. When he finally grabbed the reins of my horse, bringing us to a stop, I was afraid, as I thought him angry at my brazen behaviour."

"Oh, Anne, I hope you have not disappointed the king."

"Do not worry, he quickly allayed my fears, raising his arm to halt the rest of our party."

"Oh? And then what happened?"

She giggles, then tells me that Henry turned to her, placed his finger on his lips and urged her to silence. He let go of her reins and pointed ahead.

"I lifted myself in my saddle, and there before us was a magnificent stag, some way in front of us, at the edge of a clearing."

"Did you chase it?"

"Of course. Our arrival alerted the stag to our presence, and it was eyeing our group. Henry reached for his bow and arrow but the animal spooked and leapt forward into the thicket. Then we chased it!" She claps once, her eyes lighting up. "The king spurred his horse forward with a loud battle cry, the hounds racing along beside us, Griffin included! I followed the king and we ducked along the path, hurtling through the forest, and the chase went on for fifteen or twenty minutes before the stag tired, and began to slow. The hounds brought the creature down, tearing at its flesh."

I grimace. "I can do without the gory details, thank you very much."

"Do not worry yourself. The king jumped from his horse to inspect the stag, which was dying, and directed one of his huntsmen to come forth to finish off the beast. Most of our number dismounted and gathered around the dead stag, congratulating Henry on his prowess and skill."

"And George and your father, what did they make of the hunt?"

"Father had drawn up his horse beside me, some way back from the fallen stag, which gave him the chance to ask me what the king had spoken of in the rose garden. I think George may have said something to him." She frowns. "I tell you, I nearly shared everything! I am surprised my father does not yet know of Henry's intentions towards me. Up until half an hour ago, only you and George knew the truth of it, but after George obviously confided in him, I felt it my duty to reveal the king's desire to father. I told him that Henry is questioning his marriage to Katharine, and that he seeks a new entertainment and has asked me to be his maîtresse en titre. Father flew into a fit of ruddy anger, which he was hard-pressed not to show. I explained to him that I turned down the king's offer and sent back gifts he had sent me before."

"Did he calm himself?"

"Yes, he did. Thank God! I think he was rather impressed with my resolve."

Surely the idea of Anne being the king's mistress would distress her dad no end. From what I know of Thomas, I expect he's relieved that she turned him down. It's not like he needs to elevate his family further.

"What was his reply?"

"Father was shocked. He had hoped that Mary might continue being the king's mistress, and that eventually, it would be the making of her, despite the fact he had never wanted her in the king's bed. I confessed to him that this showering of gifts and letters from the king has left me puzzled, and I am unsure exactly how to proceed. I told him I had sent the king one of my rings and have noticed Henry wearing it on his little finger today."

"Do not let your uncle sway you father to push you into anything," I say. "I know your father will be protective of you, but I can't speak for Thomas Howard."

"I will not let my uncle persuade me to do anything I do not want. I will do as I wish. You heard me tell the king that I will not be his new mistress for anyone."

Listening to her, I wish I could save her life, take her through the portal and away from her Tudor world. I'm in an impossible situation – a witness who is personally involved.

She scrunches her toes and sighs. "Perhaps I should set my sights a little higher and make it my destiny to provide a lineage of kings." Her eyes sparkle as she realises the meaning behind her words. I gulp, wondering what has changed her mind on the matter.

"That would not be a bad idea!" I laugh, and she stares at me.

"I know you will not tell me whom you think I am to marry, and I know it crazy for it to ever be the king, but would it not be a wonder if I should gain myself a country for God as well as a crown and good fortune?"

Is she joking? – I can't tell. "But you refused the king's offer today of being his only mistress. Whatever makes you think he will ask you to be his wife? He already has a wife."

"Beth, you must keep my thoughts a secret. No one, not even my brother, must know."

"Know what?" I lean back and invite her to continue.

"If I suggest to the king that the only way I will be his…is if he marries me."

Agnes's eyes are out on stalks, hanging on every word as she helps Anne out of her muddy gown.

"He will then leave me alone because there is no way he will divorce Queen Katharine, and there is no way he will be able to make me his wife!" She laughs. Agnes looks at her in astonishment, flabbergasted that the king has taken a fancy to her mistress. I smile and roll my eyes, realising that my friend is eventually going to get exactly what she thinks she won't.

Agnes helps her step out of her kirtle, then begins drawing her a bath. Anne stands there, her linen shift creased about her tiny form, I imagine as a result of the perspiration from the horse-riding. She sits, unties her garters, and removes her stockings, watching Agnes and Mrs Orchard struggle with the large pales of warm water.

"Do you think my plan will not work?"

"It may work," I reply, the lie coming easy. "If you were Queen of England, at least you would be able to use the king's Turkish bath!" I laugh. Agnes looks at me in disbelief, almost spilling the hot water over the floor. Whatever she hears, she keeps it all inside and goes about her business. She must remember my midnight visit to the king two years ago but has never mentioned it.

Anne shrugs. "How do you know the king has a Turkish bath?" My eyes widen and I stare at her.

"Sorry, I forgot." She carries on, and Agnes suspects nothing. "Yes… a bath with piping-hot water might be a godsend, but perhaps my desire to have the king ask me to be his wife might be another, and one way of rebuffing him gently." She stretches out her toes. "He would never divorce his wife – Rome would never allow it!"

"Have you not thought that perhaps God would want you to be Queen, so you might steer the Catholic Church to reform, so it becomes more like the new faith?"

Agnes's empty bucket clatters to the floor, her mouth open in shock. "Ladies, you be heretics saying such words as that!" She passes the bucket to Mrs Orchard, who scurries from the bedchamber in her usual fashion. Anne slips off the shift and tests the water, nods to herself, then steps in and sinks below the surface, her shoulders just covered by the rose petals Agnes has added.

"Agnes, don't worry – it's just words."

"People have their hearts cut out for less than that." She scowls as she picks up her mistress's riding clothes from the floor, shaking her head to herself as she leaves the room in a huff.

"If I am as important to Henry as he says I am then he will move heaven and earth to make me his queen!" She smiles, sinking right below the waterline, letting the excess water and rose petals spill over onto the floor. Her long, wet hair is plastered against her scalp when her head breaks the surface. "Besides, sweet Beth, he will not be able to carry out such a feat. I would never be Queen – the world would never let it be."

My face burns at that comment, and I hope to God she doesn't notice. I bite my lip, knowing that I simply can't let slip details of the history I know – I remember the professor telling me I could inform Anne that she'll marry Henry, to get things moving, but I'm scared if I do that, everything will be ruined.

Anne has a spirit worthy of a crown, but I can't tell her that. Thankfully, despite the king initially showing interest in me, history is making its own way around to where it should be, and I didn't have to meddle, that much! I heave a silent sigh of relief and lay my head against the chair, eyes closed as I listen to the birds chirping in the orchard beneath the window. For now, all seems right with this world – Anne's world.

Later, as I help her dress, ladder-lacing her into her kirtle, I think of the constraints both her family and the king will put on her in later years. It's easy to forget my own problems, being concerned in this moment for Anne only.

"Tell me, why have you changed your way of thinking?" I ask, giving the laces one last tug and knotting them into place before tucking them into the sides of her bodice.

"About the king? Nothing has changed, Beth. I want a husband and will not be a mistress – that is all. I know the king will never get an annulment." She raises a brow. "Rome will never allow a king to divorce. I want to be a happy duchess, at least. I know I could never be a queen."

I guide her arms into her overgown, running the situation through my head. Today marks a change, where she thinks her plan will get rid of her king. Little does she realise that she will plunge not only a kingdom into turmoil but her own life. I can't meddle, even though I want to, and it torments me that I can't prevent her blood and the blood of so many others from flowing on her account. My mission is for history to achieve its goal. The end result has to be the one that I already know.

At dinner, the king shares with the Boleyns the intricacies of what will become his 'Great Matter'. He explains to Sir Thomas that he has asked his advisors to explore the best way to approach the possibility of an annulment. Anne keeps her own council. She has told me she will wait until the time is right to plant ideas in the king's mind about making her his wife. At least she realises that destroying his interest in her will not be an easy path to walk. There will be twists and turns beyond her current knowing but I will always be here to support her, come what may. I hope so, anyway. She hopes to marry a duke because she thinks Katharine will never agree to a divorce. I dare not tell her that it will happen, eventually – she would never believe me. Would she? No, I can't divulge such details. She will need all her strength to get through this, and it won't help if I muddle the situation with information that might change her way of thinking. Things won't pan out as she hopes, and events will not run smoothly. When the queen is commanded to leave court, and her marriage bed, she will not go quietly. It will take all of Anne and Henry's love, when they get to that point, to stay together.

She needs pushing to return to court, to be by his side, to make sure he will always desire to be close to her. However, Henry flaunting his younger, charismatic mistress-to-be right under the nose of the older queen is not the way she wants to play things.

We discuss the events of the day as we prepare for bed. "Anne, you know courtiers will be jealous of your good fortune because the king declares his love for you."

It feels strange, knowing that Henry is under the same roof, doing the same thing. Voices carry down the passageway outside, and I realise that the king is talking to Norris outside his bedchamber. He's ordering George about, too. I lay on the bed in my shift, my stomach bloated after the delights of supper. Henry has been gracious to Sir Thomas and Elizabeth Boleyn this evening, and he even enjoyed being in the company of George, who he promises he will elevate to a man of his privy chamber soon. His attentions were directed mostly at me and Anne, with whom he spent the evening complimenting and promising the fruits of favour, if we would just return to his court. Anne was witty, which made him laugh and revel even more in her company. I, for one, have never seen him so happy, and the rest of the family have noticed his jovial mood.

During the dinner, I caught him gazing longingly at Anne's pretty bosom, and, at one point, letting free what I can only describe as a low growl. The whole table heard him, even Sir Thomas, who grimaced behind his linen napkin. Later, Henry looked downcast seeing Anne and me walking up to bed – probably wishing it was him in her bedchamber, not me! I thought he would be guarded with his emotions but it was evident to see, concerning his lusts for her, that he had no control at all. As he said goodnight, I watched him looking deep into my friend's eyes with such passionate longing, I had no doubt, if he could take his opportunity, he would lead her to the bedchamber to have his way with her.

I'm so happy the situation is beginning to play out as it should. However, Anne is less obvious in demonstrating her emotions, only giving Henry the opportunity to present her with another velvet pouch containing a gift and, in their last moments together, allowing him to kiss her hand as he sat and played cards with Sir Thomas, George, Norris, and others. Jane had already gone up to prepare for bed, taking her lapdog with her.

I hope she's all right. Is she shocked with the latest proceedings with the king and the Boleyns? After all, she had once been angry with me when she thought I was coming between Henry and his wife. She was quiet tonight. Maybe, like me, she'd had too much to eat. Perhaps she retired early because she felt unwell.

As Anne gets into bed beside me, her little clock chimes midnight. The king is still talking to Norris on the landing, and now they've been joined by Sir Thomas, asking if everything is okay. I chuckle to myself, shaking my head in disbelief as I listen to their voices carry along the passageway. Men talk about women when they're alone together – that aspect of their characters doesn't change, no matter what period of history they live in.

"Norris – how do you flirt with a maid if you wish to gain her affections?" Henry asks. He has had too much wine, and his voice booms.

"Sir, there is nothing I can teach you in gaining any maid's affections. I would go as far as to say that you wrote the book. It is not for me to comment on your abilities with the ladies!" Norris sounds quite alarmed at being asked such a direct question.

"I cannot get the vision from my mind, of a maid's heaving bosom ripe for the plucking!"

"Sire, it is early morning and there will be no plucking tonight. It is time for you to go to your bed, alone. Stop these notions of young maidens' bosoms – you have a long day ahead!"

Unbelievable. To witness such chitchat between these historical figures. How must Anne feel, for she can surely hear it as well? Henry lets out the loudest chuckle I have ever heard. The drink has obviously got to him!

"Husband, will you not come to bed?" Lady Boleyn roars.

"Yes, wife!" Sir Thomas replies. "Gentlemen, I think it is a little late in the evening to talk of love, or women's breasts. I will bid you both good rest." He's trying to whisper but I think he has also had too much to drink. A moment later, a door slams.

Henry laughs. "There's a man who will be in his woman's bad books if he does not do his husbandly duty!"

Another door opens. "Your Grace, I have checked the bed for assassins, and for weapons."

"Good man, George!" Henry bellows.

"You take that arm," Norris says, "and I'll take this. He won't stumble if we guide him!"

The passageway echoes with grumbles and laughter as they carry the king to his borrowed bed.

I can't hold my amusement in.

"Why are you giggling?" Anne asks, tugging the coverlet over her shoulder.

"Nothing!" I lean over to blow the candle out.

"Do not sleep yet," she says, her voice a whisper in the darkness.

"I have no intention, I'm far too excited after that dinner."

"You did listen to what the king was saying, did you not?" she asks. "I could not believe what I was hearing!"

"I heard," I reply. "I think he was talking of your pretty duckeys."

"My breasts?" She shifts, and even in the gloom, lit by dim moonlight, I see her head tilted to one side. "Why would that be?"

"Did you not notice?" I ask. "During dinner, the king was transfixed by the sight of your heaving bosom!" I giggle again. "At one point, his eyes were almost crawling down your cleavage, and he let out a low growl – the whole table witnessed it."

"Good God!" She seems shocked at my forwardness. Hmm, maybe I went a bit too far. She turns over, and I snuggle into her back. A few seconds later, the mattress trembles as she gets a fit of the giggles, which spreads to me, and we both end up laughing out loud. Anne turns back over.

"Anne, we need to sleep!"

"My mind will not still – I keep thinking on my idea."

"Idea?" I jab my pillow to create a nook for my head.

"I am resolute in my idea of convincing the king to make me his wife." Her breathing is challenged from all the laughing. "He will never be able to make me his queen, but I will make sure I will always be his humble servant. That way, he will have to forget me."

"Ladies, please stop! All this talk be making me tired."

I sit up in shock, having forgotten that poor Agnes was asleep on her palette on the floor at the end of our bed. "Dear, Agnes, I do apologise."

"I be needing my rest!"

I turn over on my side, facing Anne. "If the king changes his mind and insists on you for his queen, you will offend the Duke of Suffolk for one, and there will be others: the Montagues, the De La Poles – those who are loyal to Katharine, as well as older families who will see the Boleyns as upstarts, reaching beyond their station. The only one who will see this alliance as a benefit is your uncle Norfolk. Without the leading nobleman in the land behind you, you will struggle. When you are queen, and have borne the king a son, your position will be unassailable. – that is the only time you will be untouchable, so until then, you need to be on your guard."

She shifts, staring at me through the gloom, taking each point with a simple nod. However, from her expression, I realise I may have said the wrong thing – perhaps she now realises who her husband will actually be.

"Mistress Anne and Mistress Beth," Agnes shouts, "I do not mean to be so rude, but would you both stop plotting, and goes to sleep?"

Anne and I look at each other, pull the sheet over our heads, and burst into hysterics. Through our laughter, I hear a tap on the bedroom door, and we both fall silent. Agnes sighs as she gets up. The flickering light from a lone candle floods the room. It's Jane Boleyn.

"Lady Boleyn told me to come and sleep in here with you."

Agnes lets her in, then returns to her pallet. Jane steps closer to the bed, sees me on the side closest to her, and walks around to where Anne is hiding under the sheet.

"Move over then, sister mine," she urges, placing the candle on the nightstand. Anne obliges, shifting into the middle of the mattress, forcing me to cling to the edge of the bed. How cosy.

I bite my lip and turn my back on my bed companions to discourage further chat. When I shut my eyes, mixed thoughts whirl through my mind. On the one hand, I want to witness this extraordinary life, watch Anne bask in the love, adoration, and affection of so mighty and charismatic a prince. On the other, I can't forget what I already know. Danger lurks where she sees potential from her rising glory. I know that, eventually, I will see and hear of enemies in shadows, and I feel helpless about how I can prevent that without changing history.

Twelve

Mid-December, Present Day – Twickenham, London

Modern life has its benefits, such as using social media to catch up with friends. Sometimes, when I'm 'away' in Anne's time, I miss the conveniences of driving my car and using my laptop. The closest thing the Tudors have to technology is the printing press – to them, it's their equivalent of the internet. George told me he thinks the printing press is a marvel. Anything new and modern to him, thrills him. How would he react to the digital age? I sometimes daydream about what it might be like to bring him through the portal and save him from his fate!

I've decided to go back home to my time, at least for a while, as Anne's fate appears to be on the right path. I also don't want to miss Christmas with my own family. Yes, I know the Boleyns will miss me – Anne and George more than the rest – but I'm homesick and need to go back to see my loved ones, and catch up with my friends, like Jessica, and others, including Rob. Then there's Professor Marshall. I need to check in with him, report on my mission's progress, and hand in those literature reviews that will be due before the end of term. It will be better if time hasn't jumped ahead too far – I don't want to have missed too much, or have my absence noticed to the extent that I have to create a credible explanation. It's not that I want to leave George or Anne, but I need to go back for my own peace of mind, and to see that I still can time-slip, and that I'm not stuck in the sixteenth century for the rest of my natural life.

My heart aches knowing how George feels about me, but he has Jane. She can try and comfort him, and perhaps the distance between us will do him good. Maybe I'm doing the right thing leaving now. Maybe it's the right time to step aside now that I've set Anne on the 'correct' path. I tried the portal, but it didn't work, so here I am now trying the ring at the same time. Maybe it will work fine, based on my need to get back? Or is it connected with my emotional state and the circumstances? I try not to think of the 'ins' and 'outs' of how it works.

I stand in the antechamber, alone. I've written letters for Anne and George this time, placing them on Anne's nightstand. The family has gone to visit the Wyatt's at Allington, which gave me the excuse to feign a headache to get out of going. I've explained to George and Anne separately in the letters that I've been summoned home by my parents. I know it's a lie but at least George knows about it from me, and this time I'm not leaving him without saying a word. I don't really want to go but, as I twist the cypher ring and it begins to heat up, I realise how long I've been away. I need to make sure my parents aren't worried, that the professor knows I'm okay and gets his report, and Rob knows I haven't dropped off the face of the earth, though I'm not too sure he's all that bothered.

As I've done previously, I think of the professor's office, and the date around when I was last there. It seems to work because the cypher ring heats up when I try the door through the portal, which opens, sending a flush of excitement through me, and I soon find myself back in the office without a rumble or a tumble. I look around at the familiar objects in the room: the desktop, with the piles of student essays stacked like the Leaning Tower of Pisa, awaiting his red pen. Anne Boleyn's NPG portrait still hangs on its spot on the wall, and she's still keeping tight-lipped. Having learnt my lesson, I've remembered to bring my canvas holdall with all those books and paperwork from my first ever time-slip experience. I also had the common sense to come back through the portal wearing my modern clothes. And I finally remembered to bring my mobile phone back, too.

I know Anne will hate that I've left her, but I had to return home, if only for a few days. She is always anxious that I won't return. To be honest, so am I. I'm never quite sure if the ring or the portal will work again. I made sure no one was around as I left; the last thing I want is to be followed. In my letter, I've tried to convince Anne that I'm missing my parents, my sister, and my friends. It isn't a lie. I came up with the excuse that I have to give my family some of the allowance her father has been paying me, and I've asked her to assure Sir Thomas that I had to show my pretend 'Tudor' family that my absence from them has been worth their while. It's the only excuse I could think of that would make my absence plausible. Anne knows, as I do, that duty is everything to her father, and he would understand my need to be dutiful to my own family.

My tummy flutters when I try the office door and realise that it's locked but I breathe a sigh of relief when I remember the spare key in his drawer. I look up at the clock on the wall. 5:00 PM – it's not too late, I will hopefully be early for tea with Mum and Dad.

End of Term – Present Day

The next morning, as I arrive at the university campus, it looks pretty with the light dusting of snow that fell overnight. Professor Marshall won't know that I'm back yet – I'm sure he'll be delighted with my academic work. At least everything looks normal. It's crazy because it turned out I was only gone a few hours. When I arrived home last night, Mum thought I'd been at college all day. My brain is scrambled thinking about the lack of time gone by here, especially when I've been away for five months in another time – *Tudorville*, as Rob jokingly calls it.

I walk through crowds of students, rubbing my eyes as I head towards the History department, having been up late finishing assignments for the end of the autumn/winter term. In the comfort of my bedroom, I analysed and critiqued the some of books on my reading list, so I'll be way ahead of my deadline for handing my work in after the Christmas holidays.

The notice board informs me that I have a lecture to attend. Professor Marshall has arranged for Dr Tracy Broman, the author and historian, to come and talk to all the early-modern history students.

I've just got here in time, with fifteen minutes to get myself settled before proceedings start. The Student Union Bar is awash with humanities' students, hanging around with blank notepads at the ready, chomping at the bit to be allowed access to the university's premier arts' lecture hall/theatre. I stand shoulder to shoulder with familiar faces as we filter through the doors to the large well-lit hall, with its excellent audio-visual facilities. It is typically used for prestigious events and visiting speakers during term time and is much sought after for conferences the rest of the year. I secure a central spot a few steps up the tiered seating system, placing myself amid the action. After fifteen minutes of hubbub, everything stills and the room is filled with buzzing anticipation.

Two chairs are set out on the stage, almost opposite each other, with a hand-held microphone resting on each one. I lean back in my seat, notepad ready, pen poised. Professor Marshall steps onto the stage, picks up his mic, and looks out into the intrigued audience.

"Good Morning!" He smiles. "Today we have a treat in store – Doctor Tracy Borman, curator of Historic Royal Palaces, author and historian, who has kindly agreed to pay us a visit to answer questions on the Tudors, and particularly on Thomas Cromwell."

He looks around, making eye contact here and there, then he spots me. The moment feels stretched but it's probably just me. He shrugs his brow at me, as if to say, 'I need to see you', then moves on.

"Once I have put my questions to Tracy, she has agreed to answer any you may think worthy to ask, so have them ready towards the end, please." He looks towards the entrance to check there are no latecomers, then back to us. "Without further ado, I'd like to welcome Doctor Tracy Borman, chief curator at Historic Royal Palaces, author and historian!"

A round of applause breaks out from the audience as she enters the hall and ascends the stage, where she lifts the microphone allotted to her. She is elegant and statuesque – a captivating character. We all watch as she taps the mic to check that it's working.

"Morning everyone!" She smiles. "I'd like to thank Professor Marshall for inviting me to come and speak with you all today, and hope that you will find this question and answer session informative." She glances at the professor, who invites her to take her seat.

"Tracy, I'd like to start by asking you what your general opinion of the Tudor period is."

"The Tudors were dazzlingly successful at not just restoring the authority of monarchy but also the mystique of monarchy. They created this division between the public and the private – appointed themselves as almost 'godly beings', so of course, everybody adored them. England was very much a sovereign state during the Tudor period – they reigned and ruled, and everybody respected their authority. There were also seismic changes during the sixteenth century: the reformation; the revolution in government – we were a vastly different country by 1603 to the one the Tudors inherited in 1485."

"Could this be called the beginning of the modern?" Professor Marshall asks.

"I think there is a transition during the Tudor period. At its beginning, England is still essentially a Medieval kingdom, though by its end it has been propelled into the beginnings of a Modern Age."

"How did the English economy and society change during this period, and with what effects?"

"Significant changes occurred in society and the economy, and there was a great deal more regionalisation, with devolution of power to local authorities, along with a strong central government. This period saw the beginnings of the Poor Laws." She leans forward on the arm of her seat. "Lots of records were kept locally – lots of sources that historians now rely on, thanks to the revolution of the Tudors."

"So how did Cromwell fit into these changes of the period?"

"As your students are probably aware, Thomas Cromwell came to the attention of Henry VIII through his chancellor, Cardinal Wolsey – I know your students have recently been studying the Cardinal." She looks up at us and smiles. "Thomas Cromwell's public image was quite different from the private man. His public image was one of a ruthless politician who would stop at nothing to get what he wanted, whereas the private man you would have wanted as a friend: he was warm, hospitable, and had a wicked sense of humour. And he would throw these amazing parties at one of his many houses, attracting people from all over the court. Even his enemies would admit he was great company." She looks towards us again, then back to Professor Marshall.

"What do you think makes Cromwell such an important character in Tudor history?"

"Cromwell came from nowhere to hold one of the greatest positions of power in Henry VIII's court." She crosses her legs as she nurses a book in her lap, the new edition of her study on Cromwell. "Admittedly," she continues, "there had been Cardinal Wolsey before him – he was also a lowly born minister – but Cromwell went even further than Wolsey. During the ten years that he was the king's chief advisor, he made truly revolutionary changes in government, religion, and society, and held more power than anyone else. But he also lost it quicker than anyone had before him."

Professor Marshall nods, then fixes his glasses on the bridge of his nose. "What do you think Henry VIII's relationship with Thomas Cromwell was like?"

As she responds, I scribble down some notes. Being reminded of these people, characters of the Tudor Court I've spent time with, evokes so many memories of my time there. Shadows of their faces cross my mind. I think of the time I sat with Henry in the rose garden at Hever, when he had his arm around me and was asking me to be his mistress. The time George took me horse-riding and I sprained my ankle. And when he kissed me – all the times we kissed– his close proximity, which always sent the most delicious waves through me; something I can't control when I'm with him. Just thinking of him has me squirming in my seat, and my cheeks burn at the memory of our clinch beneath the tree.

I struggle to focus on what's going on here, but I manage to follow the thread of it well enough. However, at times it's difficult not to raise my hand to object or contradict something that's been said. The trouble is, if I do contribute to the discussion, how can I reveal what I know to be the truth without being able to back it up? I shake my head.

"Henry VIII is well known for his tumultuous relationships with women, and he is often defined by his many marriages. But when we see Henry through the men in his life, a new perspective on this famous king emerges."

Professor Marshall raises both eyebrows. "What makes you come to that conclusion?"

"Henry's relationships with the men who surrounded him reveal much about his beliefs, behaviour, and character. They show him to be capable of fierce but seldom-abiding loyalty. Of raising men, only to destroy them later – which is certainly true of Cromwell." She brushes the cover of her book with her fingertips.

"Why do you think Thomas Cromwell made such an impression on the king?"

"Well, Professor, Henry loved to be attended and entertained by boisterous young men who shared his passion for sport, but at other times he was better diverted by men of intellect, culture, and wit. Often trusting and easily led by his male attendants and advisers during the early years of his reign, he matured into a profoundly suspicious and paranoid king, whose favour could be suddenly withdrawn, as many of his later servants found to their cost."

She flicks a strand of hair off her face as I continue to scribble down copious notes in my usual scrawl – hoping I'll be able to understand them at a later date.

"His cruelty and ruthlessness would become ever more apparent as his reign progressed, but the tenderness he displayed towards those he trusted proves that he was never the one-dimensional monster he is often portrayed as."

Professor Marshall leans forward. "What would be your one piece of advice for our students studying Cromwell?"

"Like Henry, Thomas Cromwell was not just a ruthless politician – a man who pushed through the reformation and destroyed the monasteries for his own personal gain – he was a multi-faceted personality: a family man – a gentle character – who also tried to change the lot of common folks, as well as the lives of the King and his nobility. Thomas Cromwell, despite his low birth, became a man of mark, who helped to create what we now know as a modern parliamentary system."

I continue scribbling, aware that this appears to be a quick interview.

"That's remarkably interesting. Thank you so much, Tracy!" Professor Marshall shakes her hand and looks up to us. "Can you promise us that you will come back again another time, and perhaps be able to offer us a longer session with you?"

She nods. "Of course, it would be my pleasure!"

"Can we all thank Doctor Borman for coming to see us today?"

A round of applause breaks out across the lecture hall, and Tracy smiles, a little embarrassed by our enthusiasm.

"Thank you, thank you so much!"

"Incidentally," Professor Marshall says into his mic, "Tracy has copies of her books on Cromwell, Henry VIII, Elizabeth I, and Crown and Sceptre, along with her historical fiction series, available for you to buy afterwards. They give you some useful ideas for Christmas presents, I think!" He laughs. "Tracy may even sign copies for you, if you ask nicely!" He raises both eyebrows at her. "Right, let's open the floor to questions?"

Hands fly up all over the place, and questions come from all corners of the hall, mostly on Thomas Cromwell, with some on the king, and one or two on Wolsey. As I scribble notes, I realise I haven't 'met' Cromwell in person as yet, having only seen the 'real man' in passing. Will I like him when we do meet? What might Tracy Borman say to him if she was in my shoes and had the ability to travel back to Tudor England? My mind jumbles with the possibilities.

When the question-and-answer session is over, I wait in line to pick up my copy of her book. Does she think 'her' Cromwell is the closest to the man history knows? What does she think of Hilary Mantel's fictional version? When my turn comes, I hand her a copy of her book from the pile beside her, and she takes it and opens it.

"Hello – lovely to see you! Who would you like me to sign it for?" She gives me an enthusiastic smile.

"Beth, please." She puts a sharpie to the inner title page, and the deed is done. "Tracy, I have a quick question."

"Yes?" She looks at me, probably expecting a mundane question she's answered many times before. The doctor won't get that from me.

"What would you say to Thomas Cromwell if you had the opportunity to time-travel and speak to him face to face?"

She taps her bottom lip with her marker, her eyebrows arched. "I would ask him if Anne Boleyn's destruction was his idea or Henry's." She hands me my signed copy and takes my cash.

"That's the question I would definitely want to know the answer to," I say.

"I hope you enjoy the book."

"I'm sure I will."

As I leave, I think about her answer to my question and wonder whether I will ever find out straight from the horse's mouth, so to speak. I put her book in my bag and walk out to the corridor. My stomach rumbles as I weave my way through the groups of chatting students on my way to the canteen.

A few minutes later, with a warm croissant and a large cup of tea, I look around for a place to sit. I find modern-technology noises disconcerting after being in Early-Modern England for so long. Will I have time to get used to it all again before my return? And how much time will have passed in Anne's life? I filter through the tables of chattering students, nursing my hot drink, and decide to find somewhere to sit in a covered area outside, near the Student Union Bar. It may be cold but I have my fur-trimmed coat on to keep me warm.

While the grounds only have a light dusting of snow, it's lovely to see, adding to the festive feel. The air is crisp and fresh, too. Much better than the stuffy atmosphere of the bar. I find a quiet spot under a canopy adjacent to the building, near a tree. It's nice here, with the tree's bare branches swaying in the gentle breeze. I pull out Tracy's book, flick to the title page where she wrote her signature, and appreciate the nice touch: *Dear Beth, fellow historian, and colleague. Best Wishes, Tracy Borman.*

"How nice is that!" I take a bite of my warm croissant, flick through to the first chapter, and begin reading. Shadows dance across the page as someone plonks themselves down next to me. I look up. It feels weird to see his face when I'm so used to looking at George's handsome features. Butterflies flip in my stomach but not as much as they used to. Being with George has changed things. It's not that I'd forgotten about Rob – he just doesn't create those same reactions inside. But then, who can compare to my Boleyn man? I wish he was sat here with me now. Then my mind whirs at the thought of how he would or wouldn't adapt to twenty-first-century life, and I laugh to myself, thinking how his eyes would be out on organ stops, seeing women in clothing like skinny jeans, and maybe even bikini's. It feels strange sat here with Rob, almost as if I'm cheating on George. I should have expected him to show up – it's not like he's not going to want to catch up, considering our previous experiences with the portal and all that he knows.

"Where have you been?" he asks, the old bench creaking. "Have you had a lecture this morning?"

I hold up the book.

"Ah, she's good! Is it signed?"

"Of course." I hand it to him. He stares at the message, then gives me a sideways look as he passes it back.

"Have you met him yet?" he whispers, flicking his hand through his dark hair. He takes a sip from his bottle of water.

"Cromwell?" I ask. He nods. "Not yet. Not properly." I sigh. "I'm not sure I want to."

"You've not been gone that long – no one seems to have missed you."

"The time-slip," I whisper, "appears not to affect the passing of time here. I usually return on the same day, or a day later than when I left." I can't hold back a half-smile as I take a refreshing sip of my tea. "I'm glad I've not missed out on modern Christmas."

He nods. "And what about when you return to the Boleyns?"

"Time always seems to jump forward somewhat." I glance at my croissant, not sure I'll get to eat it before it cools. "I'm never really sure when and where the portal, or the ring, will send me."

He releases a knowing chuckle. "Weird, is it?"

"You could say that!" I take another sip of my tea.

"I wish you could take me back again," he says, screwing the top back on his bottle. A couple of female students approach in big coats and woolly scarves. They catch his eye.

"Professor Marshall would kill me, like he almost did before." I'm not going to fall for it this time. "You know it's imposs—"

"Alright, Rob?" a dark-haired girl says, stopping as she passes with her friend. A pang of jealousy catches me by surprise. I'm sure Rob notices.

"Yeah, I'm fine, Georgina," he replies, all smiles. "How are you?"

She looks back and forth between the two of us. The girl is pretty, I'll give her that. Prettier than me. Well now, Rob having a female friend, other than me – how come I didn't know about this? Is she just a girl friend, or has she notions to be his girlfriend? The quirky connection nearly has me smiling: me liking George and this Georgina liking Rob. And there's me thinking he was only interested in me. How wrong have I been? I roll my eyes and take a bite of my croissant, then another sip of tea.

"Good, thanks. Can we meet up later?" She clutches a lever-arch folder close to her chest. "I need some help fact-checking and referencing that Wolsey essay. Professor Marshall gave me an extension period. Would you mind?"

Her voice is expectant, edged with excitement. Gawd, it's so obvious that she fancies him. Then it comes to me: this is how Jane Boleyn must feel when she sees George openly flirting with me. No wonder I get the feeling she must want to smack me in the mouth.

"No, of course not!" he replies, smiling up at her.

"Catch you later, then." A wide smile lights up her face. As she walks away, she nudges her friend and I catch her whisper: "He's the one I was telling you about. Gorgeous, isn't he?" She glances back, nudges her friend again, and they giggle together like two twelve-year-olds.

I nibble on my croissant to cover my embarrassment, the crumbs falling on my coat. As I brush them away, I think of Anne and George. I miss them. What would we be doing if I was with them now?

Rob stares at me. "How is Anne? Oh, and…"—he smiles—"George?"

"Anne is…well, Anne. Stubborn, surprisingly sensitive, funny, and somewhat ingenious." I remember that day she went hunting with the king. "George is married now." I push back any hint of resignation. I'm not going to elaborate on him, at least not with Rob Dryden.

"Has the King made a play for her yet?"

"Anne? Yes." A shiver runs across my shoulders. Hmm, maybe I should have stayed inside. "His pursuit of her is now in full swing." I giggle, my teeth chattering, and I swig the last of my lukewarm tea. I'm not going to share with Rob that the king also had me in his sights, at one point.

"That's good then!" he says. "History is playing out as expected."

"What?" I look at him. "Are you thinking I will mess things up?"

"Maybe, who knows?" He laughs. I daren't tell him that Henry asked me to be his mistress. That would freak him out for sure.

"I'm an observer, that's all," I say, biting back my irritation. I close Tracy's book that I've been nurturing in my lap and stuff it into my canvas holdall.

"Any chance of a drink later?" he asks, sounding hopeful. "To catch up before term finishes?"

"I thought you'd be having a drink with Georgina? You crack on, I'll see you later." I get to my feet, brushing the croissant crumbs off my coat. "I've got to hand in some of my literature reviews to get some feedback."

"Those aren't due until after Christmas," he says. "Isn't it the Wolsey essay that's due now? Why the rush?"

"I want to get the literature reviews out of the way, well some of them, anyway. I've already handed in my Wolsey piece." I shrug my eyebrows and smile.

"Get you!" Rob says. "You are bound to have insider knowledge of Wolsey, seeing as you've met the man in real life!" His tone is sarcastic. There's no need for that.

"Anyway, it seems you have an admirer who would, no doubt, jump at the chance of being taken down The Greyhound for a drink with you." I look over at Georgina, now standing at the entrance to the Student Union Bar with her friend, both gawking at us.

"I'm not interested in her!" he moans. "But I bet you want to rush back to Anne…and George." He runs his hand through his hair again, looking up at me.

"Why wouldn't I?" I stare at him for a long moment, then turn away and walk towards the university building. That's the end of that, then. I shake my head, annoyed with myself. He's not really interested in me. All he wants is the opportunity to go back through the portal.

When I get to Professor Marshall's office, I find him sat at his desk, hidden in a cloud of smoke. Such a disgusting habit. Shame on him. How is this man allowed to smoke in the building? Smoking is banned in all schools, colleges, and public buildings. I look at him and wonder how he gets away with it.

"You do know, sir, that smoking is prohibited on Uni grounds."

He looks at me and just shrugs me off, returning to his book.

"You could say hello, Beth, rather than commenting on my illegal habit! How are you?"

"Good, thanks, sir."

"Did you enjoy Tracy Borman's talk earlier?" He takes a drag on the cigarette he holds between his nicotine-stained fingers.

"Yes, thanks." I plonk down on the chair opposite him, coughing as I wave the smoke away. I really wish he'd give up. "I've got something for you." I pull a small plastic document holder from my bag and push it towards him over his desk.

"What's that?" The corner of his mouth curls in a half-smile.

"Some of my literature reviews, sir." I nod. "And my abstract draft."

"Everything?" He sounds surprised. "You've finished it all?" He grins. "That isn't due until we come back after the Christmas holiday."

"Yes, sir. I know." I manage to hold back a smile. "It's done. I don't have to worry about it now. What I am worried about is that when I left, several pages of the Ives' book didn't have any print – the history had been erased, and the pages were blank. Are they still blank, sir?"

I can't believe I never even thought to check it last night. A feeling of panic rises in my chest as he takes it down from the shelf. Has the image on the front changed back to Anne and not me? Has the title changed to its original too? I hold my breath for a few seconds as he flicks to the pages concerned and wonder if history has returned to its original course, or whether, due to my meddling, events have been irrevocably changed for the worst – for good. My objective was to go back to fix things. I hope, as Professor Marshall scans the pages, all is now rectified. To my surprise, he snaps the book shut. I can't see the cover, as he puts it back on the shelf quickly, without explanation.

I look from it to him, and I'm sure he sees my question in my eyes. Maybe it's time to give him my report of my last time-slip.

He looks at the large bag of Tudor clothing I'd stuffed next to the bookcase, in case of an emergency. "I suppose you are wanting to go back through the portal?"

"Well, I wasn't planning on returning just yet." I place the spare key to his door on his desk. "It came in handy last night." I can't hold back a smile.

"I'm glad you've completed the work I asked for early," he says, turning my folder over. "It means your time, for now, is your own. Good. Now, promise me you did not meddle any further in the history." His brows meet.

""No," I reply, somewhat sharpish. "No, sir, I told you I wouldn't. I'm a girl of my word." Does he believe me? He gets up, stubs his cigarette into his overflowing ashtray, and looks at me.

"What happened during your last visit?" He leans against his desk. "You weren't long away from here but how long were you in Tudor England?"

"February to the end of July, fifteen twenty-six."

"And...what happened? What did you see?"

I need to leave out my meddling bits, give him a brief summary. Here goes. "All you need to know is that Anne is on the right path – Henry's attentions are always on her. He thinks of nothing but Anne."

His eyes narrow as he scrutinises me. "That's it? Nothing more?"

"No, that's it."

He shrugs. "Ok."

"But, Professor, you haven't told me if the lost sections in the book have returned." I look at his face, then glance at the book on the shelf. "Are the pages still blank?"

"They're half-filled in." He raises a brow.

"The cover – has it reverted to the original version?"

"Sort of!"

"And that means…?"

"You still have work to do."

"I have to go back through the portal?" I grin, knowing that he's giving me an excuse to go back to George. "I mean, you are okay with me going through again?"

"I'm not giving you my blessing, but you have to return to the Boleyns to ensure that everything works out. The stakes are high, and you must make the history 'right', you know that."

"But I don't know what to do!" I sigh. "Everything seemed to be going right. If the missing pages of the book are only half full, what if I've altered events incorrectly, what then?"

"All you need to do is make sure Henry marries Anne, and she gives birth to Princess Elizabeth. That's it." His expression softens and he pats my shoulder. "It will work out." He gives me a smile. "Look, if you have concerns, I can come through the portal myself and check on you – once Elizabeth has been born, of course."

"Really?"

"Yes, really. You know I've time-slipped before, during Elizabeth I's reign – I can play my part now, if necessary."

"I shall keep that in mind, sir. It's exceedingly kind of you to support me – I know you are a busy man."

"Okay, I've got a talk to do for the third years." He picks up his man bag. "If you want to go back through the portal now, you can. No one is going to come in. You can change here and go back to Hever, if you like." He looks at the bag by the bookcase. "Lock the door and leave the spare in the drawer. Don't forget to leave your car and house keys in there before you go, just for safekeeping. You can also leave your modern clothes here, for when you come back through."

I glance at the door, and he smiles. "No one will disturb you. Lock it after me, to be safe."

He's good at some aspects of student safeguarding but not in others. I'm not sure the university would look kindly on a professor allowing his students to time-travel. I turn the key in the lock after he leaves, then change into my gown, ready to re-join Anne at Hever. Just as I did during my first experience of the portal, I reach for Eric Ives' book, and the cypher ring heats up on my finger as the bookcase starts to slide. Unusual. When I've used the portal before, it normally puts up a fight, forcing me to tug harder so the exposed end moves like a pulley, just as it did the first time. As before, the whole expanse of the bookcase levers itself into a pitch-black cavity in the wall, the door making its familiar creaking sound as it slides into the darkness.

I hold my breath, as nervous as the first time I entered, and my heart is in my mouth as I blink to adjust to the lack of light. When I step onto the flagstone slabs and move into the murky space beyond, I flinch when the torch to the right of me flickers into life. I should be used to it now. Then I jump when the bookcase slams shut, the sound echoing around me.

Ok, enough of this. I grab the torch from its iron holder and wave it around, thinking that if anything nasty happens to be lying in wait, I might scare it away. It kind of works because having the light close makes me feel safer. At least this time I know where I'm heading. My heart flutters, more with excitement than fear, at the thought of seeing George again.

The torchlight guides me forward like a familiar friend, cutting through the charcoal darkness. There's a mustiness hanging in the air – remnants of smells of Tudor England I've become so used to. As I continue down the narrow passageway, the sounds of students in the adjoining corridors and communal areas have disappeared. When I turn the corner, my heart skips at the sight of the large, oak-panelled door ahead of me. The silence is eerie but, as I stand before this old door, I know that beyond it, I will find a familiar friend.

I place my free hand on the lion's head handle and, using a little force, pull on it. Ahead of me, Anne's narrow stone staircase spirals upwards. I count as I ascend them, all thirteen, the excitement of seeing my beloved Boleyn family biting at my heels, egging me on towards the antechamber door. I push on it, kicking aside the heavy, tapestry drapes, expecting to hear Tudor voices. Yet, this time, all seems quiet.

Squinting and blinking to acclimatise to the change in light, I notice that my torch flickers and stills when I rest it into the empty wrought-iron cradle on the wall. The hazy light illuminates the antechamber. I lift the lid of one of the oak coffers and force my holdall into it, hoping Agnes or George will not find my modern possessions.

Where is everyone? I straighten my French hood and call out to Anne, Agnes, or anyone who might be around. No response. Most unusual. I circle the room, unable to resist threading my fingertips over the familiar walnut trunks stacked along the walls. Everything feels just as it should, comforting and familiar, apart from it being so quiet.

The floorboards creak. Rushes, gathered in corners with lavender and herbs, look like they have absorbed a few weeks of dust. They need changing. Mrs Orchard will have to sort that out. I trace my hand across the oak panelling that decorates the walls, much like the linen-fold relief carving of Wolsey's lodgings at Hampton Court Palace. Hever is so beautiful. I adore it.

I breathe in the sensuous, musky atmosphere, with the fresh pink roses on the window recess filling the air with their delightful top-notes. As I walk through into Anne's bedchamber, I'm surprised that there is no sign of anyone. The fire in the grate is low and, as I look out of the window to grasp a sense of the season, a noise from the stairs startles me and I call out again and move into the passageway.

"Anne? George?" Not a soul. "Agnes! Is there anyone there?"

My heart flips at the sound of footsteps on the stairs. It's George – I'd know his step anywhere. I peer around the bedroom door, my legs shaking. As he reaches the top of the stairs, he bows.

"Good day, Beth, I did not see you arrive. You did not send us word."

"I-I'm sorry, George, there was no time. Where is Anne?"

"You won't embrace me then?" he says, holding his arms open.

"Not now, George!" I fail to hold back a smile. "Later, perhaps."

He grins, grabbing my hand. "There is a promise I shall look forward to being rewarded with." He chuckles. "Let us go and find my sister – she will be pleased to see you."

Before I know it, he's pulling me in for a hug. Just a quick one. The man is incorrigible. I breathe in the smell of nutmeg and cinnamon on his clothes, relishing the moment. Then he more or less drags me down the stairs. As soon as we enter the Great Hall, he drops my hand like a hot poker.

September 1526 - Allington Castle, Kent

It's morning at Hever. A month from when I was last in Tudor England. Autumn, from what I can see from the colour of the leaves on the trees outside. George walks into the Great Hall and faces his family, who are settled around the dining table, at breakfast.

"See who I found looking lost on the landing, trying to find us all."

I look for Anne, who jumps to her feet and embraces me with real enthusiasm, much to everyone's surprise – she's not known for such physical shows of affection.

"Dearest friend, you are back sooner than I thought you might be!" She gives me a wide-eyed welcome, her dark eyes sparkling with delight.

Sir Thomas gets to his feet, holding his hand out to me. "Good Morning, Beth. I am glad of you being back." He smiles.

Lady Boleyn gets to her feet and walks around the table. "Good morning! When did you arrive back?" She glances at George. "You sent us no message."

"Forgive me, Lady Boleyn." I curtsy, showing reverence.

"Beth," Anne says, "I knew you would return!" She smiles, releasing me from her grip. "Come. Sit next to me." She looks at my clothes, knowing full well it's not a gown that she gave me. It's better than showing up in my modern gear. She pulls a chair out beside her, and we sit. I look at the food around the table and realise that I can still taste my croissant – an echo of a distant time. How crazy is that? Anne takes up her linen and folds it over her left shoulder. I follow suit. She leans into me. "Do not worry – you can change after we have broken our fast!" She giggles.

George tries to be discreet with his emotions as he glances at me from across the table. He picks up a platter of grapes, apricots, and cheeses, offering some first to Jane, who is sat next to him, the hint of a scowl shadowing her eyes. If she only knew how I sympathised with her not too long ago, after meeting chirpy Georgina. Another distant echo. I pour myself some of the wine and take a sip. Even so, she seems in better spirits than when I last saw her, and even George is paying her more attention, which seems to please Lady Boleyn. Maybe she has had a word with her son.

"Beth, we are travelling out today," Lady Boleyn says. "There is a need to visit Sir Henry and Lady Wyatt at Allington. You and Anne did not visit the Wyatt's last Christmastide. Methinks it will do you both good to get out and see some of our dear friends."

I recall that the Wyatt home, near Maidstone, some twenty miles from Hever, is not only a neighbour of the Boleyns but, as I have seen, they move in the same court circles. Thomas Wyatt's sister, Margaret, will go on to marry Sir Anthony Lee of Burston and Quarendon, Buckinghamshire.

"I am excited to see Margaret again," Anne whispers. "We used to be very close when we were children, and I should like to introduce you, Beth." She's obviously hoping to renew their friendship. History creates rumours that Margaret will, if it plays out that way, accompany her dear friend, when she is queen, to the scaffold, and will help Anne's other attendants bury her.

"Of course, I am certain Beth would like to visit with us, Mother." She leans towards her mother and gives her hand a gentle squeeze.

"We shall have a pleasant time, shall we not, Jane?" George gives his wife an enthusiastic smile.

She nods. "I suppose so, husband." She nibbles the last morsel of bread and cheese on her plate.

Mary and William get to their feet and pass plates to Agnes, who fusses around the table. Thomas and Elizabeth order servants about, asking some to clean the kitchens, while Robert Cranewell goes to make sure Simon has prepared the litters for our journey to Maidstone, as would have been arranged the night before. Anne and I hurry up to her bedchamber, where she and Agnes help me change into a gown more suitable for visiting family friends.

A little more than an hour later, I watch Hever Castle disappear into the distance as we make our way along the track. The miles stretch ahead of us, so we settle in, progressing at a slow pace through the country lanes. All around us, the bushes and trees are bedecked with lush green to bronze autumnal colours, and I realise that I have never felt more alive. I lean against the side of the litter, my cheek propped against the frame, drinking in every detail of the country lanes, dwellings, cottages, fields, and people walking along, as I peek around the curtain.

I'm accompanied by George, Anne, and Jane, while the rest of our party: Mary and her parents, and her husband William, carry on ahead of us in another litter. Anne and I speak in whispers as we discuss Tom Wyatt. She's worried he will come on strong to her again, and says she isn't interested in his attentions. The heat of the Indian summer stifles us in the lurching carriage but I'm thankful we're shielded from the sun.

George leans back, doublet unbuttoned, his shirt open to reveal the dark hairs of his chest. He shows no concern at exposing his flesh, even in front of me or his wife, and I don't blame him, as the heat is sweltering, even at this early hour.

"George, how do you think Tom will be with me?" Anne asks, sounding wary. "I do not want his heart and poetry." No doubt she's hoping she won't have to rebuke him for writing more verses.

"Anne, I think Tom would gladly yield and be tied to you forever with the knot of his love, as in his verses, if you gave him one chance!"

"Can you not put him off me?" she asks. "I do not want his attentions!"

The nature of Anne and Wyatt's relationship from her side seems innocent to me, apart from having witnessed his obsession with her at Hever. For all I know, this could be some game of courtly love and nothing more. She is fond of him but knows to keep things strictly platonic now that the king has taken an interest in her.

Historians will take Wyatt's poems literally and suggest that he had been in love with her, and now I'm going to witness first-hand if the struggle is real for him. I'm not that bothered if he keeps his distance or not, so long as he causes no trouble for Anne. Hopefully, the rumours that have now probably begun at Court, that Henry is interested in Anne, will make him back off. I hope he realises what a fool he's being, chasing after her.

"I can try," George says. "But, sister, I thought you liked those artistic types?"

"I do, I just do not want to be the subject of his poetry – he makes too public his declarations for me."

From the corner of my eye, I catch George eying my bosom. When I meet his gaze, he looks away, finding something interesting to study through the window. Jane pretends not to notice but I know it must hurt her. I don't react, as I don't want to give her ammunition to throw in my direction. She turns to me.

"Why is it that men get away with making certain kinds of women the centre of their attentions?"

It seems to me that Jane is the kind of woman who would cause trouble in an empty house. The insult to me is pretty clear. She talks loud enough for George to overhear, probably hoping it will place a wedge between us, forcing him to pay her more attention. She's a scheming wretch, and I can't let the barb go.

"What do you mean, Jane, by 'certain kinds of women'?"

Anne's expression is one of exasperation. She's probably wondering if Jane is referring to her. I don't think so. Her comment was directed at me. I can see it in her eyes. For such a mouse, she can be venomous.

"Well," she says, "you, for example, have no connections – but, so far, since your short time at Court, you have managed to distract my husband." The veins in George's neck look like they are about to burst, and Anne stares at me in disbelief. I knew I should have travelled in the other litter. "And," she says, twitching in her seat, "you have swayed the King's attentions from both the Queen, and Mary Carey. How do you do that?"

I shrug. "As I have said before, and will say in front of George, I am a friend of the Boleyns, and knew them all before you were even married into this family. What say you now?"

"I think you are rude, Mistress Wickers!" She looks at Anne, then to George, and back to me. "Is she not rude, *husband*?"

"I think you will find, *sister*,"—Anne's barb is clear—"that the King may have taken a fancy to Beth at one time, but now his attentions are firmly on me!"

That shuts her up, and she goes into a sulk for the rest of the journey. George, on the other hand, gives me surreptitious and sympathetic glances, probably wishing Jane was splayed out underneath the litter's wheels, instead of sat inside with us.

Anne seems happy sitting alongside me, discussing Jayne Fool. We are both wondering how the poor girl is, without us there with her at court. Anne has rightly sent money for food and clothing, so she will at least have all she needs. Anne is considered Jayne Fool's 'keeper' or as we'd say in the twenty-first-century, Jayne Fool's carer. Between us, we decide that Jayne will probably have been given to someone to keep in our absence, and is well looked after.

Even with our distractions, the journey is painfully slow. By the time we arrive at Allington Castle, I am a little nauseous from the constant rocking and jolting but delighted to finally be at our destination.

The imposing grandeur of the Wyatts' fortified family seat is magnificent to behold, and at least three to four times the size of Hever. Made of grey stone, the Medieval building is rectangular and comprises a defensive curtain wall connected at each corner by a series of semi-circular towers, each facing outwards onto a moat. We cross over the ancient drawbridge and pass under the castle's imposing barbican. I look up at the portcullis tucked away above me and wonder if it has ever been used in defence. Perhaps it has but, on this early autumnal day, all is well. The clattering of hooves on the cobblestones reverberates around the enclosed space beneath the gatehouse arch, before our litter emerges into the bright sunlight of the large, inner courtyard. In short order, we crunch to a halt opposite the main entrance of the Wyatt home. A servant dressed in blue and berry-coloured livery steps forward and opens the door, offering his hand to Anne first, then me. Jane and George follow on.

Once inside the cool shadows of the grand entrance hall, a drawn-looking, elderly woman meets us. By her rich attire and assertive manner, I assume she is the lady of the house. She wears a long, tawny gown trimmed with brown fur, its fore sleeves edged with black damask, the cuffs lined with gold thread work. Draped about her neck is a partlet, which covers her bosom, and a hood on her head with a black velvet veil. A few strands of grey hair poke out from beneath the white coif, confirming her advancing years. I find her face beguiling – deep-etched with the years of her life experience – and although I imagine that her countenance could well be stern should the need arise, on this occasion, she glows with a warm and generous smile. As she moves towards us, her frame and the bulk of her gown gives the impression that she glides rather than walks, her outstretched arms welcoming us. Lady Wyatt, for sure, and she stands beside a man I presume to be her husband.

I know little about Henry Wyatt, apart from the fact that he was on the wrong side of royalty at one time, having been imprisoned, tortured, and left to starve in a dungeon during the reign of Richard III. Scars on his face and neck betray the history of the man and are a stark reminder of the old era of civil war. The display of wealth all around indicates that he has led a successful life at court, is held in high esteem by the king, and is prominent in the new order of things. He is a much-admired public servant – diligent – and said to be supported by Wolsey.

"My dearest Lady Elizabeth!" The woman's voice is light, yet resonant, and it snaps me from my thoughts. "It is marvellous to see you all again." If she knows of Mary's reputation, she is discreet enough not to show it.

Lady Boleyn cups my elbow. "This is Mistress Wickers." I smile and curtsy. "This young lady has been serving Queen Katharine at court, with Anne."

Lady Wyatt smiles. "You are most welcome here at Allington, my dear."

"Thank you," I reply.

As she moves down the line of visitors, I notice that she lingers perhaps a little longer than she ought when she looks at Anne. Does she know what has sometimes passed between Anne and her son? Perhaps she is already aware of the king's intentions. Or maybe she's trying to fathom how a noblewoman like Anne could have captivated a prince as magnificent as Henry.

Lady and Henry Wyatt greet all their visitors in turn. After the formalities are over, and with a slight hesitation, she adds, "We have much to speak about, Lady Boleyn." With that, she indicates that we should follow her into the castle. Old Henry Wyatt bows, taking his leave of us before his wife leads us along a hallway.

She looks back at us. "My husband needs to conclude some Court business and will join us presently. And Thomas, Margaret, and some of their friends are already out in the garden, enjoying this beautiful day. Perhaps you should like to join them?"

"Of course," Sir Thomas replies, before we can answer, "that is exactly what you should all do. It is better you be with younger people than being bored by the older generation, rambling, sharing our stories of the past. Please, go – enjoy yourselves!" He nods. "When my business with Sir Henry is concluded, I shall send for you. Well, tarry not!" With a broad smile, he shoos us away. Lady Boleyn walks with us and Lady Wyatt through the castle to the gardens.

However, within moments of our arrival in the formal garden, I notice nothing seems to have changed with Tom Wyatt. He wastes no time in beckoning Anne over. George and I stand together while Tom ardently converses with Anne, who looks annoyed. I put this down to boredom as, at a basic level, chivalry is a defence against ennui and vice, in my humble opinion. As Tom is married and only separated, he realises full well he can't chase Anne, nor ask her father for her hand. He wants a piece of the pie but isn't prepared to pay the baker. The king has yet to outwardly declare his love and admiration for Anne to all his court, so Tom seems to be trying his luck, in the guise of a gentleman. Lady Boleyn and Lady Wyatt sit in the shade on a garden bench, catching up on the gossip, no doubt.

It's not a surprise to me that Anne is admired by many gallant gentlemen of the court, and a serious pursuit of entertainment is the only alternative to demoralization. Wyatt and his friends swarm around her like bees in a honeypot. He begins singing, 'Pastime with Good Company', Henry VIII's most famous song, which makes clear that courtly love is something all good gentlemen are honoured to play out:

"Youth must have some dalliance,
Of good or ill some pastance.
Company methinks then best
All thoughts and fancies to digest.
For idleness is chief mistress of vices all;
Then who can say
But pass-the-day
Is best of all?"

I sing the words to myself, in my head, but then Margaret Wyatt turns and walks towards our group. She introduces herself and makes a quick curtsy. The woman is plain but intelligent, and her manners are fine. Anne told me during our journey that she doesn't excel at playing the lute or conversing in French and Latin. Even so, I know she will be a reassuring presence in Anne's life, and her warm and generous smile and sparkling eyes make us feel relaxed, in sharp contrast to her brother.

However, my confidence has never been that fantastic, and to be around people I have never met is daunting. It doesn't help that I've just returned from my 'proper' life. At least at Court, *domus regie magnificencie*, courtiers from the nobility and gentry, grooms, pages, cupbearers, and chaplains are all on display – people from all ends of the social spectrum – which helps me to acclimatise when I return to wherever the king and his retinue will be. Although, as I watch George walk down the narrow garden path and bow before Tom Wyatt, I feel comforted by the fact that he is protective of me wherever I go, even in his wife's company. Jane is pushing her luck trying to goad me in front of him. When he's physically close to me, I forget everything else: my concerns for the outcome of my journey with Anne; for people discovering who I really am; and for my deception. I've no doubt Rob would love to be here, probably spying on George, but Rob wouldn't care if George flirted with me.

Jolted out of my daydream by someone's laugh, I focus on George, who is chatting to Wyatt, discussing Court life and the king's visit. Anne gossips with Margaret about the king's behaviour at dinner, the last time he'd stayed at Hever. Margaret gasps, taken aback by the fact that Henry must have been drunk, and that he'd been lewd in Boleyn company. It seems Anne never wrote to Margaret and told her of the king's visit. The Wyatts and Boleyns adore catching up on the intrigues of Court life. Any attention paid to a family by the king would be top of the list of subjects in any conversation, so although it's been a long while since Henry's visit, the Boleyn siblings feel it's imperative to fill the Wyatts in.

"It must have been the drink!" Anne says. "The king is normally gracious, attentive, and respectful."

"Sister, it was definitely the wine," George says. "Norris and I had such a time, even trying to undress Henry to get him to bed. Why, all he talked of was you!"

"Please, George, do not remind us," I say, having heard most of the king's drunken conversation whilst Anne and I were in bed.

Anne turns to Jane. "You see, Jane, all men, it seems, talk of women in compromising ways, not just a 'certain kind of woman'." She then turns to Margaret. "My sister-in-law needs to learn the ways of men."

"I know what men are like!" Jane snaps.

"You should do," Margaret says, "you have George, after all."

"Hmm. Have I?" she mutters, looking out of the corner of her eye at me. I ignore her and catch George's smirk. He really is so bold. I realise, as my heart flutters, that he has drawn me right in, which Professor Marshall warned me at all costs not to allow. What can I do? It's difficult to avoid my relationships with these people becoming too personal. Looking at George, in his fine velvet doublet, now buttoned-up, starched shirt and finery, he is a difficult man to resist. His chiselled features and dark eyes are so alluring. Even Tom Wyatt, admittedly the younger man, does not compare to him. However, the candle I hold for George must be extinguished.

I wonder, somewhat nervously, whether he notices the slow change in his sister, after her refusal to become the king's mistress. It was his idea, along with his uncle, to redirect the king's heart from me to Anne. It is hardly credible, even to me, a woman who knows the future, that Anne dares to presume she could hold Henry's attention and do something no woman has ever done before. No woman has ever made that step from royal mistress to a queen – pushing a reigning queen out of the way. This will be something extraordinary and will change the king, Anne, and the religious core of England. Anne will be Anne and change all the rules.

As Jane speaks of her husband, it is clear that she will do anything to keep his attentions, even if it means falling out with others. I try to pull myself towards her way of thinking – walk in her shoes so that I can understand her better – but, sometimes, her attitude makes it impossible. She is soon to be titled Lady Rochford, as, in the coming months and years, further rewards and recognition will be bestowed upon the Boleyn family.

It is clear from the chatter that George's eye is too easily distracted from his marriage bed, which doesn't surprise me. Little changes through the ages where it concerns men. While Mary's reputation suffers for her indiscretions, George's, rather unfairly, remains intact, and I wonder what his mother would think of his pursuit of me. George and Tom wander deeper into the gardens.

"Come on, ladies!" Tom cries. "Come with us!"

Anne and I pick up our skirts and hurry down some stone steps.

"Where are we going?" I ask.

"To explore!" Anne laughs. "Will you come with us, sister?" Mary refuses to come with us, staying with William, while Jane snorts at our behaviour, commenting to Margaret about how childish we are, George included. Anne and I ignore Jane, as we run passed her and Margaret, before darting through a high, dense hedge that surrounds the garden. Anne grabs my hand, laughing to herself at her joie de vivre, which is heightened today, making her company infectious. As we run after the men, the paths diverge and I'm unsure which way to go. Anne pulls me straight on, towards a garden, which is surrounded by a high, redbrick wall. From where we stand, this path winds down to an intricate wooden door that leads into an informal garden beyond. It feels like we are heading into some sort of secret meadow.

I follow her until she reaches the door, which creaks when she pushes it open, and we step into an orchard that has grown wild. I wasn't expecting this sight. This wilderness is bursting with a riot of late-summer flowers and the last of the corn crop, now cut and ready for gathering. We amble on, laughing and chattering as we go, and I feel happy brushing the flowers with my fingertips as I pass by. A marvellous array of insects, some I have never seen before, dance in the wheat. All around us is a languid buzzing of bees as they go about their work. The sound battles against the harmony of the goldfinches and sparrows who chirp from inside the hedgerows and up in the trees. Anne and I link arms as we walk towards a huge chestnut tree and, as we approach, half-hidden by the grass, we catch up with the men. George is lying in the shadow of the tree and Tom is sitting with his legs crossed in front of him, leaning back against the trunk, with dappled light flittering across his face. The scene is idyllic, like something out of a novel. The boys haven't seen or heard our approach. Their voices carry on the breeze, and Wyatt is talking of his hatred for his wife, and his love of Anne.

When we reach them, he stops talking and George looks up and asks me to sit beside him. Anne refuses to take Wyatt's hand after he jumps to his feet, but she does walk a few yards away with him. George twists his shoulders at an angle to me and rests his head in my lap. I run my fingers through his hair and begin to explain, after the morning's journey here, that we are better off staying friends.

"George, think of Jane," I remind him. "Nothing must happen between us. You know I have an arrangement." I have to say this. He's not to know how things are, especially after the way things were left with Rob only a few hours ago. He lifts his head off my lap and sits upright.

"What do you mean?" He looks hurt and bemused.

"Back home, I am in a relationship with someone. Well, sort of." I know I'm lying, but it's time to change the subject before George can say anymore. "Besides, Jane loves you and wants to be a good wife to you."

He frowns. "You know this?"

"Yes." I don't know, but he doesn't need to know that!

He turns a blade of grass, twisting the end in his mouth, then looks at me. "It is not her that I want. You know this, Beth. I should have asked your father for your hand – I told you before, that was an opportunity missed." He shifts over and leans against the tree, next to me. "We could be making Boleyn heirs by now." He smirks, then sighs. His comment saddens me, and he gives me a curious look, but I can hardly tell him that asking my dad for my hand in marriage would have presented more than a few problems. I'm itching to tell him who I really am. What if I did? The professor's warning rings in my ears: I am not to divulge my origins to anyone. Only Anne can know the truth.

Having wandered off together, Anne and Tom now return to where we sit. She stretches out, her skirts fanning from her waist, and he sits at her feet and begins to recite his memorised work to us:

"Whoso list to hunt, I know where is a hind,
But as for me, hélas, I may no more.
The vain travail hath wearied me so sore;
I am of them that farthest cometh behind.
Yet may I by no means my wearied mind
Draw from the deer, but as she fleeth afore
Fainting I follow. I leave off therefore,
Sithens in a net I seek to hold the wind.
Who list her hunt; I put him out of doubt,
As well as I may spend his time in vain.
And graven with diamonds in letters plain
There is written, her fair neck round about:
Noli me tangere, for Caesar's I am,
And wild for to hold, though I seem tame."

"I hope I have not broken your heart," Anne says, teasing him.

He doesn't rise to the bait, staring at her instead, saying nothing. George strokes my hair, which I've worn hanging down my back today. I still wear a French hood but it doesn't have a veil, so my hair hangs in plain sight. He twists a long lock between his fingers. Anne watches Tom, waiting for his answer, but he remains silent. He just stares at her, no doubt hoping she will read in his eyes what he's thinking. When he lies on his back with his eyes closed, she shrugs her eyebrows and grins at me, her dark eyes sparkling through her long lashes. I lean as close as I can to the tree trunk, so my hair is less accessible, and look out into the natural wilderness, preoccupied with my own thoughts.

"Anne, you were just a young girl, maybe ten or eleven, when I first knew you," Tom says.

"And you were tall, sir. All arms and legs as I recall, Master Wyatt."

"You were beautiful, even as a child. Your beguiling black eyes were the same then." He chuckles to himself.

George sits up. "You may have always fancied my sister but she doesn't just attract *anyone*." This comes with an element of humour.

Tom looks at George, blinking several times, as if soaking up the implied insult. "She has always attracted me. Do you remember, Anne?" He sits up. "You took a liking to me, too – you even asked me to marry you once, in the gardens at Hever!"

"I never did!" she protests. "And in any case, if I had, I must only have been a girl of ten!"

"Look at her now," he announces, flashing a broad smile at her. "She is transformed from that ungainly fawn into someone magnificent and wild. Beautiful!" Her face goes bright red, and she gives him a gentle shove to be quiet.

"Wild?" She frowns. "I am all sophistication!"

"You are sister – you have the sophistication of the French!" George chuckles.

"We should have all gone for a ride," Anne says, trying to change the subject. "It would have given you less opportunity to embarrass me, Tom!"

"Do not be like that!" Tom slumps into a sulk. "I was besotted by you, utterly beguiled, and yet…"—He looks to the sky for a moment—"you have ended my suffering. I know that you are lost to me, for…"—He glances at her necklace—"you have drunk from the cup of a king and have tasted the attentions of a mighty prince."

"Anne has not set her sights on the king," I interject, "it is the king who would catch Anne, if he can!" I'm not going to suggest that she would never be the wife of a simple country gentleman like him – that would be too cruel. He cocks his head, pondering my remark.

"What king would not be infatuated with you, Anne? You are a unique and remarkable woman." His words are full of passion, as if his manner will somehow cause her to change her mind about him.

I need to step in here. "Tom, Anne is headstrong at times, yes, but courageous, strong, and intelligent." I'm not going to say she's tempestuous, politically astute, or rash, even if it's true.

He laughs. "She is hard to fathom!"

I give him a scolding look. "Thomas, you missed out generous, devout, and loyal!"

He stops laughing. "Did I?"

"You did so, Tom," George adds.

Wyatt frowns. "Stop piling in on me!"

"Piling in on you?" Anne scowls. "You all talk of me as if I am not here!"

"Ah, but, Anne, we cannot help but talk of you, for what other woman is like you?" Tom smiles. "I should say definitely, that you, sweet Anne, are the most alluring woman in Christendom!'"

"Tom Wyatt, you talk of me, but you do not know me, really. I think you say what you do to flatter me and win me over, not because you mean what you say."

I remain silent, not daring to interrupt, but I wish Thomas Wyatt would shut up – he's getting boring now. We all get it, including Anne – you fancy her, we know! Give it a rest. Showering her with compliments will get you nowwhere.

"I am honest, is all," Tom answers.

"Foolish, more like." George laughs.

"Most men of court are frightened of you, sister. Did you know that?" George plucks another blade of grass. "And those who aren't, want to possess you – own you." He nods once as we all watch him.

"Those men are foolish too!" Anne suggests.

"You think the king foolish, Anne?" I ask.

"No, never."

"To the king, you must be like a priceless, flawless diamond – one he cannot afford." George says.

"Utterly radiant, and beguiling," Tom says, both hands out. "But Henry will find and meet the cost he has to pay for her."

The country will have to pay with their religion for the king to have her but I'm not going to mention that. "The king is passionate about Anne – I have read some of his letters to her." Oops, maybe I shouldn't have said that, because Anne glares at me.

George shakes his head. "Wyatt knows the king sends gifts to ladies he admires – it's the way of love at court, is it not, Tom?"

Good old George, trying to cover my tracks for me. I brush my hand down his arm, and the corner of his mouth turns up in a smile.

"Any attractive woman deserves gifts from a gallant gentleman – that is why I write verses for Anne in praise of her beauty, but your sister rejects me!"

Poor Tom, he looks so hurt.

"You all flatter me," she says, her tone somewhat sharp. "Now, stop it!" She sits up, not impressed.

"The king is such a man," George states. "He wants to possess you. Anne. I have seen it in his eyes."

"We all saw it, George!" I laugh. "You remember the dinner?"

"Yes!" He chuckles. "The king will have you, as he did Mary. But, instead, you will set our country in a roar, sister – unlike Mary!"

"Why do you suggest such a thing?" she asks, her forehead creased.

"For the king to try and hold you, will be a mean feat. To try to control you is like trying to keep a wave from breaking upon the shore."

"I shudder to think what His Majesty will do," I say, watching Anne shake her head.

Tom shifts about to face her. "Anne, I wonder who the king will crush, and what he will tear down to have you as his own."

George chuckles. "As you know, Tom, Anne will not give herself away to Henry as Mary did." He tugs at some late daisies in the grass.

"I am too shrewd for that, brother," she says, "and have learned the lesson of my sister well."

Tom shifts his position, and their faces are close enough to kiss. He searches her eyes, as if to implore her one last time to step away from the destiny awaiting her. George coughs into his hand to distract him, no doubt sensing the danger.

"Tom, it is the same for me with Mistress Beth." He says this as if I'm not here, and now I know how Anne feels. He glances at my shocked face. "I have loved her with all my heart for the time she has been living with my sister." My heart races at such a public declaration, and I watch him get to his feet and stand in the shadow of the tree, stretching his arms above his head.

"Jane suspects my heart lies with another but I will never confirm to her that it has always belonged to Beth."

I get up, brush my dress down, and begin to walk away. It's too much. I can't bear to hear this from him – it breaks my heart.

"I cannot bring myself to touch Jane," he continues, raising his voice so I hear, "for when I try, all I see is sweet Beth's face, her smile, and her eyes."

"My dear brother," Anne says, "this conversation is difficult for Beth, for us all, and you dwell on things that will never happen."

I turn and walk back to them. "I do not know what lies ahead for me or for Anne but I know that whatever happens will be because God wills it, and no more."

Tom gets to his feet and stands tall. "Well, whatever happens, Mistress Wickers, I will always love Anne and will always serve her. On my life and honour, I pledge it." His serious tone stuns us all into silence, until George adds that he too will honour and serve both his sister and me, with his life.

I run my hand through his hair. "I know, George. I know it well. Thank you."

Anne claps once. "Tom, let us go and fetch your sister, so we can help her and Lady Wyatt prepare the supper." She offers him her hand so he can lift her from her carpet of daisies and grass.

It's late afternoon, and I stare up at the sky, the hazy sun winking at me from behind a cloud. Anne looks back at us, her eyes apprehensive, but I mouth to her that I will be okay. I hope us not returning with them doesn't spark suspicion from Jane. It obviously will but George doesn't seem to care. Hopefully, Anne can make an excuse to her sister-in-law. When they've gone, George turns to me with a face full of melancholy and reassures me that he meant every word he said.

"I believe you," I say, my voice soft in the hope my answer will soothe him.

"Thank you, Beth."

"Anne will need you, George. Although she is a strident personality, she will need you for all that lies ahead. She has a destiny, and she needs to fulfil it, even in spite of herself. Your sister will need all our support." I take a slow breath, gathering my words. "And above all, you must be careful, George, for you and Anne will pass through the lion's den."

He looks down at me in an odd way, and I bite my lip, hoping my unguarded tongue hasn't set him wondering about me. This is a time when women who allude to knowing the future might be burned at the stake. Still, he knows that the Tudor Court can be like a bear pit.

Having considered my advice, he wraps his arm across my shoulders and we both vow to support Anne. In the silence that follows, it's clear that our friendship is set in stone. I think we both know that everything is about to change. Anne will take centre stage in history, and the carefree summer spent in the Kentish countryside will be nothing but a distant dream.

In due course, Tom and Anne have re-joined the guests in the castle, and, along with Mary, George, Jane and I, Margaret and her husband, John Rogers, and four more of Tom's close friends, all of whom have been invited for the occasion, go inside for supper with the Wyatts and Boleyns. We are all glad of the food laid out before us, as our earlier journey and garden adventure has made us all ravenous. We have a choice of salads, cooked and raw vegetables, custards, and fruit. There are two courses – one offering a selection of boiled meats and the second offering roast or baked meats. The wine has been flowing freely for some time and there is much laughter from this merry group of friends.

Tom introduces me to a couple of people I haven't met before, and would see little of again. However, amongst those present is a woman Anne will come to know well: Lady Bridget Harvey, née Wiltshire. She is from another Kentish family, and, as such, is a long-standing friend of both the Boleyns and the Wyatts. It is clear from the warmth of her greeting that she knows Anne. I'm introduced, and I dip a curtsy to all present. Except for Mary, Thomas, George, and Margaret, it is evident that the other members of the group treat Anne with a little more deference than anyone else present. Has George already shared something of the king's intentions towards his sister? I hope he hasn't been so disrespectful as to divulge her secrets. No, I dismiss the possibility. He may be many things, but I believe that, above all, he is loyal. It's probably Wyatt's big mouth. With Henry's burgeoning interest in Anne becoming more evident, rumours may have already begun to circulate of his romantic intentions. However, taking Tom's lead, the friends soon accept her presence, and everybody begins to relax into the feasting, gossiping, and merry-making. When we have eaten our fill, we retire to the main hall as the day fades into twilight.

Before long, accompanied by sweet music from the pipes and tabors, we begin to dance and twirl, as I had done at Court with Thomas Boleyn. This time, Tom Wyatt takes the lead, partnering me during an Italian dance called Rostibolli, which is danced in pairs. He watches me as I circle around and in front of him, while George sits sulking with Jane. She's red-faced, and it looks like they've been arguing. I hope to God it's not on my account! She's trying to cajole him into the dance. Instead of appeasing her, he gets up, bows to Tom, and asks to cut in. He takes my hand and leads me into the dance once more as the music resumes. It's a heavy, rhythmic, delightfully happy tune of summer, and of the harvest. I feel Jane's eyes glaring into my back as I partner her husband, but I dare not look at her, keeping my focus on Anne Boleyn and Tom Wyatt instead, who now join us in the dance.

Wyatt knows all eyes are on us. Anne is never one to shy away from a challenge, and she circles him as they glide in time to the music. As she moves up close, something catches on the hem of his cloak – a small jewel, which has been hanging by a satin ribbon from her silk girdle belt. They both stop dancing, and he tugs at the ribbon, freeing it, but hides the entire thing inside his doublet.

She scowls at him, and I want to help her. Tom makes me angry, and it's clear that he wants to hold onto the jewel as a bargaining tool, to lever his way into Anne's orbit. I should tell him it isn't going to work. Maybe he thinks that possessing it will give him other occasions or excuses to talk with her at court. She looks stressed trying to retrieve the trinket, and I wonder whether it's worth much. I break away from George and storm over to them but, as I do, Anne walks away, embarrassed by Tom's stupidity.

He takes the jewel out for all to see, holding it up by the ribbon as a trophy of his conquest. The music has stopped. The older generation looks on aghast, whilst his friends, apart from George and me, clap, and cheer.

"Thomas!" I shout. "That belongs to Mistress Anne. Give it back to her this moment!" He seems vaguely puzzled by the strength of my reaction but continues to taunt me in a light-hearted manner.

"Mistress Wickers, I claim this prize as a token of remembrance of a sweet lady! And in any case, Mistress Anne does not want it back, for she has walked away and talks to her mother." He bows low in my direction, and although he keeps up his cheery disposition, which encourages his friends to applaud, when he looks into my eyes, I see pain reflected there. There's no doubt he is angry that Anne has walked away from him. Should I fetch her and continue arguing in front of everyone, or will that heap more significance upon the stolen trinket than she might wish? I leave Tom to his friends, allowing him to keep the jewel so as not to further offend Anne.

"What was that all about?" George asks me as we cross the hall to seek out Anne. I wonder if Tom will give the jewel back, and hope that when he does, it will be the last we hear about it. I worry for Anne that the king will not like the fact that she has other admirers. However, with his ego being as it is, perhaps it will have the effect of whetting his interest further. Henry, as I have seen, has tested Anne's moral fibre by asking her to be his mistress. Although she's refused him and twists the situation to get rid of him, I'm quite sure he will pursue her with even more passion until he gets his way. His string of love letters and the way he's wearing her ring on his little finger are clear signs that he's not going to give up any time soon.

Thirteen

Late November, 1526 – Hever

I've heard all the rumours of how Cardinal Wolsey, Thomas More, and others are trying to stamp out the heresy of Tyndale's doctrine. Tyndale is now the most dangerous man in Tudor England, they say – a serious threat to the Catholic Church's influence, where scripture will dictate authority and a pope's will. Meanwhile, despite all insurrection, Henry is turning a blind eye to the anarchy and continues pursuing Anne, who is considered by some to be a sympathiser of William Tyndale.

"What does the king write?" I ask, as she opens more correspondence from him.

"He says,

> *'Time seems very long since I heard concerning your health and you, the great affection I have for you has induced me to send you this bearer, to be better informed of your health and pleasure.'.*"

"And…?" I press.

"And…" She wags her forefinger at the script, as if counting the words, or confirming what she's read.

I laugh. "Come on, spill the beans."

She stares at me, then sighs and looks back at her letter.

> "*'Because, since my parting from you, I have been told that the opinion in which I left you is totally changed, and that you would not come to Court either with your mother, if you could, or in any other manner; which report, if true, I cannot sufficiently marvel at, because I am sure that I have since never done anything to offend you, and it seems a very poor return for the great love which I bear you to keep me at a distance both from the speech and the person of the woman that I esteem most in the world.'*"

She looks at me, her brows arched, and allows us time to take in the gravity of the king's words. Then she walks to the window, so the light better illuminates the page.

> "'And if you love me with as much affection as I hope you do, I am sure that the distance of our two persons would be a little irksome to you, though this does not belong so much to the mistress as to the servant.'"

"You know that the king is suggesting he is hurt by your absence more than you are. He is clearly in love with you." I wait for her to respond but she just blinks and looks back to the page.

> "'Consider well, my mistress, that absence from you grieves me sorely, hoping that it is not your will that it should be so; but if I knew for certain that you voluntarily desired it, I could do no other than mourn my ill-fortune, and by degrees abate my great folly. And so, for lack of time, I make an end of this rude letter, beseeching you to give credence to this bearer in all that he will tell you from me.
> Written by the hand of your entire Servant,
> "'H. R'"

She folds the letter and stuffs it inside a book just as her mother enters the parlour. Lady Boleyn looks at her, her brows creased. Anne returns to her seat and strokes the spine of her book, as if in contemplation. Nothing is said. The lady of the house sits close to me in order to admire my embroidery as daylight streams through the window.

"Mother, may I retire to the coolness of the gallery?" Anne asks. "It is too stuffy here and I need a cool breeze about me to reduce my headache."

Lady Boleyn nods in assent and Anne gets up, book in hand, her billowing skirts trailing behind her, with Griffin in her wake.

"Beth, how do you enjoy your time with us at Hever?" she asks, taking up her sewing.

"I adore being here, Madam. Anne and I are such dear friends." I smile, trying to convey my appreciation of her family's favours towards me.

"And what think you of His Majesty's interest in Anne?" She keeps her voice low so none of the servants will hear.

"I am not surprised that His Majesty has noticed Anne, for she is admired by all at court."

"My husband is not happy about this current development. He has expressed his grief of it to me but to no one else. He did not like Mary's involvement with the king but, luckily, she had her husband to hide behind. Anne has no such protection."

"Anne is mindful of her reputation." I hope that will be enough to quench her curiosity.

With Sir Thomas and George still absent at Court, the castle slips into a sedate and reassuring pace of life, enhanced by the sheer beauty and tranquillity of the countryside that surrounds our little piece of heaven. We receive few visitors, and I'm glad, as it allows me to watch the everyday carry on of Tudor life. Since my first time-slip, I have become familiar with the way people speak, and by watching Anne and her mother at close quarters, I see how women of noble birth interact with all levels of society. When we receive visitors, I make sure to be at Anne's side, as a quiet and unassuming presence. And when she wants to be with her mother, I occupy some of my time in the library, devouring book after book in a quest to understand as much as I can about the world that seemed so strange to me at first, and yet is becoming my home. I no longer have a desire to return to my 'real' life, through the portal or by using the ring, at least not right now. With each passing day, I have become more ingrained in the fabric of my sixteenth-century life. As a student of history, I have never felt more alive.

On occasion, Lady Boleyn asks about Anne's intentions to return to Court and whether she would be taking me with her. She knows about the king's wishes and that he eagerly awaits her daughter's return. I confess that part of me longs for it – even if it's just an opportunity to see George again. The thought of tasting life at the Tudor Court once more exhilarates me. Yet, I sense that in my departure from Hever, Anne will be leaving the last of her youth and innocence behind, and because I am utterly entranced by every nuance of life in our country home, I am less keen to rush forward to London. Of course, I am acutely aware of the many dangers that lie ahead for Anne, and I still struggle with the notion of wanting to save her from her fate.

I know she can't wait any longer to hear news from the king, and when I re-join her, I find her re-reading his letter. Henry is clearly suffering inner turmoil at her absence. I watch and wait in silence as she opens the locked casket that holds his letters and her jewels. She removes a pouch of black velvet, releases the drawstring, and spills a jewel into her hand which, she tells me, has been crafted by the goldsmith Morgan Phenwolf. It is unique – astonishing, really. The artistry demonstrated by fashioning a ship tossed about by waves of gold with a woman on its deck is inspiring. To set off the piece, the diamonds fixed in front of the two masts are both stunning and significant.

"Anne, are you sending that to his majesty?" I peer over her shoulder as she hands me the priceless jewel.

"Indeed, I am. It will be a New Year's gift of great significance to the king, have no doubt." She allows a proud smile, heightening my curiosity.

"The large diamond is the North Star – the ship's protector as it becomes adrift in a stormy sea. The king is the protector. There is a lone woman aboard desperately seeking a port."

"Are you that woman?"

"Yes, I am. Despite the rough sea, she trusts in God that all will be well. I know Henry will understand the question the jewel poses: would he be my harbour in the storms of life?" She beams, and I know he will be elated with such a gift.

The diamonds, glittering and hard, support the masts so delicately carved in the precious metal, with three diamonds and two rubies embedded in the side, which I assume represents Anne's, steadfast love.

"This gift represents my answer to the king that I will commit wholeheartedly to him and save my maidenhead for him, so long as he will make me his wife."

I turn the gift about, feeling its weight. It seems that, for some time, Anne has begun to explore the depths of her heart, after the king's request in the rose garden – her situation presses her to examine her circumstances. She is now well beyond the age most suitors desire and has neither personal fortune nor land as a dowry. Apart from her sister's and her mother's abilities, Anne is unproven when it comes to bearing children.

She stands before her mirror, looking at her reflection. Her proud countenance with her high forehead and glittering, coal-like eyes, combine with her distinct chin to show this lady is no mouse. The woman is fearless, giving such a jewel to the king. She takes it from my hand, examines it, and places it back in its velvet nest. In this moment, she seems resolute. It's not hard to understand why this face is loved – no, adored – by one of the most powerful men in the world. I light candles with a taper against the gathering gloom as she takes up parchment and quill once more, ready to reply to her king.

"Anne, Anne, please come quickly," I shout down the hallway. "The king is almost here!" No response. "Anne, where are you? Do you hear me? He is nearly here!"

I find Anne in the Long Gallery, at the far end, reading a book. A pool of light falls around her, framing her in the brilliance of the day. Today, she is dressed in a beautiful Tudor gown with a tight-fitting bodice and voluptuous skirts. It is made of the darkest, ruby-red damask, with the embroidered edge of the linen shift beneath clearly visible above the low-cut, square neckline, whilst satin finishes the full sleeves that are turned back, and which tumble to the ground around where she sits. About her neck is strung two strands of gold chain and a pearl necklace, from which is suspended her famous 'B' initial that her parents gave her. I can't help but notice how radiant she looks.

I stand before her, out of breath from running around trying to find her. "Anne, if you don't come quickly, we will be missing all the fun!"

"What fun? Beth, why are you shouting, and what is going on?" She places the book on the chair and gets to her feet.

"The king is coming! The king is coming to see you!" As if in support, shouts echo from the direction of the inner courtyard. Then the clatter of horses' hooves resonates across the drawbridge and cobblestones.

"He's here! Anne, we do not have much time. We must go!" I almost drag her out of the Long Gallery, and we race down a short flight of stairs to the staircase gallery.

"Come on!" I say, exasperated by her inability to grasp the importance of the occasion. I peer out of an open window into the courtyard below. In the chaos, I spy the king, now off his horse and conversing with Sir Thomas.

I watch her and wish that time could standstill. It is from these experiences of spending time with her that I have come to know more of the real Anne Boleyn. If things stay as they are, I know I will comprehend the world through her eyes. I can also share her passions, feel her fears, and her hopes, and I am beginning to understand her character as I observe the events that shape and define her, which I know will eventually leave her indelible mark on the pages of English history.

The king is waiting for her downstairs. While his presence is something spectacular, I feel less terrified than before his first visit here. Anne is calmness itself, and she looks radiant. Does she know what makes Henry tick, or could she ever guess what he'll be capable of in the years to come? Courage wells up inside me and I know what I must do. For the first time, I take control. Letting go of the windowsill, I turn towards her.

"Anne, you look beautiful for the king."

"I am of no consequence, Beth. The king has come here for father, of that I am certain."

"Anne, is that what you really think? You have read the king's letters, written in his own hand – do not make jokes about yourself. You know the king comes here for you."

"I do not want to admit that the king truly desires me – it is beyond all my deserving!" She looks away and smiles. "Next, you are going to tell me that the king will end up being my husband!" She laughs, and I say nothing, too busy gulping back a nervous ball of phlegm. I say nothing.

"Are you telling me, by your silence, that the king of England is to be my husband?" She stares at me. Her dark eyes fixed. "That is the truth, is it not?" Her brows knit together. "You have known this fact all along? All this time I have known you!" I remain silent. She grabs my shoulders, shaking me. "Tell me the truth!"

"I cannot!" I shout, shrugging her hands off me.

"You are my friend, my closest friend – you need to tell me what you know!"

"Anne..." I take a deep, steadying breath and let out a long sigh. "We had this conversation a long time ago, and more than once. Do you want me to be burned at the stake as a witch? Do you want me to be accused of satanic practices, because that is what will happen if the authorities find out I can predict the future, as they see it!"

"You do not deny my question, that Henry Tudor will be my husband!" Her voice fills the space, and I look around to make sure we're not being heard. "If that is not the truth of it, you would deny it!"

"Anne, please do not be mad at me – I told you before, I could never share the truth of your future with you!" I stop myself on realising my voice is way too high. I'm shaking inside, too, and the professor's warning echoes through my head. "Now, the king is here, you need to ready yourself."

"In that case, you must help me – I need to choose some jewels to wear." She smiles now, no doubt brimming with excitement at the prospect of what might lie ahead. "Yes, of course, I know the king comes for me – I just wanted to tease you. Let's look for my casket!"

We rush to her bedchamber and she searches around the room, under the large, intricately carved tester bed, with its heavy, red-velvet hangings.

"Where did Agnes put my casket?" She asks, looking about her.

I scan the room and delve deep into a large oak cupboard. With a flourish, I pull out an ornately carved walnut casket, mounted with gold bands and hinges, which, in turn, are embellished with gold-leaf falcons, several carats of rubies, on a background of delicately carved oak. It is exquisite, and there are many complex carvings depicting scenes from the life of Saint Eustace around its sides.

When I place it on the bed coverlet, she hands me an exquisitely crafted golden key, which, in itself, is a rare and beautiful thing. I unlock it, and excitement bubbles as I lift the lid and view the treasures inside – a glittering feast of precious and semi-precious jewellery, encrusted with a rainbow of coloured gems set in gold. In my modern-day life, it is beyond my wildest dreams to think that I would one day hold any of Anne's personal jewels. At this moment, though, I realise that an entire casket of them lies open before me. I am speechless, and my attention is drawn to the pendant, which opens up like a penknife, with stunning engravings of foliage. This little item is the gift given to Anne from the king at Chateau Vert. I remember Professor Suzannah Lipscomb discussing this on her programme about Henry and Anne.

"Anne, Henry gave you this, did he not?" I hold up the priceless pendant, and she looks at it, all smiles. The golden etui is about an inch in length, richly chased, and in the form of a pistol, the barrel serving the purpose of a whistle.

It encloses a set of tooth and ear picks around the handle, with a serpent design etched and coiled around the whole piece. I had read in Strickland's work that this was said to have been given by Anne, on the morning of her execution, to the officer on guard, Captain Gwyn, as a thank-you for his respectful conduct towards her. However, the eminent historian Eric Ives wrote that there was no contemporary evidence of Anne giving anyone gifts on the scaffold, which he believed must cast doubt on the story. During my research at university, after the Lipscomb talk, I found there is no record of Anne possessing such an item and, like Ives, I never found any evidence that it had been given to her by Henry, or that she even owned it. Nevertheless, here I am, with the etui in my hand. A gentle nudge awakens me from my thoughts.

"Apparently, if I whistle, he said he'd come!" She giggles, then snatches it from me and blows into it to see if it will make a sound. I shake my head, hoping Henry doesn't hear what's going on up here. Time to get serious. I hand her a chain from the jewel case so she can hold the whistle on it about her waist, to let the king see she has looked after his gift.

"Beth, you take me too seriously! I jest, is all." She laughs again, then secures the gilt chain about her waist.

"Do you know how much that item is worth?" I'm not asking her a question, as such – I'm trying to explain to her how important a sixteenth-century artefact it is. "His Majesty is trying to show his admiration for you, and to let you know that if you ever have need of him, all you have to do is ask."

"Perhaps, Beth, but the king gives gifts to many a maiden at Court. It is just a game. A dalliance of courtly love. As I said before, Henry gave me this gift at Chateau Vert."

"Mistress, you would be wise to think on it, because I believe you will find that the King will publicly declare his love for you soon." Oops! I do my best not to show that I've said too much. "I have seen the way he looks at you."

She looks serious as she scrutinises the jewels in the casket. I take a tentative step towards her and point at one piece.

"And this, do you think…?"

"Oh, Beth, you are so clever!" she cries, her eyes wide with excitement. "I shall wear my gilt cross to show the King how I love God and the sacraments." She gives me an expectant look.

"Mistress, you know that George and I saw and heard everything when the king was with you in the rose garden on his last visit. We could just make out what you were discussing and saw your fiery chastisement of him because of his disregard for your honour. Even from a distance, I could see the anger flash in your eyes!" I can't hold back a cheeky smile. "Henry must have been taken aback by your reaction. I think he is *scared*!"

"I know he wants me in his bed as a mistress, and if he asks me again, I will say no, again. I know why he wants me always at court." She sits on the bed. "I don't want to be discarded like my sister. She has asked the king for nothing, yet has surrendered everything – even bore his children and he has abandoned her. I will not be abandoned."

After luncheon with the king and a handful of his entourage, I decide to take some air alone in the gardens. The pressure of the last few days has taken its toll, and I need to take myself out of the situation, to clear my head. I could go through the portal, or use the ring, but decide that my presence here is more important, to remain and observe Anne, as the professor has advised – to keep an eye on how things are progressing, and to make sure they don't go awry.

The winter sun is bright but delivers no warmth, and the bite of the impending season sharpens the air. I pull my cloak tighter around me as I walk towards the meadows, outside the walled flower garden. Less than ten minutes have passed when voices carry from the other side of the wall. They're familiar, and it only takes a moment before I'm sure that it's the king and Anne.

"You cannot withhold your affections from me now that I have declared my love for you!" he says. "You are in my every waking thought, and you are constantly in my dreams."

"Sire, I cannot be your mistress, as you have a wife!" she replies. "I will not come between a man and his wife – no matter how much I think of you. I cannot do it, no matter how much you may try to persuade me. I know it is wrong before God. I beg you, sir, let me return to the house!"

I can't believe I've been lucky enough to overhear them but I decide that the best thing to do is make myself scarce, before they realise I've been eavesdropping. Anne would find it hard to forgive me, and Henry would be furious. I run back to the house to keep my council, knowing full well what direction she will decide to take next.

Fourteen

DECEMBER 1526 – HEVER

A few days after the king's fleeting visit from Penshurst to Hever, Anne hears by letter from George that Henry has faced off with Wyatt whilst they were playing bowls with some other courtiers. He explains how Henry claimed that his wood held shot when it clearly did not. Indicating with his hand, on which he wore the ring Anne had given him, he said that the point was clearly his. Wyatt, however, decided on a bold response. He produced Anne's jewel and proceeded to use the ribbon to measure the distance between the balls and the jack. The king's good humour vanished, and he stalked off. When George was alone with him later, Henry exploded into a fit of jealousy, ranting on, and pacing the room, demanding to know about Anne's relationship with Thomas Wyatt and whether he, the king, had been deceived in her love and loyalty towards him.

From somewhere, George apparently plucked up enough courage to square up to him, stopping him in his tracks. He explained that Wyatt had taken the jewel from his sister without her permission and that Anne's heart was true and her body chaste. After hearing this, it seems that Henry was pacified, and sunlight was restored.

"I am furious with Tom Wyatt," she says, waving George's letter. "I wish I had recovered the jewel from him in the first place."

"I guess the King's interest in you is no longer secret?"

"I am angry at Tom for engaging in such a competition, and with the King!" She writes back to George, thanking him for his response to the king, and asks him to remember her to Henry.

When she finishes, she turns to me, still fuming. "Sir Thomas Wyatt will never succeed with me."

JANUARY 1527 – HEVER

All night, a storm has raged around the castle, with non-stop thunder and lightning competing with fierce winds and torrential rain to keep me awake well into the early hours. Inevitably, Anne and I oversleep but, when I open my eyes, I realise the rain has ceased and the breeze coming through the casement window carries clean air – sweet and fresh – much healthier than the fumes I'm forced to breathe in modern England. If anything, this prolonged stay is enhancing my health no end. It's certainly another reason for staying here. I stretch my arms out from under the linen sheets, which have become tangled in my shift and around my body.

To my utter amazement and shock, I notice a silhouette framed in the low morning light of the window and sit up, pulling the sheets to my chest. The man stands square at the foot of the bed, grinning at me as he holds a black velvet cap scrunched up in his right hand, which has left his dark-brown, wavy locks uncovered and attractively tousled.

I squint against the light, ready to cry out, but then realise that it's George, richly attired in fabrics of grey damask, velvet and silk, all of which contrast against the frill of his white, linen shirt. The light in his eyes twinkles and he moves closer to where Anne and I lie.

"Nudge my dear sister awake, Beth."

I do as I'm told, and Anne stirs from beneath the sheet, running her fingers over her plaited hair. She rubs her eyes and squints at her brother.

"Have you missed me, ladies?" He holds his arms open, hoping perhaps that I may forget myself and rush into his embrace.

"George!" Anne cries. "George, you should not be in here."

"Sister, and Beth, I need to speak with you – just for a moment." He smiles. "I have missed you both." He slumps on the edge of the bed, ignoring our embarrassment.

"Where is your wife?" I ask, hoping he has returned without her.

"Jane is visiting her family for a few days without me. Although,"—he looks out the window for a moment—"she did beg to accompany me here, to see her dear sister, and friend."

I stare at him. Jane thinks me a friend? He must be teasing me.

"How are things, brother, with you and Jane?" Anne asks as she tucks the sheet around her.

"I have to admit that things are not as good as I would wish with my marriage, but Jane is faithful and supportive, and I can ask no more than that."

"George, I wish you could find happiness," I say, hoping and wishing only for good things for his heart. Whatever I feel for him can't come between him and Jane.

"There is someone else at Court who wishes to be happy," he says as he straightens. He reaches inside a leather pouch clipped onto his belt and withdraws a letter. The heavy wax seal bears the same coat of arms as the Royal Standard – another letter to Anne from the king. With a wry smile, he passes it to her.

"The king has commanded me to ride from Greenwich, to deliver this letter to you. In fact, sister, the king is much perplexed by your continued absence at Court." He chuckles to himself. "It would not be an untruth to say that he pines for you, sweet sister. I have never seen such puppy-dog eyes when he mentions your name."

"George, do not tease me!" She growls, tracing her fingertip over the Great Seal, before slipping her finger beneath the fold, pulling the wax apart, and opening the letter.

"I want no rewards in exchange for the king having your body. I will sell myself but never you!"

"George, do not worry, the King wants more than my body, I assure you! He has been struck by the dart of love, no less."

He throws his head back and laughs.

"Do not laugh, brother!"

"Sister, please, have you listened to your vanity?" He shakes his head. "Henry only loves one person!"

She sniffs. "Who might that be, if it is not me?"

"Himself!"

"If you had seen the king, and how he looks at me…"

"We have," he says, glancing at me.

"…you would believe me. I have felt his eyes on me many a time but, until his visit to Hever, refused to meet his gaze."

"His gaze was certainly on you, sister – or should I say, on your breasts!" He chuckles. "Fancy Henry Tudor, King of England, enslaved by the chains of passion for my sister." He laughs again, looking at Anne, then at me. "Henry will never give up – if the grapes are sweet, he'll have them in time."

I take no notice of what he's saying. My attention is on Anne, now devouring the contents of the letter.

"You must reply to that letter," he says. "The king is not used to being denied."

"George, I have not denied him. I have acknowledged his love, with a gift."

"What gift?" He looks puzzled.

"Did he not show you?"

"No, he did not." He's annoyed at being left out of her plan.

"I sent him a ship – a jewel of diamonds – as a New Year gift. I know it was early…but I could not wait!" Her face lights up with a proud smile. "And with this letter, the king has now thanked me for it." Her eyes widen as she consumes Henry's every word.

"You are most lucky to get such a letter – Henry hates to write by hand."

"He writes that, henceforward, his heart shall be dedicated to me alone." Her smile broadens. "And he states that God can do it if He pleases to bring us together. Henry even prays every day for that end, hoping that at length his prayers will be heard."

"Oh, sister, where will this end?"

She releases a deep sigh. "I do not know."

"It seems that the king longs for you," I say. "It seems this can only end like any hunt, with the hunter's victory or frustration."

George laughs. "And with good sport along the way!"

"Yes, I suppose, brother." She looks a bit dismayed by that remark. "But, I think I have the king's heart in my hand."

"Take care – I thought you would have no dalliance with a married man?" He stands there, both brows raised, awaiting an answer, which doesn't come.

"Can I see the letter?" I ask, seeing that she's finished reading it. She hands it to me, with a satisfied look that intrigues me.

I stare at the heart drawn on the letter, between H and R. "What does 'Aut illic, aut nullibi' mean?"

"Either there or nowhere," George answers. "It's Latin."

"The signature means, H – not looking for any other – R." Anne smiles. "The royal H R is beautifully embellished, the heart so lovingly inscribed, and the words 'aultre' and 'ne cherse' impossibly tiny, with the whole device making a pretty picture, wrapped in the outline of a heart at the bottom of the page."

"There is no mistaking it," I say. "What a love letter, and from his own hand!" My cheeks burn with delight as I realise that Henry has accepted her gift and will wait for her, no matter what. The letter is composed with real fervour, and written with ardour by a man whose hands do not easily enable small, delicate script.

George laughs as he snatches the parchment from my hand. "The king writes like a schoolboy."

I get up and go and sit next to him.

"See." He points at the small blotches of ink on the page. "He scribbles his lovesick words."

"George, do not mock the king, for I think he conveys his sentiments well." I lean in against him and re-read the letter in his hand, conscious of his heat and scent, and the fact that I'm wearing nothing but a thin linen shift.

"Look where he writes, 'my heart shall be dedicated to you alone'. If only a man would write those kind words to me and mean them. I sigh, thinking to myself, wishing men of the twenty-first century could be as romantic as Henry has become with Anne. George eyes my shift, and I realise that I'm shivering. Anne grabs her shawl from the floor and wraps it around my shoulders, glaring at his impertinence.

"Forgive me, Beth. I did not mean to offend you or my sister. I just find it incredible that the king should want my sister as a wife, when, by convention, he should take a princess as his queen."

"Brother, the qing and I want to do what is right and correct. He passionately loves me, and I love him. I will be his queen and nothing else."

"You would be queen? Are you sure?" His head tilts to the side, both brows furrowed.

"His Majesty has agreed to wait for that moment and will do all in his power to secure it."

"Sister, you need to go back to court. Hiding here in Kent is going to drive you mad. We need to make arrangements as soon as you are packed and ready."

"Fret not, brother, the king will send word when he wants me to attend him."

I remain silent, inwardly delighted at how things are progressing. At this rate, those pages should be filling right back up again. It might be time to go see for myself.

Within days, much to Anne's cheer on a freezing afternoon, a royal courier arrives in the courtyard with a parchment and parcel, along with a message for her. She is requested by Henry Tudor to arrive at Beaulieu Palace on the twenty-fourth day of this month, and will remain there until her return to Court.

After reading the letter to herself, she whispers a prayer of thanks to the heavens and returns to her chamber to open the package. Like a faithful lapdog, I follow her up, seeing her study the familiar writing on the accompanying note, with the lines crowding each other, pressing towards the top of the page. When she's ready, she reads them aloud to me.

> *"'My mistress and friend, my heart and I surrender ourselves into your hands, beseeching you to hold us commended to your favour, and that by absence your affection to us may not be lessened: for it were a great pity to increase our pain, of which absence produces enough and more than I could ever have thought could be felt, reminding us of a point in astronomy which is this: the longer the days are, the more distant is the sun, and nevertheless the hotter; so is it with our love, for by absence we are kept a distance from one another, and yet it retains its fervour, at least on my side; I hope the like on yours, assuring you that on my part the pain of absence is already too great for me; and when I think of the increase of that which I am forced to suffer, it would be almost intolerable, but for the firm hope I have of your unchangeable affection for me: and to remind you of this sometimes, and seeing that I cannot be personally present with you, I now send you the nearest thing I can to that, namely, my picture set in a bracelet, with the whole of the device, which you already know, wishing myself in their place, if it should please you. This is from the hand of your loyal servant and friend, H. R.'"*

Anne almost sobs as she tugs at the white lambskin in which the accompanying gift is wrapped. A red leather box, long and slender, holds a delicate bracelet of fine, gold links, with a locket attached by a gold clasp. It clicks open to reveal a striking portrait of Henry against a cobalt-blue background. My scalp prickles when I realise it's the one he tried to give me. I bite my lip and keep quiet. To think this priceless locket could have been mine. The likeness is incredible, capturing his essence with that stern expression on the cusp of breaking into his special grin – his cheeks rosy and his handsome face set off by a black velvet cap, accented with white plumes. The artist is Master Lucas Horenbolte, new to the king's court, and known for creating such masterful likenesses in tiny miniatures.

I take it from her and gaze at the face for a while, inspecting the artwork, then turn it over to find engraved there the entwined initials 'H. A.', meaning Henry and Anne. He must have added these after I gave him back the locket. I show Anne, who stares at it in astonishment. She isn't accustomed to seeing her initial entwined as an official cypher. Her delicate features light up as I fasten the bracelet around her wrist.

The remaining days at Hever are now spent preparing for our trip. Henry has sent his best seamstresses and tailor, bringing colourful new fabrics, silks, lawns, and sarcenets to create a wardrobe of new spring and summer gowns as well as riding clothes for both Anne and me, ready for the new season. Paul Cotton gets to work again, sharing ideas with us, offering advice and designs he thinks we would like. I, too, am beginning to feel like royalty, being in such close proximity to Henry's betrothed. Much to our mutual delight, we discover that her mother has made plans to meet us at court on our return from Essex. I'm thrilled that she will be with us, for I suspect we will need much support at court, now more than ever.

MAY 1527

Days, weeks, and months have rolled by at Hever, at such a slow pace, and Anne is frustrated at having to wait to return to court. Her frustration bubbles over as much as the political climate is changing in Europe. According to dispatches, Rome has been sacked. I remember from my studies that this event was coming. Duke Charles of Bourbon – a Frenchman – has renounced his allegiance to King François and has offered his services to Emperor Charles, proposing a march on the lightly defended papal capital of Rome. Sir Thomas has informed Anne by letter that the duke and his forces left the town of Arezzo on April twentieth, and that the Imperialist army has attacked, captured, and sacked the towns of Acquapendente, San Lorenzo alle Grotte, Viterbo, and Ronciglione.

"Father writes that, 'as the rampaging army approached the Holy City, Pope Clement offered a sum of sixty thousand ducats to pay the rabble and save the city, but the money was nearly stolen by thieves, and the transfer was cancelled. The army reached the walls of Rome as recently as the evening of May fifth.'"

"What does this mean?" I look up at her and see that she's still engrossed in her father's script.

"The opposing forces – the Imperialist rabble – number somewhere between twenty and thirty thousand men. Many of the original soldiers have deserted but when word of the impending sack of Rome went out, many re-joined for a chance at the rare treasures of the city. Upon seeing the huge mob bearing down on them, the Roman nobility decided to comply with all demands. The mercenaries broke into their palazzi, dragged out the clergymen, and forced them to pay tribute for their lives. It seems the Roman nobility and rich merchants received the same treatment. Anarchy reigns supreme in the city. Bands of mercenaries roam the streets, stabbing citizens to death. Father says they have emptied out the villas and churches, and buildings have been torched after yielding no loot. The pillagers have even broken open the graves of saints, including the tomb of St Peter the Apostle. Looters have made off with precious stones, valuable tapestries, and even the pope's tiara. The total loss is estimated at about ten million ducats, the equivalent of thirty-five tons of gold. Mercenaries have been seen riding through the city dressed as cardinals, while prostitutes have been given golden vestments to wear."

I try not to laugh at that. She shakes her head to herself, looks up at me, then snaps the letter and begins reading again.

"Father reports that the mercenaries, when in the College of Cardinals, performed a parody of the Protestant reformer Martin Luther being elected pope. A large portion of the Swiss Guard has been massacred on the steps of Saint Peter's Basilica as they fought to protect the pope, which has allowed the Holy Father and his loyal supporters to escape via a secret corridor to the Castel Sant'Angelo, where they have barricaded themselves in, surviving on donkey meat."

"As you know," I say, "I am no Catholic supporter, but that is dreadful."

"You know why this is happening, don't you? The Emperor is trying to influence the Pope against Henry and me, so the divorce will never be granted."

"Anne, you do not know that. This could all blow over and mean nothing. How does your father know of such events?"

"A messenger came before the king and reported it. Apparently, he is furious and has not been seen with Katharine at court. They live almost separate lives, as Henry thinks she has something to do with this siege."

"Would the queen stoop so low?" I ask. The political ramifications are making my head spin. I've never come across any evidence of Katharine's direct involvement. Could it be true?

"I would not put anything past that woman," Anne replies. "She will do anything to save her marriage."

She looks angry, which makes her steely reserve even more rigid. Would Katharine lie about being uncorrupted after her marriage to Arthur? It makes me wonder if she will lie to the legatine court and to Henry over the next few years about her virginity. After all, even though a queen, she has a lot to lose, and wouldn't any mother do anything to protect her child?

27th July 1527 - The Palace of Beaulieu – Boreham, Essex

Although I know no matter how much time I spend in Anne's life, hardly any time passes back home, I still miss my parents, and even Rutterkin, my poor cat. I know my absence will hardly be noticed but my 'real life' absence from twenty-first-century life lies heavy on my heart. However, as we approach Beaulieu, I almost forget my worries, as I have never seen anything comparable, apart from Hampton Court Palace. The Palace of Beaulieu, northeast of Chelmsford, is gigantic, imposing in every aspect, and forms an appropriate setting for what is to come. It once belonged to Sir Thomas Boleyn and, after extensive remodelling, the king has turned it into a place of exquisite beauty.

Anne and I ride side-saddle through the gatehouse archway, keeping company with a bevvy of Henry's guards and stewards. In the elegantly appointed main courtyard, water splashes from marble fountains, and flowers and vines tumble from huge urns. We are relieved of our exhausted horses by stable hands, and the house-steward leads us to our apartments. The suite we are shown into comprises a lovely sitting room, a large privy chamber with a beautiful tester bed, and a bath. The master steward informs me that, once I have helped Anne refresh herself after the hot and dusty journey, I am to escort her to join the king and others in his private chamber for supper.

We laugh in delight at our private rooms, in which we can bathe and take care of our toilette. It is a luxury I imagine I will become used to in the coming months, while tending to Anne's needs and spending time in her company. Now she relaxes in the warm water of her bath while Agnes unpacks our clothes and lays out a gown of pale-yellow silk for Anne and a pale-blue one for me.

When she steps out of the bath, I sink into her second-hand rosewater. She's in a hurry, not wanting to keep Henry waiting. The bath is wonderful, and I soon feel refreshed, and once I'm dressed, my mood matches Anne's sun-coloured, lightweight gown. With controlled anticipation, we enter the Presence Chamber, whereupon the king rises from his chair, nodding to me as he hurries to Anne's side, kissing her warmly before leading her across the room to greet the other guests.

I notice Thomas Howard, Duke of Norfolk, is the first to approach and kiss Anne's hand. He stands beside his wife, Elizabeth Stafford, who seems unhappy to be here. Her only talent is ingratiating herself to Queen Katharine. Henry Courtenay, Marquis of Exeter, the king's first cousin, and his wife, Gertrude, greet Anne courteously. John de Vere, the Earl of Oxford, bows in reverence. I am introduced as Lady Elizabeth Wickers to Henry Bourchier, the Earl of Essex, and Thomas Manners, the Earl of Rutland, whilst Charles Brandon, the Duke of Suffolk, acknowledges Anne. It lifts my heart to see Sir Thomas standing behind the others, beaming at the two of us.

There is a palpable air of deference directed towards Anne, which I find curious, and I wonder what the king has told them prior to our arrival. We are seated, and Suffolk is next to me, whilst Anne sits further down the table, beside Henry. Charles Brandon is the king's closest friend, akin to a brother. He is a larger-than-life figure, as tall as Henry and equally handsome. He's a burly, blustery, and hearty man, though not as athletic as Henry, and seven years older.

"Mistress Wickers," he says, turning to me, "it truly is our pleasure to welcome you to the gathering here at Beaulieu, with the Lady Anne. I hope you are looking forward to some lively hunting and other sport during your stay."

Suffolk is popular at court, a skilled and enthusiastic jouster – a star of the tiltyard. He is one of the few men of the king's inner circle who can beat him at the tilt. When Henry was Prince of Wales, he looked up to him when he was forbidden to take up dangerous sports by his father, Henry VII. Suffolk joined the king's inner circle around the time Henry ascended the throne, and the two have been inseparable since. He's always careful not to outdo his king at sport.

"I most certainly am, my Lord Suffolk. I know that the hunting grounds surrounding the estate are excellent. Anne has told me that the king has just completed the construction of a tennis court on the site. I look forward to seeing some skilful play. So, do you think there is a chance that you will prevail over His Grace? I have heard that the two of you are mighty rivals at tennis…"—I look at him, keeping my gaze steady, but do little to hide a sly smile—"…as well as at other endeavours."

He chuckles with good-natured amusement. "I can tell you this much – I will give the matches my all, Mistress. Though it is never an easy business, nor often a wise one, to outplay the mighty Henry."

The servants of the Domus providencie, or below stairs, bring up the plates of food ready to serve for the meal. During this formal feast, roasted and baked meats are brought to the high table, preceded by the entrance of subtleties: artworks made in marzipan, depicting a large castle, and a hunting scene.

As we eat and talk, the king stands. He raises his silver cup and announces, "I would like to propose a toast to our delightful and very accomplished guest, Mistress Boleyn. I welcome her with great affection and respect for her skills on the hunt field, the card table, the dancefloor, and the many other goodly pastimes we will engage in while staying at this magnificent estate. All raise your cups!"

Somewhat abashed, Anne nods her gratitude to him while all present toast her. As this goes on, I'm reminded of the significance of this visit, although I don't know all the details. Not every meeting and visit of the Tudor Court is well documented, so I'm only reminded of what is to come as Henry addresses his allies.

"As most of you know," he continues, "there is a further reason you have all been invited to this gathering. You are among my closest friends and most trusted companions. As such, you have been made privy to my urgent need to obtain the dissolution of my marriage to Katharine. While a number of efforts are underway, they have so far proved inconsequential and ineffective. I wish to ask all of you to work with me in determining the best way forward with this, my confidential matter, to achieve the result I require in the shortest time possible."

He meets each individual's gaze one by one and is answered with expressions in accord with his – determined and assured. With a start, I realise who is notably absent from the company. Cardinal Wolsey is at this moment on assignment in France, and not privy to this gathering. As I study the faces both up and down the table, it comes to me: it is evident that most, if not all of those present, harbour a distinct dislike for Wolsey and how his power and wealth has corrupted the office of Lord Chancellor.

The remainder of the meal is punctuated with laughter and companionship as the guests anticipate a working holiday among close friends. While it's fun, and I'm delighted to be a part of it, the excitement of the day and our journey has left me exhausted. Before anyone has excused themselves, I rise from my chair and go to Anne, discussing whether we should retire for the evening. She makes our apologies and stands, receiving a disappointed look from Henry.

The next morning, a fresh, pearly mist fills the stable yard as we gather for the hunt, me included. Anne has a beautiful sorrel mare saddled and ready for her, at the king's behest. She is recently imported from Italy – an Arab-Barbary cross that is supposed to be a dream in the hunting field, impeccably behaved and agile. By late morning, the mist has burned off and the sun lights the rolling green hills. I ride alongside Anne and Henry, in tandem with George. My nerves are on edge hanging on to his slender waist but, with a broad smile lifting his cheeks, it's not hard for anyone to see that he is delighted with me being his riding companion. Thank God I am with him, because I feel safer after taking that fall at Hever all that time ago. Jane declined the invitation to ride because she said she felt unwell, with a slight headache, so I took her place. I'm grateful that we take things at a civilized pace and don't overtake our quarry. We enjoy a wonderful afternoon, where I manage to stay on my mount at all times, always relishing having George in my arms without anyone thinking it untoward.

When we return home, late in the day, Anne is invited by Henry to join him for a private supper. I help her select her apparel for the evening: a bright-green satin gown, with the sleeves set off by gold embroidery. She places a thin double chain of gold around her slender, swan-like neck, eager to spend time with her beau, and I watch with excitement as she sets off with the house-steward to Henry's chambers, her emerald skirts swishing.

It's a relief to have some peace and quiet after the noisy formality of the hunt, and a small fire provides some heat to the room as I sink into a fresh rosewater bath prepared for me by Agnes. I bask in its warmth and scent, my shift billowing out around me like a sheet, floating on the water. For a time, I am alone…until a discreet knock on the door interrupts my tranquillity.

"Sister? Beth?" A familiar male voice floats into the room, and from the corner of my eye, I see George, standing in the doorway between Anne's parlour and her bedchamber, leaning suggestively on the door casing, his doublet unbuttoned.

"George, you cannot be in here!" I yell, trying to cover myself with the thin, transparent cloth of my soaked shift.

"Beth, I have seen a woman naked before," he says, all smiles.

"George, my face is here!" I wish he was blushing, but he isn't. Goodness, I feel so exposed and unbelievably self-conscious. "You may have seen many a naked woman, but you have never seen me! Do me a favour, George, avert your gaze!" I stifle a giggle as he puts his hands over his eyes like a child, his fingers open. "This isn't a game, George – you cannot be here, with me in such a state of undress, and without company."

Agnes has disappeared. What am I to do? One thing's for sure, I can't stay as I am. No, I have to get out and bring some respectability to this situation.

I pull myself up and stand, the water dripping off me as I continue covering myself up, and not with great success!

"Would you like me to help dry you off?" He chuckles, then passes me a large sheet of dry linen, which I use as a shield as I pull the shift off. Even seeing my embarrassment, he can't help but look. I wrap the linen towel around myself and motion for him to go into the adjoining room while I dry off. What would Rob think if he saw me like this? Would I be so bashful with him? Hmm, maybe.

"Why are you here, George?" I shout into the parlour as I secure the towel around me and sit before the fire, trying to dry myself off. Agnes has arrived, thankfully after George left the room, and prepares a clean linen shift and a dressing gown for me. She lays the clothing out on the bed, then begins to brush the tangles from my wet hair. I can see that she's not impressed with George being here but I whisper to her to say nothing.

"I came to see my sister," he says from the room beyond. "I forgot that she is with the King."

Agnes helps me step into a clean shift and ties the belt of a crimson silk dressing gown in a big bow about me. Then she scurries around picking up the wet linens.

George enters the bedchamber, cup of wine in hand. "You looked better in that wet shift." He shrugs his eyebrows. "Would you like some wine?"

I shake my head, exasperated, but then nod, and he pours me a goblet of wine from the pewter flagon on the table. He walks closer, eying me up and down, as if remembering what he has seen not so long before. My face flushes as he passes my goblet to me, and while I'm uncomfortable, I'm also excited at being in the presence of this man, who I now consider my friend and loyal servant. Despite his marriage to Jane, I know I am his object of affection, and he, my courtly-love servant. That brings a smile. My Tudor thoughts come so easy now that I've spent so long here. My twenty-first-century life seems so far away at this stage.

When Agnes leaves, he flings his now-empty goblet across the room as I take a sip from mine. Knowing what's coming, I find somewhere to rest my drink before he wraps me in a deep embrace. Our kisses are divine, and convey our yearning for one another. The feeling of being wrapped in such a strong, protective embrace is something I haven't experienced before, and it feels as if this is where I am meant to be. When we draw apart, he sits on a bench near the window and beckons me to come and sit on his knee. I do as he suggests, though I'm nervous, but then his lips brush against mine, and we kiss again.

The door to the suite swings open and, from out of nowhere, Jane Boleyn's voice shocks us apart. "Oh, that is just lovely – what is this, a private party?"

She stands strong, hands on hips, scowling at what she sees before her. "Is there room for another on your knee? I cannot leave you alone for one moment, George Boleyn!"

She doesn't even acknowledge me. He jumps up, eyes wide, and whilst adjusting his breeches, tells me he will return, then runs after his wife, through the corridors of Beaulieu, calling her name. This could turn nasty. What will Anne say? I hope she will understand.

I sit before the hearth, my nerves in shreds. Agnes comes back in, probably wanting to protect my honour and make sure my reputation is intact. She starts tidying and folding clothes, then placing them into trunks. As she walks around the bedchamber, she spots the goblet George threw to the floor and picks it up.

"How are you, Mistress? Are you of good humour?" She looks at me, nursing the goblet in her hand. "Can I get you anything?"

"No, thank you, Agnes." I smile, and she leaves me alone. For what seems like a lifetime, I sit looking into the dwindling fire, waiting, hoping George will return, as he said he would.

Quite sometime later, I hear the sound of his footsteps outside the door – I'd recognise them anywhere. I have to admit that his return is a great relief. When he appears, he looks flushed and a little breathless.

"Is everything, erm...how do you fare?" I ask, remembering to speak Tudor. "Is all well?" I get to my feet, making sure my dressing gown covers me.

"I have had better days. This is not one of them. I found Jane lying on our bed crying with hysteria. There is no reasoning with her. I have done what I can, and it's now in the hands of God. I am hoping she will snap out of it – she is always looking for trouble." He plonks himself in a chair opposite me. "You were only sat on my knee – it is not as if you were in my bed." He sighs. "More is the pity. If a woman looks for a problem, then she is always going to find one!"

As I watch him poke the fire, my frustration bubbles over. Storming over to him, I pull the poker from his grip and thrust it into the holder near the grate. Anger and fear grip me as I take him by the shoulders. "After all my worry tonight, waiting for you to come back, that's all you have to say?" He blinks at me, saying nothing. "Do you not care? What about Jane? What about the potential repercussions of your behaviour – *our behaviour?*"

"Beth...my love. I care not what Jane thinks. I am past that!"

"What? You can't say such things." Tears sting the back of my eyes. I mustn't cry. "What about Jane's rights as your wife? What about her right to stand up for herself?"

He looks puzzled. I release my grip on him, shaking my head. Of course, he's not going to understand. A woman is the property of her husband in this era, and he won't get what I'm driving at. I shrug and sigh.

A long moment of silence passes before he brushes his hand over his mouth and rolls his eyes. "Sometimes, I do not understand women." He gets up and strokes my cheek. "I thought you would be pleased with a chance for some intimacy?"

"Not to be discovered by Jane," I answer. "Never at her expense!"

He growls as he slaps his thigh. "I have been tolerant and loving towards her long enough. Hang her expense!" He squeezes the bridge of his nose, then looks at me. "Why do you look so vexed?"

"Me?" I release a nervous laugh. "I'm scared of everything. I'm scared of what Jane saw, I'm scared of what we are doing, about who I am, and most of all – I'm scared that if you walk out of this room, I shall never feel the rest of my whole life the way I feel when I'm with you." Tears well up and, for a moment, I feel as if I've uttered a line from a movie, I've watched over a thousand times. I shrug, embarrassed. My face is burning but I don't care – I've told him how I really feel, in so many words. My shoulders slump in resignation.

With that, he pulls me into his arms. "Then let me reassure you, and show you how much I adore you, instead of her." His lips brush mine, then his tongue tests for resistance, of which he finds none. Our kiss is passionate and intimate, like never before. So much for us remaining just friends, for his wife's sake. We shouldn't be doing this. I need to stop it. One of his hands is about my waist, the other running through my damp hair. I catch my breath as he plants hot kisses on my neck, and as I brush my hands through his hair, he fumbles with the ribbons of my dressing gown, untying them and pushing the whole thing off my shoulders. It falls around my feet but I don't care, because his mouth is on my nipple, through my shift, his teeth grazing the tip, and I can't help but groan as my legs shake and fire sparks through my pelvis. I grip his hair and pull him up to me, and this time, I'm the one driving my tongue into his gorgeous mouth. His hands consume me, and our kisses burn like an inferno.

He pulls me closer, gasping. "I...want to see you naked." He bites my neck, sucking hard, turning me to jelly. "I want you now!"

His hands are on my thighs, pulling up my shift, but a noise comes to me beyond our world of passion, and I realise Agnes is returning. I slap his hands away and push him off me, to save his reputation and mine. He looks despondent.

"Are we always to be disturbed?" he cries, glaring at Agnes. He walks to the other side of the chamber and slumps into a chair beside the fire. I pick up my dressing gown and pull it on.

"Master George, should you be alone with Mistress Wickers? I think not." She gives us a disapproving look. "I do not think your sister woulds approve!" She walks around the edge of the room, pretending to tidy, though I think George and I are the only ones in a state. Perhaps it's not a good idea to discuss our relationship while she's present. God, I'm still shaking, and as horny as I've ever been in my life. I think she just ruined what Professor Marshall would deem 'a meddlesome and inappropriate liaison'. What if it had happened? At least I've got the contraceptive implant. George will get no Boleyn bastards from me. I shake my head, shocked that I would even think such a thing. Get a grip, woman!

Okay, I need to sit. I occupy the chair opposite George, folding my hands in my lap, hoping to hide their tremble. He seems to have composed himself, though his eyes are hard as he watches Agnes flit around the chamber like an annoying bluebottle who won't fly through the gap in an open window. Poor George, my heart goes out to him. Every time he tries to be tender towards me, or seduce me, something or someone stops us. Perhaps we should take the hint.

No doubt to take his mind off his passion and distract Agnes from the reality of what she might have witnessed, he fills me in on the politics of the day and his latest triumphs as a man of the king's privy chamber, including the latest grants, lands, and houses Henry has given him. I love listening to him, and he goes on to explain how my previous predictions had been correct, because the king has applied to the pope for the dispensation to allow him to marry again. Anne is not identified by name but, as well as raising the case, the draft dispensation includes the name of a woman previously contracted in marriage.

My mind whirs as my thoughts turn to Mary Carey and her mother. Henry never took Elizabeth Boleyn to his bed, so I presume he's covering his back with Mary, concerning the dispensation to marry Anne.

All this time, Agnes busies herself around the room with chores, until she finds nothing left to do. "I be leaving you both now, Master George, Mistress Wickers – but if you be needing me, Beth, please calls me, yes?" She gives me a nervous look, but it hardens somewhat when she turns to George. I've never seen that from her before. She bobs a quick curtsy to him, what with him being a Boleyn, and her master's son.

"I will, Agnes, fret not!" I smile.

As soon as the door closes, he takes me by the hand and pulls me onto his lap. He brushes my thigh with his fingertips, kisses my ear, then eases up the hem of my shift. I wish he'd be satisfied with a cuddle, for now.

"Where were we?" He chuckles, running the fingertips of his other hand up the back of my neck. His lips are so close to mine, nothing is stopping him from kissing me, but he pulls away and nuzzles my neck instead, planting one tender kiss after another on my too-sensitive skin. Then he whispers in my ear that he wants me, before nibbling on my lobe, his hot breath driving me close to the edge. He's gentle, which is a turn on, but his passion grows as his lips crush against mine again, his tongue not testing for resistance this time. With one of my arms around his shoulder, my other hand running through his hair, he knows he has free rein.

"No, George! Do not pull my shift any higher," I say, breathless, stopping his hand just as Anne Gainsford, a close friend and lady-in-waiting to Anne, disturbs us. Along with Agnes, she has come to serve Anne whilst we join the king at Court. Born in Crowhurst, Surrey, she is a daughter of John Gainsford by his second wife, Anne Hawte. Anne Boleyn affectionately refers to her as Nan, as she does with all the other 'Annes', Nan is a Tudor abbreviation of Anne.

I jump off George's knee before she has much chance to see what is going on, but she gives me a sharp look, and tells George he should not be in Anne's chambers when she isn't here.

"I wait for my sister, is all, Mistress Gainsford," he tells her. "Mistress Wickers entertains me, whilst I wait."

"Is that what you call it, George Boleyn?" She looks me up and down. "You two should get a chamber!" She glares at my dressing gown, untied and loose about me. I close it and pull the ribbons tight. Your love will have to wait, George. You may have branded your promise on my tongue, and you may have kindled a fire here in my heart, sending sparks to scorch my soul, but the thought of your love will be the only thing keeping me warm, besides the flames crackling in the grate. I sigh to myself, then sip my wine, a tremble still evident in my thighs. George just shrugs, gets up, and pours himself a fresh goblet.

A flurry of excitement fills the room when Anne bursts in with a smile as wide as the ocean, her jewellery glistening from the flames of the hearth. She holds her left hand out and we move towards her to take a closer look at the huge emerald she now wears on her fourth finger. Nan joins in the buzz of excitement as Anne goes on to explain that while she was supping with the king in his privy closet, he went to an ornately carved chest and withdrew a small box of crimson velvet, which he then handed to her.

"My fingers quivered as I held it," she says, "and when the king urged me to open it, I lifted the lid." She squeals with delight. "Henry slid to his knee on the floor before me and said words that touched my soul and filled me with joy – words I had thought never to hear from the King of England."

"What did he say?" I plead, as if I didn't know.

"He whispered my name and said, 'I humbly ask if you will be my wife. I will love you and cherish you with all that I am, and all that I have, forever, if you will but give your consent.'" She falters, tears of joy welling in her eyes.

"And then... And then he placed the ring on my finger, and I agreed to be his wife."

"Dear sister, I am so happy for you." George embraces her, kissing her on the cheek.

"I threw my arms about Henry and kissed him. I forgot myself completely. What a magical evening we have had together!"

"Mistress Anne, you are not the only one who has been kissing this night!"

Heat rises in my cheeks as George glares at Nan, giving her a silent warning to keep her mouth shut.

"This is a happy time for you, sister," he says, "and should not be diluted by frivolous gossip."

Nan has taken the hint because she offers Anne a congratulatory embrace and returns to her duties. That was close. Too close, and it really can't happen again. However, this moment is Anne's, and I have never seen her as happy as she is this night. We spend a few moments admiring the gorgeous ring, and how well it sits on her slender finger.

What I see is a ring full of promise, which demonstrates that Henry and Anne have an understanding that they will soon belong to each other. George embraces his sister and bids her goodnight, then bows to me, before turning on his heels and walking out of her chambers.

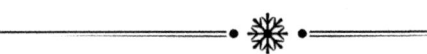

The next day, after the morning meal, the king calls a council meeting of his guests, which I am not privy to. I return to Anne's chambers, to tidy and help prepare her gowns with Agnes and Mistress Gainsford. Once the meeting concludes, she returns to us and tells us what was said, which mostly concerns Henry's attempts to nullify his marriage.

"Henry opened the floor for discussion about the existing plan conceived by Cardinal Wolsey, and its merits – or lack thereof." She sits in the window seat as Nan and I attend her needs.

"It quickly became all too apparent to those listening that Wolsey himself has dedicated very little time to the matter, and has, instead, passed off the fact-gathering, planning and execution to Doctor Stephen Gardiner, his secretary." She gets up and paces the room, which is a usual habit when she's aggravated, and seems to help her unravel and understand the politics, with clarity increasing with almost every step.

"Henry was furious, having been previously unaware of this fact. He dictated a letter to Sir William Knight, his personal secretary, addressed to Wolsey, demanding that Gardiner appear for questioning. After which, a courier was summoned to deliver it promptly to Wolsey in Paris."

How long will that take? Maybe a few weeks. Talk about snail mail. "And how did the meeting continue?"

She stops dead and looks out of the window, then starts pacing again. "The King's men hold little respect or friendship for the Cardinal." She stares out of another window. "I have decided to keep my own council, hold my tongue and my opinion for the present."

Nan and I stare at each other, knowing that our mistress is not likely to stay quiet on the matter for long. I hope she can, because she'd be better off leaving Henry to deal with his current wife, and he certainly wouldn't welcome the interference from another woman.

"It has not been openly stated that Henry and I are betrothed and intend to marry as soon as his divorce from Katharine is finalized." She turns to face us and asks us to swear that we will not tell a soul of her betrothal unless she commands us to. "I'm sure everyone in that meeting has surmised the truth between Henry and me but, even so, we must not confirm it."

We swear we will not say a word, and she continues to explain how, in letters from Paris, Wolsey claims his efforts are well underway in support of the king's case.

"I am no fool," she says. "On hearing the letter read aloud, Wolsey's contrivance was as plain as his long beak of a nose." Henry recognized the same, she believes, although she noticed that as soon as the group began to claim Wolsey's deficiencies and his unsuitability to direct the matter, he proved most loath to denounce the man. Although clearly unhappy about his chancellor's negligence, whenever others commented on the lack of attention he paid to matters important to him, Henry visibly disengaged from the conversation, sometimes rising from his chair, and wandering about the room in a fitful state.

"Why does Henry allow Wolsey to direct his matter?" I ask. "Why does he trust it to such a man?"

"I have wondered that myself. Why does he trust such a matter to one servant?" She frowns, then resumes her pacing, lost in her thoughts.

Later that day, Anne, George, and I walk about the palace gardens with their father. During our walk, George and I find a small alcove in which to sit, while Anne and Sir Thomas stand before us, engrossed in conversation.

"Anne," he says, "I am aware of the promise between you and His Grace."

She is all astonishment, looking at me, then George, to read our faces and see if we have given the game away, but we shake our heads, gripped by the tête-à-tête unravelling before us.

"How is that, Father? Henry and I agreed to keep the news private."

"He is King, Sovereign of us both, but that does not exempt him from the courtesy of involving his beloved's father in hopes and plans for a betrothal. He sought my approval before he ever spoke with you." Apparently, there is much yet for Anne to learn about her fiancé.

"By God's blood, Henry is a study in contradiction!"

I couldn't argue with her on that. The king is powerful and utterly commanding, yet tender and sentimental – quick to raise a temper but also sensitive and forgiving, if he can be influenced. It's not hard to see why she loves him so. The attraction of power and wealth is an aphrodisiac and one that will lead many women in history to a fate they have not expected.

"I assume, then, you approve of this match? If I may ask, Father, why do you believe the King to be so tolerant of Wolsey's foibles? We can all see how frustrated he is with the obvious mishandling of the nullity suit. I find it hard to justify. If the bloated Cardinal was my Chancellor, and I was to find that he gave a matter important to me such short shrift, he would have been dealt a vicious tongue-lashing. And he would quickly find himself lighter of a great deal of his cherished wealth!"

"Do I approve? My Anne, at first, I admit I did not like the fact that the King reveres and loves you, but I have thought upon it, and knowing you will not be dissuaded from such a marriage, I am now persuaded to allow the match to bring me great joy. I am made happier still by your obvious return of the King's feelings. I can picture a bright hereafter for you and His Majesty, and the creation of a noble dynasty for the Boleyns. However, make no mistake, daughter, there are challenges ahead. You must walk on the shells of eggs, fraught with peril – and the rest of us with you." He takes a quick look around.

"You must keep your wits about you, daughter. There will be many, both male and female, who will become insane with jealousy over your elevation to royal status. It will be difficult to know whom to trust. Your mother and I are, and will be, there for you always, but take care in selecting others for sharing confidences. Moreover, you must learn to read the King as you would an awfully familiar book. His grand qualities are many but he is mercurial, and his mood can change like the wind."

Anne nods in agreement, swallowing hard as she ponders her position. I sit wide-eyed as their interaction continues.

"In response to your question about Wolsey, daughter, keep in mind the extent of his influence over the King. The Cardinal has ever been a mentor, servant, assistant, and in a way, a father figure. He was at Court during Henry VII's reign, and was well in place as a key figure when he died and young Henry ascended the throne as a boy. Never underestimate Cardinal Wolsey's influence with him – they have been together for over eighteen years, and Henry has come to depend on him almost as a second father."

"But, Papa," George says, "do you not see how Wolsey plies the king to his own advantage?"

"Of course, I do!" He turns back to Anne, whose features give way to annoyance. "As do many others who are close to His Grace. However, such a revelation would be ignored, and most likely incite wrath in rebuke. That is, unless the king sees it clearly for himself." He brushes a fly from about his face. "Do not overstep your bounds with this, Anne. You'd best be patient and allow Wolsey to place the rope about his own neck."

I can't resist the urge to contribute. "Henry is unaware how cleverly Wolsey has learned to serve his own needs and desires, and all through Henry's largesse." The three of them stare at me, wide-eyed. I've started now so I may as well finish. "Anne, you should allow the situation to be resolved as it will."

She gives me a quick nod, then looks to her father. "Henry replied to Wolsey's recent letter, graciously wishing the Cardinal well, and thanking him profusely for the good work he is doing, both on his Great Matter, and for managing the increasingly tricky diplomacy between France and the Empire, on England's behalf. The praise is deceptive, Father."

"Then we must devise the replacement of Wolsey in directing the king's annulment." With that, he turns on his heels and walks back to the palace, no doubt to rub heads with Norfolk in hatching a plan to get Wolsey out of dabbling and not doing anything about Henry's annulment.

The late summer days at Beaulieu fly by but I do my best to enjoy each one and keep it tucked safely in my memory. It's a bit of a shame I hadn't thought of keeping a journal when I first started the time-slip. Perhaps I should consider buying a lined-page diary, and bring it back through from home next time. Apart from being a good way of collecting historical nuggets, it would also be an opportunity to document comments and conversations of courtiers to use for later study. I shake my head. How would I keep such a diary secret, hidden from all eyes, including Anne's? Maybe it's not worth the bother.

Anne and the king continue to delight in each other's company, and I can well believe that he will indeed be happier with her than with his previous or subsequent wives. I try not to think of the future, preferring to stay in the moment and enjoy it as best I can. Mum and Dad come to mind quite often, even Rob, but then I remember that little 'real time' will have passed, so perhaps everything is good with them.

After dinner, Henry beckons Anne, George, and me to the gardens. "Come with me. I have a surprise."

We go as commanded and follow him through the door and around the north side of the building, across the expansive lawns, until we reached the mews where the royal falcons are housed. He disappears inside for a moment, and emerges with a small leather-wrapped parcel, which he presents to Anne. She eases open the drawstring of the pouch and withdraws a fine pair of white leather gloves, embroidered in gold, and lined in velvet. The packet also contains a white hood for a hawk, which I think is made from doeskin, embellished in gold. I glance at her, then Henry, waiting to see what she will say.

He is full of excitement, and disappears again, returning with a beautiful grey bird on his gloved hand.

"This peregrine falcon is for you, Anne, so we may go hawking together with your friends and family. I cannot take the credit for this magnificent bird but know it is a gift from the Grand Prince of Moscow."

"Oh, Your Grace!" I gush. "He is beautiful."

Anne drops into a curtsy. "Please thank the prince with all my heart. What a beautiful creature – and such a thoughtful gift! However, I am not as skilled at hawking as you. Will you teach me how to handle her?" Her cheeks glow at the adulation she is receiving.

"Of course, Mademoiselle. There are not many sports, it seems, in which you require much instruction." He grunts and nods to himself. "But I do indeed relish the opportunity to be the only man to instruct you in any sport we have yet to play."

I stifle a giggle as he raises an eyebrow, and we proceed to the fields with the hawk. I can now see how difficult it is for her to resist his attentions – he is full of playful devilment, like a child yearning to open gifts on New Year's Day, with a mischievous twinkle in his eye.

During our time here, in Katharine's absence, and with few staff about, and Court protocol eased, Henry and Anne have spent much private time together, as have George and me. Our kisses are perfection, as are our clinches, but I can't express how much I desire the feel of his warm, bare chest on my soft skin. However, we have never allowed things to escalate to that degree. As much as I want it, I know it's impossible because of Jane, so I must keep my resolve. If I fail, I'm well aware that all could be lost.

I'm not the only one, it seems. Anne has confided in me that she is struggling to remain chaste and is having to use all of her cunning and discipline to escape Henry's lustful embraces; otherwise, she may lose all composure and end up surrendering herself to her master. I know she hopes against hope that the divorce will be attained, and I try to reassure her that all will be well, though I have to be careful not to give the impression that I actually know. It is patience and perseverance that she requires, and restraint needs to be practised on all sides. On occasion, she badgers me for knowledge of the outcome but, much to her chagrin, I won't give in. However, over that lush summer break, she admits that the kinder the king is to her, the more she wants to give in to him, to release all self-control and live passionately. I know, also, that even though I have sworn not to, I have to contrive a plan by which I can be close to George in private, without compromising our reputations, or coming under the intense scrutiny of others.

As day follows day, Anne and I learn a great deal by having the uncommon opportunity to watch the king and some of his chief courtiers at work. What perplexes us most is the nature of their interaction. Henry is a contradiction within his privy council as he sways like a pendulum between acting the all-powerful commander and a man who craves validation and appreciation in his role. His friends and close councillors seek the ideal plan to convince Pope Clement to allow him a divorce from Katharine in order to marry again. I tell Anne in our private discussions that Henry does not need the approval of the pope or his desired corroboration from his Council members. Against my own advice, I plant the seed in her mind that he needs to stand alone in his decision-making and be a king, but she believes he is anxious and seems desperate for the pope's assent in this situation. Henry's Catholic roots entrench him to seek the Church's approval but he's up against it because everyone in Tudor England has been brought up as a Catholic in a Church-dominated world.

Anne and I have discussed the works of Tyndale, albeit secretly. It is so hard for me as a modern woman to understand the paradox of ultimate authority between the Church and the Monarchy but, as she explains it, I begin to grasp how the Vatican reinforces this authority unnecessarily. The King of England, who bears the motto of 'Dieu et Mon Droit – God and My Right', should simply assert his God-given right to do what was best for the future of his realm. However, Anne, as a mere woman in this world, has no way of seeing how she can advise him.

She is sorry to leave as we depart from Beaulieu the next day. I am sorry, too, because it has been a time of closeness between George and me, and for Henry and Anne, with that delightful informality, I know she will miss when we all return to Court. She tells me about the developments resulting from the discussions between the king and his councillors.

"Doctor William Knight, Henry's secretary, is to be sent to Rome with direct instructions from him, instead of receiving them from the Cardinal." She passes her jewel casket for safekeeping to one of her women.

"Do you feel more satisfied with this approach," I ask, keeping my voice low, "as it will effectively remove Wolsey from the subsequent negotiations?"

"Indeed, I do. I relish the thought of Wolsey's frustrations when he learns of this dissolution of his authority."

"Do you think Doctor Knight will have some success on his mission to the Vatican?"

"I hope so, Beth, and I hope Queen Katharine will not destroy that strategy by imploring her nephew, the Emperor Charles, to help in what she deems a disgraceful affront to her integrity and her position as Henry's rightful wife."

"Indeed, Katharine represents a considerable setback to the King's plans." I know she won't step down for her rival any time soon.

"It is difficult to say what Katharine may do when Pope Clement is still imprisoned. With Rome remaining in turmoil at the hands of Charles, the Pope is unlikely to align himself with Henry and thereby risk angering both Charles and the Queen."

It has all the makings of a dire situation but is part of the history I know and has nothing to do with my meddling, so I'm confident that things are still on track. Has the professor thought to check the pages to see if they have filled up again? It might be time to go see for myself.

Fifteen

September 1527 – Richmond

I travel with Anne, her father, and a few other members of the Beaulieu company to Richmond, where Henry intends to hold Court for the coming month or so. Katharine will not join him for a few weeks yet, and I know Anne looks forward to spending quality time with him, hunting, hawking, and playing cards.

One evening, when in the king's privy closet, tucked away from all the court, I get the chance to discuss what is now commonly known as his 'Great Matter'. Anne is anxious to have Doctor Knight reach his destination in Rome and make a positive impact on the king's behalf. Henry has received another letter from Cardinal Wolsey, who is plainly distraught about his waning position of control. The letter is an entreaty for renewed confidence in his commitment and abilities.

As we sit in his chambers, in front of Anne, I pluck up the courage to speak.

"Your Grace, do you feel the Cardinal's influence and standing with the Pope is sufficient to gain the conclusion you desire?"

"No," he replies, without hesitation, "I am not certain of that at all. I will have to follow the situation with great vigilance. God's blood! Wolsey surely should have influence and access after all the time and money he has spent there!"

"Beth and I are but inexperienced women," Anne says, before I can respond, "and, as such, we cannot advise you on matters we know nothing about, but, at the least, we will provide all the encouragement we can, and be a support to you whenever possible."

Henry looks at us in disbelief, then roars a mighty laugh, as only he can. "I cannot speak for Mistress Beth, Lady Anne, but I assure you, you are anything but an inexperienced woman! Your intrinsic knowledge would do well to be deployed to rule this nation, alongside me! I would not want to go head-to-head with you on any matter. No, my dear, I both solicit and respect your views."

"Sire, Beth is far more knowledgeable in matters of politics. She is a scholar."

"Your Grace, Mistress Boleyn exaggerates!"

"Does she? I think not. You are wise beyond your years, Mistress Wickers, and yet not appearing a day older than when I was first acquainted with you." He views me with a suspicious eye, my nerves rising under his gaze.

"Sire, Mistress Wickers is blessed with a youthful complexion most women could only wish for."

I'm sure my face is purple with the fire in my cheeks. Thank you, Anne, for jumping to my defence.

"Then you are incredibly lucky, and unbelievably beautiful, as youth appears to be on your side! I have long admired your beauty, Beth."

His compliment makes me blush even more. It's clear that, when Anne's with him, he makes her feel as if she can accomplish anything. In that moment, it's easy to picture them as a loving royal couple, married for many long years, surrounded by their children; the heir and spares Henry hopes to have from their relationship. Sadly, I know the truth of how many years they'll be together, happy or not.

30th September 1527 – Richmond Palace

Cardinal Wolsey has been summoned to Richmond upon the king's command. Anne and I are sat in the window embrasure of the music room in the late afternoon. She is teaching me how to play the lute, and we're working together on a new composition. I'm all fingers and thumbs, and pretty confident that I'll never play as well as her. My concentration on plucking the strings is broken when we're interrupted by an equerry, who announces a messenger. The young man enters the room, looking dishevelled – sodden from the steady downpour. Anne frowns on seeing the mud he's trodden onto the red and gold Turkish carpet.

"Mistress Boleyn, I have come to see His Majesty," he says, bowing low. "I am sent by Cardinal Wolsey, who wishes to meet the King to provide a report of his travels. The Cardinal wishes to be advised of the hour at which he should report to the King's Privy Chamber for the meeting."

Anne blushes, and I know it's because her temper is rising. Her tongue can be sharp at times like this; she never seems able to restrain herself when her blood is up.

"You may remind the Cardinal," she snaps, "that no one joins the King in his Privy Chambers unless expressly invited." Within seconds, she sets her lute down on the window seat and marches from the room, with me and Wolsey's messenger following her through the labyrinth of corridors and passages to the king's apartments.

All eyes are on us as we reach our destination, and when we enter, the hallowed doors are shut firm behind us.

Anne extends her arm towards Henry. "His Grace, the Cardinal, shall report here, where the King is already," she says, as if it was the most obvious thing in the world.

Henry seems pleased at her sudden appearance and stands up from his chair to greet her, planting a small kiss on her cheek and nodding towards me in acknowledgement as I curtsy. The nervous, soaked messenger peers at the king for some sign of confirmation that these orders are, in fact, valid, whereupon Henry, straight-faced, conveys his agreement with an emphatic nod. The young man thanks him, looking flustered at being ordered around by a woman, but he affords Anne and me a respectful bow and retreats from the room. She places her hand on Henry's arm.

"Henry, I am most sorry to enter your chambers unannounced. I should not have proceeded here as I did but the messenger was sent to me before you. However, you must know how much it irks me when the Cardinal presumes to tell his King what he should do."

Admittedly, she never seems to realise that she often commits the same offence. My gaze darts from his face to hers as she gives him an apologetic look, then laughs. "I am sure that poor messenger had no idea what was happening, or from whom he should receive his orders. His head was moving back and forth as if he were watching a play of tennis, trying to work it out!"

Henry laughs along with his mistress. "Your invective was well worded, sweetheart. I am sure I would have said mostly the same thing. That is, had I been given the chance...?" He raises an eyebrow and they burst into laughter. Their company is infectious, and how anyone can infer that Anne's interest in Henry is anything other than love, based on their correspondence and verbal intercourse, baffles me. She is no wilting flower, and he is beginning to learn that he has met his match.

"And I am glad you are being recognized as someone of great importance to me," he continues, "even if it is at the expense of the Cardinal's messenger." He chuckles to himself, not batting an eyelid at my presence. I am much like Anne's shadow, and he is so used to having me around that I am privy to many a conversation he has.

Shortly afterwards, a crier heralds the Cardinal's arrival, and following a nod from Henry, Wolsey enters the chamber. At a glance, he looks pasty and ashen, worn out by diplomatic relations that are clearly beyond his remit. Does Henry notice the strain he appears to be under, or does he even care? I think he just wants results. Wolsey looks downtrodden. He lumbers over to his king, bowing as low and deferentially as his decrepit bones will allow. When Henry addresses him, Wolsey raises himself with great difficulty.

"My dear Thomas, how very good to see you again," Henry begins, his tone kind.

The Cardinal glances about, unsure whether to proceed with the conversation in light of the company in the room. I think he went away with the misconception that Anne would be a dalliance, at most a mistress, and definitely not wife material, and seeing the reality now, his response comes only after a perceptible hesitation. His expression is no longer one of haughty superiority but edged with apprehension. He shuffles, not quite knowing where to start.

"You can speak freely in front of Mistress Anne," Henry says, "for she is privy to all my closest secrets. I keep nothing from her!"

Wolsey's mouth opens in shock, but he checks himself and continues to deliver his message. Anne clenches her fists by her side, her knuckles white, with Henry standing beside her, his gaze bearing down on the squirming cardinal. It is uncomfortable to watch as the man delivers his report.

As we return to Hever in the jolty litter, I reflect on my time at court. Anne was in her element – fully involved. She put her all into each game of cards, merels, dancing, and hunting that the weather would allow in the last few weeks we remained at Richmond. Henry enjoyed competing with her, and later reports that they were so often merry together are true. He loves the sport of making wagers with her, and she won more often over him than he did over her. I avoided being drawn into such games and always watched from the side lines, peering at her cards over her shoulder, before walking around the table to view his. He tried to bribe me several times into revealing her hand, but I never gave her game away. She was like a wry fox as she emptied his purse with every turn of her cards. And she knows he secretly loves that about her. Of course, the supreme wager he longs to make above any other is to be in her bed, but she is always clever at keeping him at arm's length, well able to redirect him.

With the promise of the Christmas season gaining momentum, it makes me feel homesick because, when I left my 'real life', it was fast approaching the end of term and Christmas. How much time has passed? As much as I love it here, I'd hate to miss the food, booze, and presents with my family, and surely, they'd be concerned if I just disappeared and didn't show up for the festivities. I wouldn't have to be away for long, though I know I'll feel guilty leaving. Anne needs me. Then there's George. What do I do about him? But things are going so well now, and everything is back on track. And if I go back, I can check to see if the pages have filled in.

Even so, spending so long here means I've become much closer to these real Tudor personalities. I'm drawn by the lines written in Henry's songbook, and obsessed with immersing myself in the glamour, opulence, and infinite intrigues and trysts of the Tudor Court, with its rich, beguiling thrills igniting my senses and imagination. The professor invited me to travel alone, living in the sophistication of Henry's palaces, to partake in the extravagant, multi-course feasts of beast, fish, and fowl; to feel the weight of my damask gowns brush across stone floors, and witness advisors jostling for power as they scheme and squabble behind the closed doors of the Privy Chamber. I can't help but be awestruck as I observe Henry wooing Anne as he tries to lead her into the royal bedchamber, on his terms.

Then there's George. I never expected that anyone might be attracted to me in such an intense, passionate way, least of all Anne's brother. Why does he have a wife! The deeper I get into this Tudor world, the more I'm mesmerised and captivated by him, and more so the older he gets! I never expected to be transfixed by him. Perhaps, initially, I thought he'd be a distraction, but I never imagined I'd fall in love. Before him, I fancied Rob. I thought I might even fall in love with him. However, after spending the last few months here, there is no denying the fact that George has stolen my heart. If Agnes or Nan hadn't disturbed us when they did, the outcome might have been more than a bit of bodice-ripping!

I shake the visuals from my mind, no matter how arousing they might be. The litter lurches from side to side, across the hard, impacted ground. Snow is settling on the tree branches, creating a wonderful, festive vista. Anne, wrapped in her furs, looks out of the window at the crisp, white sky, watching winter hares racing in and out of their burrows. I sit opposite her, with Agnes beside me, a woollen rug shared across our laps. She's resting her head against my shoulder, snoring, which allows Anne and me the opportunity to talk.

"I thought it best to come home, now that Henry has decided the court should go to Greenwich, to spend the remainder of the season there."

"You will miss him, I think?"

"Yes, of course, but Katharine will be joining everyone." She sighs, folding her arms across her chest. "For that reason, Henry feels it will be better for us to remain out of immediate view while I wait for a positive answer from Rome."

"Hever is the right place to be – you can see your mother." Also, this visit might allow my exit through the portal to visit home for a while. I know 'real-time' will hardly have moved but I feel like I've been away for a veritable age.

She leans forward, up close, looking into my eyes. "You want to go home, too – don't you?" I have to strain to hear her whisper, but her grimace is clear. "To your time. To your family." She leans back, pulling the fur-lined hood of her cloak around her face to keep the biting air at bay. I know she hates me leaving, and she doesn't look happy about it.

"At some point, I'm going to have to. I need to catch up with my own family. If I don't, and my absence is noticed, there will be trouble."

She stiffens. "Trouble? What kind of trouble?"

Agnes's gentle snores give me the confidence to speak. "The kind of problem where your parents might think you've been kidnapped, or even murdered!" I keep my voice low. It doesn't help that she can't seem to appreciate my situation. I shake my head at myself. Why should she understand? This situation is unique, and entirely of my making. Might be best to put things across in a way she can relate to. "You know, the kind of trouble where your parents might take to their beds with worry?"

She nods, blinks to herself, and turns to look out at the passing scenery of farms, fields, and villages. Then she snaps around to me.

"Let me come back with you, through the portal? I want to experience your time."

"My era is a far more dangerous prospect than the placid Hever Castle," I say, hoping that will put an end to such thoughts.

November 1527 – Hever Castle, Kent

Anne and I pass our time together in Kent, enjoying the occasional visit from Mary and her two children, Catherine, and little Henry Carey. Their visits are a welcome diversion, as we love caring for and playing with the youngsters. When Anne is with them, it is so obvious how much joy it would give her to have children of her own. The weather, already dismal, grows progressively colder, much more than is typical for this time of year. Anne pines and sulks, finding it difficult to be apart from Henry after they've spent every day in each other's company, and it's clear that she daydreams of him whenever she can. She's been embroidering a motto onto a linen ribbon to emphasise her suffering. It's convoluted wording – 'Always towards absent lovers love's tide stronger flows' – sounds so much better in the original Latin: 'Semper in absentes felicior aestus amantes'. She bears her heartache with every stitch.

The separation also precludes her from attending a grand event being held at Greenwich in mid-November – Henry's investiture in the French Order of St Michel, which will seal the alliance between him and King François. It will be celebrated by a tournament, a grand banquet, and a masque at the banqueting and disguising houses at Greenwich, and no expense will be spared. She longs to be there, and although her status grows daily, matters of state and public spectacle still elude her.

In Kent, we do the best we can to enjoy Christmastide, but it is so cold that Lady Elizabeth limits the number of rooms we use in the house to conserve firewood and maximize heat. One day, after putting it off for so long, I take the opportunity to try the portal. With Anne's family around her, it makes me think of mine and how much I miss them. I miss my friends, too, and university, and I even miss Professor Marshall. While time may not have passed much back home, here, it has, and it feels like I've been away from everyone for way too long. I miss my friendships and the relationships with people in my modern life. I'm not a cold creature – far from it – and right now I'm feeling the need to reconnect.

I've worked hard to set things straight – to complete my mission – and I'm happy to have spent such a prolonged amount of time here to secure Anne's future, to set her on her own life path. Perhaps it's time to let her travel on ahead without me. Does she even need me anymore? It saddens my heart to think she doesn't. Would I be able to just cut myself off from everything in 'Tudorville' and return to my home life – my real life? Goodness, at this stage, I'm not sure where my real life lies.

I make sure I'm alone when I enter the antechamber. With the tapestry behind me, I step towards the portal, full of trepidation at not having returned home in such a long time. But then I smile to myself at the thought that hardly any time will have passed. It's something I'm still not used to.

My stomach flips at the sound of something shuffling behind me and, when I turn, I see the unmistakable shape of Anne in the shadows. She looks around, pressing on walls, no doubt trying to work out where the entrance to the portal is. My dream flashes behind my eyes and my neck goes cold. What would happen if she travelled into the future? How would she survive without being inoculated against the likes of measles, mumps, polio, or even the common cold? Oh, my goodness, imagine the consequences if there was a vaccine, I could give them against the sweating sickness. William Carey would survive, and so many more. I shiver as these possibilities tumble through my mind. I need to stop even considering what might happen if I interfere or meddle in her world, any more than I already have. No, the consequences are too dire, and that snaps me back to this reality.

"Anne, what are you doing?" I can't believe this. "You cannot follow me through the door. It's impossible."

"Why is it? I want to see the England you come from."

I grab her shoulder in the darkness, my dream coming back to me again – the sheer panic of chasing her over Westminster bridge.

"You can't. You mustn't!" I insist. "What about the King? Your situation is too important to abandon now."

I try to drag her back, but she keeps on, doing her utmost to persuade me to take her. There's no other way but to grip her arm with both hands and drive her back from the passageway, through the antechamber and into her bedroom.

"If you don't do as you're told, I swear on my life, I will leave you, and never return!" My voice is close to a screech, and she flinches.

"You would come back – if not for me, you'd come back for George. I know you love him!"

"Don't bribe me with love, Anne."

"Why not? It is as good a reason as any to stay here, is it not?"

She blinks several times at me, as if daring me to disagree, but I can't because she's right. And I hate that she is. I could never stay away, when my heart belongs to George. For this reason alone, I abandon my intention of returning home, for now.

———————•❄•———————

On the day following the end of the Christmas season, a courier arrives, practically frozen, with a package for Anne from Henry. The shivering man sits by the fire, warming himself as he eats some food between sips of wine in preparation for the return trip to Greenwich. Anne has gone to her chamber to compose a short reply to be taken back. She scribbles a note of thanks for Henry's kindness in thinking of her and promises to compose a longer letter the following day.

Once the messenger has been revived enough to be sent out into the grey, frozen landscape, Anne goes back to her chamber and settles herself next to the hearth to open the parcel that accompanied her new letter. I watch with excitement as she peeks inside the leather pouch to find a long, narrow wooden box lined in deep-green velvet. She opens it to reveal a breath-taking jewel – a large, clear diamond – set in gleaming gold, and hanging from a chain. Her look of disbelief says it all, and she's not sure whether to laugh or cry. Also inside the leather bag is a small scroll of parchment. When she unrolls it, Henry's strong script greets her. She reads it out, and I'm delighted to be able to witness it. I have to say, she is ever gracious with me, facilitating my desire to experience my time here to the fullest. I'm thankful that she isn't bearing a grudge after not being allowed through the portal – still allowing me to be privy to most of her secrets.

"'To be worn by my dearest love, the most beautiful woman in the world.'" Excitement carries each word, and it's obvious from her expression that she's touched by Henry's thoughts.

"Beth, I long to be his in mind, body, and soul. I am finding it hard to be patient, having to wait to hear some news of what is happening in Rome."

"Anne, I know you would rather be planning your wedding celebrations, and it has been frustrating to learn that the efforts of Doctor Knight have not been as significant as we had hoped."

She sighs, turning the jewel in her hands. "I am so glad the King stays ever more closely in touch with me and tells me how this campaign is being waged but the longer it goes on, I confess, the less I expect a successful outcome or the hope of ever becoming Henry's bride."

I laugh. "You once never wanted to be his wife – it was just a ruse to be rid of him."

"Over time, my feelings have changed somewhat," she says, holding the jewel up to the light so it sparkles all the more, the refractions bouncing from ceiling to wall. "A woman has the right to change her mind, does she not?"

One evening, sitting as close as we safely can to a sparking fire, Lady Boleyn opens up the conversation.

"Anne, as often as we have talked about your hope and plan to marry the King once he is awarded a divorce from Katharine, we have never discussed the fact that the marriage would make you Queen Consort." She doesn't look up from the tiny stitches she's making to a seam in a linen shirt for her husband but, after a short while, she stops and fixes her gaze on her daughter.

"Well, what think you on that? Is it the hope of being queen which motivates your desire to marry Henry?"

Anne puts down the embroidery she's working on and gives her mother an uncompromising look.

"Mother, besides Beth,"—she smiles at me—"you are the only person in the world to whom I could say this with the chance it would be believed. A crown is not my reason for wanting this marriage, though I am no fool and know what it would mean for the Boleyns and Howards. I have maintained my virginity, though only God knows how difficult that has been. I have valued my maidenhead enough to resist the men who wished to take it from me. I have waited long for the great love of my life, and now he is within my reach. Never would I have expected this love to come from the King of England, nor could I have planned it. Yet I do love Henry with all my heart, and I believe we are destined to be together. It is only that desire – to be a wife and, above all, to be the mother of the sons and daughters we will have together – that motivates me."

She brushes the surface of her embroidery with the backs of her fingers. It is so important that her mother, of all people, understands. "In my heart and mind, to be a queen without the true love of a husband is but an entrapment in a life of unhappiness. Do not forget, at a tender age I had the opportunity to watch closely the fates of both Mary Tudor, the French Queen, in her marriage to the ancient and ill King Louis X11, and then poor Queen Claude to King François. Both were queens, yet neither were happy."

"I do believe you, Anne, of course, I do. Because I know you so well, I do not doubt that the love you bear Henry is the root of your desire to be his wife. However, are you truly aware of how your quest will be viewed by others at Court? Not only the English Court but as far away as Rome. And in France and Spain? Look at the calamities in Rome. I have heard from your father that Pope Clement, as a virtual prisoner in the Castel Sant'Angelo, has finally escaped disguised as a pedlar. Some of the territories of the Papal States have been absorbed by Emperor Charles, while others have been taken by Italian city-states seeking land at the expense of the Pope. Clement will try to avoid any decision that displeases Emperor Charles, and that includes him granting an annulment or divorce from Katharine so that Henry is free to marry you. You will not be regarded as simply a girl who wishes to marry a man she loves. Yours will be a complicated life: you will be the object of backbiting and ridicule…and in that way, I do worry for you, daughter."

Anne gets up, invites her mother to stand, and hugs her. "I know you do, Mother. And, indeed, I know some already resent me, even though Henry's intent has not been made public. But, as I see it, there is little I can do except to walk the path that is laid before me. I love Henry and, God willing, I intend to be his wife. And if God's plan is that I become queen, I will rule with every scrap of ability He will give me."

"Then, in that case, my daughter,"—she kisses Anne's cheek—"I will be there for you, to support and defend you always. You may come to me with any confidence you wish to share, and it will be kept. And when and if I can, I will advise you if asked." She stands back then, still holding Anne's hands in hers.

"I do have one certainty: should God Almighty place you in the position of queen, together, you and Henry will create a magnificent destiny for England." Lady Boleyn has just uttered the truest words she will ever speak.

3RD FEBRUARY 1528 – HEVER

It seems Henry intends to send Stephen Gardiner, Wolsey's secretary, along with Edward Foxe, Bishop of Hereford, to Rome with a new strategy to convince Pope Clement that his marriage was unsanctioned by God. The letter Anne has just read from him describes the mission Foxe and Gardiner will take, painting it in a positive, hopeful light. In an added effort to keep her fully briefed, he has sent them here today to Hever to deliver the letter to her in person, before they set out for Rome. While the two public officials wait, she reads Henry's personal assurances that everything possible is being done to move the matter towards a favourable conclusion.

She sits in her chair, reading the letter over and over, then gets to her feet and hands it to me. I start reading it aloud. A frown dances across her forehead as she looks out of the casement window.

"What does 'ultra-posse non est esse' mean?" I ask, tracing my fingers over the illustrious and now-familiar handwriting.

She turns to me, distracted from her daydream. "One can't do more than the possible."

The messengers shuffle as they wait. I feel so privileged to be witnessing meetings such as these.

"I know you work for His Majesty," she says, "I thank you for coming, and for bringing me up to date on how things are going with the king's matter." She sits back against the plump cushion.

"As you know, Lady Anne, I am Doctor Stephen Gardiner and this is Edward Foxe, and we have come directly from Court under orders from the king."

She looks at the men with impatience, eager to fully understand the nature of their business with her. Stephen Gardiner is secretary to Wolsey, and has been present on one or two occasions when Henry had reason to parley with him. Master Stephen, as he is commonly known at court, is a complex figure, who has impressed the king with his knowledge of both canon and civil law. However, my historical knowledge of the man is frustratingly patchy, but he appears ambitious, wily, and a shrewd character who keeps his own counsel. He is a Cambridge academic, Master of Trinity Hall, and looks to be in his mid-thirties. His reputation is one of arrogance, and his demeanour emphasizes this in the way he looks down his nose at people. Everyone. Even with Henry's wife to be. He's no fan of Anne Boleyn. He is crafty, wily, and cunning, even by his own admission. The man's reputation precedes him, and his devotion to the Roman Catholic faith makes it difficult to warm to him. He is irascible, tactless, and confrontational, which, combined with his formidable intellect, makes him a notoriously problematic man to deal with. In my twenty-first-century view, a right bastard!

Edward Foxe, on the other hand, is Henry's almoner, and an entirely different kettle of fish to Gardiner, though roughly the same age as his travelling companion. He says little to nothing, although he seems a warm and humble man, who radiates a quiet compassion and kindness, while seemingly being able to see into a person's heart when he looks deep into their eyes, as if he is omnipotent. I'm assuming him to be a man of the new faith – one who can be trusted and confided in, much like an old friend. I have only ever met him in passing, and I know even less about him. However, Anne seems confident in their company and listens with interest to what they have to say.

"Mistress Anne, Doctor Foxe and I have been most anxious to see you." They flick apprehensive looks at me, no doubt wondering why she doesn't dismiss me from their company.

"Mistress Wickers can stay – she knows as much as I do of the King's Great Matter."

Gardiner bows, first to Anne, then to me. We reciprocate with deep curtsies. Then he continues.

"We are here as His Majesty's humble servants, commanded by the King to deliver to you this message you have now read, written by His Majesty's own hand." He looks at the crisp parchment, which I place on the table, at Anne's elbow.

"His Majesty commands me to convey his deepest desiring for your good health, Madam."

Anne stands again and walks in front of the roaring fire. "I thank you both, most kindly for your great pains on my behalf." She smiles at both men. "I have read the king's message and need to understand how I may serve you."

"Of course, Madam."

As Gardiner speaks, Foxe stands in silence beside him. The two doctors are being sent by Henry on deputation to Pope Clement in Orvieto, having the unenviable task of trying to secure permission to allow a papal legate to preside over an English trial alongside the Cardinal. They will fail in their quest to seek an annulment for Henry. I know this from history and my studies but I'm intrigued to find out more about their mission, and about the two men who stand before Anne, and whether or not they can and should be trusted. It's fascinating to observe individuals who play supporting roles, as they seem equally as interesting as the main characters on the Tudor stage. Some could be deadly in their manoeuvrings at court, especially when on the ascent, like Thomas Cromwell, who will soon become a central character in our lives; he will be particularly interesting to observe if he is ignored or underestimated by any of us. Anne will learn to her cost, later on, that those lethal enemies and unexpected friends will be found lurking in every corner.

Lady Boleyn enters the room and seats herself on a stool next to Anne's chair, opposite the two men. Anne sits beside her and, with our visitors giving her expectant looks, she turns her attention back to the matter in hand.

"Pray tell me, Gardiner, what is the exact nature of your embassy? In his letter, the king makes it clear that you are charged with the task of bringing to bear a solution to the question of His Grace's annulment. Are you to meet with Clement himself?"

"Indeed, Mistress Boleyn, that is correct."

"The Pope now resides in exile, in the town of Orvieto," Dr Foxe says, taking up the thread of the conversation, "since the unholy sacking of Rome by the Emperor's forces earlier this year."

Gardiner nods at this. "The King's Majesty has commanded us to do all that is within our power to obtain a decretal commission from the Pope."

"What will this commission achieve?" Anne asks, addressing Dr Foxe.

"The commission will lay down the principles of law, which will allow His Grace, Cardinal Wolsey, to resolve the matter directly with the Pope's representative here in England, without the appeal to Rome."

"I see." She looks at her mother, then at me, and I can almost see the cogs turning in her head as she tries to make full sense of the implications of their words. "Sirs, if you are successful, this will simplify proceedings enormously, freeing the King from protracted legal arguments overseas."

"Madam, if it can be done, my colleague shall be the one to successfully complete his task." Foxe tilts his head at Gardiner, his gaze not leaving Anne's.

"Do you think Pope Clement will grant this decretal commission?"

"Mistress Boleyn, fear not, as we have the keenest minds in the kingdom when dealing with the law. No one understands matters clearer than we do."

"Except the king, perhaps," she says, getting up again to pace the floor in front of the fire.

Henry had not expected the Pope to be held prisoner by the Spanish royal family, and knows well that, even though he has been loyal to Rome, writing the Assertio septem sacramentorum – the Defence of the Seven Sacraments – to Pope Leo X in 1521, it will never grant him a divorce. The Spanish royal family hold Pope Clement hostage in order to control what happens with Henry's annulment. Anne has understood this since May, showing great political acumen.

"Mistress, trust in us to fulfil His Majesty's wishes," Gardiner says, as he and Foxe smile at her.

"Then, gentlemen, with all of my heart, I wish you success." She brings her palms together. "Mother, before the gentlemen resume their journey, will you allow them to sup with us as our guests, for the night will soon be drawing in?"

"Yes, of course. I think that a wise suggestion, Anne."

The men bow and follow Lady Boleyn from the parlour, leaving Anne to ponder the possible outcome of the impending visit to Rome. On a positive note, she is overjoyed at the king's commitment to her by rallying all his resources to bring about the end of his marriage to Katharine. Part of me dreads the future for her. I know how arduous and torturous this journey from royal mistress to queen will be, and the stakes have just been driven higher.

While our guests retire to their rooms, preparing for supper, Anne and I make our way up the stairs to the light and airy Long Gallery. It has become my favourite place to sit and read or converse with Anne during our time away from court, and I am glad of its solitude. The rain rattles on the stained-glass windows, and the wind chases feathery clouds across an ever-darkening sky, highlighted with hues of pink and grey. I sit in the alcove window seat with Anne as she flicks through her copy of a smuggled, tiny translation of William Tyndale's English Bible, and we recall our conversation about his writings on the way to our first visit to York Place a few years before.

In our enthusiasm for the word of God, we fail to notice the footsteps of one of our distinguished visitors as he approaches us. As Anne almost jumps to her feet, she drops the leather-bound book on the floor, her cheeks flushing at the thought of being found with such heretical material. Dr Foxe reaches down to pick it up. He thumbs through the fine pages before snapping it shut and handing it back.

"My Lady, stay seated. There is no need to rise on my account."

She seems dumbstruck, possibly out of fear of exposing her religious leanings. Flustered, she sits back on the alcove, holding the forbidden book in her lap.

"Master Foxe, will you come sit with us a while?" she asks. "I pray you, sir, please come and join Mistress Wickers and myself, for we are starved of educated company, cooped up here. It is our privilege to have such a learned man in our midst."

He smiles back at her, then at me, seemingly pleased with her praise of his intellect. In her delight at being in his company, it seems that she forgets that she's holding a banned text, and is shocked when he leans across, plucks the book from her lap, and flicks through the pages again. I must look panic-stricken, for he turns to me.

"Do not be alarmed, Mistress Wickers, for I am of the same persuasion as yourself and your mistress. We share the same thirst for knowledge, to find the truth of God's word. We are of the same kidney."

Anne and I must still look stunned, as the corners of his mouth curl up into a large smile.

"Be not afraid, ladies, as there are increasing numbers of us at court who believe in the new faith and have been challenged by it. It brings me great joy to see you in possession of such a godly text."

The tension goes out of Anne's shoulders as Foxe continues with his praise, concurring with her on many of her beliefs.

"Do not be fooled by those conservatives at court, like your uncle Norfolk, the Duke of Suffolk, the Marquis of Exeter, and the Courtenays, they will always remain in the old faith. Do not fear, for increasingly, Mistress Anne, you have the ear of the king, and I see it as a miracle that God has opened your eyes. You are in such a position to influence His Majesty."

"Do you believe that, Master Foxe?" I ask.

"Indeed, I do, Mistress Wickers, for who but the Lady Anne is in such proximity to Henry, to be able to pull the shackles from his eyes, allowing him to see the truth in scripture and doctrine?"

Anne's eyes grow wide as she contemplates the enormity of her growing influence, but this is old news to me, and historic news at that.

"Doctor Foxe, you astound me with your words." She is still reeling from this, her 'lightbulb' moment, as if someone has removed a blindfold from her eyes and this is the first time she sees the light in a darkened world.

"There are those at court, Mistress Anne, who long for the dawning of a new era in the Church, and desire to incorporate Luther and Tyndale's teachings into our doctrine. The Church will be looking to you to be its patron, Madam, for you will help change things through your unique influence. This is why God has granted you a position of power at the king's side, and I will do everything in my power to resolve His Majesty's Great Matter, so that he may take you as his true and wedded wife."

Anne seems struck with the sincerity of the man's sentiments and her eyes sparkle with her emotional reaction, knowing she has just formed another friendship with a sworn ally. This is not about just Henry and her as a couple; it never has been. It is about her place by his side, speeding up the reformation and bringing light to a medieval world full of middle-aged superstitions and doctrine. I have tried to guide her in the great responsibility she bears in this matter but it isn't until now that her influence within the Church has been revealed to her. Foxe pulls a vellum-covered book from his pocket and hands it to her.

"I have hoped and prayed for an opportunity to give you this book, my Lady, and have spoken with your father on this matter, who is most happy for me to do so."

The embossed rectangular design on the cover doesn't hint at its contents, for such embossing is popular with most Tudor books of the period. It isn't until Anne opens it to reveal the title page that her breath is taken away: The Obedience of a Christian Man, by William Tyndale.

Sixteen

MID-FEBRUARY 1528

With the boredom of 'sameness' at Hever during the dark and cold months of winter, I decide it will do no harm to use the cypher ring or try the portal again. After the last failed experience, I'm hoping Anne won't hock my heels again to prevent me from going, or want to come with me. As I pull back the tapestry to the door, I hear her calling.

"Beth? Beth, where are you?"

She walks from her bedchamber and is soon at my side. The ring heats up on my finger as I try the door, but I stop when she rests her hand on mine.

"Do not leave me!" she pleads. She pulls me back and watches me twist the ring. Caught red-handed, I'm grateful she didn't come a little later and follow me through. "Why would you go home, when I need you?"

"I just wanted to see if the ring and the portal still worked, is all." I lower my lashes, ridden by guilt. Maybe it was presumptuous of me to think I could leave her to her own devices. Does that make me a disloyal friend? Perhaps she needs to be loyal to me, and allow me to catch up with my own family. Has she considered how I might be feeling?

She stares at me. "I am sorry, Beth. Forgive me?" She reaches out but I don't move. "As my friend, and because my situation is still unresolved…"

"You mean, your matter with the king?"

"Yes, exactly that." She tries to smile at me. "I thought you would stay and see things through with me. It makes me uncomfortable to know that you are happy to leave me at any time. I thought I meant more to you than that?" Now she's trying to make me feel guilty. "Do I have to beg you to stay?"

"No, no, of course not."

"What if I were to turn a blind eye to how you and George are together?"

I imagine my ears pricking up with that remark. "What do you mean?"

"Well, if I one day caught him kissing you, for example, I might turn a blind eye. What say you?"

I realise my mouth is hanging open. "Anne Boleyn, that is bribery!"

"Call it what you will – would that make you stay, besides my need of you?"

"You are a strong enough woman to deal with whatever history is dishing out to you. You don't need me!"

"I shall be the judge of that!"

"Now you are sounding like a queen!" I giggle, tugging the tapestry back over the door. It gives me a sense of importance to know that she feels she can't get through the winter months without me, her best friend. I resign myself to remaining here for another while.

The numbing winter is relinquishing its grip on the English countryside when Anne receives an invitation from Henry. She and her mother are invited to come and stay with him at Windsor. My excitement knows no bounds as I help Agnes pack her gowns, riding and hunting clothes, articles for the toilette, and jewellery.

"Mistress Anne," Agnes says, her voice full of nervous excitement, "then we truly are to stay in the king's lodgings?"

"Yes, Agnes, that is what the king's message requested. The note read that he would have me, my mother, Mistress Wickers and, of course, you at Windsor in the royal lodgings to celebrate the end of winter."

She looks at the two of us in such a loving way, it's hard to imagine in later years that she will develop such a savage tongue. To be honest, I'm more excited than her at the thought of leaving Hever, for as much as I love the place, I won't be sorry to see new surroundings after being closed up in this house all winter long.

"It appears the king is preparing a grand banquet in my honour!" Her face lights up, and it's clear to see how she has missed Henry's company and wants nothing more than to spend time with him.

We are all warmly welcomed by the staff at Windsor Castle upon our arrival, and shown to lodgings in the tower adjacent to the great gate. The tower has beautiful floor-to-ceiling windows in the base court, and hallways fan from it, with each containing chambers. Elizabeth Boleyn's lodging is halfway along the gallery hall, while Anne's rooms are nearer the king's. Both have stained-glass windows, which open on one side to the lovely courtyard and on the other to views of the massive and famous round tower. At the foundation of this are the tennis plays Henry has had built.

Anne's chambers include a sitting room, a privy suite, and a large and well-furnished bedchamber, along with a small chamber for Agnes, and a large bathroom, which they call a 'bayne', as well as a privy chamber. I'm happy to discover that I'll be sharing with her, on a palette bed supplied for me. I'm treated much better than poor Agnes, and my gowns are almost as sumptuous as Anne's, so we also share a closet full of fine dresses. When she sweeps in, her lips curl into a smile as if she already wears a crown. These chambers are more luxurious than any others we have experience of at court; she even has a presence chamber to formally receive guests, hear petitions, and dine in public if she wishes, and the atmosphere is so different – without the prying eyes of Katharine's women.

A discreet knock at the door shakes us from our excitement. It's a messenger, with a note summoning Anne to the king's privy closet for a late supper.

She is bursting at the prospect of renewing her romance with Henry after months of being apart, and with heightened anticipation, she gives me the agreeable task of choosing her gown for the reunion ahead.

After she has gone, the chamber fills with shadows, and I spend the next few hours reading in the flickering light as I wait for her to return. I squint into the pages of William Tyndale's book, searching for the sections I know Henry will read and be so inspired by. The priceless tome feels weighty, its crisp pages not yet aged with time. Oh, how I would love to sneak this original literary work into my holdall and take it back to university with me. How incredible it would be to own a first edition!

My solitary study is interrupted by the swinging of the chamber doors as Anne skips in full of excitement, bursting to share her tales of tonight's intimacies.

"We have behaved like two young people giddy in love for the first time!" she cries. "The King embraced and kissed me constantly, making jokes and dancing. He even lifted me as if I were a mere child, swinging me around until I collapsed in a dizzy heap at his feet."

"It sounds like you have had a wonderful evening!" I say.

"I have never had such a wonderful time with anyone like this in my life – the King never fails to surprise me! We so enjoyed being together."

"The King adores you, Anne. It's evident for all to see."

"I even asked him if he would teach me how to play tennis!"

"How can he do that, when women are not allowed to play?"

She shrugs and smiles. "I can but try to change the rules!"

I think about modern tennis attire and consider what Gina Clark, as the Tudor Dreams Historical Costumier, might design for Anne to wear to play tennis. I laugh to myself. It certainly wouldn't be a miniskirt or tight shorts.

"Mistress, I do not think it is becoming for any woman to play such a game of exertion," I say, hardly believing that I'm discouraging a woman from playing tennis. "Perhaps it would be better if you cheered Henry on from the side-lines."

"You are right. What was I thinking?" She nods at my suggestion.

The door opens and Agnes enters, here to prepare Anne for bed. We stop our chat but I'm looking forward to hearing more before we fall to sleep.

The weather's transformation is miraculous. The air is warm, and the sun gilds the damp earth. Flowers are everywhere, blooming in profusion, unfolding in their gorgeous yellow cheerfulness. Anne, Henry, and I are able to ride out together almost every day. I follow at a distance with his mounted guard to allow the couple some privacy. My equestrian skills are far more accomplished now and I feel comfortable riding side-saddle.

We explore Windsor Great Park, riding across broad meadows and lawns and into the wooded byways, which is incredible to see, without all the modern-day hustle, bustle, and architecture. There is something mystical about riding along trails in hushed, deep, evergreen, and deciduous forests, and I feel so lucky to be experiencing the expanse of parkland before the encroachment of modern man. The sun casts motley shapes on the budding leaves and across the mossy, living floor beneath the forest canopy. Our horses' hooves cut up the ground, releasing the sharp, clean scent of pine from the carpet of needles. At one point, we all dismount and lead our steeds by the reins and, from my position at the rear, I have a better opportunity to peer through the trees, searching for a glimpse of a fawn, a squirrel, a bright red fox, or, if I'm lucky, an elusive owl.

Henry and Anne are deep in conversation about his Great Matter, of course, and, from the snippets of conversation I catch, she seems to be encouraging him to trust his instincts and be less dependent on the opinions voiced by Wolsey. They talk of religion, and she bravely argues the point as to why any educated English person should not be able to read the Bible for themselves. She asks him if he knows why Arundel, the then Archbishop of Canterbury, forbade the translation or reading of an English Bible as a matter of law over a hundred years ago. Henry agrees in principle but maintains his allegiance to the Catholic doctrine, which prohibits such practices. They enjoy discussing the theories of humanism, and he says that he has always been fascinated by the works of Aristotle, especially his writings on logic and ethics as a basis for humanist precepts. While Anne has read some Aristotle as part of her early education, she has never been an accomplished student of his work and, recognizing Henry's evident interest in the subject, she determines to refresh her knowledge.

One afternoon, we are riding nose-to-tail on a narrow woodland path, when Henry turns in his saddle. "Anne, on the morrow, I wish to show you a special place. We will leave early and have a supper outdoors there if the weather is fair." She agrees, intrigued to discover what he has planned.

At sunrise the next morning, Agnes wakes us. We are to meet Henry and go to the docks, where the rowers will take us on a barge down the Thames. Once the river journey is complete, we are to ride the rest of the way. The prospect of the adventure is exciting, and I'm looking forward to seeing the countryside from the river. I waste no time rising to wash, and help Anne get ready. Agnes selects a riding kirtle of cream for her, with a forest-green velvet jacket and velvet cap trimmed in pheasant feathers. She also lays out a short broadcloth cloak in case the weather turns chilly. I'm dressed and ready but, when Anne runs out the door of her chamber, Agnes calls after her.

"Mistress Boleyn," she shouts, "you forgot your gloves. Anne hurries back to fetch them and we set off to meet Henry, who is waiting just outside the tower door.

He embraces her, placing a tender kiss on her cheek. "My darling Anne, how do you fare this morning?"

"Morning, Your Majesty, I am very well." She curtsies and gives him a broad smile as we fetch our mounts in preparation for the ride to the Thames. At a good trot, the journey will take us forty-five minutes.

"Good morrow, Your Majesty," I say, bobbing a curtsy.

The Master of the Horse and his grooms help us mount our rides, and it isn't long, after intermittent trotting and cantering, before we arrive at the Thames' riverbank. A liveried boatman greets us with a deep bow and assists us aboard the royal barge. We sit on soft cushions, with Henry and Anne under the tented canopy, while I stay a few feet away, leaning against the gunnel in the open air. Several minstrels play as we are rowed downstream, and we enjoy their music while the happy couple snuggle against each other in a tender embrace. The boat makes ripples as it glides towards our destination, and I lean over the side and trail my fingers in the shallow crests.

"You like the river, I think, Mistress Wickers?" Henry laughs, watching me play like a child with the water.

"It is so peaceful, Majesty. Not usually the way I think of the Thames." I take my hand out of the water and rest back on my cushion, meeting his gaze as he nods at me.

"You are not like other women at court, Beth. I think that is why my sweetheart likes you." He shrugs his brows at me, then looks back at Anne.

"Henry, do not tease her so," she says, brushing her hand against the neckline of his silk and gold-embroidered doublet. "But you are right, My Lord, for I have never found another woman in Christendom who would make a better friend than she who is with us now." He plants a kiss on her forehead, looking sideways at me, their compliments sending heat into my cheeks.

"Then, Madam, we should find your friend a husband. I will keep my eye peeled for a worthy suitor, as Beth needs someone who will put fire in the blood as well as you have ignited mine – for no one should be without the love of a sweetheart to warm their heart."

My face burns under his gaze, and I think of George Boleyn, but then Professor Marshall's warning expression snaps into my mind, and I come back to earth with a resounding thud.

"Perhaps, Majesty, I think we embarrass Beth." Anne nudges him. "See, you are making her blush so."

"I am happy being an unmarried woman, My Lord, and in the service of your court."

"Forgive us then, for, in our love, we hoped you would find happiness, too."

"Your Majesty, you are most gracious."

He offers Anne some apricots from a pewter plate at his side. When we reach the barge docks, he holds out his bejewelled hand to help us alight from the vessel. We steady ourselves on the bank, where three horses are already prepared for us. They flick their manes, eager to set off, the sun glistening on the brass work of their bridles. These beautiful steeds must be the equivalent of race cars back in modern England. Two equerries have brought an additional horse laden with supplies.

We trot on, until we come to a wooded area near Wraysbury. There, we find ourselves facing the most impressive tree I have ever seen, its branches sprawling and reaching for the clouds floating across the otherwise clear, blue sky. Its massive, wide, and ancient trunk remind me of a wizened old face – a sentinel that has witnessed the events of centuries. The breeze whispers through the branches, splayed out like a dancer's elegant arms.

We dismount while the equerries busy themselves with blankets for us to sit on, and baskets of food and ale. The blankets are laid beneath the great yew, the foodstuffs neatly set out, ready for an intimate picnic. Then the equerries bow to Henry, remount their horses, and ride off to a respectable distance. He pours Anne a cup of ale. As he unwraps cheeses and slices of meat from several parcels, he tells us that this tree has borne witness to events that have shaped the history of England, and of the world. The tree is believed to be almost two thousand years old and is called the Ankerwycke Yew. I marvel that this living thing has been in existence since before the time of Jesus Christ. Henry tells us that, near this very spot, King John signed the Magna Carta in 1215. As a historian, I shiver with excitement, thinking about all the history this tree has witnessed. It is a place steeped in antiquity, entwined with destiny. Courting Anne under its branches, Henry has now added to that history, and I find it to be a most idyllic setting, near the Priory of St Mary. However, I'm feeling a bit of a gooseberry while Anne and Henry share this romantic moment.

———————— • ❄ • ————————

This is how Anne and I share the first weeks of spring, in the company of the king at Windsor, and we enjoy much freedom, since Henry has only his riding household with him in residence, and that party does not include Queen

Katharine, much to Anne's gratification and relief. She hunts almost every day when the weather allows, and I exploit my time to sit in the Windsor Library, coveting and reading books that will be priceless volumes in my time. Henry teaches us to hawk in the Great Park and, in the evenings, we play cards with the friends we now share, although, much to his annoyance, Anne continues to beat him, winning hand after hand. When I'm alone, I relax by the fire in her chambers, conversing with Nan, learning about all the politics and people of the court. Any quarrels with Nan over her seeing George Boleyn kiss me seem to be forgotten. Nan seems to be the kind of woman to accept how things are and just get on with it.

3rd March 1528

Anne's necklace sparkles in the candlelight as I secure it around her slender neck. We are enjoying our time at Windsor, but the matter debated in Rome is never far from our minds, and we hold onto the hope that this latest advance, spearheaded by Masters Foxe and Gardiner, will yield a positive result. Anne has invited Thomas Heneage to dine with us in her lodgings. He is Wolsey's man, and as we walk through to her presence-chamber, I know she is hoping she can influence the cardinal in a wardship dispute. Her way of going about such influence makes me want to giggle but I have to keep my composure.

"Master Heneage, please tell the Cardinal that I would be much obliged if I could be delivered of some carp and shrimp from the Cardinal's fish pools at Hampton Court for Lent." She gives that half-smile as her eyes twinkle. This woman's beguiling nature can influence any man.

By the end of March, we receive from Wolsey an early, promising summary sent by the two ambassadors in Rome. It is Henry's intention to have them report directly to him as soon as they return to England in the coming weeks. Wolsey seems convinced that a redoubling of his efforts on behalf of the king will pay off; studious in his efforts concerning Henry and his Matter, he pays close attention to every development and becomes exceedingly interested every time an update of news is sent his way. He seems determined to stay in the king's good graces, and his behaviour towards Anne has become much more prudent as well – it is this observation that makes me think she will reconsider her personal scheme concerning him. Although she doesn't exactly like him, she realises she must put negative feelings aside and demonstrate her support of him and his efforts, even though her Uncle Norfolk may wish otherwise. I warn her that little good can come from an open disagreement with the man, as my wish is for her to always be seen in a kind and charitable light. However, I know that expressing my interpretation of events and of Wolsey will prove to be a distinct mistake.

May 1528 – The Palace of Placentia, Greenwich

Court life has resumed in full at The Palace of Placentia, Greenwich, and Anne is back in her previous placement, as a maid of honour to the queen. Jayne Fool has been well cared for by her keepers in our absence, and the queen has made some of her ladies pass clothing down to her. With Anne being back in the queen's household, although this isn't the station she hopes for, Henry sends her gifts almost daily, and it means that she can keep a close eye on Jayne. She knows full well that her role in the queen's household is for the king's benefit, and decides that, despite struggling with it, she will acknowledge his great kindness to her and write him a note to that effect.

I have my own struggles, knowing what the future holds. It is not a rumour but historical fact that in a month or more the virus called 'The Sweat' will sweep the country, and over three weeks, will take William Compton, William Carey, and the lives of fifteen-thousand English, and nearly bring an end to Sir Thomas, Anne, and George Boleyn, along with Wolsey and many of the King's servants. I need to guard the Boleyns against it, not forgetting myself. The thought of this epidemic reminds me of others my time has experienced, like dark shadows hovering over our country and across the world. I shiver at the thought of what's to come. Hopefully, as this spectre rises, I will have a plan.

Anne is struggling to assume an appropriate demeanour in Katharine's household, as you'd have to be blind not to see that the queen knows who features foremost in the king's desire to have his marriage annulled. The court is now split in half, and it is evident who the allies are around each woman.

One morning, as she and I walk through the Great Hall amongst the courtiers, everyone is stunned to silence as the king is heralded into our presence. Anne drops into a deep curtsy, not saying a word. I angle my head just a touch as I also curtsey, stunned to see him take her by the chin, his touch so gentle, and raise her to her feet. Everyone keeps their eyes lowered as he acknowledges her before the assembly.

"Anne." He smiles, looking deep into her eyes as she blushes in surprise. As they stand there locked in each other's gaze, the queen is announced, and she stands at the end of the hall staring at them in disbelief. Anne tries to turn away, but Henry prevents this by gripping her hand.

"No, wait, Mistress Boleyn," he says, and I watch the queen, who glares in disgust, turn on her heel with her waiting women.

"Tonight, I am to dine with members of your family," Henry says, ignoring his wife's departure.

"Your Majesty, my father says you honour him far beyond anything he deserves."

"No, no, I do not. Besides, being close to members of your family makes me feel much closer to you."

Her expression is of pure love and happiness. He kisses her hand, then strokes her cheek and neck. I watch, astonished – so happy to be a witness. Yes, I miss my own family, and my 'real' life, but I wouldn't miss this for the world. He whispers something in her ear that makes her smile but, sadly, I can't hear what is said. She looks down and blushes again as he leaves her and walks out of the hall with his privy servants.

She stands there in shock, not sure what to do, while all the courtiers gawp and stare, whispering to each other that she is the one the king desires beyond all others. So now it is a public matter for the entire world to see and she can't get away from it. In one fell swoop, this has made her public enemy number one, with half the court in allegiance with the queen.

Later, we attend Queen Katharine and, although little is said, looks are shared between her and Anne. In the afternoon, however, the queen and her ladies are assembled in her presence-chamber, since she plans to receive visitors. Anne is seated before her, and it's almost impossible for the two of them not to look at one another. The queen's chambers are full with the chitter-chatter of her ladies-in-waiting, while the two women stare daggers at each other. However, there's little in the way of anger in the queen's expression – more a simple air of disdain, though Anne returns the look measure for measure. Their behaviour reminds me of the childhood game of 'stares', with the loser being the first to blink. Then Anne raises her chin, almost imperceptibly, issuing a tacit challenge, daring Katharine to say something.

"Lady Anne," she says, and all the ladies of the chamber fall into a hushed silence.

"Yes, Your Majesty?"

The queen looks at the jewel about Anne's neck. "Who gave you that necklace? Show me, let me take a closer look." She beckons with her finger.

"His Majesty, the King," Anne says without hesitation. Both women glare at each other.

Katharine stiffens, her eyes narrowing to slits for a long moment. Then she leans forward, though only a couple of inches or so. "I know what you are doing. Do not think you can manipulate His Majesty and draw him away from me. He can give you gifts and tokens, and enjoy his play with you, but he cannot give you his true heart, for his heart will, and has, always belonged to me." She purses her lips. "More importantly, Henry's heart is mine in the eyes of God!" She looks Anne straight in the eyes and gives a smug smile. Little does the woman know what lies ahead of her. From the look on Anne's face, all she wants to do is run from these chambers, away from that menacing glare. However, as things stand, she is the queen's servant, so remains, forced to endure this indignity.

For a long moment, a heavy silence hangs over them, until Katharine leans back in her chair. "You are nothing but a Boleyn whore, like your sister before you!"

"I am no whore, Your Majesty. The king does not take me to his bed."

Katharine smirks. "Silence, I did not give you permission to talk. You are a servant!" She snorts a breath through her nose. "He will tire of you, like all the rest who came before you." She looks Anne up and down, her contempt burning in her eyes.

"I do not think so, Your Majesty. I believe Henry loves me, and I love him also."

Every mouth in the room is agape, including mine, at Anne's bravery in standing up for herself, though I'm sure many here see it as foolhardy. I'm astounded by her determination to be heard. Jayne Fool stands at the edge of the room, head down, hands clasped in front. She looks like she wants to say something, but I look at her sideways and shake my head.

Katharine's face has turned puce. "I warned you not to speak to me! You are too familiar with my husband's name – I know what you are up to, Lady Anne."

Everyone around the room shrinks back to their duties, all shocked by Anne's audacity. Some tut to each other, exchanging knowing glances, though not daring to look at the queen, who demands Anne now leave her presence. I waste no time in accompanying her from the chambers.

On the first Sunday in May, after dinner, Cardinal Wolsey arrives to meet with the king. They retire to his chambers, and I, since it's raining, return to Anne's new chambers nearer the tiltyard and adjacent to the banqueting house, after Henry removed her from her lodgings in the royal gallery, where many of Katharine's women are in residence. We're playing a game of chess when a knock sounds and Nan opens the door to reveal Bishop Edward Foxe, newly arrived from Rome.

Flustered but thrilled to see one of Henry's ambassadors at Greenwich, Anne mistakenly chirps, "Master Stephen! How excellent to see you! Please, do come in. Do please sit and partake of some wine." In her elation at the potential of receiving some long-awaited good news from Rome, she's confused Foxe with Gardiner.

"I thank you heartily, my lady," he says with a bow, politely overlooking the error. He seats himself before the fire. "I have sent word to His Majesty that I've arrived, and am informed that he wishes to meet me here in your chambers as soon as he can finish his meeting with the Cardinal."

Wolsey is not to be included in this debriefing, and as I hand Foxe a cup of wine, I notice Anne almost jumping out of her seat, unable to contain herself a moment longer.

"So, Master Stephen, what news do you bring from Rome and His Holiness as regards the king's Great Matter? What are the opinion of the Pope and the clerical scholars? And the lawyers – what was their view?"

The Bishop again kindly doesn't embarrass her by correcting her error.

"Mistress Boleyn, His Holiness the Pope is very much inclined to have sympathy with His Majesty's written opinions on the Great Matter. He is intrigued by the study, which supports the proposal that a papal legate be named to finally decide on the matter in conjunction with Cardinal Wolsey. He also expresses his confidence that the king's integrity is well represented in his argument."

"And what of it, then, sir?" I ask, just as excited to hear the results as Anne is.

"His Holiness has requested that the legate be Cardinal Campeggio, the Cardinal Protector of England."

I flinch when the door swings open with a force that nearly takes it off its hinges. Henry enters, looking most regal, and full of smiles.

"Your Highness."

Foxe leaps to his feet and bows to the king, who clasps him by the shoulders with a warm and hearty "Foxe! Welcome home. Do sit, have some refreshment and tell me how you fared."

I pour wine for the king and top up Foxe's goblet, and with a quick curtsey, back out of the room to leave the men to their discussion, taking Anne with me, blushing now as she realises how often she's called the bishop 'Master Stephen'. She shakes her head as she closes the door behind us.

We're only gone a few minutes when Nan comes running to find us, to say that the king wishes us back in the chamber with him and the bishop. We hurry back, and Anne sits by Henry's side and, together, they question Foxe, while I look on. Foxe recounts the entire mission, beginning to end, after which, being exhausted, he is permitted to depart while the king lingers with Anne in her chamber.

Henry gushes with excitement, delighted that he and Anne are finally on the correct path, and that Campeggio and Wolsey together will provide him with the formal support he needs to move forward and rid himself of his vexing marriage to Katharine. Anne and I are swept up by his enthusiasm, and she demonstrates her joy by sitting on his lap, literally covering him with kisses.

With that, I ask permission to take my leave, and go for a walk around the palace gardens to allow the couple some privacy and to gather my thoughts. My mind is buzzing with how well things are working out. From the way Henry and Anne are getting along, my mission is close to being accomplished. However, they're not married yet, and Princess Elizabeth is still to be born. I'm not just staying here to bear witness to historical events, and there's the thing about Anne not wanting me to go. But my 'real' life, and getting back to it, is playing on my mind. How much time has passed at home? How are my parents getting on? And though I'm in love with George, I cringe at the thought of Rob being 'distracted' by Georgina. I know I didn't mistake seeing her giving him the eye. But then there's the issue I'm most concerned about: are the pages of the Ives' book no longer blank, and what about the book title with my image on the cover? Gosh, I have a lot to think about.

Seventeen

June 11, 1528. – The Palace of Richmond

As Agnes and I unroll several bolts of silk sent by the king, we welcome the warm fragrant breeze that wafts into Anne's bedchamber on this fine summer morning. I admire the fine quality of the fabrics and glance towards Anne, asking her which is her favourite. She's in the process of penning a letter to Cardinal Wolsey concerning the annulment but looks up and indicates her choice of an intricately woven cloth of gold.

Sir Thomas Heneage, the cardinal's gentleman usher, has written to Wolsey, mentioning the Lady Anne and her rise in the king's esteem. However, even now, Henry is still appearing at public functions with Katharine, apparently in harmony. No one knows whether the divorce will happen, and as far as the courtiers are concerned, it's anyone's guess who the next queen will be. Uncertainty is everywhere, and the court is awash with talk about an epidemic that is starting to take a grip on the city. While I'm helping Agnes sort out the fabrics, I notice her face has a yellow hue, and her hands are trembling.

"Agnes, what's wrong? Are you ill?" I ask, alarmed. "Mistress, come and have a look at Agnes."

Anne gets up from her chair, takes Agnes by the arm, and leads her to the window to have a better look.

"What is it, child?"

"I am not feeling at all well," she whispers before sinking to the floor. "I be feeling dizzy, and hot. My stomach be hurting, too. Do you think I may have caught the sweat?"

"Don't be silly, Agnes," I say in an effort to reassure her, though I know well it's the case. "It is just a headache, it will pass."

"I have pains in my head and neck. Is that not a sign? I'm going to die!" she wails.

"You are not going to die," Anne insists as we guide her to the bed. She loosens the restricting garments from around the girl's body and removes her coif. Agnes's face has now broken out in a sweat, so I run to the pitcher of water, soak a linen towel, wring it out, and wipe her face, repeating this several times before placing it on her forehead and instructing her to keep it there. Anne rushes from the chamber in search of Lord Sandys, to see if he might locate a Court physician. I rush around the room trying to find some squares of linen I can fold to make masks for Anne and me. She returns to the bedchamber with the news that Sandys has hurried off on his mission.

"Anne," I say, folding the linen into a triangular shape and tying it around my head, so the cloth covers my nose and mouth, "you need to wear one of these." I hand her the mask. "It will guard you against the…masmas in the air." I just about remember to speak Tudor. "It's not entirely protective but it may help."

She looks over at Agnes after tying the makeshift mask around her face, to find her servant now only partly conscious, dripping with sweat and burning with fever. The poor woman's breath comes in sharp rasps. Anne runs over and wipes tears from her eyes as I continue to apply cool cloths to her head. When we try to give her a sip of water, she can barely swallow.

A single rap on the door signals Master Cuthbert Blackeden's entrance. He glances at us both, his eyes wide at our appearance in makeshift masks. Then he nods, no doubt approving of our Tudor PPE. He pulls his own mask up over his nose. The king's chief apothecary strides to the bedside and pushes me out of the way, his expression grim.

The cause of the disease remains unknown, but it tends to afflict richer members of society more than the poor. If I remember correctly, the humanist Desiderius Erasmus, who himself almost fell victim to the sweating sickness, attributed the sweat to inadequate ventilation, clay floors, and the unchanged, rotting rushes commonly strewn around rooms. He also claimed that excessive consumption at mealtimes was a contributory factor, as well as the use of too much salt.

Its onset is marked by a feeling of apprehension, followed by violent, cold shivers, dizziness, and severe pains in the head and neck. The sufferer is usually unable to keep warm, and will then experience hot sweats, palpitations, intense thirst, and delirium. In the final stages, they will be overwhelmed with exhaustion and have an urge to sleep.

"Mistress Wickers, please keep your distance," Blackeden cautions me. "You must already be aware there is little we can do for Mistress Anne's servant. I will offer what help I can, but she has a bad case of the sweat."

He turns to Anne and says in a muffled, low voice, "I am sorry to tell you it is likely that she will be dead within a few hours."

I'm shocked to the core at the prospect of Agnes dying, and so soon. If only I had a bottle of antibiotics or paracetamol with me from Hever that I could crush into some wine, I could save her life. Mum always keeps a stash in the first-aid cupboard. Why didn't I bring some with me?

I pull Anne to the corner of the room, out of earshot of Blackeden.

"Anne, I've still got the ring – I could return to my time, to get some modern medicine that might save Agnes's life. Would you let me go?"

"Could you do so, and be confident you could return back to us in time?"

"I know I've told you that your years here pass very fast, but if I spoke with the professor, he'd help me make sure I returned to this exact same location and time using the ring."

As far as I'm concerned, my suggestion is credible. Surely, she cannot deny Agnes the chance to live? She has been part of our lives for so long now, she's like a Boleyn family member. I glance at her, and see that her breathing has turned shallow. I need to excuse myself so I can hide somewhere to time-slip. No one must see me disappear.

"I need to change this situation for Agnes!" I plead. "You must let me go." She must sense my panic and hear the fear in my voice.

"Yes, by all means, make haste. I will make excuses for you – do I not always do right by you?"

"Yes, Anne. But we need to do right by Agnes!" I pull down my mask for a moment, kiss her on the cheek, then race out of the room. Where to go? I need to find somewhere dark and quiet, with no one about. As I hurry past courtiers huddling in whispering groups, I spot a large tapestry, which I stop at and peek behind. Lucky for me, it hangs in front of an alcove in the wall. It's dark and I won't be disturbed here. As I twist the ring, it begins to warm up. Do I think of home? Of the professor's office where I left my clothes? Yes, that's probably best. I twist and rub the cypher ring and, as I do, the heat it radiates becomes almost unbearably hot, and I screw my eyes up tight.

Cigarette butts; paperwork; laptops; essays; Professor Marshall: Office, university, Twickenham. I keep repeating the words over and over in my head. With a whooshing, rumbling, and tumbling, I find myself lying on the floor of the professor's office, my mask and hood askew, blinking at the fluorescent light in his ceiling. I crawl to the side of his desk and peer through the footwell. Professor Marshall is at the door, talking to a student. It's Rob.

I rub my head, which throbs with the onset of a migraine, probably because of my inner ear having to adjust to being propelled through time, and probably because of the brightness of the modern lighting. At least I made it. I pull my mask off my face. No time to waste.

As I get up from the floor, I bang my head on the corner of the desk. "Ouch!" Now my headache is going to be ten times worse.

Professor Marshall turns, looks down at me, and grins. "Are you okay there?"

Rob strides into the office. "I didn't even notice you weren't here this afternoon." He frowns, scratches his head, then closes the door. "You've only been gone a few hours."

I must make a great impression on everyone then, with no one noticing I've been missing. So much for that. I stand up, pull the French hood off my head, and place it on the desk. My heart is beating ten to the dozen.

"Erm, Professor Marshall need your help." I walk over to him as he stands in front of his desk. He pulls a cigarette packet from his pocket and goes to take one out. I snatch them away and throw them into the jumble of papers on the desk. "There's no time for those. It's a filthy habit, anyway!" Rob grins at my audacity.

"What's the problem?" the professor says, as if he hasn't got a care in the world.

"It's Agnes," I reply, as I thump down in his leather chair, my skirts billowing about me.

"Who's Agnes?" Rob asks, taking the seat opposite me.

"Anne's maid – the Boleyn family's servant. The young girl who always does her best."

The professor walks round to where we are sat and leans against his desk. He picks up his cigarette packet, pulls out a fag, and proceeds to light it, sucking on it and inhaling as if he hasn't had a hit of nicotine in hours. What am I supposed to do, rip it from his mouth? He really should give them up. Smoke swirls above our heads, and I breathe through my nose in the hope of filtering some of it.

"What's the problem with Agnes?"

"She's dying – I need to save her!" I blow out a breath in exasperation, my cheeks puffing. "She has the sweat." Rob looks at me, then back to the professor.

"Ok, that means Anne, George, and Thomas will contract it soon, doesn't it?"

"I'm afraid so, and William Carey will die, along with many others."

The professor flicks his ash into the crowded ashtray on his desk. It stinks! Is he ever going to empty it?

"Don't you care, sir? What can we do?"

"Do nothing."

"Nothing?" Rob asks. "Why nothing, sir?"

"Because, dear boy,"—he takes another drag of his cigarette—"if the girl survives, and has children, that's generations of people in the future who weren't meant to exist. That could change history irrevocably."

I stare at him. "I can't believe you wouldn't help Agnes, sir!"

He stares me down. "I told you not to meddle."

I get up. "Fine." I pick up my Tudor hood from his desk. "Can I have my car keys please?"

"Yes, of course." He opens the top door of his desk and pulls them out. "Here." He plonks them in my outstretched hand. "Are you not taking your clothes – your modern stuff, I mean? It's still in a bag behind the chair." He grabs the bag and passes it to me. "You can always bring some modern clothes back here and leave them, if you decide to go through another time, though you'll be happy to know that the pages of the Ives' book are no longer blank, and the cover is back to its original state. Your mission has been a complete success." He gives me a smile. I storm out of the office in full Tudor dress, with Rob now following.

Other students stare at me as I pass them by.

"Are you going home in that?" Rob looks me up and down as I stride beside him.

"Why not? I've done it before!"

He chuckles. "Yeah, I guess you have.

I fumble with the key to my front door lock. I'm shaking – fuming at the professor's nonchalant reaction to Agnes's plight. I lift the hem of my gown, stride over the pile of post on the doormat, and see Rutterkin sat in the middle of the hallway, meowing.

"Hello, my lovely!" I say, bending to stroke him. He purrs around my hem. I've missed him. Goodness, I've missed everyone.

"Where do you want me to put this?" Rob asks, holding my bag of gear. He shuts the front door.

"Just there, thanks." I smile, nodding at the bottom of the stairs, grateful to have someone with me who understands what's going on. First things first. I walk through to the kitchen, put my hood on the worktop, then fill the kettle and flick it on.

"What are you going to do now?"

"Have a quick cuppa, then I'm going to find all the medication I need before going back. We have plenty here."

"Back?" His brows crease.

"Yep, back to Richmond."

He finds two clean mugs in the drainer. "You're going, straight away?"

"Yes, Rob, straight away."

The kettle boils and he pops a teabag into each cup. "Why? You heard what the professor said."

I pass him the milk from the fridge. "He may not care about Agnes, but I do!"

"He warned you not to interfere in a way that would change history." He hands me back the milk.

"But this is Agnes we are talking about. A loving, caring soul, who would do anything for anyone. I have to at least try to save her. Anne and the physician don't know that she's definitely going to die. It only looked that way when I left." I take my tea and sip it but it's burning hot. "I need to go upstairs, find the medicine, and then go back."

"I guess you do." He blows on his tea. "Is there anything I can do?"

"Not really – all I know is, I can't hang around here for long, in case my parents come home. They can't see me like this." I walk to the bottom of the stairs and see my bag of stuff. "Actually, there is something you could do." I tilt my head to one side, hoping he won't mind conspiring with me.

"What's that?" he calls from the kitchen. His mug clumps on the worktop and he walks through to the hallway.

"Could you take this bag back to Professor Marshall's office?" He looks puzzled. "Just in case I need it?"

"If you really want me to?"

"In case I come back again through the portal, I'm going to need some normal clothes to change into. I can't keep walking through the university in full Tudor regalia – people will talk!"

He laughs. "If anyone does ask me about today, I shall use your previous ploy and say you are part of the university drama group!" He walks back through to the kitchen, and I follow.

"I'm going to use the ring to travel from here."

"You can do that?"

"Yes, it's worked a few times that way. I don't always have to use the portal."

"Before you go, at least drink your tea." He hands me my mug.

"Let's go and sit down then." I walk into the lounge. It feels weird being home, and in my Tudor gown. I put my mug on the small table and sit on the sofa. Rob sits in the armchair. Rutterkin, never one to miss an opportunity, jumps into my lap and snuggles into the folds of my gown. "Make yourself comfy then." I smile at him as I stroke him, loving the vibration of his purrs.

"He's lovely," Rob says, trying to make small talk.

"What's happening with you and Georgina?" I ask. "She seems into you."

He shrugs his brows. "Is she? I hadn't noticed."

"I know we aren't dating, Rob, but I need to ask you a big favour."

"Yeah?" He tilts his head to one side and runs his hand through his hair. "What is it?"

"Besides taking my stuff back to the professor's office, could we say I'm staying with you for a few days, just in case my absence is prolonged? Just so I can...cover my tracks?"

"I don't see why not. My dad's lodgers sometimes have their girlfriends staying over, so…"

"Don't get your hopes up. I'm not really staying over. It's just a rouse to keep my parents, and anyone else, from worrying. Okay?"

"You know I'd do anything for you."

His eyes smoulder, in just the right way. Not as handsome as George, though. I disturb Rutterkin as I pick him up, taking it easy to prevent him clawing the fabric of my skirts, and put him on the floor. He looks disgruntled as he walks away, tail twitching.

"As a friend," Rob adds.

"Yep, as friends," I reply. I pick up a pad and pen from the table and scribble a quick note to Mum:

Mum,
I'm staying around Rob's for a few days. I need to get this last assignment done. Don't go worrying about me. I'm fine. Beth ☺ *xxx*

I leave it in the centre of the table, where I know she'll see it, then pick up my mug of tea and take a big gulp. So nice. It feels like an age since I've had a cuppa.

"Right, I need to get going!"

Rob knocks back the rest of his tea and carries both mugs into the kitchen and loads them into the dishwasher. I stand at the kitchen door.

"You know your way around a kitchen, I see!" I giggle.

"It's a case of fending for yourself in my house. I told you my brother's a chef. Besides, I'm used to it."

"It's never like that here. Mum likes doing everything herself. She won't let me do anything." It reminds me of poor Agnes, fetching and carrying for me, Anne, and the Boleyns. My neck goes cold as the guilt hits me. I can't stand here chatting when the poor woman is dying. She needs my help. I walk through to the hallway, with Rob following.

"You need to get going, don't you?" He looks at me as if he can read my mind.

"You could say that," I reply. I hand him my car keys. "You'd best take my car. At least if you drive it back to the university, it will be in the car park if I return through the portal."

"Are you sure? Are you fully comp?"

"Yep." I smile. "You're covered. Don't forget to take my stuff." I hand him my bag, and he surprises me by giving me a peck on the lips. "What was that for?"

"Nothing." He shrugs. "I wanted to."

I know it means more to him than nothing – I can see it in his eyes. Not wanting to get into a full-blown conversation about 'us', I nod for him to go, and watch as he opens the front door and walks down the garden path. He turns back and smiles, then gets into my car and drives off. It seems strange, seeing him leave without me, in my little pink Figaro. I shut the door, grab my French hood from the worktop in the kitchen, and make my way upstairs to find the meds.

The first-aid box and medicine cabinet in the bathroom are my obvious targets, and I rifle through them for anything that might be useful: Antibiotics; paracetamol; aspirin; some perfume, more toothpaste – all the toiletries I know Anne loves. I pack it all in a small linen bag and go into my bedroom, which is just how I left it. Time to prepare. I look in my dressing-table mirror, secure my French hood, and check that nothing looks out of place in the way I'm dressed.

Okay, time to go. As I stand in the centre of my matt, with my linen bag on my shoulder, the ring begins to heat up, and I visualise the space behind the tapestry, thinking of Agnes, Anne, the palace, George, and the sweat. That's it, keep thinking it. I hope I return at the right time, and not in the future – too late – with poor Agnes long gone.

The ring burns as I turn it, and I close my eyes tight, thinking the words again and again. As before, I'm hurled at shocking speed, like a death eater in Harry Potter, through the air and back through time.

———— • ❄ • ————

I open my eyes, stunned and not a little discombobulated. Wow! I shouldn't expect this time-slip thing to be easy but, God, that didn't half hurt. My head throbs, as if I've been knocked out. That's all I need, to end up with a concussion. I blink a few times to clear the stars and sparks, and realise that I'm back behind the tapestry, my linen bag still on my shoulder. Great, the meds came through. I rub my lower back, then get to my feet, straighten my hood, and brush down the front of my gown. Yes, I think I'm okay, if not a tad wobbly.

Ok, time to get moving. I peer out and see the same people from earlier, except they're just a few feet further down the passageway from when I left. Strange. That means that in the Tudor-slip, I've only been gone a matter of seconds, or a minute or two at most. How very odd, but fantastic. I remember to pull my make-shift linen mask over my nose and mouth before stepping out, checking that I haven't been seen. Then, as nonchalant as possible, I walk towards Anne's chambers, where I last left her with Agnes and the physician. Am I too late?

There's an air of wariness about the palace, with several courtiers passing me in a panic, staring at my face covering. They whisper behind their hands, and I catch snippets that send shivers through me: plague; miasmas; physicians; and death. This isn't good. A priest is walking around swinging an incense holder, and as he passes me, the vapours hang in the air – a heavy scent, like sage – and I cough into my mask.

When I arrive in Anne's chamber, she is pacing back and forth, her mask still on, and doesn't notice me as she watches Blackeden administer a concoction to Agnes, who barely drinks it, with most trailing out the side of her mouth. He wipes her face. What the hell has he given her?

Anne rushes from around the bed to embrace me. "I see you have your bag with you," she whispers.

"How can I administer my medicine with Blackeden here?"

"Tarry until he's gone," she suggests.

Thinking on my feet, I begin opening all the casements to let fresh air in. Anne looks over at me and frowns, and I remember that's not the way they do things here.

My heart hurts as Agnes's breathing grows hollower and quieter. Anne and I gawk at each other, then look at the physician, then back at poor Agnes. She grabs my hand, and we stand there feeling helpless. I don't think my medicine will work now, anyway – she's too far gone. The physician leans in, holding a mirror to Agnes's lips, checking for the strength of breath. We can hardly hear her now, the movement of her chest is almost indiscernible. She's slipping away. Our lovely Agnes is dying.

We sink to our knees, close our eyes, and clasp our hands in prayer. Anne begins reciting something unfamiliar, in Latin. Prayer is the only thing that may help Agnes now. It doesn't take long before the rasping sound of her breathing diminishes…and then stops.

"Her ordeal is over," Blackeden mumbles. Agnes is gone, giving no time for goodbyes. She must have been suffering the symptoms far earlier than we'd noticed. Which means Anne and I could possibly have it. Oh my God, what if I've carried the virus on my clothing back to twenty-first-century London? The idea frightens me but then I shake my head at the realisation that I must be adequately inoculated through the innumerable vaccinations doled out to me in childhood.

We rise to our feet, our tears unchecked as Blackeden covers Agnes with a sheet. He turns to Anne. "Mistress, this poor soul is the third person in the palace who has succumbed to the sweat this day. The king is preparing even now to leave Court for Saint Albans, where he will stay at Tyttenhanger briefly, before moving again to Waltham. Your brother is leaving with His Majesty. May I suggest that you also depart Surrey and the London environs as quickly as you can? I have no doubt that this epidemic will grow." He looks at us both with concern, then repacks his bag and hurries out, no doubt having others to care for.

I am in utter shock, not only grieving for the abrupt loss of Agnes but also stunned by the disclosure that Henry and George are preparing to leave without telling Anne. I grab the inkwell and some parchment and hand it to her.

"Write to the king. Get a messenger to deliver a note to him, so he knows what is happening." I pack her wooden casket, stuff it in a travel sack, then wait while she pens the letter, glancing every now and again at dear Agnes's shrouded, lifeless body.

When she's finished, we leave the room and order the usher to deliver her message to the king. The porters are coming to remove Agnes's corpse as we run through the hallways. My tears won't stop, and I'm not sure if they're of pure sorrow or mixed with guilt for not being able to save her.

I grab one of the guards near Henry's chambers and ask him if he knows whether Sir Thomas is in the vicinity. My near frenzy startles him but he steers us towards the Chamberlain's offices.

Sir Thomas greets us, his face forlorn. "Daughter, the king has told me to take you to Hever this instant."

"Can I not see His Majesty?" she asks. "And what about George?"

"It would not be wise – I would advise against it. We will stay at Hever until such time as we know for certain you are not infected with the sweat."

"I pray to God I am not!"

"The king prays for it more. You cannot see Henry. He is going into seclusion and your brother and Jane with them. Now go and wait for me while I arrange a litter to take us home." His features are as grave as I've ever seen them.

"Anne, what about George? I swear, if anything should happen to him, I'll never get over it!"

"If I cannot see the king, then you cannot see my brother. We wouldn't want to be responsible for giving either of them the sweat, especially as my maid has just died of it." She frowns and shakes her head, releasing a groan of despair that brings more tears to my eyes. As upset as we are, there is no time to waste. We wait at the palace entrance, and, within minutes, Sir Thomas returns with a driver and litter and helps us inside as the servants load our luggage. Then, with a thunderous clatter of hooves, we set off for Hever.

June 1528 – Hever Castle

Anne continues to weep as the litter lurches and rattles over bumpy roads on the way from Richmond to Edenbridge. Sir Thomas sits opposite me, staring out through the small window. At one point, he reaches across to Anne and takes her hand in his, an everyday gesture from him but, this time, she clings to him for a long while. As I watch them, it hits me that neither of them look well, their faces white as linen sheets, with a sheen I haven't witnessed before. They both have the sweat; I can see it. I'm astounded at how fast this virus acts, though I shouldn't be, having read enough about it during my studies.

I'm hoping to God my childhood inoculations will prevent me from catching it. My immune system has to be different to these Tudor people, which might see me better able to cope with certain illnesses.

"I have touched Agnes, father. I bathed the sweat from her face, slept in the same chamber, all on the day of her death. Do you think I could have the sweat?"

"No, daughter, I think not," he replies, reassuring her as only a father can.

"And if I were to come down with the contagion, would it spread to you and mother?"

"No, your mother is healthy, my child."

She gasps. "What of Henry…? He, too, has been subjected to those who have come near to the contamination, has he not?"

Her father taps her hand. "All will be well, daughter."

"What about George, will he not get the contagion, too?" I ask.

"Beth, please." His smile is weak. "Do not vex yourself."

"It is rumoured that the king's favourite, William Compton, has in the last few days fallen foul of the sweat," I say.

Anne brings her hands to her face, her dark eyes wide. "Does that not mean Henry could be contaminated?"

"No," Sir Thomas says, shaking his head, "Sir William has died at Compton Wynyates in Warwickshire, a long way from here."

"Poor man." I wince at the thought of such an epidemic taking so many people in such a short time. We sit in silence as we consider the loss of the king's dear friend and our cherished Agnes.

"Sir Henry Norris is rumoured to be taking Compton's place as the royal favourite, a position he is said to deserve, being a popular and trustworthy man." Sir Thomas knows that Anne is familiar with Norris.

"The king needs a discreet and level-headed man of proven integrity around him," she says, her voice heavy with melancholy.

"After Compton, Norris will be the chief gentleman of the Privy Chamber, and the most trusted member of the king's private household."

"Then, father, Norris must be the best-beloved of the king," she responds, knowing Henry would only surround himself with worthy men.

Norris must be an impeccable man, and is one I admire, for he has already been granted many favours and positions, being almost as close to the king as Charles Brandon.

Anne is distraught that Henry hasn't been in contact with her, and that he plans to leave London with Katharine. I rub her shoulder and remind her that he has to do what is expected of him. As she is neither his wife, nor a member of his family, being his unofficial sweetheart is not enough to give her special rank in the eyes of the public.

"All will be well," Sir Thomas says, patting the back of her hand.

"It seems the king's fear of the sweat is greater than his love for me," she cries, shuddering in her misery. "I feel completely abandoned and more like a fool than I ever believed possible."

This is the first time I've seen her show real, unguarded emotion, and I'm relieved when we arrive at Hever, as she is exhausted. Precautions have to be taken, and we need to keep her to her chamber so she can rest. Lady Boleyn has been fussing over everyone, panicking that all the household will go down with the illness. She has told me that Sir Thomas has taken to his bed, and all he does is sleep. The poor woman checks on him every half-hour, making sure he's drinking, and watching for any change in his symptoms.

Once we ready ourselves for bed, it isn't long before Anne falls into an uneasy sleep, tossing and turning until dawn. I help her to dress but she refuses to stay in her chamber, so meanders about the house and garden all day with little purpose. It's difficult to watch but I'm glad of the modern medicines I now have, close to hand should they be needed. As we go to bed the second evening, I feel hopeful that the country air of Hever will be our defence against the disease. However, the following morning, Anne says she feels a strange tightness in her head and throat, so I dress and search for her mother, who I find on the landing, taking fresh linens into her bedroom.

"Lady Boleyn, I am sorry to disturb you, but Anne is stricken with a blinding headache. She says she aches all over and feels weak."

We enter, along with one of the servants and Mrs Orchard, to find Anne lying on her bed. Her mother takes command, and we undress her and change her into a clean, fresh shift. She trembles all over with a chill, so we cover her with a thick woollen blanket.

"Can we summon a physician?" her mother asks the servant. "Mrs Orchard, please ask the cook to prepare Anne some food!" Mrs Orchard, her eyes dark from all the crying over poor Agnes, scurries out the door, no doubt to fetch wine, freshly baked bread, clean linens, and water.

"My Lady, there will be no need of physicians. I can look after Anne. Trust me."

She gives me a sceptical look, which I ignore because she doesn't know what I know – that Henry will send his own physician to aid Anne during her sickness. Before she slips into a fitful sleep, while Lady Boleyn is checking on her husband, I fetch the medicines from my holdall and drop soluble aspirin into her goblet of watered-down wine. It's not easy but I persuade her to sip it before her mother returns. Then I sprinkle the antibiotic powder onto some bread, without catching the attention of Lady Boleyn, who is now on the other side of the bedchamber folding linens. The antibiotics might have no effect, with the sweat being a virus, but I'm willing to try anything at this stage.

Elizabeth's expression is fraught as she watches me sit Anne up against her pillows so she can chew on the bread without choking. She slips in and out of consciousness, only vaguely aware of her surroundings as I administer cool cloths, sips of wine, and other bitter concoctions. When she wakes, I try to give her hot soup, spooning the broth into her mouth. She continues to sweat, then grows chilly, her teeth chattering.

As evening approaches, I spot Lady Boleyn asleep in the chair beside her bed. Sir Thomas is semi-conscious. Mrs Orchard steps into the room.

"Is all well with Sir Thomas?"

"I'm not sure. Do you think the mistress would mind if I nursed Sir Thomas for a while?"

She glances at Lady Boleyn. "I think not. The poor lady is exhausted." She grabs a woollen blanket from a wooden trunk at the end of their bed, and lays it across Lady Boleyn's lap.

"If you be needing anything, Mistress Wickers, please let me know if I can be of any assistance." She creeps out of the bedroom, and eases the door shut.

I pull out the meds from my apron pocket, move to the other side of the bed, and drop a couple of the aspirin into a goblet of red wine. It fizzes as I turn the goblet in my hand, swirling its contents around, until they have dissolved. Then I crush up the antibiotics and sprinkle them between the slices of a cold-meat sandwich. I bet the Boleyns have never seen a sandwich before! Ready to act, I sit on the empty side of the bed and nudge the man until his eyes flutter.

"Sir Thomas, forgive me."

"Beth?" He stares at me, trying to focus. I put my arm around his shoulders as he struggles to pull himself up.

"I have a little wine for you – it might make you feel better?"

As he takes a sip of the medicated wine, Lady Boleyn stirs from her slumber. She blinks several times and shakes herself awake, then looks at the woollen blanket over her knees and pushes it onto the floor.

"Beth, I shall take care of my husband." She rubs her forehead. "You must be exhausted, child?" She takes the drugged solution from me and continues to cajole him to drink it, almost pouring it down his throat. I walk to the door, satisfied my job is done. Doctor Butts can attend him now.

"Lady Boleyn, I have left Sir Thomas a slice of cold meat between two pieces of bread that might give him sustenance." She looks at the sandwich on the plate, then picks it up.

"What an unusual way to serve meat!" She nods to herself. "My, how much easier it will be to eat!"

I can't tell her the food is laced with antibiotics. As long as he eats it, I don't care what either of them thinks but I hope to goodness I haven't caused the

Boleyns to invent the sandwich. That would be a little change to the history, that's for sure. I almost chuckle, thinking what the professor would say. Does it matter? No, it was a means to an end. My main hope is that the medication proves helpful. I make sure to administer more aspirin in his wine every four hours. To Anne's, too, though I must be careful because I know that if I'm caught, I'm a goner.

Doctor William Butts has arrived on orders of the king. He has been commissioned to treat Sir Thomas. When he's in the parlour having a snack, I take the opportunity to give Anne another dose of aspirin, paracetamol, and antibiotics, hoping it will give her a fighting chance. Doctor Butts is the second of several physicians who normally attend the king. I would consider him overweight, with more salt and pepper hair than most men of forty-two. He is calm and cultivated, and I like his soothing presence – his urbane manner matching his kindly bedside demeanour. Considering how learned he is, it surprises me that he has yet to be made a Member of the College of Physicians. His dress is sombre, made of plain black wool, giving him a studious air, maybe to mask his lack of knowledge; these people really didn't know what they were at.

Unbeknown to him, his patient is in better hands – mine. He is baffled when, later the next day, Anne wakes from her sleep, looking about as she regains full consciousness. As she tries to draw herself up in the bed, she endeavours to explain to him that the heaviness in her head and limbs seems to have lifted. At that moment, her mother walks into the chamber. When she sees Anne awake and sitting up, she runs to her, hugging her and crying, not wanting to let her go. She praises God, thinking she has just witnessed a miracle.

"Oh, Anne, my child! I thank God you have recovered." Her throat is thick with emotion. "I have feared so many times that you would be lost to us, but Beth has nursed you so very well. I am so relieved and so incredibly grateful!"

"Mother, for how long have I been sick?" Anne asks.

"Four days have passed since you fell into the sweat. For the first three days, you drifted in and out of consciousness, and after that, you slept. We did not know if you would awaken or pass from this life in your sleep."

The stress of members of the family falling ill to the sweat has taken its toll on all of us and Lady Boleyn looks pale and thin. Clearly, she has worried so much about her husband and children that she has eaten little, and I doubt she's managed to get much sleep. Anne takes her hand in hers.

"Thank you, Mother, for not giving up on me, and for doing all you could to save me."

"As I said, it was Beth's doing. We love you, Anne, as does your father. You are his most precious jewel. It is fortunate that we have Doctor Butts here, who arrived at His Grace's instruction to attend on you and your father at a vital moment. We have been instructed to send a message immediately to the king to let him know your condition if it changed. I will have the kitchen send up some meat broth for you, and then perhaps Beth and I will prepare you a warm bath. In the meantime, I will bring you the two letters that arrived from the king's messengers while you were so ill."

Doctor Butts checks Anne's forehead for any continuation of clamminess, then her throat for swelling. He nods and closes his case of medical equipment.

"Mistress Wickers, I shall inform His Majesty that the Lady Anne has made a full recovery."

"Thank you, Doctor Butts. The Lady Anne appreciates your attention and kindness." He nods again at me and takes his leave.

"I wonder if Henry really worries for me," Anne whispers. "I wonder if he has been in tears for me."

She must still be affected by the medication I've slipped into her food and drink. I touch her hand. "I'm sure he would have gladly borne your illness to make you well."

Her eyes widen, and she pushes herself up against her pillows. "Yes, dear Beth, I think he would. Henry loves me. He does, does he not?"

"Daughter, the voice of love would bear it twenty times. I know the king is concerned about you. But, you must not worry. Now, I need to go and attend on Doctor Butts, to make sure he has eaten." She scurries around the room, collecting and passing empty pewter plates to waiting servants. Then she leaves.

"How is George – is he ill?" Anne asks.

"He may be," I reply, knowing full well from history that he contracted the sweat. I give her a reassuring smile. "If he is ill, I know he will recover." I shrug my eyebrows. "He resides at Waltham Abbey with the king and queen."

Sometimes, knowing the future is a reassurance, as it allows me to share good news and hope with Anne. I know when I share small tidbits of her family history with her, she believes me because she doesn't always try to draw answers from me, but in this instance, she is persistent.

"Could that mean that Katharine or even Henry has caught the sweat from him?" she croaks. "And father, how is he?"

"Sir Thomas is still in bed – he is being attended to – and we have had no news that the king has fallen ill."

"And Katharine?" She pulls herself up again against her sunken pillows.

"Not a word."

She sighs. "Thank God!"

"Doctor Butts will make sure your father recovers, too." I touch her hand again. "Besides, in the middle of the night, once your mother was sleeping in a chair beside their bed, I dropped some medication into his goblet, mixing it with a little wine."

"Will that work?" she asks.

"It has with you." I can't hold back a smile. "Try not to worry yourself. You need to build up your strength." Her expression shows her thoughts are with her family.

"I wonder if Henry is on his knees, before the Cross, bargaining with God for my life, offering all manner of things if heaven will spare me." She tries to smile at the thought.

I think about Henry, and how he will feel when Doctor Butts relays the news of Anne's recovery. At least once he hears she is over the worst, he will know which way to proceed with his Great Matter. I'm not surprised that he has sent more letters to Hever, and I open the seal, full of excitement, and read the first letter to be delivered. Between caring for her husband and daughter, Lady Elizabeth appears on the landing, hanging around at the doorway, waiting to hear what Henry has written.

No salutation is found inside, only a dark smudge where Henry's palm has smeared the first application of ink to paper. He expresses his immense relief that she had not come down with the illness yet. Obviously, he wrote the letter days ago. The small piece of parchment is splattered throughout with droplets of ink – by-products of an anxious hand. The words don't flow freely – the script is cramped and slanted towards the top right of the page. It looks like he has written this communication in real haste. It's dated 16th June 1528.

I scan the curly scribble. "Immutable?"

"The French for 'enduring' or 'abiding'," Anne mumbles as she rests her head against her pillow. She has outsmarted death this time, while Henry resides miles away, safe and sound with Katharine, his wife and queen. We are banished to Kent, to get along as best we can.

———— • ❄ • ————

Within a week, Anne is greatly improved – eating and drinking well – I already have her up and about, wrapped up warm in her cloaks and furs. I encourage her to take the air, which brings colour to her cheeks. Her strength is returning, and she is delighted when a messenger arrives with another letter with a royal wax seal. She is greatly comforted by her lover's concern and smiles as I open it up and start reading. It was written days after the first, on June 20th, 1528.

"The king says that when his court was at Walton,"—does he mean Waltham? The Tudors spell so many words differently—"two valets of his bedchamber – your brother and Master Fitzwilliam – had fallen ill, but now they are quite well."

She stares at me, realising that I knew.

Her mother comes rushing in on overhearing my words. "George has the sweat?" she cries, the fear in her voice heightened. I get up and thrust the letter under her nose.

"He did, Madam, but no longer." I smile. "See – read here." I point at Henry's scrawl. "George is well."

She sighs, nodding to herself. It appears that neither of Anne's parents has been aware that George has been fighting for his life.

"He is definitely out of danger?" she asks.

"Yes, Lady Boleyn – the king says so."

She hugs me. "Beth, that is such a relief to hear!" She releases me from her embrace, which was lovely. I miss my dad's hugs. "I will go and tell my husband, and see how Doctor Butts is attending on him."

"Of course." I sit back on Anne's bed, the reeds crunching in the mattress beneath my weight.

"Has the king said anything else?"

"Yes." I scan the letter. "It appears Doctor Butts wrote to Sir Thomas Heneage who has now informed Henry, telling him you had caught the sweat, and that you have now recovered – he asks after your health. I quote: 'The uneasiness my doubts about your health gave me, disturbed and alarmed me exceedingly…but now,' he says…etc, etc…" I scan the text for something positive. "'I hope and am assured it will spare you, as I hope it is doing with us.' – The king seems most concerned about you."

"When he wrote that letter, he obviously was unaware of how ill I have been," she says.

"Yes, but Doctor Butts will continue to inform him of your progress. You see, Anne, the king hopes that Doctor Butts has made you well and that he will see you soon."

She sighs. "Henry has not forgotten me."

This letter, I notice, has been written in as great an urgency as the last. It's clear to see where the quill has jabbed at the parchment. I can imagine Henry stabbing at the inkwell with every few strokes. The parchment is blotched, scratchy, and smeared – rendered in terror. I translate the French, and although my reading is poor, Anne can understand me. Its contents are unbelievably heart-wrenching. In addition, at the bottom of the page, after Henry's initials, it looks like he's encompassing her in his strong arms, surrounding her with himself and his heart.

The panicked tone of this letter is so unlike any of the others. His pain and anxiety jump off the page, the ink splattered and smeared by his large hand – the writing often dark and scratchy. There are fine sprays of ink where the nib of the quill has caught at the parchment in haste. However, some of the splatters do not appear to be ink; they could be tear stains. It really is a mess, compared to the usual neat and beautiful-looking missives he has sent before. It is the appearance, rather than the words that convey his love for Anne. This is more than a lustful letter – it is from a distraught man worried about the woman he loves, and I'm finding it hard to believe that I have it in my hand. What an amazing life I am leading.

Within days, a messenger arrives with a letter carrying news. I watch as a distraught Lady Boleyn sits in her husband's chair in the parlour, reads the words in disbelief of William Carey succumbing to the sweating sickness, just as I'd blurted out would happen when I'd confessed to Anne years before. I really do have to watch my mouth. The family is grief-stricken – all were so fond of William. He has been a good husband to Mary, despite all King Henry had put them through.

Anne walks around her bedroom. She says she still feels weak, but I keep telling her that being fully dressed, and up and about, and outside, will boost her health. The more she listens to me, the quicker she seems to improve every day. Sir Thomas has also recovered, and is up and about, but stays in his bedchamber on the insistence of his wife.

"I feel sorry for Mary," Anne whispers, as she leans against the window sill, looking out into the orchard. "What will happen to her now?" She sighs, playing with her hair, which she wears loose. "And what of her children – Catherine and little Henry?" She shakes her head, the action slow, then turns to face me. "They will feel his loss – mourn him. I am devastated. I wish I could be with her, to comfort her, but Mary does not come to Hever in case she has the contagion."

Anne has been wise to spend her time recuperating. We sit in the parlour, dressed in our summer silks, reading. The warmth of the sun's rays streaming through the window cheers us. Its light dances across the Turkish carpet, and Griffin enjoys basking in its glow. The wolfhound is growing older, and is no longer so light on his feet when he ambles up to greet Sir Thomas as he enters the room. Anne gets up, as do I, and we curtsy to her father, who looks thinner, weaker, and not as robust as he once was. He lowers himself into his chair in front of the hearth.

"How are my girls?" he asks, stroking his beard.

"We are well, father." Anne half-smiles. "Should I ask Mrs Orchard to get you some wine?"

"That would be a comfort." He nods. She leaves the room, her steps soon fading down the hallway.

"I am relieved at my daughter's quick recovery," he says to me, a knowing look in his eyes. "I feel I must thank not only God, and Doctor Butts, but also you for how Anne was saved from death."

I shake my head. "My Lord, it was all Doctor Butts' doing, never mine."

"Do not be modest. I vaguely recollect you instructing me to drink a bitter concoction."

Heat surges into my face. "Sir, it was just wine, and it was my duty to care for you when your wife was resting."

He gives me a half-smile. "Not only that but, my wife also told me you nursed Anne almost by yourself."

"Sir, I—" Our conversation is broken as Anne enters the room. She sets a flagon of wine and an Italian-style glass down on the small table next to her father.

"Thank you, dear," he says as she pours the wine into the glass. "You were responsible, Beth – responsible, I tell you."

"Responsible for what?" Anne asks, looking back and forth between the two of us.

"Making you well, daughter!"

"Perhaps, sir, it was my praying?" Since spending so much time here in Tudor England, I have found myself drawn into the religious fervour of the era. Although I attend Midnight Mass on Christmas Eve with my parents every year and services at Easter, I have never experienced such a change in my thoughts towards religion and God since being here. Yes, I had faith before, and belief in God, but never to this extent. Anne's commitment to religious reform has gripped my imagination and I pray repeatedly for her, spending time at devotions clutching her book of hours, the one made in Bruges, which her father had given her. It comforts me to know I have in my possession something so beautiful and treasured by her. The prayers within are simple and heartfelt, and they seem fitting, as I have thanked God for sparing her life.

Staring out of the parlour window, I contemplate the reality of Anne's situation and her relationship with Henry.

"Is there any news of the king's health, father?" Her question breaks my thoughts.

"At present, the king is in good health – if not, we would know by now."

"And George?" I ask. "Is there any more news of him?"

"All we know is what the king has written to Anne. My boy has recovered – thank God!"

"With this contagion present here, and abroad, it seems insurmountable that Henry would be able to resolve the matter between him and me." Anne frowns. "I do not think I will ever be the king's wife – let alone his queen."

I resume daydreaming out of the window, concerning myself with issues way beyond my remit. As things are, with the odds against the couple being together, it seems like the obvious choice to encourage her to walk away from him, as, to all involved, it seems impossible she will ever become his lawful wife. I know the pope will be resistant to Henry's annulment, as are many people at court and elsewhere about the realm. Many at Court are now becoming aware of his wish to supplant Katharine with Anne, and are openly opposed to it. Over time, I know Henry continues to convince himself of the logic and soundness of his argument, that, because of Katharine's previous marriage to his brother, they have never been legally wed. In any case, who is to say she isn't lying about not having consummated the relationship with Arthur? As a woman, would you not protect your child and the succession and try to save your marriage by lying, saying that you were a virgin when you came to your second marriage bed? A mother would do anything to protect her child, wouldn't she?

Henry honestly believes his argument is justified and that it will stand under the scrutiny of canon law. I know Anne feels doubtful about the whole matter, thinking the situation will never resolve itself in Rome. I try to reassure her that Henry will never give her up. He needs to resort to the only approach that might, in the end, succeed in his wooing of her and their eventual union: the submission of the church to his will. For that to succeed, somehow, she needs to show him William Tyndale's work, which will cement in his mind the rightness of his cause.

I look at her, wondering how I'm going to convince her that showing Henry a heretical book is the right thing to do. No, I need to keep my ideas to myself for now. But as Katharine is a princess of the blood, and has been Henry's beloved and respected wife and pious queen for many years, the whole situation must feel like an uphill struggle for Anne. I know it does to me. If they knew her as I do, I'm sure there would be less opposition to her. I'm not going to be the one to pass on such negative stories to her, about her – they are only opinions, after all.

Being as close to Anne as I am, I can see she is filled with a deep sense of hopelessness. Her thoughts must be ragged, holding her in their ugly grip during her long recovery. The hours inch past and her moods vary from day to day. One persistent notion keeps her going, like a tiny flame flickering in the darkness: the idea of marriage. She has told me that her feelings have surprised her of late, and her devotion to Henry seems to have crossed a boundary from which she feels she cannot turn back. As her strength returns, her attitude rallies and I hope we will soon be able to return to court so she can access her feelings better. It seems that her illness has given her hope that, together, they possess an uncanny strength, which will give them the resilience to await the verdict of Rome. In the meantime, she prays daily to God to show her the way forward.

She writes a message to Henry, confirming that she is getting better day by day, and wishes nothing more than to be with him again – that she misses him greatly, and prays constantly that his health will remain strong. Then, after considering for a few moments, she asks on behalf of the family after her deceased brother-in-law, William Carey, that his sister Eleanor Carey be considered for an appointment to the newly open position of Abbess of St Edith at Wilton. She asks me if it is wise to ask a political favour of Henry. I tell her that he will grant anything she requests, so long as it's reasonable. Her appeal represents a new perspective in their relationship, and we have no idea how he will react.

Mary Carey is now a penniless widow with two children. Sir Thomas has refused to help his elder daughter, and she has been reduced to asking Anne to intercede on her behalf if they are not to fall on hard times. Henry's latest letter suggests he will appeal to Sir Thomas, so he can arrange for a small annuity to be paid to Mary and her family. The king also reveals that he has awarded the wardship of Henry Carey to Anne, presumably so she can protect her nephew, who might also be Henry's own.

His correspondence, this time, is neatly written, with a well-executed script. It appears business-like as if he has written it while overseeing and signing the many documents that make up his daily routine. It is dated June 22nd, 1528.

The morning sunlight plays across the ceiling of the bedchamber as I put off getting up to dress. While it looks like a bright day is dawning, I want to remain curled under my covers for a little while longer, until I pluck up the courage to make a start of it.

Anne grabs a wrap and places it around her shoulders as she walks to the window, which she unlatches and pushes open to view the orchard below. It is indeed a lovely summer's morning, and there is no more beautiful place on earth to appreciate it than from the heart of the Kentish countryside. I sit up and stretch. The night-time mist, billowing over the lawns that slope towards the river, is beginning to dissipate and, when I get up and look over Anne's shoulder, the bell of St Peter's tolls in the distance, its peal piercing the silence beneath the morning sky. Below us, the apple trees are busy with young fruit, the beautiful blossoms long gone, and I'm delighted to see the swans and their cygnets glide on the stream beyond the castle. The swans remind me of home, when I sometimes walk down to The Ponds at Carshalton to watch the family of swans there. Living close to the stream, does Anne and her family follow the progress of their local cygnets through each summer? Such a wonderful day – yet it will be difficult for us to enjoy.

Anne and Wolsey are not at loggerheads as history often documents them – at least not at the moment – for the cardinal has marked her recovery from the sweating sickness by a 'kind letter' and a 'rich and goodly present', which she acknowledges directly, along with her indebtedness to him for his help. On this bright morning, she takes her quill and pens a letter thanking him for his kind thoughts, pleased that he has taken the time to send her good wishes. For all his goodness to her, there's still the reality of who and what the man is really about. Wolsey will try to cling to power for as long as he can – he may even think he could claw his way back to power even when he's dismissed. I'm the only one who knows that his time is running out, if history continues to run along its proper path.

Eighteen

Hever Castle - Kent

Sir Thomas paces the parlour floor, stroking his beard and muttering to himself, whilst his wife, Anne, and I wait for him to speak.

"I've been informed by letter today that the queen is expected to appear very soon before the legates to present her testimony against the divorce." He sighs, looking at Anne. "I did not think this matter would be so serious, or go so far." He shakes his head.

"Father, initially I thought that if I suggested marriage to His Majesty, he would tire of me, and eventually forget any thought of leaving his wife. But since the king's mind is now so decidedly resolute in this matter, I find my feelings for him have quite changed."

"I know. I know." He continues to nod.

I have to get in here. "Sir, do you not think that the king would have still sought a divorce even if he did not want to marry Anne?"

"Who knows the king's mind, Beth? I'm sure none at court do!" He sighs again, his shoulders slumping.

"What the king wants, he shall have," I say.

"I understand the matter of the verse in Leviticus has weighed heavy on the king's conscience, but you all know I have never been happy about him pursuing you, Anne."

"I never considered Henry would try to push through an annulment for my sake," she says, shaking her head. "However, now that the matter is gathering pace, I am resigned to my fate. However, I wish it could be easily concluded, for everyone's sake."

I've never heard her talk so decidedly before. She's quite the diplomat. I hope she can stay that way because it will stand her in good stead when she becomes queen.

"That one day you might be queen?" Lady Boleyn says, wringing her hands.

"Yes, mother." She shrugs. "As I said, I had hoped that the matter would have been concluded by now." She looks at me, her brows arched. "I thought that some weeks after I left court for Hever, the legates would have come to a decision on the matter." She grimaces. "I know, too, the king is most anxious for things to be resolved for us." She turns to her father. "I never encouraged the king, sir."

"Daughter, I understand." He leans against the fireplace mantle.

"Now that the king's love for me has been established, and his will is being pushed, I feel I am growing more and more accustomed to the idea of being his wife."

"And queen!" I add. She arches a brow at me and smiles.

"I fear this will not turn out well," her mother says beneath a deep frown.

Sir Thomas waves her remark away. "Whatever we may think about the king's desire for an annulment, it matters not, because once His Grace sets his mind on a course of action, or, indeed, having our daughter as a wife, there is nothing any of us can do to dissuade him."

"Nevertheless, father, it is frustrating that the preparations for the hearing have moved ponderously, and the official business has only just got underway. Reluctantly, I am beginning to believe that God's great plan for me includes mastering the art of patience."

"It is proving a difficult lesson for us all, to be sure – especially for our king."

The serenity and peace of Hever, of being in Edenbridge, as opposed to the noise and clamour of court, should offer a welcome respite, but with news being brought daily from court, it is the opposite. Would it be better for Sir Thomas to return to court so he can hear the news first-hand, as it happens?

"I grow impatient, father. How am I to concentrate on anything while events that will shape my future are being determined by the legal proceedings at Blackfriars?"

"You must not worry yourself," her mother says.

I touch her arm. "Anne, stop imagining disastrous outcomes!"

Sir Thomas taps the mantle. "Ladies, all will be well."

Later, Anne chases her mother through the castle when the king's courier arrives unexpectedly. As always, I'm not far behind her. We meet the equerry, who stands fidgeting beside his horse in the courtyard, and Anne nearly grabs the package from him. Back in the house, she sits at a desk in the library, sometimes used as her father's estate office, and clears aside a pile of bills and ledgers to open the thin, crackling parchment. I recognise the familiar hand of Henry's quill. It's hard to miss Anne's smile – it's as if she's in the company of the man as she reads to herself.

Looking over her shoulder, I see the ease of his scrawl and the degree of familiarity with which he now writes. This letter is penned in English, not the usual, formal French. He seems to have put quill to parchment in a less-proscribed manner, with the messages being composed much faster. The ease with which they communicate shows how they have grown comfortable with their relationship – not how it is always portrayed in history. Anne is often considered the unwilling participant, cajoled into it by her overbearing relations, but pressing for marriage, she had hoped to dampen Henry's interest, not realising he would push for an annulment to have her. Now, it seems the tables have turned, and she has been surprised by Henry pushing for something she thought he wouldn't want. His love and affection for her is instantly apparent from the prose on the page and, now, it seems from her response, her affections are beginning to match his. Thank God things are continuing to go to plan, historically speaking, just as the professor wants it, and I need it to.

Within days, a courier arrives with yet another letter for Anne, dated after July 6th, 1528. Henry writes of Walter Welshe, Master Browne, Thomas Care, and John Coke, the Apothecary, who had fallen foul of the sweat but who have now recovered. The king goes on to discuss the matter touching Wilton.

Anne reads aloud as if it will help her feel closer to Henry.

> *"'As touching your abode at Hever, do therein as best shall like you, for you best know what air doth best with you; but I would it were come thereto (if it pleased God), that neither of us need care for that, for I ensure you I think it long. Suche is fallen sick of the sweat, and therefore I send you this bearer, because I think you long to hear tidings from us, as we do likewise from you. Written with the hand de votre seul, H. R.'"*

Henry is hopeful the sweat will yet pass him by. Concerning Anne's request, he writes that Cardinal Wolsey has looked into the matter, and has discovered that Dame Eleanor Carey has borne two children by two different priests. Even worse, that she has also been intimately involved with a servant of Lord Broke. These unfortunate facts render her unfit to hold her position but, in order to please Anne, he offers his assurance that the other candidates under consideration would not be selected by Wolsey alone but, instead, they would search for a 'good and well-disposed woman' not affiliated with the cardinal or any other political ties. With Dame Eleanor's blighted background, she has to find a new patron. What is most important to Anne is that Henry has accepted her suggestion, and does not chastise her for speaking beyond her station. Three further letters follow in rapid succession, each bemoaning the fact that Anne and he are still apart, and he promises his efforts on the Great Matter to be unrelenting.

> *The approach of the time for which I have so long waited rejoices me so much, that it seems almost to have come already. However, the entire accomplishment cannot be till the two persons meet, which meeting is more desired by me than anything in this world; for what joy can be greater upon earth than to have*

the company of her who is dearest to me, knowing likewise that she does the same on her part, the thought of which gives me the greatest pleasure. Judge what an effect the presence of that person must have on me, whose absence has grieved my heart more than either words or writing can express, and which nothing can cure, but that begging you, my Mistress, to tell your Father from me, that I desire him to hasten the time appointed by two days, that he may be at court before the old term, or, at farthest, on the day prefixed; for otherwise I shall think he will not do the lover's turn, as he said he would, nor answer my expectation. No more at present for lack of time, hoping shortly that by word of mouth I shall tell you the rest of the sufferings endured by me from your absence. Written by the hand of the secretary, who wishes himself at this moment privately with you, and who is, and always will be, your loyal and most assured servant, H. no other AB seek R.

George has returned from Court to visit Anne. I've not laid eyes on him since before he caught the sweat, and I've got to say, I'm thrilled at seeing him. However, he doesn't look as robust as normal, though he has some colour in his cheeks as he alights from the litter. His parents greet him under the portcullis. Sir Thomas's embrace is firm and almost drains the air from George's lungs.

"Father, it is so good to see you!"

"And you, my boy."

Lady Boleyn envelops her son in a gentle hug, then strokes his cheek. "I thank God you are well – I am so relieved you are home again, although it looks like you need some of my good home cooking."

"Don't fuss, Liz," Sir Thomas says, his face alight with a smile. "Give the boy a moment."

Anne hugs her brother. "It is good to see you, George."

"I have missed you, sister. It is good to see you, too, have recovered."

I curtsy to him, and he nods, his gaze never faltering from me. "I have missed you also, Beth." Anne takes a sideways glance at him, and smiles first at him then at me – maybe her attitude towards us as a couple is changing?

Her father walks into the shadows of the castle, with his wife beside him, and George follows. John, his valet, is unloading his trunks from the litter, and Simon, the stable boy, has unharnessed the horses and is leading them beyond the outer courtyard, towards the stable block.

Robert Cranewell, Sir Thomas's body servant, waits at the castle door with a flagon of wine and several goblets on a tray.

"Thank you, Robert," Sir Thomas says, nodding as he picks up a glass. He strides through, heading towards the parlour. In turn, we all take a glass.

"I need this!" George says, patting Robert on the shoulder.

By the time I enter the parlour, Sir Thomas is already reclining in his chair, his wife standing beside him. Anne and I sit on the settle, prodding the cushions into a comfortable spot at our backs.

George takes a sip of his wine as he stands before his parents. "The contagion is rife in London, and on its outskirts. Uncle and I have been lucky to recover but so many have not."

"Who else has fallen ill?" his mother asks.

"Wolsey, some members of his household, and William, of course."

"From his letters, it seems the king is anxious for his health," Anne says.

"And for the queen," George adds. "We Boleyns should rejoice in our good fortune that we have survived."

"Except for William, and our servant Agnes," Sir Thomas whispers. It's clear that he's affected by members of his household succumbing to the illness.

Lady Boleyn squeezes her husband's hand. "I am glad my children have pulled through, and have come to no more harm."

"'Tis all because of Beth," Anne says. "Helping Doctor Butts nurse both father and me back to health."

George looks at me. "Beth?"

"Yes," his mother replies, "Beth was instrumental in tending to your sister, and helping me to take care of your father."

He arches both brows and nods at me. "Then perhaps, Father, we should speak with the king and suggest that Beth Wickers be given a title, or some kind of reward. What say you?"

"Oh, no, please don't – I do not deserve such acclaim."

"You know the king will be the judge of that!" Sir Thomas says. He looks at his son. "And what of Henry?"

"The king keeps moving from one bolthole to another for fear of the plague. Many of his people have died of the sweat within three or four hours but we have heard that of the forty thousand who succumbed in London, only two thousand are dead." He shakes his head, the action slow.

"Are there any remedies for this sweating sickness?" Lady Boleyn asks.

"Nothing seems effective, mother, and the terror it causes is more fatal than the disease itself." He takes a sip of his wine. "Children, in consequence, we have heard are less affected by it than persons of riper age. It rages mainly in Kent and Sussex, and the neighbouring counties. Out of England, it is unknown, nor is the infection carried by merchants, or others into foreign parts. Among the sufferers is Bryan Tuke, the king's secretary, one of the few persons admitted at the time into the king's presence."

"I pray to God the king does not get the sweat." Anne holds her cheek.

"We all do, Anne," her father says.

"George, I am relieved the king did not visit me in my sickbed."

"Would you have wanted to receive him, shivering, sweating, and writhing?" he asks.

"Goodness knows what treasonous scandal I might have repeated in my delirium." She moves her hand to her mouth.

"Did you rant, sister?"

She looks at me. "Beth said I did!"

"I did, too," he says. "Jane said I had no restraint as she supervised my nursing. Heaven knows what I gave away." He ruffles his fingers through his hair, flicking a glance at me that has my face burning. "She hasn't looked me in the eye since my recovery."

His mother sighs. "Oh, George."

"I could not have borne it if you had died," I say, unable to hold it back. His mother stares at me, alarm in her eyes. Oh, God, I need to shut up.

"Sister," George almost shouts, "have you ever known such longing for sleep, as if heaven was beckoning?" He shakes his head and chuckles. "Jane even threw water on my face, several times! She literally shook me – even held my eyes open!"

"I somehow held a fear of sleep," she says, "and fixed my mind on the starlings outside my window. And I tried to concentrate on Beth's face."

He nods once at me. "Our sister has lost her husband, and I haven't seen her. I am worried about her children. William was only twenty-eight, and he died greatly in debt. We need to find a way to help our sister."

I'm so glad he was quick to change the subject and take the focus off me. As I watch him, concerned for his sibling, I give thanks it was William and not George who fell to the sweat.

Within days, George has returned to court, taking with him bundles of letters and papers bound in a leather folio for the king. Anne and I didn't want him to go but, as we waved him off, she felt confident he will try to influence Henry in a favourable way regarding her situation.

After helping Lady Boleyn with some chores, Anne now sits beside me in the library, reading a pocket-sized copy of the New Testament. While she thumbs through the bold print of red and black, I read and re-read other papers smuggled into England, and passed to her at Hever over the summer, including a pamphlet of Lutheran writings. I break the silence, to discuss the contents with her.

"How completely logical it seems to me that man answers directly to God, with the singular intervention of Jesus Christ. It rings true that God alone could determine the vindication of sin, forgiveness, and salvation." As a believer, I know we are saved by grace, but I want to hear Anne's opinion on it.

Anne looks up from her bible. "Such profound principles of life and hereafter are certainly not appropriated by clerics who are appointed by man. It is well known that many are corrupt…sinners of the highest order." The lines on the bridge of her nose wrinkle.

"Do you think you could be brave enough to discuss these concepts with Henry?"

"In my heart, Beth, I believe this thinking, and I believe it could provide the answer the king seeks."

She puts down her bible when we hear a rider approach, and voices below. A quick look through a window into the shady, summer light of the inner courtyard has the two of us running along the hallway to see a courier pulling a sealed letter from the leather panniers attached to his saddle.

The servant eyes the royal seal with some familiarity. Lady Boleyn walks into the hallway, embroidery still in her hand, wanting to find out what the commotion is all about.

"Bring the lad in for a cup of ale and a slice of bread," she says. "Then, once he has been fed, he can be on his way."

She waves both men through to the kitchen but, before she has the chance to interrogate Anne about the letter, we rush out into the gardens to read it. When she breaks the seal and begins to read, she realises that George has been questioned by Henry about her health, and has told him that he longs for her to return to Court. We sit together under a tree, in the dappled light of the warm sun, surrounded by a sprinkling of daises. The letter was written on July 21st. She reads it aloud:

> "'Darling, I heartily recommend me to you, ascertaining you that I am not a little perplexed with such things as your brother shall on my part declare unto you, to whom I pray you give full credence, for it were too long to write. In my last letters I write to you that I trusted shortly to see you, which is better known at London than with any that is about me, whereof I not a little marvel; but lack of discreet handling must needs be the cause thereof. No more to you at this time, but that I trust shortly our meetings shall not depend upon other men's light handlings, but upon our own. Written with the hand of him that longeth to be yours. H. R.'"

I assume from the letter that George has reassured him that all is well with her. Within days, as we sit in the parlour, we are disturbed by another royal messenger, who arrives with yet another letter from the king, this time pleading with Anne to be with her. Again, she reads it aloud to me:

> *'Mine own sweetheart, this shall be to advertise you of the great elengeness that I find here since your departing; for, I ensure you methinketh the time longer since your departing now last...'*

"What else does he say?"

"He talks of my kindness, and his fervency of love for me."

"And?" I ask, my patience tested.

"He says it grieves him for us to be apart but that soon we would be together, and the pain of not being together would be gone."

"And...?"

"He's been studying the case of his matter, in his library, for four hours. Which is why, he says, his letter is shorter."

I nod at that, seeing him in my mind surrounded by piles of books. "Anything else?"

"He says he has a headache from writing, but..." She falters.

"Yes?"

She smirks. "I'm not sure I can read it aloud."

"Yes, you can – I'm a modern woman!" I giggle, having an idea what's coming.

Her cheeks redden. "He wishes himself, especially of an evening, to be in my arms...and he trusts shortly...that I will allow him to kiss my breasts!" She giggles. "I cannot believe I have shared that with you!"

"You know you can tell me anything. Anyway, I know that Henry is obsessed by your bosom!"

She looks at me and laughs again. "Then he signs the letter...

> *'Written by the hand of him that was, is, and shall be yours by his own will
> - H. R.'*

Her eyes are wide, jaw dropped, as she traces his words with her fingertips. She re-reads sentences to me, almost to reaffirm what he has written.

"The king astounds me with his words. His sentiment is so touching, it almost makes me want to weep."

I look at her, knowing that she doesn't often show her true emotions when it comes to him. It is only me, and George, occasionally, who gets to see what she really thinks of him. From her demeanour, it's clear that she pines for her beau, or perhaps she's depressed because she wants the matter of the annulment resolved once and for all. I try to reassure her, telling her that things will change and that she will be Queen of England one day, but she must persevere, as Henry must be patient, too. Her eyes are wide like saucers on hearing confirmation of her future from my lips, and I hope she isn't bubbling with anger at me for never confiding in her.

Within days of this last letter, another arrives, bearing the promise of change. Anne doesn't waste any time in replying, expressing her most heartfelt thanks for his generosity, and, importantly, to inquire about the latest status of his matter, and asking and urging when they can be together again. She also asks if there is any news of Campeggio, and what of the Legatine Court? When will they likely hear any news, and can Wolsey not override the court on Henry's behalf? The questions go on, until she has exhausted the ink from the well. She sprinkles her words with drying powder, blows the excess off, then seals the letter and returns it to the waiting courier, requesting it be given to the king with her deepest devotion and love.

George has also sent a letter, and as she reads his familiar, cursive writing, he tells her that the king is restocking the royal library. It is Henry's resolution to take his Great Matter into his own hands by thinking differently about it, and transforming the outcome by reading the books he is gathering into a research library, created from scholars' works purchased on the open market. Henry has asked his librarians to order the books alphabetically by sticking Arabic numbers on the spine of each tome, cataloguing them so each volume is cross-referenced.

From all accounts, he has become something of a scholar, looking at sources of thought on England's history, its theology, and on marriage. According to George, it is Henry who comes up with such ideas to resolve his matter, and, as I already know, Cromwell will eventually be the thug who reconfigures the idea of England itself, because of it. Henry is acquiring new books of literature, like Chaucer, and he envisages a great navy for England so she will no longer be invaded once every fifty years, as she has before. It seems that Anne has changed the king forever, causing this great shift in thinking and behaviour, and the whole court is flabbergasted by the change in him.

Nineteen

WEDNESDAY, SEPTEMBER 16TH, 1528 – HEVER

Anne knows Henry dislikes spending long periods bent over his desk writing, and we could only imagine the headaches he has developed from hours of researching on his 'Matter'. This has most probably been the reason for keeping him from writing a longer letter, but I doubt it stops him from imagining himself in her gentle embrace. We all await the arrival of Campeggio to London. He is the Papal Legate designate, and we are assured he is expected soon. There are numerous reasons, we have been told by the king via letter, why he has not made better time, including poor weather, poor health, poor roads, and so on. Only I know how disheartening this situation will prove to be. Anne wants to vent her growing frustration and resentment on Wolsey, and her father and uncle are encouraging her to do so. Now that they know she won't be dissuaded from marrying the king, they want to use the situation to their advantage and have Wolsey supplanted.

Thank God her rational judgement prevails, and she doesn't go for it. I encourage her to look to the future and forget about Wolsey, Campeggio, and the court for a time because, with Henry's promise that he and her father have secured and renovated lodgings for her and her growing band of servants in Durham House on the Strand, we know this means we won't have to return to court to serve Queen Katharine. Henry has ordered an inventory to be taken of the furniture in Durham House and extra furnishings provided from York Place. Anne is grateful to her father and the king for this and writes to them, thanking them for their diligence and work on her behalf.

Durham House is where we are to stay on our eventual return to London. We've heard through George that it was the cardinal himself who suggested that it might not best for Anne and Katharine to be under the same roof. Thankfully, Anne is no longer required to provide service to Katharine. The knowledge of not returning to the queen's service has given her great peace of mind, lifting her spirits, and the two of us can't wait to return to the city and become settled near to Henry.

A royal messenger arrives to deliver a prompt response to her reply to Henry's last letter. A fine leather wrapper protects the thin parchment, which has been folded twice. She opens it and is greeted with a smudged scrawl.

> *"'The reasonable request of your last letter, with the pleasure also that I take to know them true, causeth me to send you this news. The legate which we most desire arrived at Paris on Sunday or Monday last past, so that I trust by the next Monday to hear of his arrival at Calais: and then I trust within a while after to enjoy that which I have so long longed for, to God's pleasure and our both comforts. No more to you at this present, mine own darling, for lack of time, but that I would you were in mine arms, or I in yours, for I think it long since I kissed you. Written after the killing of a hart, at eleven of the clock, minding, with God's grace, to-morrow, mightily timely, to kill another, by the hand which, I trust, shortly shall be yours. Henry R.'"*

Sir Thomas has also informed us by letter that Campeggio actually arrived at Calais on Monday, September 14. He has it on good authority from the ambassadors at Court that the legate will soon be arriving in England, much to Anne's delight.

LATE SEPTEMBER 1528

Anne and I are sat at breakfast when Lady Boleyn enters the room, waving a sealed letter in her hand. She gives me a curious look, hand on hip.

"Beth, a messenger has called with letters for me, and amongst one from my husband is a letter addressed to you from my son, no less!"

My jaw drops. "George has written a letter to me?" I rise from my chair, my tummy in a whirl. She offers me the letter over the table. "Thank you, madam." She folds her arms. I hope she's not waiting for me to open it, in front of her. "May I take my leave of you? I have broken my fast."

"Very well," she says, frowning.

My skirts swish behind me as I race as fast as my gown will permit to the top of the castle, to sit and read his letter in the autumn sunshine of the Long Gallery. Lady Boleyn's voice carries along the hallways as she calls for Mrs Orchard to come and clear the breakfast table. Within minutes, the rustle of silken skirts outside signal's Anne's arrival. This time, like my loyal lapdog, she has followed me.

I find a quiet spot – a window seat – and lean back against the velvet cushions. My mouth is dry from my nerves, and my hand trembles before I slide my thumbs over the wax seal, applying a little pressure and snapping it apart. Then I flick open the thin, crackling parchment and recognise, from the dedication in the book he gifted me, the familiar hand of George's quill. I smile to myself as I begin to read his words – it's as if he's in the gallery, sat here next to me. It's a pity he's not.

'My own darling Beth,

'I hope you did not think me rude in writing to you. I want you to hear good news of me, and to know you are well. Since my return to court, His Majesty has appointed me Esquire of the Body. I am delighted to be rising in favour with the king and wanted to share my good fortune with you.

'Jayne Foole asked me to send news of her, that she is well. She wants you and Anne to know that she misses you, and cannot wait for you both to return to court.

'Since our parting, I have been melancholy. My happiness is to be near you. I think often of you, and wonder how you fare, at Hever with my sister. I play over again in my mind our kisses and your caresses, and our affection. You are incomparable to any woman I have ever known. You kindle a burning flame in my heart. When free from all the cares of court, I look forward to passing all my time with you, having only to love you, and to think only of our happiness, and of proving my love to you. My feelings for you makes me selfish. You must know how much I adore you. I cannot exist without you – I am forgetful of everything but seeing you again.

'From the hand of your servant, George.'

WINTER 1528 – HEVER

George has written again, sending messages by courier, that, on 15th November, he has become the keeper of the Palace of Beaulieu. The funny thing was, in 1516, before Thomas Boleyn was a Lord, he sold New Hall (now the Palace of Beaulieu) to Henry VIII for one thousand pounds. Henry has now rebuilt the house in brick for seventeen thousand pounds. The king has a desire for fine things, and isn't afraid to spend his father's money.

When the candles are spent in Anne's bedchamber, I lay awake thinking of George. Lady Boleyn was not best pleased that her son has been writing to me but it warms my heart that I am in his thoughts. Anne has read his letter to me and has kept her promise not to make comments on her brother's affairs. She need not worry because, so far, my relationship with him has been that between a lady and her courtly lover, though I'm eager to take it further at some stage in the future, especially with things between him and Jane being so bad.

Anne awaits news of the Legatine Court, as Katharine and Henry go head-to-head at Blackfriars before Cardinals Campeggio and Wolsey, to decide upon the validity of their marriage. She says she can't bear to witness the proceedings herself and feels that she may be a target for hatred and therefore ridiculed by the crowds in London if she's seen in the area. Sir Thomas sends us detailed, written accounts of the trial, and what was said. Anne sits beside me in the parlour, reading the contents of his letter. His writing is neat and small, like George's. She sounds astonished with the contents.

"I cannot believe the sheer determination and audacity of the queen to appeal to the king directly during the court proceedings!"

"She was recalled by the court, wasn't she?" I ask, looking over her arm at the letter.

"Yes, by the lawyers who wanted the proceedings to continue." She shakes her head. "The queen has ignored everyone. She said that she will only take the decision of the pope in Rome as her answer to the annulment, and nothing more, and she is adamant that she remains the king's true and loyal wife!"

Her exasperation is clear as she leans back on the settle, her eyes closed. If she's stressed about this, she'll need to gird herself for what's coming.

One afternoon, as we wile away our idle time reading, sewing, and chatting, I bring up a subject Anne probably doesn't want to discuss.

"Anne, I have not returned to my time for such a long while. I am concerned about what is happening with my parents, with my education, and whether or not I will actually be able to return home at all. Yes, I know it worked during the sweat but who's to say it will now? I need to try, even for a short while? You know I will not abandon you. There is little we can do, shut up here at Hever, and matters will progress naturally without me."

I could so easily step into a dark corner to activate the cypher ring but I feel guilty leaving her like that.

She looks at me through her thick lashes, her black saucer eyes unmoving, as if piercing my core. "If you must return home, then I will allow it. But you must promise me one thing." One corner of her mouth lifts, and I know she's up to no good. "I want to go with you at some point – I want to see what the future looks like!"

I stare at her, almost afraid to contemplate the implications of such a request. After her scare with the sweat, I wonder about all the other viruses and diseases she'd be open to. Things like the common cold – the flu – measles – mumps – chickenpox – shingles. I'd feel responsible for her if she were to come back with me, and I'm more than aware of the potentially disastrous consequences, not just to Anne but to early-modern England.

"Anne, I am not sure it would be permitted but I can ask my tutor if it would be safe and give you an answer on my return." I sigh. "I know you want me to stay."

"I would rather you did not go – you said you would support me."

"I did. But if I do go back, it is not because I do not care about you, be assured of that."

"I know." She nods. "And do not tell me when you are going, as I may be tempted to follow you." She gives me a playful smile. "How about this? And I say this with an honest heart. Will you swear not to leave me alone until the annulment has been concluded?"

"I will think on it." If I stay for a while longer, it will give me an extra reason to focus on the political proceedings and to be a friend to her when she has few true supporters. However, if I did go back, I doubt she'd follow me. She's so in love with the idea of Henry being in love with her, it's inconceivable that she'd want to be out of his orbit for too long a period. Therefore, for now, I know she'll stay put. At least, I hope so. I haven't forgotten my dream – my nightmare – of chasing her through London.

9TH DECEMBER 1528 – BRIDEWELL PALACE, LONDON

Anne and I have once more returned to court, where the king has lodged us in sumptuous chambers, arranged so they are close to his own. Greater reverence is now paid to Anne than has been given to Queen Katharine in a long time. Bridewell Palace is set on the west bank of the River Fleet, south of Fleet Street, with a connecting covered gallery that links the palace to Blackfriars. This is one of the king's principal London residences, since Westminster Palace had been devastated by fire during his early reign. The palace has two brickwork courtyards, with the inner court containing the royal lodgings.

We are in the gardens, linking arms, standing by a fountain. Jayne Fool is following on behind, with one of the court lapdogs on a lead. She dawdles as the dog sniffs around the flowerbeds. I check every now and again to see if she's managing the dog by herself.

"Beth, I want to tell you most earnestly just how grateful I am to have you here. You brought me through the sweat, helping me recover. I need your support more than ever, with the hearings soon to come. I know my father is grateful, as is George. Please do not leave me, at least not yet?"

"I know how much my friendship means to you, truly I do, otherwise would I still be here with you?"

"You are like a sister to me," she says. She really knows how to guilt-trip me. "And I know I should have been more understanding of your feelings for my brother, especially when I too am pursued by a married man."

Her dark eyes soften as she looks towards Henry's privy chambers. I'm grateful that she recognises the agony of my situation with George. As I follow her gaze, I see Sir Thomas and George looking down on us from a window. They seem deep in conversation, until he smiles at us and waves. He says something to his father but I can't make it out. Then he bows and walks away, out of sight.

Anne waves back at Sir Thomas, who nods at us. I'm comforted by their relationship. I hope he will be a great support to her when she becomes queen. The Boleyns know how to keep me grounded in Tudor times. I'm sure they are quite capable of manoeuvring through the details of Henry's matter but it seems both Sir Thomas and his two younger children want me in their close circle, so here I am to remain, for the time being.

Someone calls from behind us.

"Ladies!" George cries. "Wait for me, before you walk away – I am a maker of fortunes." He laughs. "You need me in your company!" He smiles at Jayne Fool as he passes her, and she blushes.

Anne turns about. "Oh, brother – will you relent, and be less arrogant?"

He catches up with us. "Arrogant, me? Never!" He chuckles, then kisses his sister's cheek. "Father has told me we are to do a good work for you this day, helping the king on his matter."

"I thank you, for your due diligence." She smiles, and we carry on walking around the courtyard.

"How do you fare, Beth?" His teeth gleam when he smiles. Then he puts his arm about my waist, not caring that his father may be watching from the window.

"I'm very well." I smile back. "It is good to be at Court with us three together again."

"It is that, Beth. It is that!" He leans in to kiss me, but Anne stops him.

"Brother, you should be more careful. You know the Court has spies everywhere!" She glares at him, and he takes the hint, dropping his arm to his side.

Jayne catches up with us, having let the lapdog off the lead. It toddles off and she steps after it.

"Come on, doggy!" She picks up a stray stick and throws it. "Go fetch the stick!" she cries. We all watch as the dog picks up the stick, and rather than bringing it back to Jayne, he runs off with it. "Hey, you! Doggy, come back!" she calls. As she runs after it, Anne and I fall into a fit of giggles.

"I shall be a gentleman," George says, "and go and help the girl." He chuckles, then runs after Jayne and the dog.

Our focus switches within a second or two when, from this principle courtyard, we are delighted to see Henry wave to us from the window of his presence-chamber, when he should be paying attention to matters being thrown at him by eminent courtiers. He gives us a wry smile as we walk arm in arm towards the privy gardens, wrapped in our furs and giggling like schoolgirls.

CHRISTMASTIDE, 1528 – GREENWICH PALACE

On 8th December, Cardinal Campeggio arrived in London, sent by the pope to stall the Blackfriars proceedings. Wolsey and the king are hoping Queen Katharine will gladly retire to a convent of her choosing, an offer she continually refuses. She is a woman standing on her status – her right as a queen – and she would rattle the casements from London to Livorno to get her way. Her belief is that Pope Julius II's original dispensation is true and correct, and nothing will dissuade her otherwise. She is obstinate, stubborn, and proud.

The whole court has retired to Greenwich, where open court is kept by both the king and the queen, as it always has been. A cocktail of smells hangs in the air, of raisins, almonds, nutmeg, mace, cloves, liquorice, figs, and ginger. The storerooms are full of expensive ingredients ready for the feast. Anne is there, too, holding court in her own apartments, away from the queen and her household. Henry and Katharine are leading separate lives, even though they are living under the same roof. I watch at dinner, as they remain courteous in public, however uncomfortable the situation feels. Katharine watches him like a hawk, which is obvious to all in attendance and makes them painfully aware of the ménage á trois in their midst.

On Christmas Eve, I stand in Anne's privy chamber as a large log decorated with ribbons is carried in and placed in the hearth, ready to burn for the twelve days of Christmas. Her company of friends gather to watch it being lit. George, Jane, Norris, Mistress Cobham, Brandon, Sir Thomas, and even the king stand around watching, with Jayne Fool squealing with delight as the flames begin to lick the back of the chimney breast.

Before dawn on Christmas Day, we all attend Mass, with each member of the congregation holding a lit taper. More masses are held later in the day. As we stand in rows, we begin singing 'A Virgin Most Pure'. Anne stands in a pew opposite the king, alongside her father. I'm stood with myself and Jayne between him and George. Every so often, Henry's eyes twinkle in the candlelight, and he slips a surreptitious wink at Anne, who tries to hide her smiles behind her song sheet. Sir Thomas scowls at her, while George nudges my elbow, trying not to chuckle.

He leans in and whispers. "Yes, she's vergin' on the ridiculous!" His shoulders shake as he fails to stifle a chuckle. Does he think it's crazy that his sister is a virgin, or is he questioning my chastity? Knowing George, probably both.

The men sing exuberantly at the chorus, and I look up at him and smile as his voice rises above everyone, except the king, who is loudest of all. George's joy is catching. He holds me in his gaze, then winks, the corner of his mouth curling in a subtle smile. Jane, stood next to him, nudges him just below his ribcage, evoking a grunt from the man between us.

"Take a day to rest, woman. We are all entitled to lighten our load and have some cheer, even you. It is Christmas!"

She glares at him but carries on singing. I turn away, so as not to encourage him. Jayne Fool bellows at the top of her voice, not singing in time to the music, which makes me giggle. Bless her heart.

Later, I sit with Anne, George, Jane, Nan Cobham, Jayne Fool, and others as we are served plum pudding in Anne's chambers, to line our stomachs in preparation for the main meal of the day. I dip my spoon into the thick broth of mutton, spices, dried fruits, breadcrumbs, and wine. George sits opposite me, with Jane next to him, and I notice him eying my bosom. I wish he wouldn't. Jane notices his behaviour, too. He's so blatant. Hmm, maybe I should match him, measure for measure. I lift my foot to find the inside of his calf, and stroke his stocking with the silk of my slipper. Then I take another mouthful of pudding and, as I do, I ease the spoon from my lips, giving it one long lick. His eyes are out on stalks, and he doesn't know where to look. Maybe I've gone too far. I shrug my eyebrows and turn away. Jane jumps up and thumps her wine goblet on the table, the liquid splashing up the front of her dress.

"That's where being spikey gets you!" George says, laughing.

She doesn't see the funny side, pushes her chair back, and storms off, no doubt to change her gown. George gets up, and I think he's going to follow her, but he goes to the fireplace and snaps some holly off the mantle decoration, then walks over to me. With a wink, he offers me his hand, which I accept, then he leads me to the corner of the room, where he pins the holly to an oak beam in the ceiling.

"What are you about, George?" Anne asks.

"I am afraid I could not find any mistletoe, so this will have to do!" His smile lights up his face. "Anything for the ladies!"

"George would do anything for attention," Norris says, leaning against the edge of the fireplace.

"You give the wrong impression of me, Norris – you are but jealous!" George looks back at me. "'Tis only one lady's attention I wish to have."

"Yes, and she's just gone to change her dress!" Norris snaps, trying to come across as quick-witted, only to fail. Anne ignores the goings-on and leans across the table to talk to Nan Cobham. George gazes deep into my eyes, then grips my waist and draws me to him. My heart is doing somersaults and my legs are trembling. Our lips meet, the touch soft and gentle, until he presses down and gives me a strong, hot kiss. As his tongue touches mine, I taste the fruity, intoxicating punch of mulled wine.

"Boleyn has Mistress Wickers where he wants her!" Norris cries.

My eyes are closed, and I'm on my toes, hooked to George's gorgeous mouth, lost as our tongues explore each other. Someone coughs, and I become aware that the room has fallen silent. We part and I open my eyes. The musicians have stopped playing their lutes, and all focus is on us. Ok, maybe such a public kiss was a mistake.

Someone enters the chamber, and I turn to see Zouche, one of the equerries, his tray rattling as he carries a couple flagons of fresh mulled wine. George still has his arm around my waist.

"A lifetime is not long enough to love you," he whispers.

I blink at him in disbelief, trying to comprehend what he's just said.

"Mind your backs!" Zouche shouts, breaking through us, and the moment. George's face is flushed, as I'm sure mine is. His expression is victorious, and his eyes sparkle.

"Just the man!" Anne cries, jumping up from her seat. "I think it is someone else's turn under that holly! Master Zouche, here is Mistress Cobham – I think she deserves a Christmas kiss.

We look on as Zouche leads Nan by the hand beneath the holly, and everyone claps when he kisses her. The chamber door swings wide open, and in strides the king, who looks about the room with a broad smile.

"What goes on here?" He chuckles, his blue eyes twinkling in delight. Nan and Zouche break their embrace. Henry looks up at the holly and pulls it down.

"I have brought a gift for Mistress Anne." He smiles. "Something better than holly." He looks directly at her. "I have mistletoe, mademoiselle!"

"How wonderful!" Anne replies.

"I have also, another gift."

"Really?" Anne asks. All those gathered in Anne's chamber stop talking or eating to see what else the king is giving to Anne.

"Lady Anne, may I present, all the way from the French Court – Mademoiselle Delphine Dubois!" Out from behind the king steps a woman in her late twenties, with long blonde hair. She has large brown eyes, soft features, and an hour glass figure. Delphine is dressed from head to toe in the French fashion, and she is carrying a leather portfolio. When she sees Anne her mouth curls up in a huge smile. They obviously know each other.

"Mademoiselle Anne!" Delphine exclaims, forgetting all protocol. Anne runs to her, and they embrace. Talking in French, until the king interrupts them.

"Yes, ladies, I thought you would welcome seeing each other, but I have brought Mademoiselle Dubois to you, because we have been practising a song I have written especially for Christmastide." There are audible gasps around the chamber, as Henry and Delphine stand next to one another.

"Your Majesty, what is the song called?" I ask.

Some gentlemen and women sit about the room.

"Mistress Wickers, it is one you have never heard before. 'Tis titled 'Green Groweth the Holly'." Henry smiles, as myself, George and others stand and watch, as Delphine and the king begin their duet.

♪ *Green groweth the holly,*
So doth the ivy.
Though winter blasts blow never so high,
Green groweth the holly.

As the holly groweth green
And never changeth hue,
So I am, ever hath been,
Unto my lady true.

As the holly groweth green
With ivy all alone
When flowers cannot be seen
And greenwood leaves be gone,

Now unto my lady
Promise to her I make,
From all other only
To her I me betake.

Adieu, mine own lady,
Adieu, my special
Who hath my heart truly
Be sure, and ever shall. ♪

When the king and Delphine finish singing together, the king has a huge smile on his face. Delphine curtsies. Those watching burst into a round of applause.

"You liked it?" Henry asks. Anne rushes to him, planting a kiss on his cheek.

"We loved it, sir. Your song was beautiful."

"Then I am happy." The king replies. "Lady Anne, I take my leave of you and your guests, I have matters of state to attend to. Delphine can stay with you!"

"Majesty!" Anne and the rest of those present either drop into a curtsy, or bow, and the king leaves.

Anne takes Delphine's free hand, and drags her to a window seat, and they sit down together, conversing very fast in French. "Madame Anne, we much speak English while I am a guest in your country!" Delphine smiles.

"I cannot believe you are here." Anne says and she beckons to me to come closer. "Delphine, this is my good friend Mistress Wickers." I curtsy, not knowing quite what to do.

"Bonjour, Mistress Wickers."

"The king remembered me when he has been en France. He thought you would appreciate my company over the Christmas period."

"The king is very thoughtful." Anne replies.

"I have heard about the king's matter and your predicament and have brought you a gift of my own." She begins to undo the tie on the leather portfolio on her lap, and takes out a piece of sheet music. "I thought the words in this are a message to you, and the king." Delphine begins to sing a solo, in French, and George comes over to listen.

🎶 *Jouissance vous donnerai*
Mon ami et vous mènerai
La où prétend votre espérance.
Vivante ne vous laisserai;
Encore quand morte serai,
L'esprit en aura souvenance.

Si pour moi avez du souci
Pour vous n'en ai pas moins aussi,
Amour le vous doit faire entendre.
Mais s'il vous grève d'être ainsi,
Apaisez votre cœur transi;
Tout vient à point, qui peut attendre. 🎶

I recognise the melody, but not the words, as my French isn't that good. I think

this song is written by French composer, Sermisy, and is one of the melodies from Anne's songbook. This songbook is now an artefact, which in my time, is currently kept at the Royal College of Music in London.

Anne sits and listens, knowing exactly the meaning of the words. When Delphine finishes her performance, George turns to Delphine and says, "If your lips taste as sweet as your voice sounds, your husband is a lucky a man!" Delphine blushes.

"George!" Anne snipes.

"Can I not give a lady a compliment?"

"Yes, but..." Anne looks at me.

"It matters not." I lie, but not very well. "I am going to get myself something to drink." I walk over to the sideboard and pour myself another glass of mulled wine. I hold the glass to my nose, and take in the aroma of heady spices. The smell transports me back to my time, when standing in my Grandmother's kitchen when she had been preparing and baking her home made mince pies for a Christmas Eve treat. I take a sip. It tastes like a concoction of dried spiced fruits. As I swallow the wine, I can feel it coating and warming my throat. I'm glad there's no mead here, as when I drink that it tastes stronger than paint stripper!

Suddenly, I can feel the flickering feeling of a couple of fingers stroking the back of my neck. I'd recognise that touch anywhere. Its George.

"Beth, open your eyes, if the mulled wine has such a reaction, I know something that has twice the body, and is contained in a far better vessel than that – and you would want to keep your eyes open when drinking it!" He whispers.

I take a sharp intake of breath. "George why does everything revolve around physical intimacy, with you?" I shake my head. I can't stay mad at him for long.

"You drive me wild with desire, as everything about screams woman!"

"George, that's the drink talking, tell me on the morrow when we are alone, and sober!" George looks like a little boy scolded. He touches my cheek with the back of his index finger.

"Forgive me?" He asks. "And I was only being kind, giving Mistress Dubois a compliment, I did not mean to hurt you."

I sigh. "George, if you do not mean it, then do not do it – otherwise I shall think that your

intensions towards me are meaningless."

He pulls me to him, embracing me, gripping my waist, and drawing me to him. Another public kiss! I don't think my heart can take anymore somersaults and my legs begin to tremble. This time, George is fiercely insistent as our lips meet this time, and his is not as soft and gentle when presses down and gives me a strong, hot kiss. As his tongue touches mine, he can taste the fruity, intoxicating punch of spices on my lips. My eyes are now closed, and I'm wrapped in his arms, hooked to George's gorgeous mouth, lost as our tongues explore each other. I forget we aren't alone, until I hear a few people cough, really loudly.

"Beth!" I hear Anne call, and I break away from George's embrace. My cheeks feel flushed, but George doesn't look ashamed at all. He might, if his wife had caught us. Now most of Anne's close circle knows that there is something going on with George and me. "Would you like me to translate that song into English for you?"

I walk over to Delphine and Anne, and they begin to sing the same song, this time in English. George stands beside me with his arm about my waist. Everyone must assume I'm his mistress.

♪ *Love's climax will I give to you*
My friend and I will lead you to
The target of your deep desire.
Alive I will not you eschew,
E'en when my time on Earth is through,
Love's spirit will remain afire.

If you should have a care for me
For you I'll care the same degree,
On this Love will you educate.
But if you chafe that it should be,
With me you need not now agree:
For good things come to those who wait. ♪

Everyone gathered claps, as Delphine and Anne finish the song. George looks down at me and whispers. "Our time will come."

"Delphine your singing is beautiful," I say, "but I am afraid I cannot sing at all."

"Your lute playing is not so bad," Anne laughs.

"I need more lessons, Anne."

"Perhaps, Mistress Wickers, Lady Anne and myself can teach you not only to play the lute, but to sing too?" Delphine suggests.

"Yes, that would be wonderful."

"Beth, I do not need to teach you any lessons, as we already make wonderful music together!" George chuckles.

Anne glares at George. "Yes, brother, we all noticed!"

Anne now accompanies Henry everywhere. To my relief, I no longer have to wait on the queen, either, though she sometimes eyes me with suspicion when I'm in the same room as her, which makes me uncomfortable, and I'm thankful it isn't that often. It's at the stage now where Anne rules her own household, and Jayne Fool is in permanent lodging with us, travelling in our entourage whenever we are on the move. Anne is kind, and never forgets to include her in all that goes on. She commissioned John Skutt and his apprentice to make particular garments for Jayne, who now has an assortment of colourful gowns, kirtles, and silk coifs to show her social status as a member of Anne's household, so nobody thinks she's a servant.

Interior designers have made our private living areas as exquisite as possible. Anne now has her own sumptuous lodgings at Durham House, a separate suite of rooms at Greenwich, along with lavish rooms at Hampton Court. She is Queen in all but name, and she and Henry are inseparable.

4TH APRIL 1529 – GREENWICH PALACE

Several months have passed and life carries on as normal for most courtiers, except Anne, who has not given up hope of the pope resolving matters of the divorce in favour of Henry. It is with this mindset that she dips the nib of her quill into the inkwell, the bright spring sunlight streaming across the floor, illuminating the intricate designs of the Turkish carpet.

I lean over her shoulder. "Who do you write to, Anne?"

"Master Stephen Gardiner. What think you of it, have I got the tone right?"

I pluck the offered letter from her hand and start reading, noticing the hope she has placed inside.

> "'Master Stephen.
>
> "'I thank you for my letter, wherein I perceive the willing and faithful mind you have to do me pleasure, not doubting but as much as is possible for man's wit to imagine, you will do. I pray God to send you well to speed in all your matters, so that you will put me in a study how to reward your service. I do trust in God, you shall not repent it, and that the end of this journey shall be more pleasant to me than your first, for that was but a rejoicing hope, which ceasing, the lack of it does put to more pain, and they that are partakers with me, as you know. Therefore, do I trust that this hard beginning shall make the better ending.
>
> "'Master Stephen, I send you here the cramp-rings for you, and Master Gregory, and Master Peter; pray you to distribute them both, as she, (that you may assure them) will be glad to do them any pleasure which shall be in my power. And thus, I make an end, praying God send you good health.
>
> "'Written at Greenwich the 4th day of April,
>
> "'By your assured friend,
>
> "'Anne Boleyn'"

"What think you?"

"You believe he will still be able to influence the Pope, with a second meeting?"

"This is a mission to Italy. The Pope must resolve such matters. Henry and I have waited for so long. The Pope cannot ignore us, for if I lose hope and faith, then all is lost."

If that's the case, a resolution may be closer than I thought. My tummy fizzes with excitement at the thought that it might be time to suggest a quick visit home.

Twenty

I stand with Anne in the servants' chamber, checking through my trunk that all my essential personal belongings are there. This time I'm leaving nothing behind. I stuff any remaining toiletries into my linen bag.

"Can you not leave the toothpaste for me?" she whispers. I don't know why she's whispering, as the room is empty.

"No – what if someone else opens the trunk by mistake, or sees you holding the tube? It is such a foreign object; you'd never be able to explain it away."

She shrugs. "I understand." She passes me my mascara, perfume, and the remaining items tucked at the bottom of my trunk, then closes the lid. I give her the key.

"Lock it and keep my things safe, for when I return. I will need all my gowns and shifts."

"You have my word," she says as she tucks the key inside a purse that hangs from her girdle belt.

"Now, what will I tell George?"

"We can use that letter you composed, from your 'family'. George will…" The door swings open, and he walks into the room.

"I heard my name mentioned. 'George will…'?" He looks from Anne to me, and back again. "I have been searching for you both everywhere! Why have you been hiding?"

"It's nothing, brother. We are not hiding."

"I thought we could go for a ride?" He arches his brows and smiles.

"In April, with this changing weather?" Anne looks out of the window at the gathering dark clouds.

"Perhaps not." He shrugs. "A game of cards, or chess?" He looks at the bag hanging from my shoulder and frowns. "Where are you off to?"

"Home," I reply.

"Home? Do you have to go?" His eyes betray his need of me.

"George, Beth has to tend to her sick and dying cousin. Her family sent word this morning." She hands him a scrap of vellum from her purse, a note I composed myself, written in my scratchy cursive hand. He glances over the scant-detailed request and hands it back to her.

"Besides, Beth has not seen her family for such a long while, it would be remiss of us not to allow her some time with them."

"I suppose not." He sighs. "We have been rather selfish in that regard, keeping her with us. I hope your cousin fares well under your care."

"As you have read in that letter, besides going home to care for my cousin, father has requested I give him some of the allowance that Sir Thomas has awarded me. I think it only right that I support them." I hate lying to him, pretending I have this sixteenth-century family, but what else can I do? I need to preserve my true identity from him. He'd never understand who I really am.

"If you must go," he says, his shoulders slumped. "Is there nothing I can do to change your mind?"

"No. I'm sorry."

"Stop plaguing the poor girl, George! She already feels bad enough about leaving."

"Forgive me?" he asks, putting one hand behind his back as he leans in to kiss my cheek.

I should be used to his attentions by now, but my insides quiver and heat rises through me as his breath brushes my skin. He bows to us both, then turns and walks out of the chamber. I hate lying to him. However, I'm glad Anne has understood my need to see my friends and family and is allowing me to return home.

I'm on the floor of Professor Marshall's office. My head hurts, as does my backside, but at least I haven't broken a bone. The professor jumps up from his desk in surprise, sending a pile of assignments and his full ashtray across the floor. It's a shame there's no way of warning anyone I'm on my way in.

"Ah, not to worry," he says, "the cleaners can deal with that." He looks down at me, his brows creased. "You know this is the same day, right? You appeared earlier, panicking about Agnes."

"Really? So not much time has passed at all?"

"No – a couple of hours, if that." He gathers up the essays and binders strewn across his office rug.

"Wow! No change in date then?"

"Definitely not. Did you managed to save poor Agnes, or did she pop her clogs?" He lays the paperwork in an untidy pile on his desk.

"I'm afraid there was nothing I could do."

"Ah, right." He offers me his hand and helps me up. "I hate to say it but perhaps it was for the best. The girl still being alive could have really messed with the history." He buttons up his coat, casting a look over the scattered butts and ash on the floor.

"You don't have to sound so pleased about it!"

"I'm not – I just think that fate has intervened and helped the situation run its course...naturally." He shoves the pile of essays into his bag. Why doesn't he mark them online? It would make his work so much easier.

"Have you come back for good this time?" he asks, sparking his lighter to the tip of a cigarette.

"No, sir. I just needed a 'modern fix', to see my family, enjoy a steaming hot shower, listen to twenty-first-century music, maybe even watch a decent film, and catch up with you, Rob, Jessica. That kind of thing."

"Okay, well, Rob left your car and house keys with me." He nods at his desk. "They're in the top drawer."

"Thanks, sir."

"He said he parked your car in the usual spot." He blows smoke up to the ceiling. "You know what? You must be mentally and emotionally exhausted. Why don't you finish the term now? You've handed your work in already. Go home – have a break – enjoy Christmas. If you want to go back to Anne, she can wait."

It's not a bad idea. The thing is, will George wait? He's going to miss me but Jane Boleyn won't. Professor Marshall hands me a reading list for next term.

"Have a look at this – I'm sure you've got most of them. If you fancy doing some work, reading is never wasted."

I smile at him, take the list, and shrug. "Professor, before you go, could you answer a question?"

"Yes, what is it?"

"How do you deal with the time-slip? Mentally, I mean?" I'm aware my eyes have become slits. "I don't appear to have aged but I have 'lived' in the early-modern era, and you can't say that won't affect a person. I have to be affected by it.

"I can't explain the ageing process, and how that does or doesn't work. If I could, I'd make a fortune as a cosmetic expert. Look, I haven't got time to share my experiences with you now but I will. I promise."

Before he picks up his bag, and keys, he looks at me, his head tilted. "You are okay, aren't you?"

"Yes, sir. Thanks."

"Use the spare key to lock the door after you." He nods, then walks out of the office.

I change out of my Tudor garb and leave it all folded neatly in a bag behind the professor's chair. I've swopped Tudorville for my modern life, for the time being, and it feels weird slipping back into skinny jeans, a T-shirt, and my coat. I find my watch, bracelet, earrings, and scrunchy in the professor's top drawer, tie my hair up in a top knot, then put my jewellery on, which feels weird. I shake my head, looking down at my legs. It's been a long time since I've worn such tight clothing. So odd.

———————— • ❄ • ————————

The feeling of lying between clean, fresh-smelling sheets, and under a feather-filled duvet, is wonderful. Rutterkin meows when I disturb him as I pull the duvet over my face. I press the fabric to my skin, exhilarated by the floral burst of jasmine. Then I throw back the duvet and hop out of my comfy bed.

What time is it? I grab the TV remote from my bedside table and switch on a terrestrial channel. Ah! Breakfast telly, with the familiar presenters smiling back at me, bringing the latest news of the day.

It's 7:30 a.m., and I'm going to do what Professor Marshall suggested and chill for a while. I spend ages in the shower, exfoliating, softening, and plucking, trying to make myself feel like the modern girl I am, and not a Tudor woman with hairy underarms and legs. Anne had shown me how to shave my legs and armpits with a Tudor version of a cut-throat razor, but the job was always laborious, so I gave up in the end. I study myself in the mirror. My eyebrows haven't been threaded in an age. I'm going to need to do something about that. While getting ready, I hear the front door slam. Mum must be needed for something important, leaving this early in the morning. Ten minutes later, Dad is calling 'goodbye' to me up the stairs. I lean over the banister in my dressing gown.

"Bye, Dad – see you later! Love you."

"See you!" he calls in a cheery voice. "Have a good day, Beth."

Within an hour of both my parents leaving for work, I'm dressed, my hair is dry, and I feel ready for the day.

As I wait downstairs for the kettle to boil, I check the clock, happy enough that it's just gone nine. Rutterkin purrs around my feet, wanting to be fed, so I give him kibble and fresh water. Then the doorbell rings, and I rush out to see who it is. My friend Jessica is on the doorstep, wrapped in a thick, woollen coat, scarf, and hat. She's on the same course as me.

"Hi!" she says, her teeth gleaming as she smiles. "I saw your car and wondered whether you fancied going into town, or down the High Street?"

"Are you not going to Saint Mary's this morning?" I ask, waving her into the hall.

"No, I thought I'd give it a miss." She follows me into the kitchen. "I think the last few days of term are usually for people behind with their work, who maybe haven't handed assignments in."

I shrug, glad I don't have such things to worry about. "Fancy a cuppa?"

"Yes, if you are." She sits at the table.

I get another mug from the cupboard. "One sugar, as always?"

"Yes, please."

I pour milk into both our cups and stir the sugar into hers.

"So, what are your plans today?" she asks, pulling off her hat and ruffling her hands through her hair.

"I've got a list of stuff to do. Look at the state of my brows." I lean forward for her to inspect them.

"Blimey, they're not exactly 'on fleek'. Not like you to neglect yourself. Too much coursework?" She giggles.

I pick up my mug and sip the steaming brew. Tea never tasted so good. "I know, right?" I roll my eyes on thinking about how little time has passed since my first time-slip, yet so much time has slipped by in Tudorville. It's no wonder my beauty routine has gone out the window.

"What else did you have planned?" She cups her mug in both hands.

"I could do with a haircut but the chances of getting an appointment with a hairdresser this close to Christmas is slim to none. Ah, it can wait."

She screws her nose up at me as I sip my tea, staring at me in a way I'm not too comfortable with.

"Your hair's growing really fast. What are you using on it – some secret serum?"

Yikes! She hasn't seen me for a couple of days in 'real-time', yet I haven't set eyes on the girl for two years or so. God, it's so strange, I can't get my head around this time-travelling lark!

"It's just my bed-head, Jess, you know how it is?"

"Hey, I'm not that bad, am I?"

"Only joking. What have you planned for today?"

"Do you mind if I go to the bookshop in the High Street?" She arches her brows. "I've got to pick up some books I ordered that the professor advised us to get from his reading list." She glugs down the rest of her tea.

"Yeah, I don't see why not." I close my eyes, savouring the flavour of my favourite brand of tea, the strong, English Breakfast kind they sell to visitors at Hampton Court.

"Come on then!" she says, passing me her empty mug.

I swig down what remains of my brew and open the dishwasher. Hold on, the two mugs Rob placed in there yesterday afternoon haven't been washed. Weird. And Mum and Dad must have had fish and chips from the wrapper last night, as there's no sign of a dirty dish anywhere. I pout to myself about that. How I'd love a good, battered sausage and chips. What a shame I missed it arriving home so late.

297

I grab my handbag from the kitchen worktop and find a decent coat to wear from the hooks in the hallway. It's cold out, and there's a bitter wind blowing, with a few snowflakes drifting on it. Yep, it's becoming quite Christmassy.

Jessica jumps in the passenger seat of my car as I hop in behind the wheel. She plugs her phone into the adapter and finds something cheerful and loud to listen to. She's not an eighties' fan like me or Mum, so she puts on the latest song from the charts and starts singing along – out of tune, I might add.

"Where is your mum?" she asks over the din.

"Fashion College," I answer. "Still lecturing. It's the last week of term there, too, I think."

"And your dad?"

"He finishes work for the Christmas break this week, too, so we shall all be home." Sometimes, I don't feel as if I have parents. They leave for work before I get up, most days. I barely see either of them. I might get the odd text from Dad during the day but never from Mum. She's more of a workaholic than my dad.

"I love Christmas, don't you?" she asks.

"Yeah, it's a magical time!" I switch the wipers on to disperse the snow, which is becoming heavier. I think of Anne, and Christmastide with the Boleyns, and Court. Then George comes to mind and my heart flutters at the memory of him kissing me under that holly. What did he say? 'A lifetime wouldn't be enough time to love you.' Wow! If my heart could melt, like the snowflakes as they hit the wet tarmac, it would. I don't half miss him.

"You're deep in thought. What's on your mind?"

"Nothing." I shrug, hardly able to tell her George Boleyn is on my mind – she'd never get it. Why did the professor choose me, say, over Jessica, or any other student to experience this extraordinary life I'm now living? What makes me so special in his eyes? No matter, I'm lucky to have the opportunity. He has brought me to the love of my life, though I never thought my man would be over five-hundred years old, and now headless! Oh, Beth, stop! What am I like? I can't focus on the here and now, even when I'm here, because I'm always thinking about George.

"Are you thinking about the Christmas presents you need to buy? Because I know I am." She bobs her head to the tune – the noise. "Every year, it's the same. I never know what to buy my family. I end up getting them the same thing almost every year."

"At least we historians are easy." I giggle. "Book tokens. Amazon vouchers. Annual membership passes to Historic Royal Palaces."

"You aren't wrong there!" She taps her hand on her knee. "Are you buying anything for Rob?"

I snap a look at her. "Rob? Why would I buy anything for Rob? We're just friends."

"Oh. Funny that, because I saw him driving your car into the university car park yesterday. Is there something you're not telling me?"

"No!" I reply, screeching to a halt into a parking bay on the High Street. "He picked it up from the garage for me. It went in for a service." Gawd, I'm a terrible liar. Can she sense that? Hmm, she's looking at me like she doesn't believe me. Crikey, I need to keep my mouth shut. I'm always getting myself into a shitload of trouble with my big mouth, here, and five hundred years ago.

We grab our handbags and I lock the car, and we walk towards the beauty salon. When we get there, I'm chuffed to see that they do walk-in appointments. Jessica grabs a seat in the reception as I have my brows tended to. I'm so glad to be getting de-fuzzed. After twenty minutes, I come out of the treatment room and pay my bill. Jessica looks at me.

"Have you seen yourself in the mirror? It's like you've been smacked in the eye by the therapist. She's done a good job there. You looked like you needed a going over with the lawnmower!"

"Give over! I've only had my brows shaped and plucked. The redness will go down."

She nods, then smiles. "Where to next?"

"Sutton High Street, for the bookshop?"

"Sounds like a good plan!"

Jess blasts her music out as I drive to our next stop. It's not far, and I soon find a bay in the multi-storey car park. As we walk down Throwley road and turn onto Sutton High Street, I find all the concrete and glass so stark. It's all pedestrianised and modern, which is fine, but what I really notice is the lack of nature – of greenery. Being with Anne and George in their time, the natural world is everywhere. What would they be doing if I was with them now?

The wind bites, pulling me back to my present. We wrap our coats about us as the snow keeps coming. And it's settling. Flakes melt on my face as we pass all the same old shops you see in every other high street in the country: charity shops, banks, and supermarkets. Christmas carollers try their best, standing in the cold, to bring some festive cheer to shoppers. Perhaps I should bring Dad up here, when the daylight begins to go, so he can see the Christmas lights. He always used to bring me here when I was a child. Besides, I need to take him to the jeweller, so he can choose a decent Christmas present for Mum. As we turn onto St. Nicholas Road, the bookshop comes into view.

"Are you coming in?" Jessica asks.

I hold my scarf up to my face. "Yes, anything to get out of the cold."

The heater blasts warm air as we enter, and it's lovely. So many distractions in here but I'm not going to be tempted to look at any new titles, not even in the History section.

I follow Jessica up the stairs to the second floor so she can pick up her order – the books from that reading list. As usual, when we reach the top, I'm hit with the delicious smells wafting from the café – the scent of ground espresso: hot, fruity, woody, and nutty all rolled into one, inviting me to stay awhile, to enjoy the atmosphere. There's a little nook to sit with friends or indulge in flicking through the first chapter of a newly purchased novel.

"While you collect your books, I'll just have a quick look around." I don't want to buy anything. I can't – I already own so many books, and I haven't any room for more.

I meander up and down the aisles and, as I reach the end of the last one, where the history books are, someone laughs, and I stop cold. Hold on, I know that laugh. I've been away for a while, in Early-Modern England, but…

The laugh comes again. Okay, what's going on here? I peek around the end of the last bookstand, towards the nook and, to my astonishment, see Rob Dryden sat with…Georgina?

It is her, and he's got his arm around her, and they are nuzzling each other. No, they're kissing!

What the actual…? My face has gone cold, and goosebumps have erupted across the back of my neck and shoulders. How cosy! And how close they seem to be, on a leather sofa, their frothy cappuccinos in front of them, no doubt going cold with them being so busy, with each other!

Hmm, interesting. I know we're friends, and not dating, but I liked the idea that we were beginning to come round to admitting we liked each other in that way, even if we hadn't done anything about it. To see him here, with this other girl, hurts me, even angers me. But then why should I be jealous? This isn't me. Not really. And I do have George. Don't I?

Jessica calls to me from the service desk, and I try to hide my face behind my scarf but it's too late – I know I've been spotted.

"Let's get out of here," I say.

"Why?" She frowns. "I thought you were having a mooch around?"

"No. We need to go – we really need to go!"

"What's the matter with you all of a sudden?"

"Don't look,"—I nod towards the nook—"but Rob is there, kissing Georgina Whatshername."

Jessica, of course, takes no notice of what I've said and looks over at them. In that moment, I get the impression that she's going to shout *hello*. Please don't.

Too late. We've been seen, for sure. Georgina gets up and walks towards us.

"Hello, you two. What are you doing here?"

"Buying books. It's a bookshop, eh?" I'm mortified, stating the obvious. She rolls her eyes at me. "Rob's helping me with that Wolsey essay."

Witch. "Is that his idea of mentoring you, by snogging your face off?"

Her eyebrows arch as she gives me a smug look. "You're just jealous!"

"Girls, don't argue, especially not over a bloke." Jessica shakes her head. "Georgina, if you don't get the essay finished soon, you'll miss the deadline."

"And you'll fail the module," I snap. I need to put my claws away. She ignores what we say, shrugs her hair back, and walks into the toilet.

"Hi, girls."

Oh, God. Chatting to Georgina, I hadn't noticed Rob coming over.

"Hello," Jessica says, her usual enthusiastic self.

"How's your revision session going?" I ask, the snark in my voice clear to everyone with ears. "From here, it looked like she got an 'A'."

His face turns red, but I don't care anymore. Or do I?

"Erm, I think it's helping," he replies, not quite knowing what to say.

"What are you doing with her, anyway?" I ask. Jessica looks at me like she doesn't understand what's got into me.

"What do you think?" he snaps.

Jessica doesn't know where to look, so she wanders off down one of the aisles, pretending to look at the titles, though staying close enough to hear the conversation.

"What are you having a go at me for?" he asks. "I helped you with your car yesterday, and what thanks do I get? You can't blame me." He glances around and leans closer. "You're like the bloody scarlet pimpernel – one day I see you, and the next I don't!" He looks down at his shoes, shaking his head. "Probably shagging George Boleyn!"

I clench my hands by my sides until my knuckles burn. "If I was a bloke, I swear, I'd punch you!"

"You wouldn't dare!" He chuckles, brushing his hand through his hair – a nervous tic I quite like about him. Liked! Past tense!

"Don't expect a Christmas present from me, because you won't be getting one!" I storm off before he can get another word in. So much for keeping my cool. Out of the corner of my eye, I see Georgina return from the toilet and sit back on the sofa. She turns her nose up as she sips her cold cappuccino. Serves her right for wasting all that time kissing!

Jessica apologises to Rob as I walk away from them.

"You didn't even say goodbye," she says when she catches up. "What's the matter with you? And what's going on between you two? And why on earth would he mention George Boleyn?"

So, she was listening.

"Hey, I like studying the Boleyns, what's the big problem? It takes time, and he just can't deal with it."

Seeing Rob with Georgina, stuck together like limpets, I realise something that I hadn't over the last while, what with my Tudor distraction: I like him more than I thought. But there's nothing I can do about it. If he likes her, I should let him go. It's not as if I have any kind of claim on him. He hasn't professed his undying love to me, unlike George. We've made no promises to each other, so I've lost nothing. Yes, I value his friendship but that's all it is. All this scenario has done is reinforce my desire to find some solace in George's arms.

I'm sitting on the sofa in the lounge with Dad, having a cuppa, studying him. He looks tired and I'm glad he's on holiday from work for the Christmas break. He's got his nose in The Times, as usual.

"Are you doing any research over the holiday," he asks, not looking up, "or are you giving things a break?"

"I'm researching Anne Boleyn, and Henry VIII's 'Great Matter'. In particular, I'm looking at events leading up to the annulment." The holidays will allow me to read up on events so I can refresh my knowledge of what's to come. Dad glances up at me and realises that I'm looking at him.

"Darling, are you okay? You seem at little…distant?"

"I'm grand. I just feel like I haven't seen you in 'ages'."

He chuckles. "You only saw me the day before yesterday. But we are like ships passing in the night."

"We need to change that," I say, putting my arm around him. He cuddles me back. "I'm so glad it's Christmas." I'm going to spend as much time with Mum, Dad, Jo-Jo, and my niece as possible.

AUGUST 1529

I've returned from my Christmas escape to my 'real' life, where all went well, apart from Rob and his witch. Professor Marshall advised me on my next steps in Anne's journey and is pleased I didn't give in to her demands to come through the portal with me. The ring is continuing to work without a hitch, though I'm surprised my finger isn't blistered from the heat it generates.

Back in Anne's life now, where four months have passed, and I've missed the summer progress. She and Henry have continued pressing for a resolution to their matter. They are still much in love, which adds certainty to my observation that she isn't operating out of cold ambition. She's still playing the game well, acting cool around the court, not wanting to show her enemies any weakness.

In my absence, she has accompanied Henry on his visits across the counties and seems happy as she tells me all about their adventures.

"How are you and the king?"

"We visited Waltham Abbey in Essex two weeks ago, and the weather did not disappoint us." She arranges roses in a vase as she tells me her news.

"Is the king in good health?" I'm hoping she'll open up a little more on how things are going with them and how he's treating her.

"He is preoccupied with the legatine court, which has now adjourned from Blackfriars. I could not be separated from him at such a delicate stage in matters and we went on to Wolsey's residence in Barnet." She lifts a rose to her nose to smell its sweet fragrance.

"If you are willing, Beth, would you join me in visiting Henry Carey at Buckingham? He feels the loss of his father so acutely, even though a year or more has passed since he departed from the sweat."

"Anne, I would love that!"

She repays my response with a small smile before placing the rose back into the vase.

"What of Mary?" I ask, looking out of the window from the embrasure.

"Mary is with little Henry, and so you shall see her also."

"For that, I am glad, Mistress." I smile. "What of George?"

"My brother fares well. In late July, he was appointed governor of Saint Bethlehem hospital."

Oh, does George becoming a higher officer of the court mean I'll see less of him? "Will your brother visit Mary and his nephew and niece?"

"I expect so," she replies.

This gives me a sliver of hope that I might get the opportunity to be alone with him. It feels like an eternity since we last shared such a moment. We are never far from prying eyes, or company at court.

11TH AUGUST 1529, BARNET MANOR –ESSEX

We have such hopes for the day as Nan Gainsford, Anne, and I take a stroll around the gardens of Barnet manor with lapdogs in tow that belong to some of her ladies-in-waiting, enjoying the late-summer sun and the fragrances given off by the last blooms of the rose gardens. On our return inside, we prepare Anne for Mass, then lunch, before the dancing master arrives to teach us the steps to a new dance.

Nan tidies up the table, ready for Wolsey's servants to bring sweetmeats and fruit for luncheon. I notice her face turn white, as if she's seen a ghost. She looks as if she's about to faint. Anne walks around to where the poor woman is gripping the edge of the table. I push a chair up behind her, taking her elbow and urging her to sit. Anne pulls an open book towards her, pressing the page flat to take a closer look at the drawings inside. She laughs.

"Nan. See here a book of prophecy – here is the king." She points to his image. "This is the queen, and this is me with my head off." She shakes her head and chuckles. "Nan, please do not worry yourself, it is but a bauble, nothing to be concerned with."

She doesn't seem to take the book seriously, which I'm surprised at because these people are mighty superstitious. If it were me, I would be alarmed, even frightened. But, then, I know things, don't I?

"Anne, this worries me," I say, wanting to know who was responsible for leaving such a book there for us to see.

"'Tis obviously some joke!" she replies.

"Please, do not take it as a joke. You know many at Court do not appreciate your elevated position."

She snaps her head up. "If I shall marry the king, nothing will touch me. I am protected. I think on the hope I have that the realm may be happy by my issue. I am resolved to have him whatsoever might become of me."

"Mistress, are you not worried by who may have done this?" I ask, worried about her lack of concern.

Nan is still in an alarmed state. "If I thought it true, though he was an emperor, I would not myself marry him."

Anne flicks her comment away. "That matters not, for it is foretold in ancient prophecies that at this time a queen shall be burnt. Who is to say that it is not Katharine who will be put to flame?"

Her ladies look shocked by her statement, yet her face shows no emotion. I have to admit, I'm puzzled by her manner. The court can be a dangerous place, with many hidden agendas and cabals.

19TH SEPTEMBER 1529 – GRAFTON MANOR, NORTHAMPTONSHIRE.

Anne and I move from chamber to chamber in her apartments, with her lapdogs following us. I forget they are so close on our heels that, when I step back, I almost trip over them. Their soft faces and adorable eyes look to lure us into a game of fetch. One little spaniel is sat in the corner of the bedchamber chewing one of Anne's expensive silk slippers. I try to grab it off the rascal before his teeth tear the fabric. All the dogs have been with us at Hever, learning to be well-behaved house dogs, but some are still babies. They make wonderful companions for us.

Anne laughs. "I can tell anything I choose to them, without fear of judgment, but I am not happy when they ruin my shoes, or take a piss on my carpets."

Arm in arm, dogs following, we walk into the adjacent sitting room. There we come upon Nan Gainsford and George Zouche locked in a passionate embrace. Shocked at being caught, she stumbles away from the young man, apologizing to everyone, blushing like a strawberry.

"Oh, my Lady, I am most sorry!" she blurts out.

She has no reason to act prudish, considering she was the one who chastised me for sitting on George Boleyn's lap. I look from her to Anne, then to Zouche, surprised I hadn't noticed there was something between them before now.

He grins. "Mistress, I do wish I could say that I am sorry but, in fact, I am not. My crime is well worth any consequence."

A long silence follows, until Anne begins to laugh, the beautiful sound filling the room, gathering up the giggles of those around her, and soon, all of us fall about laughing, with the dogs' tails wagging as they yap in tune with us.

"Nan, you'd best attend to the unpacking and allow Zouche to stable the horses. The king will not be so cheery if things are not attended to."

Nan curtsies and leaves the room, whistling as she goes.

"Nan, stop that immediately! A whistling woman or a crowing hen shall call up the devil out of his den!"

She steps back in. "Lady Anne, whatever do you mean?"

"What she means," I say, "is if you keep on whistling, you'll have a shitload of bad luck – the devil will come and scare the life out of you!"

The woman stares at me, her brows furrowed, and I realise I've forgotten to speak 'Tudor'. She turns her back on me but not before tossing Zouche a saucy look. I like her. She is fun to be around and a good friend to Anne, and despite not being able to show George Boleyn how much I care for him in public, it's easy to wish that same good fortune on Anne's friends.

The trunks holding Anne's clothing and other belongings have been placed in the centre of the chamber, and when all is assembled, Nan and I begin sorting hoods and headwear. A sudden cry from Anne in her bedchamber makes my heart skip.

"Anne, what ails you?" I call.

"Beth, please hurry!"

I scurry into the room to see her standing before her large wardrobe.

"Beth, did you move the coffer which holds my private belongings?"

"I did not. Why?"

"If this is where it has been, then it is here no longer."

Her distress is evident. I move her aside and search the wardrobe, going through it again to be sure. The casket is gone, the space in the bottom, where it used to lie, is bare, and the fine settling of dust where it was kept proves that it has been missing for some time. Anne keeps jewels, gloves, and some other small trinkets and ouches in it, along with all her love letters from the king. Only a few of us are aware of its contents, and I'm alarmed that anyone would steal such precious sentimental items from her. The other thing that is so strange is that the key to open the locked casket still lies in the drawer where I placed it days ago when we arrived at Grafton.

Anne looks at me in disbelief as she takes the key from the drawer and waves it around in dismay. A tear slips down her cheek as she realises the enormity of the theft and its implications. A chill runs across my shoulders when I remember that these letters will end up in the Vatican. Damn it, I should have made it my responsibility to protect them.

We are mystified by their loss, and Anne brings both hands to her chest as she starts palpitating, her breath becoming shallow at the prospect of her treasured letters from Henry being lost forever. She has always kept them from prying eyes and, from the expression on her face, I begin to grasp the enormity of what has happened. Distraught, she collapses back in a chair, clinging to her breast for breath. I kneel before her, my hands on my knees, and implore her to inhale deep and slow to calm herself.

"Anne, who else would have access to the key and the casket apart from your mother, Nan, and me?" I search my memory to identify anyone else who may have been aware of the casket's existence, apart from Anne's closest confidantes. She leaps up from the chair, her breathing restored, key still in hand.

"Perhaps it was my aunt, Elizabeth Howard, Duchess of Norfolk!" She begins to pace the room.

"Why would Norfolk's wife know about the casket?" I sit back on my haunches again. Nan stands in the doorway of the anti-room, listening.

"I swear, Madam, it was not me!" she says

"I know, Nan. I know." She holds her hand up in reassurance, then turns to me. "Beth, you remember the maid the duchess recommended to me, the one who was so vigilant with everything?" She places the key on the table.

"Yes, she was very observant. I noticed how she had an uncanny and almost unnerving ability to anticipate your every need."

"And she made herself familiar with my belongings, too, so she could provide me with the best possible service. She proved to be a skilled maid, to be certain, but she is no Agnes. There was something about this child that I could not quite identify – she made me feel uncomfortable, at times." She continues pacing the room, acting like a detective trying to solve a murder case, or a disappearance.

"Lady Anne, you should have said!" Nan cries from across the room.

"Maybe, but I thought I could trust my aunt in her recommendations, although I felt the new maid overly solicitous, almost scheming, and so, after a few weeks, I dismissed her – and I would have removed her from my service sooner had I realised before now that this innocuous event of my missing belongings occurred. You remember my dismissal of her?"

"Yes," Nan answers. "You had returned from an afternoon out, and upon removing a diamond brooch from your bodice, placed it back in the coffer, and while it remained unlocked, you re-read one of Henry's early letters."

"Yes!" Anne says, her forefinger in the air. "I absently settled in a chair and pored over the letter while Agnes busied herself in the chamber, straightening and brushing my clothes before taking them down to be stored in the royal wardrobe."

"Do you think this new maid saw the letter with the royal seal?" I ask, visualising the unfolding scenario.

"Perhaps," my lady, Nan says, "she noticed the open coffer from whence the letter you were reading came, and saw the other letters within?"

"Yes, perhaps that is what happened." Anne sighs. "Then this girl told the Duchess of Norfolk, who has now taken the casket for herself." She shakes her head in disbelief.

"You think the Duchess of Norfolk is capable of that?" Nan asks, her eyes wide.

"The new maid – Martha, her name was – was to return to the Duchess of Norfolk over a week ago, and she has obviously lifted the casket and taken it to my aunt before we travelled."

She looks pale, which is unusual for her. I'm shocked by the possibility that someone in her family would look to betray her so. But why should I be so surprised, when in years to come, Jane Boleyn will be unfairly added to the list of people who, as the re-writers of history have it, will be pressurised by Cromwell and others to turn against Anne?

Nan walks to the closet, wipes the dust away with her hand, and checks the empty space at the bottom, as if to reinforce in her mind that the casket is gone.

Anne collapses back in her chair. "Why would my aunt want Henry's letters? She knows how precious they are to me!"

I kneel before her again and lean in to whisper without Nan hearing. "Mistress, I think your aunt may support Queen Katharine's cause."

Her mouth opens in silent astonishment, then she leans towards me, her lashes fluttering like butterfly wings. "Why would you say that? She is my family." She is so close, her delicate breath brushes my face.

"The Duchess is unhappy and has been for a while. She wants to crush the joy out of everyone's happiness. Gaining possession of your letters means she has a power over you – she may do anything to get back at her husband. You being his niece, she knows the only thing that stands between you and your family having power, is Rome. The Pope will want the letters for evidence. Evidence against you and the king, in case they decide to excommunicate him."

Seventeen of Henry's love letters were locked in Anne's casket; ten in French and seven in English. I have a strong suspicion they have been passed on to Cardinal Campeggio, on his visits to England, and forwarded to the pope to let him see how things were developing. I know they will eventually be stored in the Vatican Library – a fact, as a historian, that will always incense me. But I can't share this information with Anne; she would be mortified by it. She must never discover the truth.

Anne sighs, leaning back in her chair, her eyes closed, no doubt wanting to shut out the world and its calamities. The duchess – Elizabeth Howard – was married at fifteen. Anne's uncle was old enough to be the woman's father. However, Elizabeth's own father, the Duke of Buckingham, wasn't bothered by the age gap and approved of the marriage. The duchess felt forced into it, according to Anne. Norfolk described her as difficult and wilful, wanting to exercise her own demands within the marriage, much to his disgust. To outsiders at court, the marriage had previously been viewed as successful as, within the first year, Henry, the future Earl of Surrey, was born, followed by Thomas Howard, 4th Duke of Norfolk, then Thomas Howard, 1st Viscount Howard of Bindon, who will be created a Viscount by Queen Elizabeth I of England in 1559, followed by a daughter, Lady Mary Howard, who will marry Henry VIII's bastard son, Henry FitzRoy, 1st Duke of Richmond and Somerset, followed finally by Lady Katherine Howard.

Elizabeth, in the beginning, appeared to have been an obedient wife, travelling with her husband on two military campaigns to Ireland. She was also deemed a success at the court by becoming a trusted lady in waiting to Katharine of Aragon, and that is where the problem lies with Elizabeth Howard – her loyalty to the queen.

Nan steps over to us. "Anne, you know that your uncle Norfolk has for three or four years been quite blatantly keeping Bess Holland as a mistress, and…she is one of your ladies. Your uncle has humiliated his wife by trying to move his mistress into official apartments in one of their homes."

I say nothing at her effort to justify what has occurred and why the duchess has embroiled herself in a cold war against Anne.

"Yes, I know, Nan." Anne sighs, keeping her eyes closed. "But I am neither my uncle nor my aunt's keeper – they are adults and can do as they wish."

"The duchess is very sensitive about her status and dislikes the fact that you seem to take precedence over everyone," I say, trying to rationalise how her aunt may feel hurt and put out, but she continues to lie back on the chair with her eyes closed.

"I also think she resents your interference in the marriages of her children," Nan adds, her tone gentle. "Especially your insistence that her daughter should marry the Duke of Richmond." She steps closer. "Outraged, she has complained to everyone, about everything, loud and clear."

"Ah, well, Ladies." Anne opens her eyes and looks at me, before raising her head and taking in Nan. "If my aunt does not like being part of my household or supporting her niece, and going behind my back to support Katharine, then perhaps I should ask the king to ban her from court."

The stronger her anger, the thicker her French accent becomes. Nan and I look at one another, shocked by the idea that our Anne is so powerful, she can bend the king's will whichever way she chooses.

"I could have banned you from court, Nan, when your suitor George Zouche snatched my book, Obedience of a Christian Man, from you. That Tyndale book was mine." She throws her hands up and shakes her head. "My belongings always seem to go astray."

"Madam, I apologised to you profusely for that folly. I was most aggrieved at appearing disloyal."

"Talking of belongings," I say, wanting to make sure she understands why her letters have been stolen, "did you not hear that your uncle has taken away all your aunt's jewels and frequently locks her away in her apartments so she cannot cause any trouble? Is it any wonder she gets her maids to do her dirty work?"

"Mistress Gainsford," she says, ignoring me, "you are fortunate that I had intended the book for the King, since there is no doubt, he would find it enlightening, and you are even more fortunate that His Majesty retrieved the book from Wolsey."

The fact that young Zouche gave the tome to Wolsey doesn't say much about his loyalties to Anne.

She and Henry have spent many hours in recent weeks poring over its intriguing propositions. Reading this material encourages the couple to know that they are not alone in their growing mistrust of the papacy, and how it interferes with critical matters of state in England. Anne, being the acknowledged owner of such a banned text, proves to the whole court that she has become a religious dissident and firm supporter of the new faith's cause.

She gets up from her chair and embraces Nan, who is almost in tears. "Dear Nan, you may have done the King and me a great service, if you would yet know it. Do not fret, I went directly to Henry and explained to him what had happened." She gives her loyal servant's shoulders a reassuring squeeze.

Nan blinks as she stands back. "I would never wish to offend you or the king."

Anne waves her away. "The book has opened the king's mind to the corruption of the Catholic Church, and what has been read cannot be unread. He has suggested the book is a great one – a book for all kings to read. So, you see, things have worked right in the end."

"Changing the subject," I say, in the hope, she will forget about her aunt's disloyalty for a while. "I have heard that Suffolk has concerns that the Cardinal's magic might still work on the king. Suffolk, I hear, has arranged for Campeggio alone to be given lodgings at Grafton."

"Really, Beth? Do you think the Cardinal's supporters may flock to welcome him and warn of the latest situation?"

"Perhaps, Mistress, who knows with Cardinal Wolsey. His luck can turn on a coin, can it not?"

"Hmm, time will tell." Nan and I then set about preparing her to attend Henry in his privy chamber.

Twenty-One

19TH SEPTEMBER 1529
– THE MANOR OF GRAFTON REGIS

We have all witnessed or heard about the collapse of the Blackfriars trial, much to Henry and Anne's disgust. A clarion sounds as the two legates are called to the presence-chamber, which is packed, with every courtier and lord of the council standing in a row, in order of rank. Anne and I witness polite greetings all the way, sincere and insincere, because Wolsey, who is fast falling out of favour, is struggling to secure Henry's annulment. The cardinal has arrived from The More, so that Campeggio can take his leave and return to Rome. He is in a state of anxiety, as no chambers have been allocated to him to facilitate his change from his riding clothes. I heard that Henry Norris, always the gentleman, gallantly stepped in and offered his rooms. However, Wolsey kept us all waiting while he changed, and Anne kept tutting, speculating in my ear whether or not the king would receive the prelate.

To our surprise, when Wolsey and Henry are reunited, the old magic between them kicks in. The king raises the kneeling cardinal and takes him from under his cloth of estate to one of the great window embrasures, making him put his hat on. They engage in a long and earnest conversation, much to the annoyance of Suffolk, Norfolk, and Thomas Boleyn.

When their talk is finished, Anne seems furious, and I follow her and Henry out. She berates him as they storm off down the hallway.

"If any other nobleman had done what Wolsey had done, he would probably have been executed!" Her voice is raised but Henry just shakes his head.

"Wolsey has promised me he is my most loyal and faithful servant. He understands my impatience." He stops in his tracks and turns to her, glances at me, then places his hands on her shoulders. "I assure you, my mistress, I am doing all I can to bring this annulment about, as is the Cardinal. I shall speak to him as soon as I have visited my privy closet, and will make progress in this matter before midnight." He kisses her cheek and takes his leave of us. Anne watches as he disappears into his rooms, and rolls her eyes heavenwards, shaking her head.

"How long do we have to wait? How long must we endure these papal courts, its bishops, cardinals, and Rome?"

She storms off towards her chambers and I have a job catching up with her. There is no hope of Henry visiting her to play cards tonight, for there is no doubt he will be badgering Wolsey until the early hours to put pressure on Campeggio and Rome.

20TH SEPTEMBER 1529 – GRAFTON REGIS MANOR

This morning, we arise early and break our fast on apricots, sweetmeats, and wine, before preparing to pack and ride out with Henry. An usher announces his arrival as servants clear away the pewter plates. Henry looks resplendent in red and black velvet, his chains of office glistening in the bright morning sun, and the plumes in his hat dancing as he embraces his beloved.

"How do you fair, this fine morning, my love?" He towers over her, and she raises herself on her toes to plant a delicate kiss on his cheek.

"I am well, my lord. But I see you look tired, for no doubt you have been up all night with Wolsey, Suffolk, and others."

I know she's holding back from giving him a telling off.

"I promise, I was in my bed before one of the clock!" He beams at her. "I did request Wolsey come here first thing this morning, so that we could continue our conversation, but overnight my mind has been in much turmoil that the Cardinal is the one lying to me, delaying things, pretending to be on my side, when he is not."

Anne looks concerned as the veins at his temples bulge in frustration. "What will you do?" She takes his hand in hers, trying to alleviate his anger.

"When he comes from Euston, I shall pretend I have not seen him. I have already granted Campeggio his leave and have ordered Suffolk to instruct Wolsey to return with the Papal legate to London."

"If that is your desire, my love, then we shall go out riding and not return here until the Cardinal and Campeggio are gone."

Within the hour, Henry, Anne, and other members of the court, including myself, ride out through the gates of Grafton Manor, in plain sight of everyone. Unbeknown to Anne, it will be the last time the king will see his first minister.

9TH OCTOBER 1529

Wolsey's luck is not to last, and it is a coup for Anne and her faction that, within two years, she has almost singlehandedly brought down the second-most-powerful man in the realm. I feel much more at ease now as we make a fleeting visit to Durham Place, then on to London and to the Tudor Court, which is awash with stories of the downfall of Wolsey, as a writ of praemunire has been filed against him in the Court of King's Bench. Also, Cromwell is a touchy subject on everyone's lips. A writ of praemunire is a law that prohibits the assertion of papal jurisdiction against the supremacy of the monarch, and it is because of this law that the cardinal takes the easy way out by resigning the great seal nine days from now.

As his star is descending, a new man's star is ascending. After the collapse of Cardinal Campeggio's hearing this summer, Thomas Cranmer, the Boleyn family's new Chaplin, suggested switching focus from the legal case at Rome towards a general canvassing of university theologians throughout Europe. As well as advising removal of the pope from the equation, Cranmer suggests this strategy has the added benefit of being more cost-effective than the protracted and futile negotiations Wolsey had spearheaded. The king has agreed, and Cranmer has undertaken the task with diligence.

Realising his potential, Anne and her father have taken him under their wing, offering him lodgings at the newly acquired Durham Place, the Boleyns' lavish Thames-side mansion, so that he might have some quiet time to reflect and apply his mind to the concerns of the king's Great Matter. Although Cranmer has embarked on his theological career as a conservative, his efforts on Henry's behalf has already encouraged him to question papal authority. As chaplain to the Boleyn family, he is guiding them towards the reformed religion, hoping to take Henry the same way.

Cromwell and Cranmer will eventually become firm friends, which is a likely alliance owing to Cranmer's changing religious zeal. They instinctively know how to work together, urging the king to petition the European universities about his divorce. Henry has been drawn into the idea, likes it, and thinks it will give his Great Matter more gravitas.

Cranmer is an introverted man, quite the opposite of Cromwell, who is now the one to watch out for. Having risen from the ranks of the lowborn, he had, for some time, been in the service of Cardinal Wolsey, and has now, of course, been noticed by Henry, who has taken the lawyer into his service and will later make him his secretary, elevating him to the peerage. The man is becoming increasingly powerful and rich, and will grow wealthier than half of the court's nobles. Cromwell knows that England is a heartbeat from disaster.

The pope and most of Europe oppose Henry, and into this impasse stepped Thomas Cromwell, a wholly original man, a charmer, and a bully, both idealist and opportunist, astute in reading people, and implacable in his ambition. Nevertheless, Henry can be volatile; one day tender, one day murderous. Cromwell will help him break the opposition, and his men are everywhere. A man like that is dangerous, and I remember Professor Marshall warning me to keep a close eye on him, as he has a tight hold over the king. He will come to believe that he rules over Henry, and such a mindset will become a dangerous thing, especially since the king often listens to him. However, I advise Anne to support the man, since he is willing to aid her cause. While it's not always easy to like him, I know he is of the same religious persuasion as us, and I see no wrong in promoting such an alliance.

I have seen the portrait of Cromwell at the National Portrait Gallery, which was painted by the celebrated Tudor master, Hans Holbein, depicting a man who divides historians as much his contemporaries. In a few years, he will be reviled by many as a Machiavellian schemer, who destroys England's monasteries, ousts one queen, and has another executed. Henry stops at nothing in his quest for power. Five hundred years later, he will be viewed by some as an enlightened, pious, and dedicated royal servant, whose intelligence, wit, and hospitality endears him to friends and enemies alike.

My first impression of Cromwell, up close, is that he is a pensive and rather grumpy lawyer, with a bulky frame and of middling height, with prying grey eyes which stare out from under slightly raised, questioning eyebrows, giving a vaguely cynical attitude. He has wide, thin lips, always pressed into a hard line, giving him a mean appearance, which is finished off with a large, bulbous nose and double chin that hints at his age. Although he dresses moderately, his clothes are beautifully made of fine, high-quality fabrics. His cap and gown are hardly the attire of a fashionable courtier, yet both are in sombre black, a dye which is expensive and hard to reproduce in Tudor England. He has a distaste for ostentation, and this is not just a pragmatic choice in attire.

Henry has always laid down a strict set of guidelines to regulate dressing for Court, all of which are closely tied to a person's status. The royal family alone can wear purple. Dukes and marquises can fashion the sleeves of their cloaks from gold silks, while earls can wear sables. Barons are entitled to a mantle of fine cloth from the Netherlands, trimmed with crimson or blue velvet, and knights are permitted a shirt of damask and a collar of golden tissue. Cromwell is still a man of lowly birth, with none of these titles, so he is denied the privilege of wearing the rich colours and fabrics that accompany them. His no-nonsense character is evident from his need to choose such plain clothes and suggests he prefers that style of dress. From what I have observed of him, he does not display his feelings when dealing with political matters at Court, and airing his emotions in public are rare, although in private, he may show his feelings more openly. I know that when Wolsey dies, Cromwell will shed tears for the king's chief minister, yet he will cry as much for himself as for his beleaguered master.

In happier news, Anne has told me that George is to be knighted. I am proud of him. Will I get to witness his Investiture? Oh, I hope that I may even have time alone with him, to have an opportunity to 'chat'. I've made the decision not to 'chase' him, but I can't deny my feelings. For those alone, it's natural to want to see him, even be teased and annoyed by him, much to Jane's annoyance. It goes without saying that he'll try to flirt with me. I hope.

22ND OCTOBER, 1529

Anne stands at the window of her apartments at Durham House, looking out into The Strand, pressing her palms on the sill as she watches her father mount his horse to go and attend to the business of the king. We have settled back into the routine of visits from Henry, Anne's family, and from George, who always seems to be here whenever he gets the chance to break away from the tedium and routine of the court.

"Did you know Wolsey has surrendered all his property to the Crown?" Anne says, continuing to look outside with a cold and unemotional composure.

"Henry will protect him against complete ruin, will he not?" I ask, knowing the answer already from my research. I give nothing away, knowing that Wolsey will be offered the choice of answering to the king or parliament. Anne laughs at my comment, turning her back to the window to face me as I sit in a chair by the hearth, her dog at my feet.

"But Henry's affection can be notoriously fickle, and courtiers have been quick to conclude that Wolsey's prospects are not favourable." She picks up her book of hours and shakes it in my direction. "God has his hand on this situation, I can feel it. Three days ago, Wolsey was deprived of the Great Seal, and I have it on good authority that the Cardinal threw himself on the King's mercy. Rome will not be of such importance to Henry now the Cardinal has been put away to his country house at Esher. Let us hope he can do little damage to the King's cause now he is away from court. Uncle Norfolk says that he is still cultivating the Cardinal's good graces, in case he should ever return to court. I cannot believe he would be so disloyal to my family and to the king by doing such a thing!"

"Anne, all will be well for the good of the kingdom and for the spiritual prosperity of this realm. You will see."

She gives me a pensive look, probably wondering what secrets of the future I'm keeping from her. I'm glad I have her trust as, after seeing how she so subtly contributed to the Cardinal's undoing, I would hate to be her enemy. Maybe that's something I should take heed of during my time here.

Today, George's ceremony is taking place in the king's audience chamber. Everyone of note is assembled, including the Boleyn family, and the Howards – all standing transfixed as the investiture to confer a knighthood goes ahead. Henry stands on his dais of red and gold, wearing his crown, and in the full ceremonial dress of cream and gold. He towers above George, who kneels before him on a knighting stool. All hold their breath as he taps the side of his knighting sword's blade on George's right shoulder. The monarch then raises the sword just over George's head, and I wince as I watch, reminded of the fate that awaits him at Tower Hill…if history stays on track.

The room is hushed as Henry flips the sword counter clockwise so he can place the same side of the blade on George's left shoulder. George gets to his feet, proudly receiving the insignia of his new order. Henry smiles down at him and grabs his shoulders.

"Viscount Rochford, you are now prepared as my ambassador to attend your first embassy to France!"

France? George can't go to France, it's so far away. If I were his wife, I'd be asking the king's permission to accompany him everywhere he went. But no, I will have to stay put, and be alone for weeks, maybe even months.

Most of the room erupts in applause, wishing George well. I notice a few from the corner of my eye who whisper behind their hands, probably that he has only been elevated because of his sister. Jealousy is a dangerous thing.

Throughout November, Henry is being kept busy with matters of state. He has regular audiences with the new Chancellor, Thomas More, as well as with Dr Cranmer, who continues to work on a treatise regarding the Great Matter. Parliament has convened, and in the speech customarily given by the Lord Chancellor on this occasion, Thomas More seizes the opportunity to denounce Wolsey and all he came to represent. More, Anne tells me, has made it clear that, under his appointment, the clergy will act with propriety and Christian temperance. He has affirmed a return to the commandments and the values that Catholicism represents.

The king has taken yet another step towards the ultimate separation of himself and Katharine by sending her to stay at Richmond. He's gone a step further by sending her daughter Mary to Windsor, maintaining a distance between both, in case they get any ideas about plotting against him. Anne and I remain at her favourite Palace of Greenwich, while Henry travels back and forth, conducting business in Whitehall Place while parliament is in session. Hampton Court and York Place, now named Whitehall, have been gifted to him by Wolsey.

He has visited at Whitehall for a royal walk-through, accompanied by Anne, Lady Elizabeth, and Henry Norris. As well as interior decorating and refurbishing Whitehall and Hampton Court, Anne is kept busy making alliances and enemies of her own. Since Dr Cranmer has taken up residence at Durham House, she has become something of a student of the learned man, visiting him often. His tutelage largely consists of engaging us both in elucidating theological discussions, as George used to do with us at Hever. Anne's friendship with Cranmer grows steadily and she respects and admires him for his gentle manner and discourse. Our knowledge of the birth and movement of the Lutheran faith grows, and we begin to understand how it is destined to either reform the church, or prompt a compartmental approach to religion.

We sit in her rooms, where she is teaching me to beat her at cards – I am losing – when the steward who announces the arrival of the king interrupts our calm. Henry had agreed to have a private supper with Anne after he'd dined with Katharine during the day. He looks agitated as he enters, and Anne drops her hand of cards on the table before rising to greet him in a deep curtsy.

"Your Majesty."

"There is no need for such ceremony, my love. To your feet!" He takes her hand, raising her and guiding her back to her seat.

"How is the queen?" she asks. "And how can you be so friendly to him?"

"What, sweetheart?" His mind is elsewhere, and he seems in a daydream as her question breaks his chain of thought.

"To Wolsey, after he has failed you?" She's quite insistent, and I'm praying she doesn't go too far. I'm always worried she will overstep the mark.

"It is not entirely his fault." Henry rests his hand on the hilt of his sword.

"He was your chief minister, he controls everything, so whose fault is it you cannot get a divorce?"

She tilts her head to one side and glares at him. I can't get over her audacity in his company – I have never seen anyone speak so directly to the man, and she gets away with it. For Henry, the way she talks to him must seem exciting, as no woman has ever effectively given him orders.

"I know him better than you," he retorts.

"You are blinded by affection." He sighs but allows her to continue. "Wolsey is the Cardinal of a Church that will never free you and he keeps you coiled in its arms like a serpent."

Henry towers over her but it doesn't deter her.

"I have just come from Katharine," he says, probably hoping the change in subject will relieve the pressure of her offence.

Today is St Andrew's day – 30th November 1529 – and most at court are celebrating with those in their families who have Scottish connections.

"What is wrong, Henry?" Anne pleads.

He paces the floor in front of her, before the hearth, trying to warm his calves after his journey by barge on the frosty Thames.

"Katharine has just told me that she has long been suffering the pains of purgatory on earth, and that she is very badly treated by me for refusing to dine with and visit her in her apartments."

Anne remains silent, no doubt understanding that her man needs to vent his spleen.

"She has no right to complain," he says, resting his hands on the surrounding mantel of the fire, stretching his arms out and leaning his weight against it as he looks into the beckoning flames. "For she is mistress in her own household, where she can do what she pleases." He goes on to explain, without interruption, that he has not dined with her because he has been busy with 'affairs of government'.

Anne looks on, knowing that she is his distraction, because he has plenty of servants ready and willing to do his bidding at any given moment. It is the distraction of securing an annulment that grieves and grates on him, and all Anne wants to do is produce for her king the long-awaited prince, born in wedlock and of a regal bloodline. Henry resumes his pacing, looking at her, then at me as I tidy pewter goblets and plates away from our earlier meal.

He then stands tall, hands on hips, and lets out a long sigh. "She ought to know that I am not her legitimate husband, as innumerable doctors and canonists, all men of honour and probity – and even my own almoner, Doctor Lee, who has once known her in Spain – are ready to maintain."

"What if the Pope will not agree with these doctors?" she asks.

He looks down at her, as if the thought of someone saying no to him is a complete surprise.

"Should not the Pope, in conformity with the opinions so expressed, declare my marriage null and void, then, in that case, I will denounce the Pope as a heretic and marry whom I please! And,"—he holds his forefinger up—"I have told her I will do this, if I need to."

"She is a stubborn woman, my love. Perhaps she would have been better to accept your most gracious offer of retreating to a nunnery."

This is more a statement than a question on Anne's part. I've tried to warn her and Henry on many occasions that Katharine will not go quietly. I catch myself rolling my eyes, realising this couple before me, have underestimated the queen, and will do for some time to come.

"I dare not ask what the queen replied," she says, waiting to see how Henry will respond.

"The queen says that, without the help of doctors, I know perfectly well that the principal cause alleged for the divorce does not really exist, as I myself, have owned upon on more than one occasion. The queen continued to say that, as to my almoner's opinion in this matter, she cares not a straw. She says my almoner is not her judge in the present case – it is for the Pope, not for him, to decide. She also says that she respects those of other doctors, whether Parisian or from other universities, and that I should know very well that the principal and best lawyers in England have written in her favour."

His face is growing more indignant with every sentence, and Anne and I take a sideways glance at each other, wondering when he will blow into a rage. She gets up and stands in front of him, taking his hands in hers as he goes on.

"Indeed, she has asked me to give her permission to procure counsel's opinion in this matter and she has stated that she will not hesitate to say that, for each doctor or lawyer who might decide in my favour and against her, she shall find a thousand to declare that the marriage is good and indissoluble."

I'm amazed when Anne's countenance changes in a split second before our eyes and she pulls away from his delicate embrace. She strides over to the window, a few feet from him, then snaps around, her nostrils flaring and her eyes blazing.

"Did I not tell you that whenever you disputed with the Queen, she would surely have the upper hand? I see that some fine morning you will succumb to her reasoning, and that you will cast me off!"

She jams her hands on her hips, and I wish for her sake she would close her mouth and let the king speak, before she regrets anything she might say. But, no, she rants on, and I realise that I am way out of my depth in this situation, knowing well that, once she sets her mind to something, she's like a dog with a bone that won't let go.

"I have been waiting long, and might in the meanwhile have contracted some advantageous marriage, out of which I might have had issue, which is the greatest consolation in this world but, alas, farewell to my time and youth spent to no purpose at all."

Henry rushes to her side but she shakes him off, looking him straight in the eye, as only she can do.

"Oh, Anne!" He looks dismayed, almost heartbroken, as she storms from her apartments and out into the gallery beyond in an attempt to control herself before her temper blows. I know she feels she has a legitimate complaint; she has remained loyal to the king, and she loves and honours him. Despite all this, she has no guarantee at all that she will ever become a wife or a mother, though I know I've already told her this will happen.

"It is I who may well end up alone years from now!" she shouts from the gallery, her voice choked with emotion. I wish she'd keep in mind exactly what I told her – that she will marry Henry.

Before she says one more word out of place, I spin round to face Henry. "Majesty, the Lady Anne is concerned she has no reassurance that you will not give up on this quest to be with her and simply go back to Katharine, or even taking mistresses as you please."

They like to quarrel and do so frequently, if only to allow them to enjoy making up, as they always do. He stares at me, his eyes blank, not knowing what to say.

"Your Majesty, I will talk to her."

He grabs my hand. "Mistress Wickers, you are a loyal servant to both myself and Mistress Boleyn, I will not forget it."

He half-smiles at me and, in that split second, I am reminded of what it is like to be caught within the full heat of the sun. With that, he leaves the room and walks into the gallery to find Anne with her head in her hands. I watch as he touches the nape of her neck, his face a mask of anguish. He folds her into his embrace, and they cling to each other for a long time. No words are exchanged as they share the same feelings of despair, longing, desperate hope, and, above all else, love.

1ST DECEMBER 1529

The court has failed to achieve attainder against Cardinal Wolsey, and a confession by him has been submitted to parliament instead. Sir Thomas More, the newly appointed Lord Chancellor, is taking an aggressive stance as he denounces him. The cardinal's adversaries proceed to record his faults in a series of forty-four articles, which have been presented to the king today. These faults include violating the liberties of the church, subverting the 'due course and order' of the law, and, most serious of all, claiming equality with the king. The cardinal, no doubt under intense pressure, has put his signature to the document, thereby acknowledging his guilt and preventing any restoration of his titles and offices.

Sir Thomas Boleyn – Lord Rochford – has told Anne that Cromwell spoke in the cardinal's defence. She's concerned that Henry still feels affection towards him and doesn't want to see him brought so low. This, together with Wolsey's submission, is enough for him to avoid attainder. It has been a struggle, with momentous consequences, but, despite everything Wolsey has tried to achieve, Henry feels the man didn't work hard enough to win the annulment. Maybe I should have brought back a journal to document events, because I'm witnessing so much of importance that hasn't necessarily been correctly documented by historians. No, it wouldn't work. I'd never be able to hide my scribbles and notepads anywhere. And if it were found, I would have some serious explaining to do. It could be the end of me.

9TH DECEMBER 1529 - WHITEHALL PALACE

The Great Hall of the Palace of Whitehall glistens with torch and candlelight, warmed by the hearth-fire on this dark winter's evening. I will never forget what happened the day before, as this was when the king's radiance shone on Elizabeth and Thomas. Sir Thomas has been created Earl of Wiltshire, an old and aristocratic title, as well as the Earl of Ormond in the Irish peerage – nobility of the highest order. Lady Elizabeth has become a Countess. The ceremony was elaborate, with all the peers decked out in their ermines, furs, and finery. George has been restored to the king's Privy Chamber, as a gentleman of the chamber. Right now, the Boleyn name is riding high.

Afterwards, Henry enters Anne's chambers with Wiltshire and Suffolk in tow. Anne and I curtsey as the lords and the king line up in front of us.

Suffolk steps up to me, his chest out. "I am come here to bestow on Mistress Wickers," he bellows, holding a large scroll of vellum with the widest, longest red ribbon I have ever seen attached to it, "by orders of His Majesty the King, letters patent awarding her land in Ireland, for her particular use."

Hanging alongside the ribbon is a heavy wax seal depicting the king's likeness. I know my jaw has dropped, because I can feel it. My face is boiling hot, and Anne stands next to me with a huge smile lighting her face. She must have known about this – I can't believe it. I rest my hand on her arm to steady myself. Suffolk rolls the letters patent up, ties the ribbon, and hands it to Henry, who is now standing in front of me.

"I knew you would not like me to make a public spectacle of such a gift, so I thought it best to bestow such a token to you in private." He smiles, towering over me.

"Your Majesty, I do not deserve it. I have never owned anything except—" I was going to say my car but manage to cut myself off in time.

"This plot of land," he says, "is for your services to both myself and to my future wife – it is no more than you deserve." He hands me the scroll.

"I am truly honoured, Your Grace." I curtsy, knowing this gift has been given to me, in part due to Anne's relationship with him, and partly for my friendship with him.

"You qualify for this honour in your own right – it may also mean that we can find you a worthy husband!"

It's a good job the man can't read my mind because, if he could, he would know the only man for me, at his court, is George – Viscount Rochford. But there is no way the king would ever agree to such a match, seeing as George is married. I will never let Henry agree to marry me off to anyone, and I won't be slow in telling Anne so. No, I haven't set out to achieve any material gain. I'm here for Anne – I have been all along. Even so, it seems my star is ascending, as is Cromwell's. He's not only feathering his own nest but is working consistently to rehabilitate Wolsey with Henry so he might avoid being charged with treason. The disgraced cardinal has been effusive in his thanks and has unrealistic expectations of what his protégé can achieve in restoring him into the king's good graces. It seems he has difficulty accepting that his glory days are over, as he constantly seeks a return to royal favour and claims that Cromwell is the only means by which he can achieve this. He has placed Cromwell in an intolerable position, that most men would reject, but not his man, who has learnt the art of diplomacy from his years on the continent, as well as during his service to Wolsey, and he is already an excellent judge of the king's character and moods.

While Cromwell is part of the device for pushing the annulment, Henry passed Cranmer over to Sir Thomas to be cared for at Durham House, to get on with the writing, which, after completion, he is asked to take up an appointment as royal agent, to solicit the views of the Italian universities. This will be no small task for him.

With these few weeks, and now months passing, Christmas has come and gone and so has New Year, and Henry and Anne grow impatient waiting for news, as Cromwell solicits the advice of theologians and intellectuals across Europe.

He left England in January, in the entourage of Sir Thomas, who is being sent to argue Henry's case yet again, this time to Charles V and Pope Clement VII at Bologna. Cranmer has become a new and incredibly important member of the Boleyn cohort. At last, Anne is backed by a first-rate politician in Cromwell, and a man of the new faith in Cranmer.

12TH FEBRUARY 1530 – WHITEHALL PALACE

The court has moved palaces in the last month, and I am at Whitehall helping Henry and Anne oversee the building work and decorations. He has inspected each building plan before it goes forward, and Anne is as involved as he is in overseeing the design of the new palace, taking a tremendous interest in its architecture as well as the stylish details. She may as well be the project manager, possessing the sort of sophistication and taste that comes from serving the French queen as a teenager. As a couple, they share a fondness for

French and Italian decor. She likes antique touches, such as classical columns, ceilings, and patterned grotesque work.

When Henry begins the extension at York Place, Anne, and her mother, now the Countess of Wiltshire, make frequent visits to supervise the building work, which goes on round the clock. New galleries and chambers are being built, with extensive gardens, jousting and tennis yards, a bowling green, a cock-fighting pit and, of course, the magnificent Holbein gatehouse, with its chequered pattern and fleur-de-lis. The two women are lodged in the chamber under the cardinal's library, and it is in these sumptuous surroundings that Anne continues to deliberate on her brother as well as Thomas Wolsey.

"Have you heard that George's good luck continues?" she asks as we walk in the palace grounds. "Eleven days ago, he was appointed chief steward of Beaulieu." Her brows arch as she smiles. "The king has sent word to him in France."

"It is not luck, Mistress. George is a talented man, and now an experienced diplomat for his years, and, yes, his connections to you assist his elevations." I can't help feeling proud of him, knowing the way history will paint him will be wrong.

"I have heard that the master secretary has secured Henry's pardon for Wolsey."

"Is that not a good thing, after his loyal service to the king?"

"I hope it is all Henry will do, for I cannot abide the man. I hope he never returns to court."

"The king will not let him return, not now that Sir Thomas More has been raised further to favour."

"Hmm." She purses her lips. "The king can be so changeable in whom he trusts. Thank God I am his mainstay and confidante, as I do not think he would know which way to turn if he was without me."

It's true, Anne's power and influence are second to none with the king, which works well for me, as I know that if I plant a seed in her mind, she usually acts on it. I just have to let her think it's her ideas that encourage Henry.

"Would it not be beneficial if the Cardinal were to be restored to the church, away from the court?"

She glances at me. "Perhaps. He could do less harm to me if he is away from London."

"Why not suggest to Cromwell, or even His Grace, that the Cardinal be restored to the Archbishopric of York, with all its possessions except York Place?" I watch her expression as she eyes me.

"Do you think that would work?"

"Make the men think it is their idea. Plant the seed in their minds – especially that of Cromwell, who will consider it an extraordinary achievement to restore his former master to a position of power, no matter how insignificant a post."

She looks up and nods to herself. "Hmm, maybe it would be a wise move to keep Wolsey in our favour – a way of controlling him." She giggles at the sudden excitement of her plan, and, in as little as over four months, Cromwell will have transformed Wolsey's position from the disgraced minister on the verge of a conviction for treason to one of the foremost prelates in the land once more. Little does anyone know that it will be Anne's doing to encourage Cromwell from a standing start, and him with no position and precious few contacts in a court filled with the cardinal's enemies. Now, not only Wolsey but Cromwell himself will enjoy the king's good graces.

However, Wolsey is not satisfied, as he is too ambitious for his own good. A less ambitious man might be content to secure nothing more than a pardon so he could spend the rest of his life in peace, if not prosperity. He is too used to riches and luxury, and he petitions Cromwell, urging him to protect his assets. Such an approach worked for him at the height of his powers but not now, as Cromwell is not yet close enough to the king and therefore opts for a more diplomatic approach, assuring Wolsey he has done his best for his former master. Still, the cardinal isn't content, even though Henry has pardoned him.

With Wolsey out of the way, his properties are reverting into the crown's hands, and rumours are reaching him that his former protégé has betrayed him by profiting from the dispersal of his lands. The cardinal has complained of this to others, which reveals the cracks in the relationship between him and Cromwell, and the episode has demonstrated just how susceptible the two men are to court intrigue and power. Even though Wolsey is far away from the court at Esher, Surrey, and with apparently little chance of regaining any influence, his alliance with Cromwell is still viewed as a threat by their enemies, who are intent on destroying it altogether.

Queen Katharine is now virtually separated from her husband, with Henry refusing to see her or behave kindly towards her.

George has secretly written to me whilst in France, which helps ease the pain of not having him near. I've written back, reporting on what's happening here at court as if I'm some kind of political correspondent – keeping him informed on all matters, The only thing I keep close to my chest is how I feel about him – I will never tell him how I miss him. I have thrown out feelers to see how things are between him and Jane, but she only ever shares that she misses him, too, and that all is as it should be between husband and wife. If I'm being honest, I long for him to return to court. I can't wait for it, and look forward to an event when I'll get to spend some time with him to talk. At odd times of the day, I stop and realise that I miss his eyes, his laugh, even his childish humour. Occasionally, I think of Rob, wondering if he and Georgina have become an item, now that I've been living my life in Tudor England for all these months, though time probably hasn't moved more than a couple of hours back home.

Most of the time, Henry is living with Anne and the rest of his court at Whitehall. The pope insists that the divorce case can only be heard in Rome and has ordered him not to interfere; the academics might be bullied into backing the divorce but there is still popular support for Katharine.

At last, George has returned from France, from his four months of diplomacy at the Court of François I. I haven't seen him yet but am sure it won't be too long before he visits. Need I say that I'm looking forward to seeing him?

SPRING 1530

Anne has created for herself a new motto, a defiant defence which she has adopted for herself: Ainsi sera groigne qui groigne (Let them grumble; that is how it is going to be). Her defiance as a mistress is seen when the livery coats of her servants are embroidered with a version of the arrogant motto she learned from Margaret of Austria. Her attitude at times seems counterproductive and the device doesn't last long. After I rationalise it with her, she removes the motto within weeks. She is certainly behaving as a mistress should, as Henry finds himself facing a person prepared to stand up to him. She wants Katharine gone from Court, which is understandable, as the queen has her own spies and Anne is making many enemies for the king.

"I have complained to Henry," she remarks to me one afternoon as we sit on the lawns in the palace gardens, playing with her growing brood of dogs, "that the queen must not make or embroider shirts for him any longer."

"What did he say?"

"He has told me that 'they are just shirts'." She mimics his voice. "I have told him that the shirts are not just shirts but a symbol of the relationship that still exists between them, but alas he does not seem to understand me." Her tone is bitter. "Henry has told me I make too much of it and has reminded me of all he has done for my father, for George, and all the gifts and tokens of affection he has bestowed upon me." She takes a deep breath and shudders. "He treats me as if I am ungrateful."

"Mistress, I know you did not expect all the king has done for you."

"Indeed, I did not welcome it at first, but since he has chosen to elevate me and now wants me as his queen, who am I to refuse him? If you remember, in the beginning, I did not expect that Henry would be able to make me his queen. All I had expected to be was his loyal and obedient servant."

"Yes, you have always been that, madam. You and the king work so well together."

"We do, indeed!" Her face lights up with a broad smile.

"The love you have for one another shines through everything." I'm so relieved that, finally, everything seems to be going to plan, but one thing does worry me: Anne seems to be changing. Over the last few months, she is becoming egotistical, and sharp. Is this because of her growing influence and power? The cliché comes to mind, and I wonder is it true that power corrupts the individual?

Saturday, 12th November 1530

I wonder where the summer disappeared to. Sadly, for Anne, the summer has passed, without any real progress politically, though I've enjoyed spending time with Anne and Jayne, at Court and walking around all the king's rose gardens. Anne is hoping for a day of leisure, as her ladies-in-waiting attend her, dressing her in a lavish gold gown and the most beautiful, black-worked shift. Silk rustles and writhes as her black damask sleeves are pinned in place, and rubies set in gold with diamonds sparkle on the neckline of her kirtle, winking their facets in the bright morning sunlight. She looks resplendent, almost royal, as Margaret Wyatt, recently Lady Lee, places a black velvet hood on her dressed hair.

We all sit about the breakfast table in her privy chambers, chattering and gossiping, as women do, about what Maria de Salinas was wearing yesterday and how solemn and sombre she looked, always in black, always dower, always tragic. Queen Katharine's women are too pious and contemplative for Anne's liking, and the way she and her entourage carry themselves at court could not be more different than that of the suffering Katharine.

Maria wasn't among the original Spanish ladies to accompany Katharine to England to marry Arthur Tudor. She came a few months later, as part of the second wave of Spanish attendants, after the young Princess of Wales had been widowed. Isabella of Spain sent them as a sign of her support for the newly made arrangement that Henry VII's second and only surviving son, Henry, would be wed to Katharine.

Maria's devotion is always obvious but then the two women keep themselves closeted away, the majority of the time from public view, much to Anne's delight. On the days the Spanish do appear, it is a frustrating game of chess to keep Anne and our faction of attendants as far apart from Katharine as we can. Anne's dislike of anything Spanish not only runs to Katharine and her attendants but to those ambassadors who would work to keep Charles V and his political concerns at the forefront of Henry's mind.

Henry's mood matches the colour of Anne's gown as she enters his privy chamber, dipping before her betrothed as he sits on his dais, looking the height of regal in sapphire silk, with gold and ruby ouches. Henry Norris and

Charles Brandon stand beside the dais, doffing their caps to us as we enter. The king, blown away by Anne's appearance, observes her small, yet heaving bosom with some delight, the lust twinkling in his eyes, and he rises to his feet to greet her, taking her hand as they promenade the room.

Jane Boleyn sulks in a corner. Ever since that incident with George at Beaulieu, when she discovered me on her husband's knee, she's given me the cold shoulder. I watch as she sits whispering with Mary Shelton, while Lady Lee and I take a turn about the room, stopping at a small window that overlooks the gallery. Mary – we like to call her 'Madge' – is a younger cousin of Anne's, and is pretty, sweet-natured, and many men at court, including the king, are just that little bit in love with her. She is a great admirer of Tom Wyatt, and regularly contributes to a book of court poetry known as the 'Devonshire MS'. Being a clever little thing, she delights in editing the said book, much to the admiration of Tom.

Henry, ever the flatterer, brings Anne towards our huddled party, smiling, hand on hip. It's no great surprise that he remembers the name of every woman in the group. He stops at Jane.

"Lady Rochford, why do you hide in the corner? Come and bid us good morrow!" He is in a fine mood as he takes her reluctant hand. She then shrinks back, blending into the colours of the tapestry, probably wishing she was anywhere but the king's chamber. Mary Shelton is the next one to be caught in his radar, as he cups her cheeks with his hands before planting a kiss square on her lips. Anne watches, loving his tender manner towards her attendants.

"Who do we have here?" He beckons for Margaret to come closer.

"Lady Margaret Lee, Your Grace." She dips a quick curtsy before he pulls her forward to plant a kiss on her cheek. Then it's my turn.

"I know you, Mistress Beth! I must say you look exceptionally fine today, and that teal-coloured gown suits you so well. Brings out your colouring." He traces his big paw over my cheek and bends to kiss me, the bristles of his beard brushing against my delicate skin. Then he takes hold of Anne's hand, looking like the sultan of a mystical harem.

"I swear, my lady, the older I get, the lovelier all you beautiful young women become!"

Anne laughs. "Age will have advantages, Sire!"

Before Henry can make a reply, a gentleman usher announces the arrival of the Spanish ambassador, Eustache Chapuys. The king looks at the throng of women about him, then dismisses them, asking only myself and Anne to remain. Lady Lee, Jane Rochford, and Mary Shelton take their leave, with Chapuys tipping his cap to them, then to Henry. Anne and I watch as he approaches the king, his nerves evident in his shaky bow. The show of anxiety belies the reality – the man possesses courage by the bucket-load. He is an arch-conspirator for his master, Charles V, Holy Roman Emperor of Spain, and nephew of Queen Katharine, and his confidants are the old Catholic families who support Katharine and Mary. Chapuys takes notice of them, misinterpreting what he hears, then reporting incorrectly to the emperor, urging him to invade England, when, in fact, the families like the Poles and the Exeters have little popular support. I know from history that this 'little man', as Anne likes to call him, will be ineffective – a brave man on a failing mission.

"Your Majesty," he dutifully addresses Henry.

"Chapuys." The king motions him to approach, while Anne and I stand beside the small window, looking on. The ambassador eyes us, as if he is afraid to speak with us in the room.

"How is your master?" Henry asks, speaking in French, as does Chapuys, for it is a mutual language they share.

"Charles is well, Your Grace, and enquires after your own health and that of your Queen."

"I have heard that your servant has died of the plague," Henry says, changing the subject. "Have you sent your condolences to the family?" He knows about everyone, from the highest lord in the land to the lowliest of servants.

"I have, Your Grace."

Anne whispers translations into my ear but my French is getting better day by day and I'm confident in interpreting the conversations myself. While talking on a myriad of subjects, the king tries to introduce the subject of his divorce at every opportunity, and speaks eagerly and not without cause, for every few minutes he looks at Anne from the corner of his eye, hoping to impress her.

"Your Grace, please do not enter into such a delicate subject, for I am resolved not to say anything more on this matter, without express command from Your Majesty."

The more Chapuys tries to avoid the subject, the more Henry presses him on it.

"Charles thwarts me in every possible way you can imagine!"

"No, Your Grace. Never!"

Anne nudges my elbow and I struggle to keep a neutral face.

"Charles expects from me, the King, what is dishonest and unreasonable."

"Your Grace, as to the dishonest demands to which you refer, there is no one in the world to whom this could apply so little as to Your Majesty, who has always acted as an honest, honourable, and most virtuous prince."

Henry leads him by the elbow to the middle of the room, so they cannot be overheard, in case Anne is offended, but as I take her goblet to a nearby table to refill it, I can still hear it all.

"If I have spoken so unceremoniously about Charles, then I have done it to induce you to reprimand your ambassadors in Rome and in France, who are inventing numerous falsehoods about me. Despite it all, I will carry my purpose through."

Chapuys stares at him, not knowing what to say. Henry glances at me while I'm refilling the glasses.

"You, yourself, have frequently sent advice from this country to Rome which has greatly embittered my case. I have heard that the Pope has mentioned this to our ambassadors in Rome."

"Your Majesty, I report only what I see and hear. I do my job with duty and care to both you and my master."

Henry grumbles a little about France, before Chapuys bows and takes his leave. He never acknowledges our presence, and will only ever refer to Anne as 'the lady', or 'concubine' in his dispatches to Charles V.

Early December 1530

The king is visiting Anne, as he often does, between being entwined in Court politics, religious matters, and advancing his Great Matter to a conclusion, along with juggling the accommodation of the queen against his mistress's wishes. The day is bright and clear, and a light dusting of snow covers the ground as we prepare ourselves for Christmastide. I'm reminded of my last visit home, and of the world, I've left behind, when I spent Christmas with my family.

I am like an innocent child, sucking in the atmosphere of each syllable as Henry sits with Anne on the couch. He never minds my quiet presence and often allows me to join the conversation, if he values my opinion on a subject. Anne is delighted that he takes me into his confidence and has assured me that, before long, he will wish to bestow more accolades on me, though I always assert that I am undeserving of such things.

"Dearest Anne, sweetheart, I have intelligence to impart to you, which I think will please you." Henry's scent fills the room and appears to intoxicate Anne when he leans in close.

"Do tell me, Henry, we would delight in some good news." She looks over to me as I stuff some sweetmeats in my mouth, then nuzzles closer into his chest.

"Well, then, this is for your and Mistress Wickers' ears only. You may not share what I am about to tell you until I have done so first."

My curiosity is piqued as I swallow the last morsel of food left in my mouth. Anne smirks and sits up straight, giving him an expectant look.

He looks at me with a twinkle in his eye, and it's obvious he has plotted a scheme to please her. "I intend, my darling Anne, to honour your family and your father by creating him, Lord Privy Seal. I do not think it enough that I have already created him Earl of Wiltshire and Earl of Ormond. Not only that, but I also wish to bestow a gift upon Mistress Wickers here."

"Henry, that is so very generous of you and absolutely magnificent for my friends and family!"

I'm stunned to silence as Anne throws her arms around his neck, and I know that, soon, I will be ushered from the room to allow her the privacy to permit him the opportunity to give his hand an advance above her knee. Cash or presents are the only things that will authorise Henry to explore her curves, and she takes much persuasion in giving an inch and will never condone him spoiling what she refers to as her secret parts. She would confide in me if they had done so and I'm confident they have never gone that far; her virginity means everything to her.

Twenty-Two

4TH DECEMBER 1530 – GREENWICH PALACE

Anne and I are alone in her chambers when we hear a tapping at her door and Thomas Howard, third Duke of Norfolk, is announced. It is unusual for him to visit Anne personally, as he tends to bark orders at her through his brother-in-law. There isn't much love lost between them, as is evident from the look he gives his niece on entering. The man is a leading counsellor and Wolsey's deadliest enemy, and, at fifty-six, one of the most distinguished and longest-serving members of Henry's court. He has the vigour of a man half his age and appears to run on rage. It's well known that he served Henry VII faithfully, proving an able soldier and leader of men, and he continues to enjoy favour with Henry VIII, who made him a Knight of the Garter, the highest order of chivalry in the land and an honour he would justify when he played a prominent role in defeating the Scots at Flodden in 1513.

In 1514, he was made Earl of Surrey, and on the death of his father in 1524, he succeeded to the dukedom of Norfolk. From what I have witnessed, the man has never manipulated the king to notice Anne, nor has he had any influence on the situation in any way. Thomas Boleyn, now titled Earl of Wiltshire, has ever declared himself; on the contrary, he tried to dissuade Henry from the marriage. Although, ever since Anne began to encourage the king's affections, Norfolk probably hopes it will serve to enhance his standing at Court even more. He appears to back Anne's efforts but is also quick to turn on her if she doesn't listen to his advice.

He seems an earnest man, bold and witty in all his matters, sharp as a tack, rather than humorous, and tends to profanity when he's angry. Unlike Cromwell, Norfolk is not known for his sparkling wit or conversation. Proud and arrogant, he may be, but Anne has told me that he also possesses a violent temper and lashes out at anyone who causes offence. He jealously guards his favour with the king and harbours a bitter hatred towards those who rival his own influence.

I keep an eye on him from my seat across the room. He appears stern, with a menacing face and cold, dark staring eyes. Physically, he's the opposite of Cromwell, who carries bulk much like Henry. He's small and spare in person and his hair is jet-black, though greying at the temples. I can see where Anne gets her dark looks from, and possibly her temper, as Norfolk is always the most outspoken advocate for an aggressive, warlike foreign policy, which has at times set him at odds with Wolsey, who tended to be more cautious. Norfolk took a dim view of this lowborn butcher's son from Ipswich, who he believes had no place in either the council or the court. Now he takes a similar view of Wolsey's protégé, Cromwell, the lowly brewer's boy from Putney. His wife tells Cromwell that he beats her, and she also complains that his mistress treats her cruelly. Norfolk dislikes that Cromwell knows everything and is everywhere he looks, which he accepts through gritted teeth and a sprinkling of false bonhomie.

Cromwell seeks Norfolk's assistance, which is an indication of his own audacity. He rightly judges Norfolk, that his star will rise in direct inverse proportion to Wolsey's fall, and he apparently has no scruples in petitioning his master's adversary. Indeed, with Norfolk in the ascendancy, securing his favour is an essential prerequisite to promoting Cromwell's interests at Court. Pragmatism has once more won out over principle, as befriending his enemy is simply a means to an end. Pure Machiavellian.

Nevertheless, Wolsey's enemies, triumphant at his fall, now dominate the court. Principal among them is the duke of Norfolk. Given his kinship to Anne Boleyn, he has a close stake in the king's Great Matter. Together with his nephew George Boleyn, Viscount Rochford, and Charles Brandon, Duke of Suffolk, he is determined to engineer Wolsey's complete failure and downfall, one that is usually attributed in history to Anne. However, as Norfolk and Boleyn see their kinswoman is so set on becoming queen, they manoeuvre around the throne and in court to assist the king in ridding himself of those who would stand in the way of the annulment of his marriage.

Norfolk considers Wolsey below his station, referring to him as greedy, pretentious, and common. It is evident from his demeanour that he delights in the disgrace of Henry's first minister.

"Niece, I have…I have come to tell you of news of…the Cardinal." He is flushed in the face, tripping over his words in his excitement as Anne stays firm in her seat.

"What is it, Uncle?" She looks anxious, as if expecting to hear the news that Wolsey has returned to court and has been restored to power. "Spit it out!"

"Wolsey set out for London, to The Tower, but his progress was…was hampered by a fresh bout of sickness, which drove him to a state of near… collapse." He tries to regain his composure. "It has been reported that he was barely able to stay on his mule, when, on the evening of the twenty-sixth of November, he arrived at Leicester Abbey."

"Yes, Uncle, go on," Anne urges, her hands clasped together.

"Early the following morning, he made his final confession, and he died shortly afterwards on the twenty-ninth." Of course, I knew Wolsey's death was coming, but it wasn't my place to tell anyone what I knew, for fear of too many questions or accusations.

Anne gets up, grabbing her uncle's hands to steady herself. The shock of his news hits her as she realises her old adversary is now dead. "Is this really so?" She sits back on her chair, staring up at him in disbelief. "I wished him out of favour because of the damage he has done to the king, but I have never wished him dead."

"It is as true as I stand here before you," Norfolk says with a wry smile. "Niece, our great enemy has fallen before us, without our having to lift a hand to it."

Henry and his court regularly attend Mass in the royal chapel, sometimes more than once a day. The king often uses the time before the consecration to transact business but, on this bright December morning, he has scribbled in a book of hours and asked his messenger to go to Anne's chambers with the prayer book she'd left in his chambers. Anne is still being prepared for Mass when the manservant arrives. I stand next to her as she interprets, quoting Henry's writing:

"'If you remember my love in your prayers as strongly as I adore you, I shall hardly be forgotten, for I am yours. Henry R. Forever.'"

"The king is a little lovesick, Mistress," I say, pointing to the illustration on the page depicting the flayed Christ, the man of sorrows, under which Henry has written his dedication. "Anne, why do you say nothing?" I take her hand and squeeze it.

"I cannot help it, Beth. The king puts such a burden on me, one which I hope and pray I can fulfil." She stares back at the words, resting the Flemish book of hours on the table beside her as she prepares to pen a reply.

The king's man waits, not uttering a single word as Anne turns to a page showing the miniature image of the annunciation, with an angel telling Mary she is to have a son. She has chosen the illuminated page with deliberate enticement by promising Henry, she will give him a son. Under the intricately brilliant depiction of the Annunciation, she presses her quill to the bottom of the page and replies with a couplet in English:

By daily proof, you shall me find

To be to you both loving and kind.

Someone taps on the door, and I go to open it, finding George standing on the threshold. He smiles, and I do my best not to react to his gorgeous scent like a lovelorn teenager.

"Can I come in, Beth?"

I turn to Anne, who has just put the quill back into its resting place on the table. George eyes the king's messenger, who coughs into his hand.

"Come in, brother!" she says.

He walks to the table to see what she's doing, as she blots the ink with sand, blowing the remnants into the fireplace.

"What secrets are you hiding for me?" he asks, looking over her shoulder. He snatches the book up and thumbs through its pages to find where Henry has written. The chamber smells of woodsmoke, as the fire crackles. He reads the couplet to himself.

"I'm ashamed – the book is spoiled by a royal quill!" He smirks. "Look... 'If you remember my love in your prayers as strongly as I adore you – I shall hardly be forgotten. Henry R, Forever.'" He chuckles.

Anne scowls. "I am not sorry – clearly, it is written in black and white – the king loves me!"

"This is amazing. What is he saying? Echi Hommo – he's written under the image of the Crucifixion – the pangs of love he is suffering are akin to the suffering agonies of our Lord!" He looks at Anne in amazement.

"Can you find where I countered him?" she asks.

"Where is it?" He flicks through the delicate pages. Anne pulls the book from his fingers. "Let me look!" he asks, watching her find the page. He leans down to read it. "By daily proof you shall me find, to be to you both loving and kind." He scrunches up his face. "What a terrible couplet!"

"George, it's not bad poetry!" I say.

"The book has only just been brought to me – it happened so quickly, I did not have hours of leisure time to while away like you, when you and Wyatt write poetry!"

He grins. "I cannot wait to see Wyatt's face when I tell him!"

"No, George!"

"I won't – of course not. 'Twas a joke, sister."

"Henry will be struck by the position of my epigram." She raises a brow.

He stares at the page. "Anne Boleyn – the fertile virgin." He straightens. "How could you profane Our Lady with such a comparison?"

Her eyes widen. "Henry will like it."

"How could you write such a thing in the very book of Hours I gave you?"

"Trust me, George, the king will like it!"

"You are brilliant as ever, sister – but fertility is nothing without legitimacy!"

"He wants me more than ever since I nearly died from the sweat. But our campaign with Rome is foundering – we extend into months and years. Sometimes I despair that we will never convince the Pope to ever turn this false marriage to Katharine."

"The Pope is persuading and pleading in just the way that we are told to pay for our soul's passage through purgatory, but perhaps that is not the right way?" He hands back the prayer book, and Anne passes it to the king's messenger, who bows and hurries out of the room, no doubt well aware that Henry will be impatient for a reply.

"I bought you a present, Anne."

Her interest is piqued. "Let me see it!"

He lifts a book he'd placed on a sideboard near the door, and hands it to her.

"This book, if we dare show it to the King, could hold the secrets we've been looking for. We can reject the Pope without rejecting God, or the true Church."

Anne turns it over. "Simon Fish – Supplication for the beggars?"

"Beggars are people – needy, impotent, lame, and sick, that only live by alms. Half the wealth in England is owned by the monasteries but they comprise only one out of a hundred of the population. Instead of helping the poor."

"Henry knows their arrogance and lechery," she says.

"Monks catching the pox and leprosy from one woman and bearing it to another. Squalid and dirty, unholy in the extreme. Celibacy – I've seen them in the stews." He runs his hand through his hair as Anne flicks through the pages of the book.

"I would not trust them with one of my dogs!" she says.

"Here's the thing – the church in England usurped the power of the king. You, sister, have the power to inspire Henry to truly lead his people and to reject the corruption and superstition of Rome." He sits next to me at the end of the four-poster bed.

"What if we are wrong?" he asks.

"George," I say, "there's not one word spoken of purgatory in the Holy Scriptures, and we have no command from God to pray for the dead, and yet, the church extorts coffers of gold for the saving of souls." I think I sounded more than adequately Tudor, with that remark, and smile. George notices.

"Beth – and what of God? What if we are wrong and the church, as it is, is the only way?"

"What you speak of, I believe, is the way to an enlightened, reformed church." I reply.

"An enlightened way that serves our purpose, too?" Anne looks at me. I suspect she means: will this enlightened way serve the king's purpose?

"Why not, Anne?" George asks. "Our purpose will champion the beggars!"

"And make Henry into the king he's always destined to be?" I suggest.

"Exactly!" she replies, smiling.

"His destiny..." I say.

George jabs his thumb into his chest. "And ours!"

"And England's!" I can't hold back a smile.

On that positive note, he stands, bends to kiss me on the hand, then goes to kiss his sister. "I am attending His Majesty. I shall see you both later."

Once we're alone, Anne continues the conversation. "Henry is tightening his grip on obedient Roman Catholic England." She flutters her lashes. "Beth, have you noticed how the rituals of the Latin Mass are subsiding, even though the King once believed that the English language was not fit for the word of God?"

"Yes, I have." I sit in the window seat, opening the casement to let some air into the room.

"The Latin language is beyond most people's comprehension and therefore makes the bible inaccessible to them." She sits beside me, nursing the book George gave her in her lap. "This enables Henry to control who understands the word of God. If people cannot understand the bible for themselves, then it gives the monarchy and the other courtiers control of the people."

"Religion and politics are different sides of the same coin," I say.

"But do you see now, how times are changing, just as you said they would all those years ago? William Tyndale, the man whose life's work would be translating the bible from the original Greek into English, is slowly becoming the most dangerous and wanted man in England."

I tap her arm. "Did I not tell you his influence would start ascending because of his biblical ideas?"

"'Tis exactly as you said. Those smuggled copies from Stuttgart he has released to readers and scholars of the common tongue."

"Tyndale's words and phrases will reshape and change the way men and women express themselves and what they believe. But Henry will try to write him out of history because of the savage truth Tyndale's work will reveal about the men and women in his court." The words are piling for release, and I have to let them out. "Tyndale's words will expose the king for the hypocrite he can be." Hmm, maybe I shouldn't have said that. I'm sure people have lost their heads for saying less.

Anne raises a brow. "You cannot say such a thing of the king!"

"Look, Henry wants to control the ploughman's every thought and deed. He can do that easily through the Catholic Church because they have control of the reading of the Bible as it is written in Latin. Do you not understand, Anne? This fact is crucial in maintaining the church's structure and power."

She stares at me, flabbergasted by my knowledge. "Go on…"

"The rulings of popes through the centuries of canon law, with the devices of purgatory, penance, confession, and the hierarchy of the Church, hold the layman back in getting past the Latin language to read the bible, to understand it and challenge these concepts so that he can be liberated by reading and learning from this sacred text."

"But what will this mean for the king?"

"You know what Henry is like – he will sway like a pendulum, from being opposed to such texts, to supporting them openly, especially once you and George have explained your points to him."

2ND JANUARY 1531

As we enter the Great Hall at Greenwich, the room is alive with the chatter of men waiting to petition the king. Some play cards and board games, while others gossip in corners, carrying their little lapdogs under their arms. To one side of the entrance stands a huddle of Katharine's ladies-in-waiting. Anne, incorrigible as ever, can't resist goading them as she passes. She is fiercer than a lioness, not aiming her loud comment at anyone in particular.

"I wish that all Spaniards were at the bottom of the sea."

The attendant, whose name I forget, looks shocked.

"And there to stay!" George whispers to Anne.

"Mistress Boleyn, for the sake of the queen's honour, you should not express such sentiments!"

"I care not for Queen Katharine, nor any of her family. I would rather see her hanged than have to confess that she is my queen and mistress!"

George smiles at her. "Do not be afraid of them, Anne, for they no longer have the king's ear as you do!"

She leans closer. "I have heard, brother, that the Bishop of Winchester is being sent on a mission to France, so that he may rally support from François in gaining permission from the Pope for the divorce case to be heard and tried in England."

"At least something is being done, although ambassador Chapuys is staying away from the king – his visits are less frequent."

"Henry is hoping his marriage will be dissolved during the next sitting of parliament."

Anne is playing a risky game here, making more enemies among the queen's attendants by exposing herself to hateful gossip.

"George, I have been so worried about Anne," I say when we're away from Katharine's ladies.

"Why?" he asks, leaning in. "That mob of women?" Anne overhears what George says.

"The thought of it makes me tremble," Anne says. "That mob would have torn me to pieces, George, if I hadn't got away on the river barge. Where would Henry have been then? Why is it people love Katharine so?"

He grimaces. "You were right to banish my wife from court – she was part of that mob! I cannot explain her attitude. Banishment from court will teach Viscountess Rochford a lesson."

"George, let's not quarrel over her."

"Sister, I have failed to understand why Jane would be so disloyal to you."

"I know, I do not understand it either."

He nudges me. "Let's look on the bright side, Beth. The only benefit of this sorry situation is that, with Jane gone, I now have more opportunity to openly flirt with you."

I want to thump him but hold myself in check.

"George, stop it!" Anne says.

"Sister, no, these people are dirt. Men dressed as women, screeching like cats. I swear, they will hang, every one of them! Henry will make sure you are closely guarded from now on. I will make sure of it myself!"

"I swear, brother, I am wasting my youth on that man!"

"You must be patient."

"Henry treats me like a mere dalliance!"

"Sister, I swear, the king has begged me, with tears in his eyes, to mediate with you." He looks to the ceiling. "Begged me! The most important king in Christendom."

"It warrants nothing, George, nothing, while she still carries the name of Queen. However, with Brereton's petition with all our diplomatic efforts – Father, Uncle – we will prevail."

"Henry adores you!"

She blinks a rapid sequence. "He does want me. First, I thought he wanted you, Beth, but now, I know he really wants me."

"Only for now is she still queen in name," I say.

"I swear, Beth, Katharine is no queen of mine."

"She should be in a nunnery, out of the way, or dead," George says, his expression grim. "She must make way for the new Queen of England!"

"Tell Henry I will not come to him tonight. Tell him not to expect me. Tell him I am overcome with grief at my treatment!"

George bows. "Take care, sister."

6TH JANUARY 1531

Anne is in a foul mood and paces the floorboards in her apartments, as she often does when anger or frustration hits her. My only remedy in such situations is to be a listening ear, for that is what she needs.

"Did I tell you of the farce of a masque that my father put on to entertain the king?"

"No, my lady, you did not."

"Cardinal Wolsey going down to hell! I was shocked at first but then, as I watched the king, my father, and brother revel in the entertainment, I had no choice but to join in with the applause and show appreciation."

"Why did your father show such a masque?"

"It was at a private dinner for Claude la Guische, the French ambassador, to stress the king's new, more hostile attitude towards the Roman Church and all its agents, while tacitly reminding the French of their own supposedly 'special relationship' with Wolsey, and their alleged involvement in his plotting immediately prior to his fall."

"Ah, an opportunity for your newest and dearest to show the ambassador their importance and status now that Wolsey is gone, perhaps?"

"Indeed. Wolsey's time in power is over and now France should deal with Father and Uncle Norfolk. However, la Guische was offended by the play and by Norfolk's idea of having it published." She frowns at me. "Apparently, the ambassador mocks my father and uncle and laughs at their new power in government. I thought I had friends at the French Court, but it seems my family makes enemies everywhere. Truly, I despair of them!"

"Oh, Anne!"

"On top of that, I have found out that Katharine insults me."

"Why? How?"

"I asked Henry to make sure that Katharine stopped making his shirts, but it appears he has not spoken with her, and she is still embroidering his shirts, Beth!" She snorts in a sharp breath through her nose. "I found servants taking her a bolt of cloth. That woman knows no bounds and has no pride."

"Do not worry, Anne – a seamstress is all she is to him!"

"I cannot believe she is still making his shirts!" She shakes her head. "I dismissed the servant who was pandering to her. I threw him out. The dogs can have him! I do not need to be told by Henry – they've had twenty-two years of sewing that is valuable to the royal wardrobe. She has ever been more of a mother than a wife to him. And he still keeps her close."

"Strange, I know, but I expect it is custom. The king must like his shirts just so."

"Beth, saying things like that – God's bones, you make me burn with fury. Henry is a fool to let her work him in this way." She sighs, though it comes out like a growl. "He makes a fool of me. Sometimes, I see her as another Wolsey in his life. He can't shake off their influence – he's like a child."

"Stop worrying, Wolsey is gone. It took some time, but he's gone."

She releases a nervous giggle. "I said I'd have him in the end, did I not? He called me 'the high crow' or was it the 'black crow'? I paid no mind to him in the end, but he should have never called me such, because I plucked out his eyes and will do the same to Katharine!"

"Anne, calm yourself!"

"Henry doesn't want another simpering fool of a woman – he needs someone in this world who will demand the best of him."

As she finishes her sentence, someone taps at her chamber door. I go and answer. It is Jayne Fool.

"May I come in?" she asks.

"Of course, Jayne," Anne calls to her, "come sit with us." She sits on a stool, and Anne's little lapdog comes and snuggles around her skirts.

"What be you ladies talking of?"

"Politics," Anne answers.

"Hard to understand, for me!" she says, smiling, brushing her hand over the top of her linen coif.

"You demand the best of Henry?" I ask.

"Yes, and why not?" Anne says.

"Push him, but not too far. Let others do the work, too."

"Push him! Push him!" Jayne repeats.

Anne smirks. "That Thomas Cromwell is my man now!"

"Ah, the blacksmith's boy?"

"Yes, Beth, let him wallow in the mire for us. God knows, I heard his father's nails are black with the dirt of his misdeeds – no doubt, the son is of the same kidney?"

"Under those silken gloves? I doubt it very much. No, he's a clever fellow."

"Clever fellow! Clever he be," Jayne says.

I nod. "Cunning."

"He wants greatness, too, and power." Anne stands beside Jayne. "He thinks I see him as a friend – that we Boleyns think him an honest fellow, with honourable intentions, not the schemings, and lies of a lawyer." She arches her brows. "Am I too hard on him?"

"I know him from history for what he is."

She glares at me, willing me to keep quiet so I don't give the game away to Jayne.

"He is ready at things – good or evil. Hear my warning."

"Cromwell is a dog to bait, Beth – the likes of Thomas More and all his popish fellows."

I shrug. "As I said, he is a clever dog."

"Clever dog! Clever dog!" Jayne says.

Perhaps it's not wise for her to be here while we discuss politics. She continues to play with the lapdog, which is snapping at her fingers.

"Yes, Cromwell is clever, as are many who yap at the king's heels – just like his dogs Cup and Ball."

Someone knocks at the door, only this time it is more forceful. It opens, and a page stands, shuffling from one foot to the other.

"Lady Anne, Viscount Rochford is here."

My heart skips a beat as George enters the room.

"Ladies." He bows with a flourish, then walks over to Anne, bending to kiss her on the cheek. He then turns to Jayne and takes her hand. "You are a more beautiful Jayne than my wife!" He smirks, and she blushes, tugging her hand away before he has the chance to kiss it. "And Beth, my most favourite jewel of all!" He pulls me to my feet and plants a huge kiss on my lips, his arm around my waist.

"Brother, behave yourself!"

"I am all good manners, sister." He plonks himself in a chair beside her.

"What are we discussing, ladies?"

"Life," I answer, running the tip of my tongue across my bottom lip to catch his taste.

Anne groans. "George, why does the King suffer the country to spit at me?"

"They will never do such a thing when you are queen."

"You are QUEEN! QUEEN! QUEEN!" Jayne nods as she repeats the word. I think she does this because she's unsure of how to make her way in the conversation.

"Nan Boleyn," Anne says. "Plain Nan!" She smooths down her skirts. "I have waited years for the king, yet they still say I am a whore. I have a reputation like Mary, even though I have never earned it. This waiting to be married is drawing me to madness! I tell you, I can stand it no longer."

"Stand it no longer?" Jayne says.

"Sister, if there is no plan, maybe we will end up in Bedlam one day?"

"Don't say such things!"

He laughs. "I will be able to say I used to be a governor of this place, you know!"

"And you know what I can say?" She prods his arm with her forefinger. "I can say I used to be that Nan, Anne Boleyn, that Great Whore, or black crow, who once thought herself to be queen one day!"

"There is a wretch in Bedlam who thinks he's Henry VIII, you know," Jayne says.

"Shush, Jayne. How do you know of such things? To say such a thing is treason, surely?"

"Only treason to the man in Bedlam who dare not behave himself!" George says, chuckling to himself. "The person in there who thinks he's the king, sits on his closed stool all day, every day. He's covered in his own shit, yet still gives his commands. I feel sorry for the fellow, and I hate the place – the noise is hideous."

"In Bedlam?" I ask.

"Yes," he answers. "The place is great enough to drive a man that has his wits, right out of them."

Anne glances at Jayne, and mouths "George," as if to make him bite his tongue and not offend.

"There is money in it – keeping those poor souls in Bedlam. The amounts some people will spend to place family members there is gigantic, to get their relatives out of view."

"George, I always thought that Tudor society was tolerant of the mad?" I ask.

George leans across to the table beside him and pours a glass of wine from the flagon. "To a point, society is. However, sweet Beth, I am tempted to throw Viscountess Rochford in there, out of harm's way, so she doesn't cause a riot." He sips from his glass. "It might be one way to get rid of a wife!"

"Perhaps the king should put his wife in there also?" Anne says.

"And maybe that sulky daughter of theirs can join her also!" He takes another sip of his wine. "The girl will be sulkier still, if you give her a little brother."

"If God be willing," Anne says.

"God willing! God willing!" Jayne shouts.

"God does will it, sister – I know it to be true." He nods a couple of times, his eyes wide. "When you are queen, there will be one king, one law, which will be God's ordinance in every part of his realm. We Boleyns have come so far, we need to take care." His brow furrows. "You, sister, need to take care of your temper. The King will only be pushed so far."

"There are people at Court who resent me for my hold on Henry." She looks at me. "Do you remember that crude drawing, that prophetic sketch that was left in my chambers, all that time ago?"

"The one showing Henry, Katharine, and you, with your head cut off – the one that Nan found?"

"I remember it," George says. "The trouble is, Anne, many people are affected by jealous tempers. Forget about it. Mary used to be jealous of us two playing games or taking riding lessons together. She was sickened to her stomach when you made her watch us, remember? We used to ride through the meadows and up in the long grass, then ride past Saint Peter's during those hot summers at Hever, before you went to France."

"How could I forget?" she says.

"You were the best horsewoman for a girl your age."

"Always. And, brother, you were the best jumper. Especially of ditches, and ravines!"

"Mary felt left out watching and waiting at the gatehouse. She always thought it right she should be teaching us, and not one of father's servants."

"Is she jealous now, do you think, of the closeness between the two of you? As siblings, I mean?"

Anne snorts. "No, of course not, she has her children."

11TH FEBRUARY 1531

Everything is changing in Tudor England. Having failed with the pope, Henry now seeks the power to annul his own marriage to Katharine by asking parliament to declare him Supreme Head of the Church in England. The 'Pardon of the Clergy' in the opening months of the year is the second triumph for Anne Boleyn and her supporters – Wolsey being the first, and the pope being the second. It is not, however, a conclusive victory for Henry and Anne, as there is no divorce. Instead of applying the logic of his new title, Henry wastes time and effort by trying to block any hearing of the divorce suit at Rome to secure papal approval for a trial elsewhere.

These policies should never bother the king, as he ought to trust in his new title: Head of the Church in England – except this title has been awarded by the church and parliament, with the rider 'so far as the law of Christ allows', which means in truth that he really has no power over the church at all. Henry being Henry, I expect him to push on with a hearing before the authorities of the church, despite any such provisos. Convocation grants him the title of 'Singular Protector, Supreme Lord, and even, so far as the law of Christ allows, Supreme Head of the English Church and clergy', and much to the delight of Anne's father, it is George Boleyn, Viscount Rochford, who plays a prominent role today in persuading convocation of the scriptural case for the king's supremacy.

The convocations of Canterbury and York are the English Church's legislative body, which, like parliament, is made up of two houses: the upper house of bishops and the lower house of general clergy. The king's articles were introduced to them on February 7th, following which, convocation met on five consecutive days, with the last being today, February 11th. George is now a member of the Privy Council, chosen by Henry to express his growing anti-papal sentiments and parliament's arguments in favour of supremacy.

Anne and I sit at the fire, studying Tyndale's 'Obedience of a Christian Man', and discussing the implications on the Church and the changes taking place for Henry.

343

"George was sent to convocation yesterday afternoon," she says. "He delivered various tracts, announcing to the legislative body that the King's supreme authority is grounded on God's word and ought in no case be restrained by any frustrating decrees of popish laws or void prescriptive of human traditions." She's acting out George's part, as he would have addressed the convocation, and it's difficult not to giggle. "But that he may both order and minister, and also execute the office of spiritual administration in the Church whereof he is head."

She laughs, holding both hands out to the heat of the fire. "George was better than I could have been at addressing them, but convocation did not want to deal with my twenty-six-year-old brother, they wanted to deal directly with the king." She shakes her head. "I heard he did very well, and when they sent members of the lower house to see the king, he turned them away and instructed them to deal with my brother."

"The King is happy to use George's talents as a buffer between himself and convocation, and this, I have no doubt, is to the extreme satisfaction of your father." The position in which Henry was happy to put George will have done nothing to temper his pride, and it is hard to imagine that Sir Thomas is unmoved by his son's extraordinary prominence at such tender years. I, for one, feel so proud of him, and I'm determined to tell him when I see him next.

Convocation initially baulked at the idea of recognising Henry as Head of the Church but a suggestion by Cromwell, Thomas Audley, and George to qualify the demand with 'as far as the law of Christ allows' seemed to iron out objections. Although this is a victory for the Boleyns and their supporters, verbal acceptance by the clergy and actual compliance are two different matters, and any act of convocation must be agreed on by parliament before it is enforced, and it seems Henry, still loyal to his catholic roots, would secretly prefer Rome's approval. Meanwhile, those openly loyal to Rome are battling against the advancing tide of heresy. Chief amongst them is the Lord Chancellor, Sir Thomas More.

Twenty-Three

MAY 1531 – WHITEHALL

The Duke of Norfolk is incensed, swearing, shouting, and parading himself around Anne's chambers, railing about the calamity befalling the Boleyn clan. Francis Bryan has summoned Thomas Cromwell from Austin Friars to assist in matters that perturb the duke. It is Henry Percy, or his wife Mary Talbot, causing the trouble. Henry Percy who, less than five years ago, inherited the Northumberland title on the death of his father, is depressed, it seems. His marriage to Mary Talbot is in utter turmoil, the relationship has broken down irretrievably. Northumberland has complained about his wife's malicious acts and lies, while her father is worried that he is abusing his wife and might even consider poisoning her. Percy is outraged at Shrewsbury's suspicions and has refused to permit his father-in-law's servants to see or speak to Mary.

When the countess's brother-in-law, William, Lord Dacre, asked the Duke of Norfolk to defend her, Northumberland told Norfolk that he never wants to see her again, as long as he lives. The couple have been separated for a while, and Northumberland has announced that he is bequeathing his entire inheritance to the king, since he has no children and he and his wife are not likely to have a legitimate heir. He is estranged from his brothers, and doesn't want them to inherit his property. Mary Talbot hates him and seeks a divorce, accusing him of having a pre-contract with Anne Boleyn. She has confided her alleged grievance to her father, who has now mentioned the matter to Thomas Howard, 3rd Duke of Norfolk, hence his anger.

We all stand on the edge of a precipice, waiting to see who will be pushed first into the pit by the allegations. Anne consults Cromwell for advice, frustrated that the king has left her standing in her chambers this morning, after they had a row. It's not a great atmosphere to walk into, as the king is furious and won't speak to her. She's beside herself with frustration, knowing that Wolsey broke any kind of promise she had with Henry Percy. The memories of that day at York Place come flooding back to me, remembering the spittle that spewed from the cardinal's lips as he gave Percy a good dressing down. A pre-contract or betrothal is a serious matter; it is almost as binding as marriage itself. The king wants to order an inquiry, but Norfolk has other ideas.

Francis Bryan escorts Cromwell into Anne's chamber but his voice can't be heard over Norfolk's stomping and shouting.

"This matter will bring the whole family down!" he says, his face red with temper. Cromwell bows, then removes his hat, before stroking the anglets on his doublet.

"Shut the door, Francis, and do not let anybody in!" George instructs. "I can see Wriothesley loitering outside." He flicks a wave at the open door. "He cannot be privy to family conversations." With that, he stands between me and Jane, who has returned to Court from her recent disgrace. His sister Mary sits on a chair near the fire.

Norfolk tugs the fur collar of his coat over his shoulders, puffing himself up to display his importance. Clothes seem to make the man in this instance, as his bony frame can only be improved by fine cloth, braid, and fox fur. Cromwell exudes a calm confidence as he assesses us one by one. Daylight floods the room, illuminating the gathering with its gentle warmth. The atmosphere, however, is frosty as Jane speaks.

"I think we should pack Anne's bags and send her back off home to Hever. What say all of you?"

I'm sure she's delighting in putting Anne down, knowing I would accompany her back to Kent and she would have George to herself.

George isn't impressed. "One more word, JANE, and I will send you back to Kent myself. You can go instead of my dear sister!"

She isn't deterred, looking to Cromwell. "The King has said he might force an inquiry into this Percy matter, before the whole council. If Anne has concealed a secret pre-contract, then—"

"I wish there had been a clause to annul my pre-contract and marriage with you," George snaps, "because I would have forced Father to make sure I could get out of it!"

This is the first time I've witnessed such a huge gulf between the pair. He looks at me but lowers his gaze before Jane takes notice. She now keeps quiet, realising she's said enough.

Anne paces the room in her usual fashion, her silk skirts trailing and swishing behind her with every turn. Her head is bowed, and she is deep in thought, her hands clasped in front of her. She snaps her head up and turns to Cromwell, looking him square in the face.

"Master Cromwell, I deny all allegations that Mary Talbot has made against me in this matter." She stands motionless before him.

The floorboards creak as he leans back on his heels. His shoulders heave once, and he nods. "Good. That is the thing to do." His voice is low, calm, and direct, unlike everyone else in the chamber.

"Harry Percy spoke of his affections for me, even love – I will allow that – but there was nothing more. I assure you there was no pre-contract, least of all any marriage between us. Wolsey put a stop to the matter, did he not Mistress Wickers?"

I nod in Anne's general direction, not wanting to be involved in the argument.

"And no joining of bodies in consummation!" Mary interjects.

Anne scowls, glaring at her sister for being so direct. "Yes, Mary, everyone knows I am an untouched woman. As a queen to be, that is what the king expects."

"How was the king when you last conversed?" Cromwell asks, changing the subject. Anne makes no reply.

Mary almost jumps with frustration. "What is the use of calling on Master Thomas Cromwell if you do not tell him what has occurred, and you deny him the opportunity to help you?" She seems overly vocal today.

"He said nothing, Master Cromwell, and he walked out of the room, leaving me, exactly where I stand before you."

She is remarkably calm, considering her predicament. Perhaps she trusts Cromwell more than anyone realises. Maybe they have reached an understanding. He may have considered his position; indeed, if Anne were to be crowned Queen of England, then the possibilities for Thomas Cromwell could be endless. Thomas Boleyn looks frayed at the edges as he walks into the middle of the mayhem.

"It seems to me," he says, "there are several approaches in this situation. Surely, Anne, you can placate the king, you have done this before have you not?"

"Oh, God's blood!" Norfolk shouts at his brother-in-law. "While you are selecting the way to deal with the king, your daughter, sir, my niece, is being slandered and abused. Not only that, but the king's mind also is being infected towards her, and this family's fortune is going right down the privy before all of our fucking eyes!" He throws his weight around, hands on hips, making everyone feel uncomfortable. Cromwell raises his brows and shrugs.

"Uncle, will you let me, or my father speak?" George asks, much to the annoyance of Norfolk who grips the hilt of his sword. "Harry Percy was convinced once to forget any thought of marrying Anne."

"What if he could be persuaded again to forget any claim he thinks he had on Anne?" Thomas asks.

"Wolsey once fixed that situation," Anne responds, her tone sharp. "He interfered all too easily. Warned Percy against me. How Mary Talbot thinks I was pre-contracted to her husband, only the Lord above knows!" Anne sighs. "Sadly, now we may need him to satisfy the Talbot girl's worries, he is no longer of use." She clasps her hands together, playing with her emerald betrothal ring, twisting it this way and that on her finger. My friend is anxious, which I don't like, so I negotiate the perimeter of the room to get closer to reassure her. George watches me as I stand near her. Cromwell picks up what looks like a shard of glass from the carpet. I wonder where that is from? He then places it on the small table at the side of her fur-strewn chair, before returning to his place and standing before Anne. She continues to twist her ring until she creates a red mark on her skin.

"Lady Anne, you will be Queen of England one day, I know it." I wonder how Cromwell knows of such things? Maybe he has a crystal ball tucked away at Austin Friars that no one knows about? I laugh inwardly, because I'm the only one here who knows the future.

Cromwell continues. "I think the Pope cannot stop it. Worry not about Henry Percy, as he is a spider that can easily be squashed under a glass, should you wish it – he will not stand in your way. I dare to think that even God, or his angels would deny yours, or the king's wishes, let alone stop you from what you want."

She blinks at him and smiles. Cromwell is set to be the original working-class hero, and the original self-made man if he can pull off removing Percy, using his scheming heart to impress the Boleyns and Norfolk. Standing before Norfolk, he is throwing down a gauntlet, challenging him that he can achieve the desired result by flinging off his humble origins and charming himself all the way to the king's side. He's a compelling figure but with a hard, ruthless, and ambiguous streak. Anne seems intrigued by him, drawn in by a charismatic figure who has dragged himself up from the gutter of Putney. She can't seem to fathom how he has done it. How has he risen so high in His Majesty's estimation? Now that he's in a position of authority, I know how he will use that power to get Anne where she needs to be – sat on the throne of England. While I'm staring at him, I'm also reminded of already knowing how he will, or probably might orchestrate her downfall. I can't take my eyes off Cromwell.

"So, Cromwell, you must be able to shift Henry Percy out of the way!" Norfolk exclaims, stepping up to him. Cromwell responds with a half-smile, then bows and takes his leave.

Anne sweeps into her chambers, owning them, taking pride in her status at court. The rooms I share with her are large, with a presence chamber and her parlour flanked by our respective bedrooms. She also has a private room and a bedchamber for her servants. Rich burgundy drapes adorn the windows, and we are blessed with a view of the beautiful gardens.

I hand my cloak to another one of her ladies, who folds it up and puts it away. Then I walk to the windows, opening them to let in the breeze. I need air. My kirtle is pulled tight, squeezing my ribs. I wave to the waiting footman for him to bring us some wine, then drop into a chair near the hearth. The man hurries over and hands me the goblet – the metal feels cool, the wine soothing. Anne paces the room, running her hands through her dark chestnut hair. She removes her gloves and sets them on the table, then accepts wine from the footman and quenches her thirst, gulping it back, before pressing the goblet into his waiting hand. Unlike Anne, I savour my wine, letting the rich flavour fill my senses and settle my nerves.

"I sometimes wonder," she begins, "whether life would have been easier if I had been the wife of a simple man, as my sister Mary."

I shake my head. "Anne, do not wish such things, lest such desires should come into being. God has dealt you your hand in life and it is a rich and rewarding one, if you put Him first in all that you do."

"I try my best to put God first, but the courtiers are as ravenous as a pack of rabid dogs. They hover on the outskirts of the field, pacing and pawing, growling, waiting for whatever scraps our lion king leaves, and then they fight for the best pieces, the most succulent, and the most sought after. The Boleyns are lucky as, thanks to my favour with the king, we have all we need as a family, and I find us to be the key to which people open the door to the king's favour. Everyone is false with us, judging us and waiting for us to slip up, so they can take our places in the rays of the king's sunlight."

"Anne, you will not mess things up." I lower my voice. "Promise me you will always listen to the little counsel I give. You may not act upon it always but promise me you will listen to me."

"Sweet Beth, I promise. Have I not taken heed of your counsel before?"

I nod once. "You have indeed."

"The king has shown me such favour this year. Look at all the gifts he has bestowed upon me. Courtiers look upon me with envy and greed."

"Mistress, is it not your right as the king's fiancée to receive such gifts? Surely, these same courtiers will have to give you such honour and respect as their queen one day?"

"You are right, I had not thought of that. However, it has come as such a shock to me, as the king's wife-to-be, to have near-unlimited finances and for Henry to spoil me so. Look at the gifts I have already had: nineteen diamonds for a headdress – two bracelets, each crafted from ten diamonds and eight pearls – nineteen diamonds set in trueloves of crown gold – twenty-one rubies artfully arranged in gold, shaped like a rose. Not only that but did you not see and feel the two borders of cloth of gold for the sleeves of a new gown which had been trimmed with ten diamonds and eight pearls?"

"Yes, Lady Anne, I did – it was exquisite. I have been astonished by the lavish gifts the king has bestowed on you. His generosity is unending."

"I have also had six large golden buttons, two diamonds crafted into the shape of two hearts to wear in my hair, twenty-one diamonds, and twenty-one rubies, amongst other treasures. The king most definitely spoils me."

The conversation comes to an abrupt end when Henry breezes into her newly appointed chambers. Mary Shelton, Lady Lee, Nan Gainsford, and Jane Rochford dip in a unison of curtsies as Anne approaches the king. He offers his hand, and she kisses his ring. Dutifully, I drop to a curtsy beside her, but he prompts us up.

"Why, my lady, have you quarrelled with Guildford? He has resigned his office as Comptroller of the Household." He looks perplexed and draws a chair under him, dismissing the four women from the chamber.

"He is not very partial to me, Your Grace."

Henry's brows knot together, as if he can't understand why anyone would dislike Anne Boleyn. "He told me you said that once you become my queen, you would have him punished and deprived of his office. Is this true?"

"Henry, he was rude to me. The man does not like me, and, in any case, he told me he would resign his office." Henry chuckles. "What is it?" she begs. The laughter isn't infectious.

"I told him not to take any mind of women's talk!"

"And?" she quizzes.

"He has resigned, anyway!"

JUNE 1531 - WHITEHALL PALACE

I feel uneasy, saddled on the side of a chestnut mare, as Whitehall recedes into the distance. The king, Anne, and his retinue ride away with the rest of the court, and none of us will ever see Katharine of Aragon again. I see her watching from a casement window and can clearly detect the sorrow in her expression – she must know what lies ahead, being separated from her daughter, and her husband, and an end to her royal life. She has been told by the duke of Suffolk that she is to be installed in a series of castles, with limited access to those who might visit her.

Cromwell rides beside Anne and me this morning as we follow the dry dusty roads away from the palace, through the city streets of Tudor London. As we pass the throngs of people mooching around market stalls, hanging around tavern doorways, and gossiping on street corners, I feel uncomfortable and wish we'd taken a litter to our next destination. The king rides ahead of us with

Suffolk, Norris, and others, taking in the adoration of the assembled crowds. Some rush up to him, touching his cloak, trying to reach for his hand. Others dare to ask him for alms. Norris and Suffolk ride on either side of him, using their horses to beat the crowds back. Armed, liveried men circle the group, making sure the king is safe. Some voices in the crowd bellow, "God Save the King!" or "God save His Majesty!", while other brave souls, especially the women, shout, "Boleyn whore!" as we ride by. Henry glares around to see where these comments come from, and his soldiers search through the crowds, dragging suspects away to be nailed to the pillory or shoved in the stocks.

"How are you, Cromwell?" Anne asks, raising her voice over the crowd.

"I am well, Lady Anne. And how do you fare?" He looks around when someone else shouts an insult at her.

"I could be better, sir, but I am glad to be with the king, and away from Queen Katharine."

"Madam, I can understand that – the matter will soon be resolved."

"I hope so, Master Cromwell." She smiles. "And what news do you have for me?"

"Tyndale still refuses to support the king with his annulment, even from Antwerp, and will not bend a point of principle to be in favour but says that he will only come back to England when the scriptures are translated to English and freely available to all."

"Foolish man – does he not consider that the King might help him?"

"It appears not, Madam Anne."

"I would have thought Tyndale would try to make a friend of the King of England," I say.

"Tyndale will not come back, Mistress Wickers." He turns to Anne. "Thomas More has told the king he does not have to keep the promises he makes to a heretic and will not agree to William Tyndale's safe-conduct back into England."

"I see." She nods. "It appears that the only people safe at court are the Boleyns, or anyone associated with us."

"Your patronage and support have done me favours, madam, as it has for Doctor Cramner."

"Sir Henry Norris has also benefited from your support, Anne." I feel I can talk freely of reformers in front of Cromwell. "I know Norris feels it wise to show support for you, as he has much in common with you and your circle, being of a reformist persuasion." She glares at me, willing me to shut up. I take the hint and keep my focus on the road ahead.

"I know," Cromwell says, "that George Constantine, a manservant of Sir Henry Norris, is a zealous Protestant and trafficker in forbidden books." He pulls at his horse's reins. "I have it on good authority that Constantine only escaped being burned as a heretic by Sir Thomas More this year, by fleeing abroad."

"Yes, but you must keep this to yourself, Cromwell," Anne says, her voice low, "that it is Norris who has persuaded Constantine back to Court, under his protection." She looks worried. "And I also know that Norris is helping him bring back a copy of Miles Coverdale's English translation of the Bible for me."

Cromwell stares at her, his expression fixed. I catch a glint in his eye. He is of the same religious leanings in terms of reform as Anne. So, it seems they are allies, for now.

Greenwich Palace

Flaming torches light the Great Hall of Greenwich Palace and, tonight, Anne sits next to Henry on the dais – queen in all but name. Up in the gallery, the minstrels are making discord, tuning their instruments in readiness for the king's entertainment. I can smell the simmering, burning wicks of a multitude of candles that stand proudly in sconces, and candelabras about the hall. The candlelight flickers bright, welcoming the wishes of the night, as I glance about at the assembled courtiers. Norfolk and Sir Thomas huddle together watching Henry with Anne. Wriothesley, Cromwell, and Ralph Sadler are deep in conversation, whilst George, Jane, Tom Wyatt, the Courtneys, and several ambassadors are all on the periphery of the dancefloor, observing the dancers.

I turn, smiling at Anne, who looks resplendent in a dark-green damask and silver-tissue gown. Henry claps to his musicians and orders them to play a melody suitable for a basse dance. The notes float up into the hammer-beam ceiling, and it isn't long before Henry takes the floor, guiding Anne in the first steps of the dance, her gown pooling around her as she glides forward in the king's masterful hand.

Beside me, George and Jane are talking. The drums are so loud, their conversation is barely audible, which isn't such a bad thing, as it irks me to see them getting along. Probably out of a sense of duty, he takes her hand and leads her to join his sister and the king on the dancefloor, her expression smug as she shoves past me. To the left of me, Margery Horseman, Nan Gainsford, Jayne Fool, and Anne's other women stand alongside the dais, in case Anne needs their assistance. They are hoping to be drawn into the dance, and it isn't long before the floor is full of people, filtering through the gaps of circling dancers.

I move to the periphery, nursing the fourth goblet of wine, watching George dance with Jane. He's got good legs, and dances well. She looks thrilled at being the centre of his attentions but doesn't see him scanning the crowds standing on the side lines. Every so often, he holds Jane's gaze, and they exchange brief conversations. Ah, to be a fly on the wall. Hmm, maybe not.

The loudness of the music, combined with the wine, has my head thumping. I need air. As I walk towards the entrance, I see Tom Wyatt leaning against a carved screen, his focus fixed on Anne as she circles the room with Henry.

"Mistress Wickers, would you like another drink of wine?" he asks. I rub my temples, shake my head, and carry on towards the door.

Once out in the fresh air and the stillness of the evening, I look up at the starry sky, reminded of the evening Rob took me for dinner to the Greyhound pub. Was that a date? It feels like a lifetime ago. I wonder if he will he take his girlfriend there? Would he have the cheek? Is it any of my business? And who am I to ask, considering how things are with George and me? How are things with George and me?

I realise I'm still clutching my cup of wine, and I place it on the top of a low stone wall, hoping one of the pages will pick it up. The evening breeze is cool on my face as I descend the stone steps and walk through the cloisters that lead to the knot-planted, walled garden – the music fading into the distance.

After five minutes of peaceful walking, footsteps echo behind me, and my heart surges at the familiar tread. I turn to see George bearing down on me. He doesn't give me time to say anything, grasping my waist, his lips hot on my neck. Within seconds, I'm being pushed against a recess in the cloisters, his mouth now on mine, his strong tongue searching. When he breaks the kiss, I gasp in a breath, my legs trembling and my stomach swirling.

"George! We…can't do this! What are you…doing?"

"You know exactly what I am doing!" he says, his voice muffled as he plants a flurry of kisses on my neck. "I can bear it no longer. Every time I make love to my wife, it is your face I see!" My legs nearly give way when his teeth clamp on my neck, and he pulls me hard against him. "I need the real thing," he cries, "to make me whole."

He kisses me again, and this time I meet his tongue with mine, something I've been wanting and needing for such a long time. Half of me is screaming a warning in my head, while the other half is wondering how this is going to go. He pushes me further into the recess, up against a door. I try to ease him away with my left hand, reaching down with my right to stop him from pulling my skirts any higher.

However, the reality is, I want him as much as he wants me. I know it's wrong but I'm going with it. He manages to turn the handle on the door, and we stumble into a dark room, with a huge ebony table at its centre. I guide us towards it, our mouths latched together – his hands are everywhere. Then he lifts me on top of it, as if I weigh nothing. Books and parchments fly everywhere and, as I look into his eyes, I realise that he means business, and not the courtly kind. He's a man on a mission, and I'm determined to match him.

"Why does a woman's clothing have so many layers?" He laughs as he lifts my gown. "Your skirts are more difficult to peel back than an artichoke!"

We burst into a fit of giggles. I reach towards him, trying to kiss him, biting his lower lip, then sucking on it as I fumble to undo the small buttons on his doublet. In between stolen kisses, he tugs at the lacing of his codpiece and, once undone, his breeches fall over his buttocks, which I waste no time getting my hands on, gripping and kneading the firm flesh, his body heat burning into my palms.

His impatient hands ride up under my skirts and, through the fog of my passion, I'm aware that my thighs are being parted. He groans and, in a boiling moment of madness for us both, he's on top of me, then inside me, thrusting, pulling me to him, moving with me in the hottest embrace I've ever experienced. I grip him between my legs, meeting his rhythm, evoking a loud moan when I bite his lower lip again, then pulling his hair and sucking his sweet tongue. This pours fuel into his tank, and he drives into me, time after time, and I'm with him – climbing, climbing – and we cry out, our groans filling the room as a golden tsunami crashes through me, leaving me shaking as if electrified. My God, never in my life have I experienced anything like this.

He collapses onto me, spent, the deed finally, and truly, done!

In that moment, the door flies open, and who should be standing there but the king! I grip George's hair, keeping his head still so he stays on me with his face hidden. Henry Tudor stands there, looking at me, his eyes lit above a broad smile. In the darkness, I'm unsure if he realises it's me. I would die with embarrassment, yet he doesn't bat an eyelid, as if he has witnessed this kind of shenanigans many times before. He stretches his arm out to stop his party from entering the room, and I watch with enormous relief as he turns and walks out, slamming the door behind him.

My hands begin to tremble with the realisation of what has just happened. I continue to hold George close to me, and he remains motionless, in case we are disturbed again. George is stuck to me like glue, as we both listen for Henry's voice echoing, as its sound resonates from the passageway outside.

"This room is already occupied with game-playing, sirs. I suggest we find another to continue our game of cards!" Someone chuckles, followed by Henry's booming laugh. "Norris, I'd rather be playing the game they are playing!"

"What game is it they play, Your Grace? May we join?"

"Suffolk, this is a game only for two!" Their laughter reverberates through the cloisters as they go on their way.

George lifts his head – sheer terror in his eyes. "It could not have been any worse if it had been Jane herself at the door. It could only happen to me!" He stands and fixes himself up. I hop off the table and straighten my skirts, my legs like jelly. He has his hands to his face in mortification.

"What shall we do?" I ask, my voice trembling, partly from fear but also from the wonderful experience we've just shared.

"We cannot walk into the Hall together – people will suspect something."

He's flustered, as am I – my heart beating so hard in my ears, I'm sure he can hear it. If Henry recognised us, this could be a real problem. I fix myself up as best I can and leave the room first, pretending that I'm looking for the house of easement – the bathroom – and make my way out into the cloisters. Lucky I did, because, as I hold back in the shadows, I see George intercepting Jane halfway across the courtyard.

"Where is she?" she screams. "I know you have been with her!"

"Quieten your voice, woman. People will hear!" He keeps his voice low, no doubt to lessen the chance of attracting attention, all the time holding Jane by her shoulders.

"I do not care if they hear!" she sobs. "Let them hear!" She slaps one of his arms away. "I get no affection from you, yet you give your love freely to others! My goodness, I can smell her off you!" George puts his arm about her and forces her to walk back to the revels in the Great Hall.

I give it a couple of minutes, then make my way back towards my chamber. My heart is still pounding, again partly through fear of what might happen, and partly because of what just took place with George. What have we done? This scenario is impossible. I've got to get back home. I can't face Anne, or Henry.

Did he recognise me? Was it too dark to make me out? A whirlwind of thoughts flies through my head as I ascend the stone steps to the chambers. My hands are clasped, and I feel the ring, which I turn for comfort, simply because it's a connection to home. Something flutters in the branches of a tree behind me, and I look up but my weak ankle twists on a step and I lose my footing and fly backwards, tumbling and falling until I land, hitting the back of my head. It hurts, like my brain has been slammed off the inside of my skull. When I open my eyes, I have to squint and blink as I stare up at the fluorescent strip-lighting in the ceiling of Professor Marshall's office.

The room isn't empty. The desktop computer is whirring, and someone's fingers are tapping the keyboard. It must be Professor Marshall. I curl up behind his big chair, not wanting him to see me. How can I explain why the ring has sent me back to my time?

My heart jumps when the handle on the door creaks and someone enters. I try and peer around the chair without being seen, groaning inside when I recognise Rob's black, shiny brogues.

"Professor Marshall, have you seen Beth?" he asks, his voice conveying his agitation.

"No, Robert, I haven't seen hide nor hair of her. Forgive me."

I know the blood is pumping around my veins fast because the sound of it reverberates in my ears. What am I going to do? I really don't want either of them to know I'm here.

"She's gone through that portal again, hasn't she?"

What's going on? He seems to be here every time I arrive back. And why is he discussing the portal with Marshall?

"Is it any of your business?" Professor Marshall says.

"Erm, no, but Beth's my friend, and something's happened."

"What?" I groan as I struggle to my feet, and both men gawk at me.

"You're back!" the professor says, his glasses hanging off the tip of his nose.

"I'm glad to see you!" Rob says. "Why do you look so…dishevelled?"

"Huh? Erm…"—God, my inner thighs are all sticky —"what the hell are you doing here, Rob, asking questions about me?"

Professor Marshall stares at me. That must have sounded rude.

"Jessica texted me, trying to get a hold of you. She said there's been some kind of accident – something to do with your dad. It might be nothing but…"

My face goes cold. "How can it be nothing? Oh, God. Mum must have tried to contact me, and telephoned Jess when she couldn't." I hold my face with both hands, my heart burning at the thought that something terrible has happened to my poor dad. "I need to get out of this bloody gown!" I shout. "Can you both bugger off for a minute while I change?" I grab my bag from behind the professor's chair.

I've let my family down, being away so long, though I know time hasn't skipped too far ahead here. Oh, how long have I been away? Too late, the door is closed and I'm alone. My poor dad, what the hell has happened?

I struggle out of the gown and shift, and whip out my jeans and top, wasting no time getting into them. My finger is marked under the ring, no doubt from the heat of transition. Strange how it happened. I suppose it's inevitable that, at some point, my Tudor adventure had to end. It obviously knew, or sensed in some way, that I had to return home. Is it all about my dad, or did I go too far, with George?

Oh, my goodness, does this mean I've lost control of it? I take it off and turn it over, and it heats up. Oh, no, no, no – I fling it into the top drawer of the professor's desk – I'm not going back to Tudor England. I'm not going anywhere, not before I've seen my dad.

Want to carry on Beth Wickers adventure with the Timeless Falcon Dual Timeline Series?

COMING SOON:

Volume Three: A Turbulent Crown.

Volume Four: An Enduring Legacy.

A NOTE TO THE READER

Dear Reader,

Thank you for reading *The Ring of Fate.*.

Welcome to the world of Beth Wickers. This is my third novel, and my second historical novel, which is now part of The Timeless Falcon Dual Timeline Series. Beth's journey began from my interest in history years ago, with Anne Boleyn and the dramatic story of her fall, reading the likes of Jean Plaidy when I was a child of nine. My study of Anne and history has never diminished. I know that Anne's life history is an interest shared by many: the crowds who visit His Majesty's Royal Palace and Fortress, The Tower of London, who feel compelled to see the supposed site of Anne's scaffold, imprisonment, and eventual judicial murder, or walk around with other visitors who flock to Hampton Court Palace where Anne stayed in the triumphant days of her coronation in June 1533, or even to Hever Castle, which was her family home for a time. The fascination with everything Anne Boleyn is evident in numerous websites on the internet. The insatiable appetite for everything relating to the Tudors, from raunchy television series to opulent films, to the Westend musical, Six! continues unabated.

I have consulted academic works and research on Anne Boleyn and personalities of the Tudor Court by successful historians like Eric Ives, Suzannah Lipscomb,, Elizabeth Norton, David Loades and others, to frame a number of real events in Anne's life, to bring her story around Beth to life. Primary sources are also fantastic devices to learn of historical context, and analysing sources is the closest we will get to remove the veil between these historical personalities and events, in order to conclude anything which remotely resembles the truth. The highlight of my research was looking through and holding the twenty-six pages of Anne Boleyn's indictment of her trial, and seeing the indents in the vellum where the Duke of Norfolk had ticked the jury off with his quill as they entered the king's Great Hall at His Majesty's Royal Palace and Fortress of the Tower of London. My primary research included documents from websites such as British History Online, and The National Archives at Kew. The icing on the cake in terms of research, was having the opportunity to sit in the front row of The Aldwych Theatre and watch Ben Miles as Cromwell in the stage adaptations of Hilary Mantel's *Wolf Hall* and *Bring Up the Bodies* — on the last night's performance — and knowing Hilary Mantel was in the audience. What an incredible experience that was. The play was an atmospheric-inducing device, and historical aspects of the drama were thought-provoking.

It is this insatiable appetite by both historians and enthusiasts for Anne Boleyn, that compelled me to write a completely different take on her story, rather than the usual regurgitation of Anne, from her point of view. Moreover, it is my protagonist's story, which enables us to observe Anne in a different light. What would we do if we had the ability to time-travel back to the Tudor period and meet Anne? Would we behave ourselves and not tamper with history as we know it, or would we wreak havoc and try to save Anne from her well-documented downfall? These are the dilemmas that face Beth Wickers. Her story is one I felt obliged to write, and although I include primary events, it will never be close to the truth of Anne's life, as unless we were there at the time, we can never know all the facts relating to Anne Boleyn. I did consider, at times, what I would ask Anne, Henry, or other key players of the Tudor Court, and speculated what I might try and do to change history if I could time travel. In hindsight, would I allow such prominent Tudor personalities to play out their destiny as history intended? This book has been a labour of love and an exciting and fun retelling of Anne's story, as close to the truth of who I imagine Anne to have been. But this is fiction, after all, and I won't pretend any differently.

For those reading Volume Two, we are continuing with Beth Wicker's time-travelling story together; thank you for being here. You have two more volumes in The Timeless Falcon Dual Timeline Series to go, unless I decide to add further stories. For those that haven't read *The Anne Boleyn Cypher'* (Volume One), you can read it to find out exactly how Beth ended up in sixteenth century England from the present day. My protagonist, Beth Wickers, has often woken me up in the middle of the night, screaming at me to finish her story. I think most authors end up with their characters talking in the heads of their creators? Beth has often told me the outcome of her adventures, clamouring at me to get up out of bed, so I would type her thoughts into my manuscripts as they formed in my head.

While researching the key figures of the Tudor period, tracing their journeys through the primary sources, I saw the potential of weaving a modern-day, fictional character like Beth into the Tudor world to represent the eyes and ears of modern readers who love history. I wanted to integrate Beth Wickers into the Boleyn world and simultaneously set her apart from it. I am a great fan of fiction, television series, films, and their prerogatives. It allows writers, authors, television studios, filmmakers, and readers, to transcend the veil of time, space, and reality, providing the ultimate way to escape the routines of our everyday lives. Series such as this can perform a kind of magic in our mind's eyes, and these fictional tales' only responsibility is to themselves, to be good versions of historical fiction. However, authors cannot hope to please every reader simultaneously. As a genre in its own right, historical fiction has its freedoms and limitations. It also offers the greatest thrill of transporting readers to another realm, the closest we can come to witnessing the past. Growing up reading historical novels, I quickly understood how much the genre could also be educative and deeply rooted in the facts of history.

The Wickers family, Rob Dryden, Professor Marshall, and others from the modern world are fictional. Still, I would suggest that Beth Wickers is also representative of many historians who imagine what it might be like living in the sixteenth century. Although Beth is closest to the Boleyns, in more ways than most, I created her by assimilating the lives of many other historical figures around her and how she might interact with them and them with her – this is especially true of Jane Parker, Jane Boleyn, or Lady Rochford, (whatever title you choose to call her) - George's wife.

We all have ideas of what historical figures may have been like based on evidence and sources, but there is little evidence of Jane Boleyn's character. With some historians suggesting George was promiscuous, or homosexual and a bit of a cad, I wanted to show George in a different light. Yes, he enjoys the company of women, and yes, he has probably had a few dalliances (but not many), yet he is NOT homosexual, not in this story anyway. Jane tries to be a good fiancé and eventual wife, by turning a blind eye to his misdemeanours. Still, through his interactions with Beth, Jane observes that there is more to her husband's relationship with Beth than meets the eye. Jane hates the bond Beth has with George, and it makes her angry. She wants to be loved by George the way he loves Beth – that's what makes her spikey.

I had to make Jane Boleyn spikey, but in Book Three, Jane's backstory will be revealed. I didn't want to follow the usual tropes about Jane Boleyn, without good reason, and however, she's such a wonderful character to as spikey, and her reasons for being so, may be revealed later in the series. I will stress that Jane's backstory, is purely speculation on my part, because unless you were there to actually witness what went on, we will never know the real truth of what happened, but the way I have implied a backstory in George's and Jane's relationship is a good one to explain Jane's later behaviours.

Another figure I took historical liberties with was Jayne Fool because we know so little about Jayne. We do not know when Jayne came to live in the household with Anne Boleyn or how old Jayne was at the time. We only know of Jayne's life experiences through accounts in the records of her attending Anne Boleyn's coronation and the painting of the Family of Henry VIII c.1545 that hangs in the Haunted Gallery at Hampton Court. I had read about disabled people at the Court of Henry VIII through my non-fiction research, writing, and PhD work. I wanted to show how compassionate and open-minded the Tudor Court could be towards disabled people whose experiences are known to us.

Other characters close to Beth are fictional, especially those relevant to the romantic plot line, such as Robert Dryden. The way I have portrayed Henry VIII's character, and other courtiers, allows me greater scope to flesh out their roles without altering what is known about existing people. It is also worth mentioning that, as Beth Wickers is a modern woman, of our time, that she is bound to be far more attractive to many of the men in the Tudor Court, including the king, than Anne Boleyn's contemporaries because of the modern products Beth uses in her hygiene, and beauty regimes, (which rubs off on Anne), and her usual good, healthy diet and use of modern medicines in her own time, that it is obvious Beth, would have many male Tudor courtiers throwing themselves at her.

Whilst I have researched the lives of individuals like Henry VIII, Katharine of Aragon and Anne Boleyn in detail, a gulf remains between biographical works and the creative fleshing out that allows them to come to life as characters in fiction. Thus, there will be times when historical fiction authors have to take the liberty of putting words into their characters mouths, describing their conversations and deeds that they believe are compatible with what is known or can be inferred about their characters, and events over five hundred years. Individual readers' views on Henry, Katharine, Anne, George, and others can often be unshakable, though, surprisingly different. Still, I have tried to change them from these historical characters usual tropes, and show them as well-rounded, actual human beings dealing with the politics of their day. It may be that a writer's presentation of known figures at this moment in their lives does not always fit with that of readers, but writer's always have sound reasons for writing their characters as they do.

The same is true for locations and events of the era, as well as details such as clothing, food, furnishing, protocol, and behaviour. Writers embellish the known facts, fill in the gaps, in keeping with their essence. The Beth Wickers and Anne Boleyn of 1521 will not be the same as their depiction towards the end of the whole series; their characters will grow and change through the experiences of their lives.

Furthermore, I wish to stress that although the historical aspects of this book are loosely based on original sources, digital archives, and academic accounts, Beth's character and her experiences in the Tudor period were used as an entertaining device to creatively retell Anne's story, and is written purely for the readers' enjoyment, and to entertain, which I hope, as a reader, you will enjoy.

Best Wishes, Phillipa Vincent-Connolly

Reviews by readers these days are integral to a book's success, so if you enjoyed The The Ring of Fate I would be very grateful if you could spare a minute to post a review on Amazon, and I love hearing from readers, and you can talk with me through my website or on Twitter (@PhillipaJC) and follow my author page on Facebook (Phillipa Connolly Historian).

ALSO BY PHILLIPA VINCENT-CONNOLLY

THE TIMELESS FALCON SERIES:

Volume One: The Anne Boleyn Cypher
Volume Three; A Turbulent Crown
Volume Four: An Enduring Legacy

Disability and The Tudors: All the King's Fools

ACKNOWLEDGEMENTS

Firstly, I want to thank my readers who have supported me by reading and reviewing this series, for believing in me and my work, and for loving Beth Wicker's story enough to continue reading the whole Timeless Falcon Dual Timeline series. Secondly, thanks to Eamon Ó Cléirigh from Clear View Editing, who persevered and supported me in slowly transforming this volume, and the subsequent volumes in the series, into their final incarnations. Thank you for your patience.

Thank you to Richard Jenkins for his beautiful photography for the cover of the book, and for Megan Sheer for the beautiful design of the covers for the series.

Thank you to John Gillo for his belief in my work, and the support and encouragement he has given me to publish this series.

I also want to thank historian Dr Tracy Borman for allowing and approving a cameo of herself to appear in this book, and for letting me know that she thought this story to be 'This pacey, and engaging novel offers a fresh perspective on a much-loved historical period. Fans of The Tudors and historical fiction will be enthralled.'

I want to thank Gina Clark from Tudor Dreams Historical Costumier for her unwavering sense of humour, continued support, balanced with copious tea and champagne drinking, giving me some witty one-liners ideas, and spicing up the sex-scenes as I was reading the first draft of Volume Two to her. Gina's sense of humour, enthusiasm and love encouraged me to keep going, because we know, as Bob used to say, *"Set a goal to achieve something that is so big, so exhilarating that it excites you and scares you at the same time."*

Lastly, thank you to my two boys, Joshua, and Lucas who at times, have run out of patience with me for the amount of time I am glued to my MacBook Pro, in an event to get Beth's story out to readers.

Thank you to everyone for your support, as you are all wonderful!

Phillipa Vincent-Connolly, Poole, Dorset. January 2023

ABOUT THE AUTHOR

Phillipa Vincent-Connolly is an historian, writer, and published author of historical fiction and nonfiction. She is a consultant on many exciting projects across a broad spectrum with a special interest in disability and is becoming the 'go-to' broadcaster on this subject, especially recently with the publication of her book, 'Disability and the Tudors'. Published by Pen and Sword history imprint, currently, this is the first book in a series on disabilities in specific eras and benefits from Phillipa's own experience of living with Cerebral Palsy.

She achieved her degree in History and Humanities in 2011 and her PGCE, QTS, in 2014, and NQT 2019, in teaching (secondary), and part of her MA Graduate Diploma in History in 2020, and is currently working towards her PhD at Manchester Metropolitan University specialising in Tudor disability history. She has spoken at the National Archives and the British library to great acclaim. Her experience in teaching makes her an authoritative and engaging public speaker. She is a Fellow of the Royal Historical Society.

Phillipa has written for History Today, Blitzed Magazine, has been interviewed regularly for BBC radio, and has appeared in mini-TV documentaries.

Among her many interests, she has a deep and abiding love for all things historical, archives, artefacts, architecture, fashion, and royalty. Phillipa is also a keen activist, giving a contemporary voice to disabled people of the past, and those who currently feel disenfranchised. Her own disability has allowed her to identify and empathise with those who have not been heard and she is passionate about equality for the disabled. She lives in Poole, Dorset, but is not solely UK centric, as she has a broad spectrum of knowledge and research on which to draw.

A rising star in historical fiction too, with her eagerly awaited 'Timeless Falcon' historical fiction series of books, Phillipa has both the research and writing abilities to adapt to any project and is the future of the past.